JILLIAN HART

CHAPTER ONE

Don't think you're getting out of this alive, McKenna.

The bounty hunter's threat haunted him, as Luke McKenna gritted his teeth and took another stumbling step head-on into the howling fury of a mean Montana blizzard. The frigid wind knifed through the layers of wool and flannel, cutting to his bones with ease. The snow plunged in a gray-white gale that cut off the world from his sight.

The one good thing about this storm was that if he couldn't see his way through it, then neither could Moss.

"P-Pa? I'm c-cold."

"I know, darlin'. Just hold on tight to me."

"Okay." Beth's thin voice sounded tiny and frail compared to the howling fury of the wind. Tiny arms clenched around his neck as she burrowed against his chest. She might be safely buttoned inside his coat, but she was shivering hard.

He had to find shelter and soon. Beth couldn't stand this cold much longer, and neither could he, not with the way his bullet wound was bleeding.

He'd survived ten years as a Texas Ranger; he'd fought Indians and renegades and the toughest outlaws in three territories, and by God, he'd survive this storm, too. He'd survived what he couldn't bear to live through, and he wasn't about to fail now, not when all he had to fight was a blizzard. His child depended on him, and he

3

wouldn't let her down. Not ever again.

A boom exploded behind him. Gunfire? Had Moss tracked him in this storm? Luke clutched Beth tightly and ran, kicking hard in the deep, unpacked snow. He sank up to his thighs but kept going. Then lightning flashed, and another boom pealed overhead, eerily muffled by the gale-force snowfall.

Thunder. Not gunfire. Relief burst through him in an icy wave, and Luke slumped to his knees, breathing hard. The child cradled against his chest began shaking with sobs.

"P-Pa? I'm really, really c-cold."

"I know." It tore him apart. "We're going to be warm and safe soon."

"You promise?"

"You can count on it." He'd go to hell and back for his daughter. He pressed his hand against the growing stain on his jacket. The blood was freezing solid and turning the ice driven into the fabric a bright red.

He stumbled forward and stared at the snow at his feet. The shod half circles of horse tracks were fresh and deep. *Moss.* That black-hearted killer had followed him into the storm after all.

Black fury roared through him. The child tucked against his heart sobbed again, her cries pitiful. Torn apart, he knew he'd gone as far as he could. His hopes of getting Beth out of this territory to someplace safe had ended. Moss had proven relentless, and now, cloaked by the storm, Luke could walk straight into the bounty hunter's sites and not know it until it was too late.

Hide and wait. It was the only solution. *That, and hope Moss doesn't hunt you down.* Luke pressed his lips to his daughter's brow, and the layers of wool didn't diminish the sweet love he harbored for his child, helpless and innocent, or his fierce vow to protect her from ruthless men.

"It won't be much longer," he whispered, backtracking as the storm shoved him forward. He stumbled, pain shooting through his side, and he felt the hot, wet glide of blood on his skin.

He had to keep going; he had to keep his daughter safe.

A shadow jumped up out of the darkness. Then, quick as it appeared, it vanished. Luke tore the Colt .45 from its holster and aimed, thumbing back the hammer. Lightning cracked overhead, and thunder rumbled, eerily muted by the thick blanket of falling snow.

Where was Moss? Where had that bastard gone? The winds shifted, and there it was again—a dark splash of gold in the unrelenting gray-white world of wind and snow. A horse. It wasn't the bounty hunter's black gelding. The pretty palomino disappeared again behind the veil of white. There was a road ahead, and he could follow the tracks to shelter.

"Hold on, darlin'." Relief gave him strength, for they were no longer lost in the storm. He found the horse's tracks, and marveled at the force of wind already trying to wipe them clean. "It won't be long now."

"Do I getta have hot cocoa?"

"Absolutely." He pressed his lips to her brow and took off after the blur of gold that disappeared and then reappeared again much farther away, taunting him. Running with the last of his strength, he felt his wound tear wider. Hot, sticky blood warmed his skin from waist to hip.

He lost sight of the golden horse in the thick curtain of snow and wind. His vision blurred, and he couldn't seem to find the tracks he'd just been following.

Beth. He had to keep going for her sake. She was all that mattered. He couldn't control the weather and he couldn't control the forces driving evil men in this world, but he would find a way to get his daughter to safety.

Or at least he'd die trying. His knees buckled, and he hit the snow with bone-rattling force. The howling fury of the storm filled his ears, and he breathed in icy snow. The bitter cold wrapped around him and hurt like a knife paring through every inch of his body.

He was lost and losing hope, but the child buttoned inside his coat, next to his heart, kept him going. He stumbled until he couldn't walk, and then he crawled until the light faded from his eyes and there was only darkness—until not even his body responded to his driving will to survive.

Then there was only Beth's sorrowful cry and nothing, nothing but cold and death.

Molly Lambert shook the snow from her coat, shivering from the bitter storm. The house was cold and dark, but not as cold as the trepidation filling her at the unopened letter in her pocket

Her hound danced around her in excited circles as Molly hung her cloak to thaw. Iced snow tumbled like shards of glass and *plinked* against the wood floor. She patted her dog and hurried to stir the banked embers in the kitchen stove.

The hinges squeaked slightly as she opened the door. The unread letter felt like a lead weight in her pocket. She hadn't wanted to open it in town, and then a storm blew up on the road home and she'd barely made it to the stable before the blizzard struck with full force.

The scent of cured pine tickled her nose as she fed the weak coals. The dog nudged her; the wind howled against the north wall, and soon the flames snapped greedily as they grew in strength. All the while the letter felt heavier, as if it were dragging her skirt pocket down to her knees.

She wasn't ready to read it, not yet—good news or bad. The letter was from her mother, a woman whose heart was distant and cold and growing bitter as life passed her by. Molly didn't feel strong enough for more heartache, not today. Maybe she wouldn't read it. Maybe she would tuck it into the flames and watch the words burn.

The dog shot through the kitchen and lunged with both front paws at the back door, barking high and sharp.

"What is it, girl?" Molly opened the damper wide. The metal hinges squeaked and iron *clunked* against iron as she shut the door tight. "I'll let you out in just a second."

The dog whined louder and scratched harder.

"All right, all right. I'm coming." Maybe the white-tailed deer had returned, taking shelter in the lee side of her stable, knowing she would fork out bales of sweet alfalfa for them. "Is it time to feed the deer?"

Lady barked high and sharp—the animals must be close.

"Don't chase them," she ordered as she shrugged back into her icy cloak.

Lady didn't seem to be making any promises this time. Molly opened the door to the blast of ice and wind and stepped out into the harsh Montana blizzard. The dog loped on ahead, already lost in the gale-force snowfall.

This was her first Montana Rockies winter—she'd heard from Aunt Aggie how cold and hard they were. Well, Aunt Aggie was right, Molly thought as she struggled through the thigh-high drifts and kept her hand on the clothesline, which was tied from the back door to the stable so she wouldn't become lost in a storm.

Montana was a rugged place, but it was free, too. Free from the past, free from her mistakes. She was proud of this new life she'd made for herself—and this beautiful land she'd homesteaded.

Lady's sharp bark of alarm penetrated the howling wind and driving snow. Something was wrong—the dog didn't sound anywhere near the barn, and she'd never bark like that at the deer. Molly didn't dare let go of the rope; many a person had been blown off course by the wind and blinding snow and froze to death, but alarm beat through her, hot as flame.

Then she heard it, the painful rasp of a child's sob, faint and small when compared to the storm's mighty fury. Molly let go of the clothesline and tried hard to follow the sound of that sob and Lady's intermittent barking. The powerful wind tossed her around, and she wasn't certain she was making any progress at all.

Then all of a sudden there was the corner post of her split-rail fence. High drifts nearly hid it from sight, but a dark splash of color marked the snow.

Lady leaped up, grabbing hold of Molly's jacket hem to tug her along. The dark color became navy blue, then the shadow of a man's unbuttoned coat. He lay slack and unmoving, and the dark stain in the snow surrounding him looked like blood.

"Pa's dead," the little girl sobbed. "Just like my ma. He's all dead."

Lady reached the child first. The girl's eyes widened, but before she could react, the dog swiped at her freezing tears with a warm tongue. She buried her face in the dog's silky coat and cried.

"Come here, sweetheart." Molly reached out her arms, and the little girl moved from the dog's warmth to hers, wordlessly, her wrenching sobs of loss and grief heart-breaking.

Why, the child felt as fragile as a bird and shook from head to toe with those sobs. Molly cradled her tight, chest filling with sympathy. She pulled off one glove and laid two fingers against the father's throat.

A faint pulse beat against his cold skin. Relief shivered through her. He was alive, but with so much blood lost, how could she save him? He looked like such a big man. How on earth was she going to get him into her house?

"He's dead," the little girl sobbed.

"No, he's still alive."

Lady nudged her hand, and Molly knew she had to act fast. The temperature was dipping as the blizzard grew stronger. There was no way she could fetch the doctor in this weather. Chest tight with regret, she carried the child back toward the house, but the storm confused her. Where was the clothesline? All she could see was the white-gray swirl of snow, but then Lady's bark led her to the safety of the clothesline. Fighting the winds, Molly ran as fast as she could until the faintest glow from the window told her she was almost home.

"My papa," the child sobbed.

"I'll go back for him, but you have to be a big girl and help me. Can you do that?" Molly tumbled through the door and into the warming kitchen. "You have to stay right here by the fire and keep warm, so I can take care of your pa. Can you do that? Lady will stay with you."

"I want my papa." The child shook with terror and grief, and Molly held her tight, wishing she knew how to soothe away such deep, genuine pain. With every second that passed, she knew the child's father was closer to death.

Molly thanked heaven for the hound that nosed the child gently, intent on washing away those half-frozen tears.

The girl began to cry harder, filled with need, and it was all Molly could do to walk away. Again, she thought of the unconscious man bleeding and freezing in her backyard. Leaving the child safe and snug here was the father's best chance.

Suddenly Lady leaped away from the girl, snarling. The door smacked open, driven by the wind, and a shadow broke from the curtain of snow.

A man stumbled through her threshold, gun in hand and blood staining the front of his coat like a wide patch of crimson paint.

"Papa!" the girl cried just as Lady lunged, and the shadowed man tumbled to the floor, unconscious, his blood pooling on the snow-covered floorboards, his gun clattering to a stop beneath her lace-covered table.

Faster than lightning, the girl darted to her father's side and knelt, fingers curling into his coat. "Don't die, Papa. Please."

Molly pushed the door closed against the bitter wind and knelt at the big man's side. His face looked haggard and gray. His breathing came in short, struggling gasps. He was dying right in front of her. Right in front of his daughter.

She tore at his jacket buttons and ripped open the garment. Both dried and new blood stained his shirt and trousers, and the single charred hole in the fabric gave a clear indication of his injury—he'd been shot. By whom? And in this peaceful part of Montana?

"Papa, wake up." Heartbreak in those words. "Please wake up."

Lady did her best to comfort the distraught child while Molly's heart broke. She didn't know if she could save the man's life. There was so much blood, and since the skin around the charred wound was raw and torn, she figured that the bullet was still inside him.

What was she going to do? She knew nothing about treating a serious wound like this, and there was no way she'd be able to make it through the blizzard to town. Even if she could, this man wouldn't live that long with-out treatment.

Just use your common sense, Molly. She grabbed a clean dishcloth from the counter and pressed it against the flow of blood. She'd need to take out the bullet and sew up the wound, and her stomach dropped, suddenly nauseous.

Don't think about it. Just do it. The dish towel was soaking red. The man was running out of time.

"Lady, fetch my sewing box." The dog looked at her with pleading eyes, standing protectively over the sobbing child, not wanting to leave her. But when Molly repeated her command, the hound darted off.

"What's your name, sweetie?" She hopped up to fill a kettle with water.

"Beth." The little girl turned frightened blue eyes upward. "Are you one of the bad people?"

Bad people? "No. My name is Molly." She set the kettle on the stove, then knelt to drain the water from the reservoir. "Can you feel your fingers and toes?"

"They're cold." Beth swiped at her eyes with both fisted hands. "Is my papa gonna die?"

"I don't know." Molly knew the pain of being lied to—she wasn't going to make promises she couldn't keep. "I'm going to do my best to help him."

She sent the child into the kitchen to warm by the stove, and when Lady returned, carting her sewing basket by the handle, she sent the dog to watch over the child. Beth didn't argue, but continued to sob quietly in the warm corner.

Wishing she had more time to comfort the girl, Molly moved fast. She brought two lamps to the floor beside the stranger and lit them, then fetched a flask of whiskey from the pantry. Heart pounding, she knelt down beside her patient, this handsome stranger with a rugged face made of sharp angles and even planes. She couldn't help noticing his straight nose and his chiseled chin.

She pulled down his gun belt and trousers enough to expose the span of his hip and startled at the lean muscular make of him. Dark hair fanned across his stomach in a soft downward swirl toward his groin. Blushing, Molly vowed not to think about that any further. But his hard male body was a mystery, and she couldn't help wondering...

No, that wasn't a decent thought at all. Blushing harder, she moved the lamp closer to the bullet wound in his lower side, just above his left hip. She ran her littlest pair of sewing scissors through the bright flame, then knelt over him.

His skin was hot, and her heart thundered with fear of what she was about to do and the awareness of the man. *Breathe deep, and do this right.* She gathered her courage, then pulled the soaked dishcloth aside. The blood was slowing, surely that was a good sign. She nosed the tip of her scissors into the wound.

"Beth," he murmured, his voice slurred by dream and shock, and his head thrashed to one side and then stilled. The tension drained from his big body; the pain eased from his clenched jaw.

The scissors hit something hard. Molly gritted her teeth, steeled her stomach, and dug out the bullet as gently as she could. Blood welled up fresh and fast, and her gut clenched hard.

Don't faint, she ordered, even though her entire body was shaking. She applied pressure to the wound, then reached for the whiskey and splashed it across his abdomen. The hard roped muscles beneath his bronzed skin clenched in pain, and he groaned low in his throat, a sound of agony even though he was unconscious.

Beth started sobbing again on the other side of the cabinets, a sound as hopeless as a lonely winter wind.

Tension gathered at the nape of Molly's neck as she kept working—she couldn't stop now. As she threaded her needle, she spoke softly to the girl, and the crying stopped. Beth talked in a low voice to Lady, who was no doubt offering the girl her own brand of comfort.

Molly caught the edge of the ragged flesh with her needle. She winced, knowing it caused pain. Her stomach clenched again, and she felt her head start to swirl. Fighting for air, she pulled the knot through the skin and knotted it again to make sure it would stay and not pull through.

More blood sluiced from the wound, faster than she could stem it. She edged the needle into his flesh again and tugged the thread taut. The yawning wound closed a fraction, and she kept working, bringing the skin together, trying to make the seam she sewed tight enough.

She knotted her thread well and slumped against the back wall, breathing heavily. Sweat soaked her, and she felt shaky. Exhaustion gathered like an ache in the tensed muscles of her shoulders, neck, and back. She felt so weak, she didn't think she could stand.

But she'd done it—the wound was sewn tight. Gazing at the man, who was both shivering and sweating at the same time, she feared he wouldn't live, feared that her best was, once again, not good enough.

B eth gazed up over the bowl of steaming stew, watching Molly's every move with wide eyes. Even though she was warm, bathed, and dry, the child still looked peaked. Exhaustion bruised her delicate skin and hung on her slim shoulders. She sat as silent as a ghost at the table and didn't touch her food.

"Are you going to eat that?"

Beth shook her head, her dark hair brushing the shoulders of Molly's warmest sweater, which was draped over her reed-thin body. The sleeves were rolled up in fat cuffs, and the garment engulfed her. She looked forlorn, as if she were losing her entire world.

"It's early, but you look like you need your rest." Molly held out her hand.

Silently, Beth nodded, and her fingers closed around Molly's, tight with need and fear.

Molly tucked the child into her spare bed, safe and warm, and left the door ajar, just enough to be able to check on her. No more sounds came from the room.

The poor child. She understood how seriously her father was wounded. Molly ached for her, and when she next peered through the nearly closed door, she saw that Beth had fallen into an exhausted sleep. Maybe her dreams would be sweet, without cold, injury, or fear. Lady had curled up on the foot of the bed, keeping watch.

The hinges in her door squeaked, and she set the steaming basin on the nightstand. The man on her bed remained unmoving except for the barely perceptible rise and fall of his wide chest. He still lived.

Pulse drumming, she turned up the wick. Her knuckles jarred the lamp's crystal teardrops, and they tinkled like chimes, tossing glimmering fragments of rainbows across the embroidered pillow slip and the man's pallid face.

He was handsome; there was no denying that. Her heart tripped as she pulled the blanket down the breadth of his chest. Roughly textured skin stretched taut over well-defined muscles. He was a strong man, one who worked for a living; anyone could see that. His hands bore old calluses across his palms, and his skin was rich with the deep bronze from many summers spent beneath the sun.

As she wet and soaped the washcloth, she couldn't help wondering why he was wandering on foot through a dangerous blizzard with a child so young. Was he homeless? A drifter? But he had so many guns. He'd dropped one on her floor. She'd found one in his shirt pocket when she'd removed it, after stitching his wound. Now two more were strapped into holsters tied snug to both powerful thighs.

Four guns. She tried not to think about that. Tried not to think about what kind of man he might be. He was injured and she would help him, but she wouldn't trust him. No, she *couldn't* trust him.

This man bore a hard-set face, handsome but powerful, even in his sleep. She could feel his masculinity, like heat radiating from his well-made body. What was she doing noticing? She was a decent woman, a *schoolteacher*, for heaven's sake. She didn't go around gaping at men's handsome bodies.

She set the soapy cloth to his face and gently scrubbed over the proud blade of his nose, the ridges of each high cheekbone, the soft slope of his cheeks, and the unyielding line of his jaw. She felt the shape of him through the cloth and again as she rinsed off the soap and dried him.

The rough stubble of several days' growth rasped against her fingertips and caught on the terry towel. He smelled like winter wind and man, and as she laid the cloth to the base of his throat and caressed the width of his broad chest, heat licked through her. Like kindling to flame, she felt engulfed from toes to brow, from inside out.

What was wrong with her? This was an injured man, a stranger, hewn of muscle and danger, who looked as hard as stone fast asleep on her ruffled, pink and green sheets.

Wringing the cloth out in the steaming basin, she took deep breaths, filling her lungs with fresh air, trying to drive out the heat. Awareness tingled through her body, leaving a fine trembling that radiated straight through her abdomen.

Her gaze drifted back to him. She couldn't remember ever seeing a man's bare chest before, unless she counted her neighbor who'd worked out in his fields the past summer shirtless beneath the glare of the bright sun. And even from a distance, she'd been prudent enough to keep her gaze averted.

But *this* man, he drew her like a moth to light, and she couldn't help being fascinated by the sight and feel of him. Bronzed skin gleamed in the lamplight, dusted with soft hair that fanned across his chest and gathered in the center of his ridged abdomen, where it arrowed down beneath the edge of his denim trousers.

Her gaze lingered there, where the sheet curved mysteriously over that part of him. She blushed even thinking of it, and approached the foot of the bed, not sure what to do. The very thought of washing his...his... Heat flamed her face, and she turned to the basin, to soap the cloth.

He was asleep, not unconscious. Although weak from losing so much blood, he wouldn't be helpless when he woke. Maybe he ought to take care of such a personal task. The white bandage that wrapped in a tight band just above his hips contrasted against the black sheen of dried blood, and she knew she couldn't leave him like this. He had to be cared for, and there was no one but her to do it.

She reached for his gun belt and loosened the buckle at his hips. He stirred, his head thrashing from side to side against the pillow and a moan tearing from his throat. Her knuckles brushed the hot skin and soft fur on his abdomen as she began slipping the leather strap through the plain silver buckle.

Lady's bark echoed in the parlor, sharp against the wood walls and alarming even above the constant roar of the blizzard. The dog barked again, and Molly left the stranger, dashing into the lit parlor. The Regulator clock on the wall chimed the hour as she grabbed the Winchester from its pegs above the fireplace.

"What is it, girl? What's wrong?"

The dog lunged at the door with both front paws, teeth bared.

The rifle's wooden stock felt clammy against her palms. Maybe the bear was back, determined to try to break in her door this time. Or maybe he was trying to get at the horse in the stable.

She eased back the corner of a lace-edged curtain. Even though it was late afternoon, the world was nearly dark from the storm. The gale-force wind drove the snow to the ground like bullets, making the swirling grayness so dense she couldn't see past her top porch step. The hairs on the back of her neck stood on end, and warning prickled down her spine.

The hinges squeaked behind her. She turned to see a tall, broad shadow lurch out of the dark, avoiding the light. Molly grabbed Lady by the collar and ordered her to be quiet as the nose of a revolver glinted for a flash of a second, reflecting the lamplight. His step, uneven and halting, knelled on the puncheon floors as he approached, shadowed face set, broad shoulders tensed into a steely line.

Molly shrank, and the gun she clutched so tightly felt useless against his overwhelming male power, predatory and territorial, as uncompromising as death. He pushed past her and nudged the barrel of her rifle toward the floor. Lady went wild.

"Lock her in the bedroom."

Molly took one look at the fresh bandage already stained crimson and went to do as he asked, but she was shaking from head to toe. He'd looked dangerous asleep but awake he was lethal, and although he didn't stand straight, he radiated power and not weakness, strength and not injury.

Molly remembered the guns she'd found and eyed the one he held. "It's not a bear out there at all. What kind of trouble have you brought to my house?"

"Too much, and I'm sorry, ma'am." He said no more and offered no further explanation.

The rumble of his voice, resonate and cello-deep, echoed inside her. She stepped back, not sure what to do. He towered over her and the lamplight, barely touching him, gleamed darkly off his skin. Like a knight of old, like myth and legend, he braced his broad shoulders and lifted one arm, gazing out through the dark window.

"Are your doors locked?"

His gaze latched on hers, and although she couldn't see anything more than his shadow, she felt his gaze probing straight through to her heart, as if he could read all her secrets. Exactly how dangerous was he?

"Bar the front and back doors." His shadowed jaw clenched as he stared out at the storm. "Hurry."

She hated it when a man thought he could tell her what to do, but with the way Lady's hair bristled around her neck and tail, she knew the danger outside was greater than the one inside her house. But she couldn't stop the spark of anger as she shut her dog in the bedroom, then grabbed the bar from the corner and laid it across the metal brackets on either side of the stout pine door.

A boom rumbled through the thick walls; the muffled crash could be either thunder or gunfire. Luke leaned one shoulder against the window casing, gritting his teeth against the pain that burned in his left side just above his hip. Weakness radiated down his left leg and washed through every muscle in his battered body.

He listened to the tap of the woman's step through the house and the scratch of the dog's nails against the closed bedroom door. The storm outside roared like the devil himself, and if Moss followed him here, then the storm camouflaged him well. Luke swore, anger building. If Moss was out there, then Beth still wasn't safe.

Damn. He couldn't see anything but darkness and the harsh veil of swirling snow washed with black now that night had fallen. Moss could be out there, no more than three feet away, and Luke wouldn't know it, couldn't see him. Fury tore through him like the swift edge of night.

He hadn't come this far to fail Beth.

The dog's startled bark split through the dark. He let the curtain fall, the lace feminine and soft against his knuckles, and charged around the perimeter of the room. His left foot dragged just enough to catch his toe on the edge of a braided carpet. Pain jolted up his leg and into the wound.

He gritted his teeth and kept running. The distance across the parlor seemed like a mile. He heard the crack of a door breaking, the slam of wood striking wood, and a woman screaming.

His adrenaline pumped, and he tore around the corner, revolver steady, calm from the years of working behind a gun. He saw it in a flash—the rifle on the floor, the re-flected glint off a revolver's nose, the swing of that revolver straight toward Luke's heart—

Where is the woman? He dove behind the thick wood wall as a gun fired and a bullet bit into the curve of the log wall not an inch from his brow. He could hear the rasp of frightened breathing. Moss had her. The bounty hunter he'd been ducking since crossing into Montana Territory. The coldhearted bastard who'd put Beth's life in danger. He had the woman.

"I've got a gun to her head, McKenna," a man's voice—not Moss's—boomed above the howling wind and the barking dog. "Toss me your Colt and come out, hands up and empty, or I'll shoot her. You know I will."

Hammond. Moss's right-hand man. Luke leaned his brow against the wall, breathing hard, shaking from weakness and pain. He was in no position to fight. Hell, he couldn't even hold his gun steady, and he knew Hammond would kill the woman, either way. He couldn't surrender, even if he wanted to.

"What's it gonna be, McKenna?"

"I'm coming out, Hammond." There was no other solution. He tossed down one gun and listened to it slide across the polished floor, metal gliding on wood. "I've got Beth in the next room. I don't want a fight."

"Sure, McKenna. Anything you say. Just step out with your hands up. I'd hate to put a hole in this little lady, not before I'm finished with her." Cruelty glittered like a rare jewel in the dark, as heartless as the storm, as dark as the night.

"Is Moss with you?" Luke tugged his second revolver from his gun belt, speaking to hide the click as he thumbed back the hammer.

"Get the hell out here or I shoot."

Luke shook like a son of a bitch, but he took a deep breath, willing his right hand to be steady for just a few seconds, just long enough to squeeze off one shot. *You can do this.* He had to, for Beth's sake and for the woman's.

"You win, Hammond. I'm coming out."

Luke flew around the corner. Pain blurred his vision as he squeezed the trigger, and his aim was sure and true. He saw Hammond's look of surprise, saw his gun tumble out of his hand, firing wild. The woman, hazel eyes wide with terror, opened her mouth in a silent scream as she realized the bullet had whizzed right past her neck to lodge in the middle of the bounty hunter's heart.

Luke waited, revolver cocked, as the big man tumbled backward already dead, hitting the floor with a sickening, lifeless thud. He didn't so much as twitch.

Staggering, Luke leaned against the counter. Relief swept through him, cold as a north wind. "Are you all right, ma'am?"

She shook her head. She trembled so hard, her teeth rattled. Wide eyes locked on his, and she looked ready to faint. "You could have shot me. You could have killed me."

"No. I'm a sharpshooter. I never miss." Pain exploded with every step, and he pressed the flat of his palm to his left side, where fresh blood warmed his skin. "I'll take care of the body."

"The body," she repeated dully. "You killed a man. Right here in my kitchen."

"A man who had no problem playing with your life." Luke retrieved his Colt from the floor and holstered both weapons. "You don't want to think about what he was going to do to you."

"You killed a man in my kitchen," she repeated, her hands beginning to fist. "You brought violence here, to my home."

"I'm sorry about that." He grabbed Hammond by the wrist. He knew the bounty hunter was already dead but checking was old habit. The blizzard hurled cold and ice through the open door and sheered straight through him. He debated about hauling Hammond's body away now because the woman hugging herself and shaking looked ready to faint.

He pushed the door closed with a bang and stepped over Hammond's body. Her back was to him, and he could see the rage in her clenched fists, see her fear in her rigid spine, and hear it in the constant rustle of her skirt as she trembled.

"You saved my life and my daughter's." He lingered in the shadows not knowing if he should approach her. "I had no right bringing trouble to your doorstep. I owe you more than that."

Her chin shot up. She looked ready to fight. She looked ready to crumble. She was a gently raised woman, he could see that right off. In the soft curves of her face, classically beautiful, her complexion was as smooth as cream. She was tall and willowy, but when her gaze locked on his he saw no delicate blossom easily damaged.

He saw hurt, he saw fear, but mostly he saw strength.

"Keep your distance from me." She knelt to retrieve her rifle, the fragile curve of her neck white and vulnerable in the flickering lamplight. She straightened, fingers curled hard around the wooden stock, her knuckles white. "If it wasn't blizzarding outside, I would lock you out. Look what you've done."

"Aren't you going to thank me?"

"For what?"

"Saving your life." He laid one hand on her shoulder, the other on her elbow. "And now you have to thank me for keeping you from fainting. Come, sit down."

"I don't need any help." She twisted away from his grip, but he tightened his hold on her elbow. She felt like fine china, far too fine for a man like him to touch.

"I don't understand where he came from." She let him lead her to the table and chairs by the window. "There isn't another house for half a mile, and it's impossible to travel in this kind of storm."

"Not impossible for men like Hammond." He held out the chair and waited until she settled into the polished wooden seat, skirts rustling, before he released her. His fingertips sparked with awareness. "The devil can travel anywhere, ma'am. Lower your head and try to breathe deeply."

"I'm not going to faint." She didn't heed his advice, but propped her elbows on the table instead, setting the crystal teardrops on the lamp tingling, and buried her face in her hands.

It had been a long time since he'd been this close to a woman. He liked the way she smelled faintly of lilacs sweetened by spring sunshine, how her lace-edged petticoats whispered, and the feeling of gentility, of something soft and feminine in a world cold and unforgiving. She reminded him that there were places where life was valued and killing was seen as an unbelievable sin.

He shook with weakness, but managed to step away. What did she see when she looked at him? What did she think of the worn clothes and his four guns? Of the bounty hunter dead at his feet? Of the child he couldn't provide for? What did she see?

He grabbed the dead body by one ankle, opened the back door, and tugged him outside into the black howling storm. The wind's force nearly knocked him to his knees. Luke gritted his teeth and kept going. But not the frigid temperatures or the brutal wind could drive the despair from his heart. He was a wanted man, and the next time a bounty hunter fired on him, Luke knew he might not be lucky.

He had no future, but for Beth's sake he would make peace with the woman inside the house, haloed with lamplight, frightened and alone. He was at her mercy for his daughter's safety until the blizzard blew out and he was on the run again.

CHAPTER TWO

Molly listened to the beat of his step, a faint clump-clump above the storm's howling fury. He was coming back. Her heart kicked in her chest, and she started shaking again. A part of her wanted to leap up from the table and bar the door tight. The sensible part of her knew she had to offer shelter to a man trapped in the storm, however dangerous.

Her skin prickled with warning, with both fear and awe, as the door opened and he strolled in with the blizzard to his back. She didn't need to look up to see that not even the storm frightened him; the wide line of his shoulders remained level and braced.

The wind roared with fury, and all the heat drained from the room. He barricaded the door using the bar, since the doorknob and lock were broken. His efficient, powerful movements echoed in the empty, still room.

"How's my daughter?" His low voice thundered through the kitchen.

"She's asleep. After being out in the cold like that, I was afraid she might become ill—"

"She's ill?" His face twisted with fury or pain, she couldn't tell which, as he strode past her, jaw set, limping. A bright stain spread across the waistband and left front pocket of his denims. "Where is she?"

"Sleeping." Molly stood, rifle clenched in both hands. The man

20

had lost so much blood, how could he be standing? "She looked peaked and exhausted, so sleep was the best—"

He blended with the shadows in the parlor so that only the uneven knell of his boots striking the floor then padding against the braid rug marked his progress. The bedroom door whispered open, and his gait silenced. She heard the squeak of the old rocking chair and then nothing but the storm and darkness. And the fears in her heart.

The rifle in her hands felt useless. She knew how to operate the weapon, but her skills were nothing compared to his. The image of him racing into the room, all might and power, his gun raised, and the flash of fire left her breathless. Once again she could feel the bullet whiz past her neck, feel the bruising grip of the bounty hunter's hand to her throat, choking the air from her. She smelled the stale sweat and gunpowder, then the fresh blood...

She leaned against the counter and hugged the rifle to her. Who was he? Surely, he wouldn't hurt her. She clung to that thought, remembering that her skin was still bruised from the dead man's touch. She set the rifle on the pegs over the mantle and dropped to her knees.

Her stomach twisted hard, but she wasn't sick. Molly wrapped her arms around her waist and held on tight. The smell of the dead man's blood and sweat remained on her clothes, and the bruise on her throat throbbed with pain. She remembered another man's hand to her throat, and the memory blurred and in the snapping flames she saw Arnold's face, twisted in fury.

She willed away the fear and the memories. And the sour, bitter taste of remembering the man who'd sworn he loved her.

Don't remember. She squeezed the images from her mind and willed her eyes to see only fire and flame and her skin to forget the pain of the violent man's touch.

"Thank you for taking care of her."

Molly gasped. Was he part ghost? He'd made no noise this time as he'd closed Beth's door and crossed the parlor. He clung to the darkness, as if afraid of the light, and all she could see of him was the dark mop of his tousled hair, the broad span of his chest, and the dull gleam of reflected light off the handles of his revolvers.

He flexed his hands, loose at his sides. "Looks like you took good care of her."

"It was easy enough." She stood, smoothing her palms against her skirt. "Are there going to be any more men like that breaking through my door?"

"I hope not. And if Moss comes, I won't let him hurt you or Beth. You have my word on that." He took one step, silent in the shadows.

"Who's Moss?"

He didn't answer, his step a whisper. "I'll clean up the blood and repair your back door. You have my word of honor, we'll be gone as soon as the blizzard breaks."

How long would that be? Molly hugged herself harder as he towered over her, near enough to see the stubble of several days' growth along his jaw and the dark sheen of his eyes.

"You never told me your name."

"It doesn't matter. We'll be out of here by dawn." His shadowed gaze met hers, inscrutable, uncompromising.

Yes, he was a hard man, but there was softness there, too. She'd felt it in his touch when he'd helped her to the table and heard it in his voice as he'd tried to keep her from fainting. "I have to call you something."

"Ma'am, it would be best if you forgot you ever saw me." His big hands fisted, hands that could handle a gun and deal out death, looked gentle somehow.

Molly knew she was only imagining it. No man was truly gentle at heart, at least, no man who looked and acted as he did. "What about your little girl? Should I forget I saw her too?"

"Beth would be safer."

"So, what do you do, take her with you, drifting from homestead to homestead?"

"That really isn't any of your business, ma'am." His words were polite, but they carried the knell of warning. "I appreciate what you've done. Don't get me wrong. Beth and I are just passing through, and tomorrow we don't want to be even a memory to you."

"This night will be easy to forget. Gunmen have shoot-outs in my kitchen all the time."

His hard mouth curved into the faintest grin. "Where are your bandages?"

"I'll have to make more."

"I can do it. Just need a strip of muslin." He limped into the pool of lamplight, golden against the dark blue of his denims and gleaming on the red stain of the once white bandage wrapped tightly around his washboard abdomen.

Molly took one look at the ashen hue to his rugged, stone-hard face. "Sit down before you fall down. And leave your guns on my table. I'm confiscating them until you leave."

"I'll need them in case—"

"I watched you kill a man in front of me. I felt him die. I don't know what kind of man you are, but I know enough to be afraid of you."

"I'm no threat—"

"I don't care. I won't have an armed man in my house."

He was twice her size. He towered over her, all male might and strength. Beneath his bronzed skin kissed by the lamplight, muscles stood in great ridges, prominent and powerful. He looked like an outlaw. He acted like an outlaw. He shot like an outlaw.

Seconds ticked by, stretched long by the growing darkness on his face. Uncompromising, he hitched his chin higher, and his eyes turned a shade darker.

His frown deepened, bracketing his unsmiling, unforgiving mouth. Then he withdrew both revolvers and laid them on the lace tablecloth. The lamplight glinted off the deadly metal weapons, placed next to her wreath of holly and pine that hugged the base of the crystal teardrop lamp.

"Keep one where I can get to it." He eased down into the chair, his face gray, and his mouth twisted against pain.

She remembered what he'd said about the other man and nodded.

Her hands trembled as she opened the bottom drawer in the kitchen and withdrew clean muslin. *Just take care of him now, so he can leave in the morning.* That's all she had to do. Maybe the blizzard would be a brief one.

But as she tore the muslin into strips, she knew that Beth, tucked safely into bed, dreaming sweetly, would leave with him, too. The wary-eyed little girl who'd cried so hard for her father— for this man. Danger radiated from him like heat from a fire. She grabbed the whiskey and poured a basin of warm water.

"Didn't your husband make it home before the storm?" He watched her, measured her.

She felt self-conscious as she set her armload on the table in front of him. "I don't have a husband."

"Do you mean you live on this land all by yourself?"

"Well, me and the dog."

"Isn't that dangerous, ma'am?"

"Not until you came through my door." She knelt before him and laid the scissors on his hard, broad knee. The lamplight seemed to worship his shoulders and chest, and Molly felt her gaze linger there, tracing the hard planes and ridges, remembering how he'd felt. Her fingertips tingled.

You're lonely, that's all. It was the only way to explain it. Angry at herself and at him for being so handsome, she grasped the scissors and snipped at the blood-soaked bandages beneath his waist.

"I'll unbuckle this for you." His arm brushed hers as he reached down and shucked off his gun belt. She watched his throat work as he unbuttoned his denims.

Heat washed over her face. It wasn't as if he were naked, right? As she peeled back the soaked left-front corner of his trousers and pushed down the waistband of his drawers, she could barely see his curved hipbone, let alone anything lower.

She peeled back the thick pad of muslin directly over the wound, and her stomach twisted. The injury was seeping blood in a steady stream between the stitched-tight edges of red, inflamed skin.

"Just wrap me up tight."

"I've done my best, but I'm a schoolteacher, not a nurse." She folded a length of muslin end over end to make a decent pad. "I could correct your long division if you needed me to, but I'm not sure how well I stitched up your wound."

"It looks to me like you did just fine." His voice sounded strained.

He was worried about the amount of blood, too. He was soaked with it. She applied pressure, waiting, as the pad filled. She folded another and held it tight. Finally, the bleeding slowed enough for her to begin bandaging.

She rolled the strip just below his waist, holding the muslin tight. He smelled of snow, winter wind, and man, a pleasant combination that made him seem less dangerous as she leaned close to roll the muslin strip around his back and hip, then tugged it tight across the taut hardness of his abdomen. She bound him well, taking care; all the while his scent seemed to fill her nose and head, and her pulse drummed in her ears.

"Thank you, ma'am." He stood before she could offer him a cup of coffee or a meal and before she could bring her heart rate back down to normal.

He ambled toward Beth's room, leaving her alone in the pool of lamplight, feeling strangely moved.

This man was danger, and she'd be best keeping away from him. But when she looked in on him later, he was nothing more than a shadow at his daughter's side with both elbows propped on his knees, a part of the darkness. She couldn't see anything but the faintest outline of him in the unlit room, but she could feel him, feel his protection, his vigilance, and most of all his devotion to his daughter.

Arms empty, she fed the fire and sat down in front of the hearth, hoping the heat could drive the chill from her heart. The memories had been real today, and her body still thrummed with fear—with too damn much fear.

She listened to the first blizzard of the season, late this year, and let the darkness of the December night wrap around her. She knew she couldn't sleep, and it was just as well. She was afraid to close her eyes on a night like this, afraid of what dreams might come.

The vicious storm swirled around him, a thousand grains of hard ice scouring his face. Freezing, he was freezing to death. He had to get Beth to safety. He had to hurry. He had to—

Luke's eyes snapped open. The storm howled, but not in his ears. Ice scoured solid log walls, and he was safe. He wasn't dreaming. He was wrapped in a warm blanket in a dark room. And he wasn't alone.

He sensed her presence, for there was little to see in the black shadows of the bedroom. It was a woman; he could smell that powder-soft scent of a woman's skin and the brighter scents of lilac and cinnamon. There were other smells—the aroma of a hearty beef stew and the doughy freshness of heated bread.

Her skirts rasped with each careful step. She kept her distance, moving through the dark, and stiffened when she had to lean close to set the tray on the small nightstand. The crystal lamp chimed, sending shock waves through him. He rubbed his hands over his eyes. "I can't believe I drifted off."

"You're weak and injured and slipped out of the chair. That's when I covered you up," she answered, her voice a soft whisper to keep from waking Beth. "You've lost so much blood, I don't know how you're still kicking. You should eat, then get some sleep. You said you intended to leave in the morning. You need to be strong enough."

"I don't need sleep. I swore to protect you."

"And I say no one else is going to travel through this storm, not now. My guess is the temperature is about minus twenty degrees, maybe colder. No man can survive in that for long, and it will only grow colder through the night."

"What did you do with my Colts?"

"I set one on the mantel."

"Within easy reach." Still, he was glad for the fifth revolver lodged in his boot, a boot he was still wearing. "You believe me about the man after me, don't you? He's a tough bastard, and it'll take more than a blizzard to stop him."

"What did you do? Rob a bank? Kill a man?" She met his gaze, a strong woman used to being alone. Light crept across the threshold to shine in her russet curls and illuminate the judgment in her eyes. "I figured out you're not just a drifter, someone come upon hard times. Not someone who can shoot like that. Kill like that."

"Believe what you want. I don't care. As long as my daughter can stay until the storm breaks."

"Your daughter? What about you?"

"Only Beth matters." He stood, gritting his teeth as pain washed through his left hip and speared down his thigh.

She said nothing, and fear shadowed her eyes.

He hated that fear, hated having to look at her and see what he'd become. "Look lady, I'm not going to hurt you. I'm grateful for your helping me the way you have, I—"

"What kind of man are you who can't protect a child better than this?" The words cut like a newly sharpened knife, crisp, clean, and deep. "Didn't you have the sense to get her out of the weather before the blizzard hit? What kind of father would jeopardize—"

"You don't know anything about me, ma'am," he bit out, temper flaring hot as flame in his chest, hotter than the pain, and it drove him forward, toward her. "Don't judge me by your comfortable little principles. You don't have a husband and you don't have children, by the looks of it. Don't pass judgment on what you don't know."

"I know a child your daughter's age needs a home and security. By the looks of it, you don't own a horse or a house, and you can't have a legal job." She took a step back, all fragile woman, small compared to his strength, yet her chin was set, and she met his gaze with a depth of anger that could frighten any man. "I don't have children, and I probably never will, but don't judge me either. I can't believe I wanted to save your life. I can't believe—"

She spun away, small hands fisted. Such small hands. He noticed it now, the delicate cut of her knuckles and the slim shape of her fingers. Of how silk-white skin stretched over the bones at her wrist, and how frail that wrist was. Why, he could easily wrap his forefinger around the width of it.

"I am what you think." He took a step forward and stopped, his chest heavy, aching with the grief of what he'd become. "And I'm not what you think."

"Are you going to hurt me?"

Her question rang with both honesty and fear and lingered in the empty chambers of his heart. "I told you. I won't hurt you."

"Just bounty hunters?" Her spine straightened, and her gaze was full of suspicion, dislike, and fear.

"That's right, ma'am." He told himself he didn't care if she believed him or not. It didn't matter that he felt out of place here, in her carefully decorated home with the matching green rugs and furniture, wall hangings and curtains. "How long do storms like this last?"

"I'm new to this part of Montana myself. I've heard blizzards like this can last for days, sometimes the better part of a week." She took another step back, keeping distance between them—a solid and distinct distance.

He didn't know what hurt more—the bullet wound an inch above his left hip or seeing what he'd become. An outsider. A man not to be trusted. And worse.

Just keep her calm. That's all he had to do. Reassure her. He might not need the shelter of her home, but Beth did. And Beth needed him.

"Thank you again for the meal, ma'am." He took a step back and another. Weakness washed through him. He felt sick and feverish. But he kept stepping back when he saw the relief drain the tension from the woman's shoulders and the worry lines from her soft brow. She didn't want him near her, and the pain in his chest grew fiercer, as sharp as a scythe.

You don't belong here, McKenna. They both knew it. He belonged out in the stable with the rest of the animals.

He pushed Beth's bedroom door closed behind him and let the click of the doorknob echo in the darkness. The image of the woman in front of the fire remained, her russet curls burnished and her woman's curves brushed by the firelight.

His groin kicked, and he couldn't believe that even hopeless, exhausted, and in physical pain his body still responded to the sight of a woman. He leaned against the closed door and caught his breath.

She's not for you, McKenna. Just sit down and eat the stew. Weakness washed over him, and he stumbled to the chair at Beth's side. He could hear her breathing, slow and even, lost in dreams. Love warmed his chest, sweet like morning sun after a snowy night. He felt the sweetness fill him, and the saving grace of loving his child made him remember that he was more than what the year in prison had made him. There was still a place in him that could feel and love and care.

He lit the lamp and left the wick low, the weak flame just enough to illuminate the meal the woman had fixed for him. His gaze scanned the still-steaming bowl of hearty stew, the generous plate of sliced bread, the fat slice of apple pie, and the cinnamon tea dark in a flowered china cup.

She'd gone to a lot of trouble. His conscience bit hard He'd remained self-reliant on the long trek from Texas, on the long hard flight across the plains, sleeping wherever he could find shelter for them.

That was the only life he had to offer Beth. If he closed his eyes he could see the orphanage, see the fenced yard that looked like a prison courtyard and the daily march of the children to work in the fields. He could still see Beth in that line, chin down, the light gone from her eyes, her spirit diminished.

What was he going to do? He was a week's journey on horseback to the Canadian border. He couldn't take her across with him, and guilt tore at him. Guilt made fresh by the look of censure in the woman's eyes. From a woman who lived in a house this fine, with her crystal lamps and upholstered furniture.

He forced down the food, even if his stomach was clenched

tight. Even if he felt ready to tumble onto the floor. He was overcome with a weakness that he couldn't shake. He was all at once nauseous, dizzy, and so thirsty he couldn't chew the spicy stew or the yeasty bread with-out pouring one glass after another from the pitcher by Beth's bed.

He finished every crumb of the food, but he didn't feel any better. Exhaustion and pain battered him like a living thing, like an enemy, but he'd learned something from his year of hard labor. He could push his body farther, and he would. For Beth's sake. For Beth's safety.

His heart came to life looking at her, like the first bud of spring breaking free from winter's harsh grasp. His child stirred, rolling onto her side toward him, toward the light. Her dark curls curled over her brow, and he stroked her princess's face with his gaze, memorizing the slope of her nose and the curve of her cheek for the long nights to come when he would be alone. When he wouldn't be watching over her and protecting her from harm.

When the time came, he didn't know how he would be able to endure leaving her again, how he could walk away and not see her grow and change, always wondering who she would become, always aching for the sight of his daughter's smile.

But for her protection, he would leave her. And he would never come back.

The clock in the parlor gently belled the hour—midnight. Luke bit back a groan and stood, facing the pain. He ambled to the window where the ruffled curtains, edged with lace and made with care, hid the dark panes of frosted glass.

He could see nothing. The dark and storm hid the world from him. Moss was out there somewhere—and too damn close. Luke could feel it like the ice on the glass. He leaned his brow against the frosted panes and tried to have faith, tried to believe that he would find a safe place for Beth and that he'd cross the border alive.

Luke McKenna didn't believe in dreams. His faith in the world and in people had been destroyed the night the deputies had torn Beth from his arms and led him away in cuffs and chains. When no one cared about an innocent man's life or a little girl's heart, every illusion shattered.

A light rap sounded on the door, and he waited as the new hinges squeaked mildly. Light slashed into the room, revealing the woman and her dog. The animal ambled into the room, nails clicking on the wood, and, after checking his plate and finding no crumbs, leaped up onto the foot of the bed. With a sigh, the dog circled, then curled up in a ball, watching the little girl as she slept.

"I brought you a few things." Molly tapped into the room, nearly as quiet as a shadow. "I thought you might want to wash off the blood. These are Christmas presents I bought early for my uncle, but they might fit you."

"Thank you, ma'am." The empty places in his heart felt bigger as he watched her shadowed form, accented by the thick fall of her hair, back toward the door. "Beth and I owe our lives to you."

"You owe me nothing." She hesitated in the threshold, and he couldn't help tracing her woman's curves, the rise of her breasts, the dip of her waist, the slope of her hips. She was like a fine piece of china, delicate and beautiful and far finer than he had the right to touch.

"You need your rest, too." Gentle words, as sweet as any dream. "If you need my bed—"

"I'll keep an eye on my daughter."

"But you're injured."

His throat ached at the concern in her words, spoken past prejudices and fear. He wondered if she was truly that good-hearted or she just worried that he might not be strong enough to leave the moment the storm broke.

"There will be no sleep for me tonight." He thought of Moss out there in the dark. The bounty hunter would have found shelter by now, but not for long. Luke hardened his heart. All that mattered were his promises and responsibilities to Beth.

He would watch and wait and make certain no harm came to her.

Without another word, the woman slipped from sight, pulling the door closed behind her. Her step tapped faintly along the wood floor, leaving him in the dark, right where he belonged.

Molly stared at the sheet covering her bed, where the stranger had slept only hours before. Before the bounty hunter had broken into her home. Before *he* saved her life.

Seeing him with his daughter had made him human, made him seem less like a dangerous outlaw. She'd seen the tenderness in his eyes when he'd looked at his child and the way his throat worked when Lady had settled onto the foot of the bed. She couldn't help but be confused.

This is what had torn her apart during her engagement. How Albert had been so real, a man of heart and vulnerabilities, of tenderness that made her begin to believe in that fairy-tale love only found in fiction. But over time that tenderness began to fade, the vulnerabilities turned to mist, and she was left without illusions, staring at the true man and his cold heart. A man who thought he could dominate her with commands and violence. She'd believed in romance, but he'd expected obedience.

She would not believe in a man's tenderness, in his softness again. Not that the man in the room next door could be described as soft. Hard as steel, rugged as Montana, he looked every inch a threatening man. The softness in him was small and brief—and she wouldn't think of it and let it lessen her fear of him. She would hold her heart still and not see goodness in another man capable of harm.

She folded the sheet. His scent clung to the soft, wash-worn flannel—the salty musk of his skin and a hint of something restless and clean, like the winter wind on a clear, cold day. She looked at the melted snow from his boots on her floor and the splashes of blood from his wound and knew she couldn't forget him that easily.

A sensation tugged tight in her stomach, a twist of desire that left her confused. Surely, she wasn't attracted, *physically* attracted, to a man like him? She dropped the sheet in the laundry basket, unable to forget the sight of his chest gleaming like burnished bronze in the lamplight. No, she was absolutely *not* attracted to the man. To any man.

And even if she spent nights alone aching for a man's touch, for the feel of his body covering hers, she wasn't going to admit it. To think, a woman her age still dreaming of romance even when she no longer believed in it.

Still, she couldn't help thinking of him on the other side of that wall. Wondering how he was faring, if she'd sewn his wound well enough or if he continued to bleed. Was he worrying that the storm would last and trap him here, with her, for days?

Molly closed her eyes. The bruise at the base of her throat throbbed. *Please, let the storm be brief.*

She unbuttoned her bodice and slipped the warm wool dress down over her hips. The weight of one pocket weighed down the fabric, and she remembered the letter. Could it be? Had she truly forgotten?

Remorse settled hard and heavy beneath her breastbone. Molly pulled the envelope from her pocket, hung the dress to air, and sat down on the corner of her bed. The ropes creaked, and the soft feather mattress sank beneath her weight. As the single flame tossed weak light across the corner of the envelope, Molly stared at it. Did she have the heart to open it? Would it be better to leave the words unread?

Maybe Mother had reconsidered. She hadn't always been so harsh. There was a chance she would be able to forgive. A small chance, but how could Molly throw it away? She had always wanted her mother's love.

Armed with a hairpin and as much courage as she could muster, she slit open the envelope and pulled out the single sheet of paper. Parchment crackled as she unfolded the printed rose stationary. Both of her parents' names were scrawled in black printer's ink across the top of the page, embellished with silver and gold.

Daughter, Molly read. *After much consideration, your father and I have decided to ask you one final time. This is your last chance to mend the shame you've caused us. Albert is still willing to marry you, and you are such a plain girl that you should consider...*

Molly closed her eyes and felt a cold emptiness settle in her chest, felt it spread through every part of her, body and soul. Her parents would never forgive her for breaking her engagement the morning of her wedding.

It was no apology, after all. Molly refolded the letter and slipped it into the envelope. She should have burned it. She should never have let the hurt back in, never dared to hope...

Ashamed of being so foolish, of wanting to be loved so much, she turned down the wick and let the tears fall.

The faint thud startled Luke awake. He'd drowsed off again, comfortable in the warm parlor. Beth was sleeping sound and safe, and he intended to keep watch over the house through the night. But every time he sat still, his body tried to trick him and he'd dozed off.

He bit back the moan of pain and fought the dizziness. Standing made every muscle in his body go weak. He'd lost too much blood, and he knew it. How was he going to be able to keep two steps ahead of Moss now? And without a horse?

Remembering how the bounty hunter had shot out the animal from beneath him kindled the rage banked in his chest. Black and fierce, it drove him now. He grabbed his Colt from the mantel and headed through the dark dining room toward the back door. Every step was agony, but he didn't care. Moss had dared to shoot him. Had he missed, Beth would have been hit. The rage darkened and grew hotter than flame.

I'm not going to let you win, Luke vowed, *even if it costs me my life.* He would find a place for Beth, and he would make damn sure men like Moss couldn't harm her. His daughter's life was worth his own freedom.

The thump sounded again, faint and rhythmic. He stepped over the dried blood on the floor. He heard a light click behind him— the dog coming to check out what he was up to in the kitchen, no doubt. The animal didn't seem alarmed. Remembering how the dog had barked when Hammond broke through the door, he figured they were safe enough.

He pulled back the edge of the lacy curtain and saw only darkness. He waited for his eyes to adjust until he saw an old fir's limbs waving angrily in the strong wind, one low bough banging against the eaves. Relief spilled through him. He wasn't strong enough to fight, not tonight.

The dog eyed the cookie crock set high on the counter. Luke set his gun on the table and knelt to inspect the dried blood. Not so bad. The water was still hot in the reservoir, even though the coals had been banked. He found a cloth in the bottom drawer and soap in the dish near the sink.

Such a fancy kitchen. He ran his fingertips across the porcelain sink. Smooth and cold. The water pump stood over it, the new metal shining faintly, reflecting the scant light from the parlor. He looked around. Everything was in its place—the matching lace curtains, the varnished wood countertops, the cabinets polished smooth, porcelain knobs painted with delicate purple flowers.

A real life. It was here, in this log home. Just like it was in all the homes he'd passed since he'd broken out of prison. He'd stayed away until now, feeling like a wild wolf always on the outside looking in. He didn't belong here in a world of braided rugs and crocheted doilies, where a woman's softness made a man's heart warm.

He heard it then, the indistinct rise and fall of someone weeping. It faded away, and he knew it wasn't Beth. He knew the sound of her tears. The big dog swiveled past him, long ears quirked. The animal dashed through the house, sliding across the polished floor and darting around furniture. A door squeaked open, and he heard the murmur of the woman's low voice.

His chest tightened with remorse. There was so much packed inside him, it was hard to believe there was room for more. But there was. He fought his way through the house to her darkened room. Her tears were nearly silent now, but the stifled sob still rasped above the keening howl of the blizzard.

He'd done this to her and hated himself for it. Wishing he could make things right, he pushed open the door and lumbered into the room. There was little to see in the black shadows except for the faint outline of a ruffled pillow slip and the slumped curve of a slim shoulder.

He knelt down beside her, gritting his teeth against the pain in his side and in his heart. "I wish I could change things. Make it so that Beth and I didn't get caught in that storm. So that you would never have been attacked in your own home or be forced to shelter a man you're afraid of."

"If you didn't find my house, then you and your daughter would have frozen to death. There is no place else to take shelter nearby."

"So, in other words, you're glad I found my way here?" He knew he couldn't coax a smile from her, not when her voice rang heavily, laden with grief and pain.

"That's right. I was hoping for a little excitement in my life. It was just too calm and boring."

"Glad I could help out. Liven things up a bit."

"You certainly did that." She sniffed, and he heard the rustle of a handkerchief.

"I owe you more than I can repay, ma'am. I know that. I don't want to cause you more grief."

"At least we agree on that." A sob rattled through her.

"I'm sorry I made you cry. You don't deserve that, ma'am. Not after all you've done for me and for my daughter."

"I feel old when you call me ma'am." She sniffed again. "I'm

Molly."

"Molly, then." His gaze had adjusted to the darkness, and he could see the tilt of her head, the curve of her slender neck, the tumble of thick curls his fingers ached to touch. He would bet that beautiful hair would feel like fine silk against his callused skin.

It had been a long time since he'd touched a woman intimately. His body betrayed him, even weak as a kitten he felt the heavy throb in his groin, and his denims grew tight. Yes, it had been too damn long. But a wolf didn't belong here, with a woman of lace and kindness.

"Are you going to be all right?" He couldn't leave until he'd tried to make things right.

"I'll live, trust me."

He heard the crinkle of paper and only then did he realize she held an envelope in her hand. Bad news, he figured, and felt a flicker of relief that he hadn't made her cry a second time. "Is there anything I can do?"

"Not one thing." She sighed, sounding lost as a winter wind. "I can take care of myself."

"Then, good night." He stood, her words gentle but firmly spoken echoing in his ears. Of course she didn't want him, didn't need a man like him.

She might not be as afraid of him as she'd been earlier, but she was still afraid. A smart woman should be. He'd brought death to her door. Lord knew what else would follow him here. Even if he left, maybe Moss could trail him here. Luke's guts clenched tightly and he closed his mind against that possibility.

Whatever happened, he would make damn sure no harm came to Molly for taking them in. He owed her that much. Hell, he owed her everything.

He closed the door with a click that rattled through the empty parlor. Hopeless inside, hopeless down to his very soul, he stood alone in a room of simple luxury—comfortable furniture and the extra touches that made his eyes hurt.

It was different from the stone cell he'd lived in for a year, and through the misery of that year came the glimmer of memories, bright and painful, which he did not want to see or feel. So he closed off his heart, fetched his gun from the kitchen, and settled down to make certain no harm found them on this cold winter's night.

CHAPTER THREE

Molly heard the tap of metal against wood. Although it was dawn it was still as dark as night, for the blizzard still raged against the thick log walls. Nothing but firelight guided her through her parlor and toward the back of the house. The faint tapping grew louder, and the pool of light up ahead in the darkness illuminated a man kneeling before her back door, shoulders braced, muscles rippling beneath a blue cotton shirt.

He tilted his head to one side and continued to work. "Did I wake you?"

"No." Her stomach tightened at the sight of him. His shoulders were tight and his sleeves rolled up to expose strong bronzed forearms dusted with a scattering of dark hair. The shirt stretched across his broad back, straining as he screwed the knob back into the door. The denim trousers, like new, hugged his lean, muscled backside.

She blushed, ashamed at herself for noticing. She was not interested in this man, in this gunman or outlaw or whatever he was. And yet, the fall of his dark hair over his high, intelligent-looking brows made her hesitate, made her remember the father who'd sat at his daughter's bedside and the man who seemed to care that he'd made Molly cry.

She took a deep breath. She would not be afraid of him. She would not be afraid in her own home. She walked right past him, as if he were no more a threat to her than Lady was, and knelt down to open the bottom cabinet. "How is Beth this morning?"

"Still asleep." He groaned as he climbed to his feet, all steel-hard six feet of him. "Didn't want to wake her. She feels a little warm, but I figured the best thing for her was more sleep. It's been a long time since she's had such a comfortable bed. Thought she should enjoy it."

"Is that so?" Molly thumped the frying pan on the burner. Heat radiated from the stove, and for some reason it infuriated her that he'd taken the liberty of lighting the fire.

It wasn't rational, it wasn't what she was angry about, but she couldn't help the way she let the drawer slam when she grabbed a fork or the way she clunked the bowl on the counter. "Don't light my stove again."

"Sorry." He didn't sound sorry. "Your door is fixed."

She couldn't bring herself to thank him. She heard the clink of tools he must have found in the shed just outside the back door. His step rang, heavy and uneven, and the hinges squeaked.

Alone, she closed her eyes. He was gone, but reminders of him were everywhere. The freshly washed floor and back wall shining damp from a good scrubbing, the deadly revolver on the mantel, and the scent of the man, sharp like the winter air and pleasant, were all reminders of him she couldn't seem to shake.

What was wrong with her? Molly cracked an egg against the rim of a bowl with too much force. The fragile shell crumbled from her fingers, mixing with egg white and yolk. Yes, this man definitely scrambled her common sense. A part of her still wanted to believe she could find a man with gentleness in his heart instead of anger.

Well, it wouldn't be a man who could kill without remorse. Molly tossed the last piece of shell into the waste bucket and cracked another egg. The door squeaked open and there he was, dusted with snow and larger than life.

"It's blowing worse than yesterday out there." He closed the door with the heel of his boot.

She clamped her mouth shut. She couldn't talk to him. Anger built like a new fire in her chest, spitting and popping, and she turned away when he knelt down beside her and emptied the wood piled high in his arms into the metal bin by the stove.

His presence radiated heat, and awareness telegraphed up and down her body, leaving her hands shaking. She beat the eggs hard, the steel fork striking the enamel bowl with force.

"Is there anything else I can do to help?" He brushed the moss and bark clinging to his sleeves neatly into the bin. "I took care of your horse. Can't think of anything else—"

"I don't expect you to do my chores." She knew her words came harsh, but the emotion whirled like a tornado in her stomach and heaven help her, she didn't want a man, any man, telling her what to do. If she wanted that, she could have married Albert. "I'm only offering you shelter from the storm. Do you understand that?"

"Yes, ma'am." He sounded contrite, puzzled, his voice ringing low and somber. "Thought I'd help out, that's all."

"I don't need any help." She hated how ungrateful she sounded. "I don't need anyone."

"Yes, ma'am." He released a pent-up breath, a sound of frustration. "Didn't mean to offend. If you'd feel safer, I can head out to the stable—"

"That's not what I meant." She grabbed the flour canister and found it nearly empty. She set down her measuring cup, feeling the edges of her control fray. What was wrong with her this morning? The bruise at her throat no longer throbbed, she'd had no dreams last night, but she felt as she had just last year, engaged and trapped and miserable. It didn't make sense.

She pushed past him, her chest cold, her entire body trembling.

"I can do that." Suddenly he was behind her, then beside her, his iron-hard arm brushing the outer curve of her shoulder, leaving a sizzling trail of heat and confusion. He grabbed the heavy flour sack from the bottom shelf and carried it to the counter.

She shook as he upended the sack, carefully filling the canister. Flour puffed in a chalky white cloud, and his arm, muscles shaping the blue cotton shirt, cradled the sack easily.

He was true to his word, just trying to help out because he was grateful for shelter. But that didn't explain the rage in her chest, building and pulsing, pulling tight every muscle in her body.

A muffled cough shattered the tension, and he put down the sack. His gaze arrowed to hers, and Molly felt her rage crumble.

"Papa?" A thin voice warbled, uncertain, afraid.

"I'm right here, Beth." He took off, his limp evident but it didn't stop him. "Darlin', don't be afraid."

"You weren't by my bed when I woke up."

"And I'm sorry. Molly needed me to do a few things for her.

She's making breakfast."

"I ain't hungry, Papa."

Molly eased around the corner, holding back her heart. He'd scooped Beth into his arms and now held her safe against his chest, his chin resting on the top of her tousled hair the same shade as his own.

Father and daughter. Her chest tightened, aching with a force that could make the blizzard outside weak. Once she'd dreamed of holding a child of her own. Her arms felt so empty; her life felt empty. This man, with no home, without even a change of clothes, had more than she ever would.

"What are you making for breakfast?" He snared her gaze again, his dark eyes filled with a silent pleading.

Whatever he'd done wrong in his life, despite what he'd become, she could see he loved his daughter.

"I was going to make eggs, biscuits, and ham." Then, she saw how Beth frowned, and her face looked pale. "When I was a little girl, I loved pancakes. I could make those, if you'd like."

"I hate pancakes." Beth buried her face against her father's shirt.

"Beth, that's no way to treat Molly, who's been kind to us." Although he spoke to his daughter, his gaze returned to Molly's, dark and steady. "If it weren't for her, we'd be frozen as solid as two snowmen."

"I still don't like pancakes."

"Molly, I'm sorry." He held the child tight. Troubled lines eased across his face, adding years and severity. "I don't think she's feeling well."

"Does she have a fever?"

"She feels hot." He leaned his cheek against Beth's brow. "Not too bad."

"I'll steep some tea and honey." Any fever could be dangerous, and Molly couldn't help the twist of concern in her chest. She stepped back into the kitchen, out of sight, and heard Beth mumble, "I don't like tea."

She filled the kettle, her hands trembling. The fire blazed, thanks to the man who'd built it this morning. The wood stacked in the bin nearby warmed, spreading the pleasant scent of pine and winter into the air. She set the nearly empty sack of flour back onto the pantry shelf, remembering how he'd towered over her. She closed the door and wished she didn't remember the feel of his arm brushing hers.

"There's no excuse for her behavior."

She startled, spinning around. Grim, fists loose at his sides, he seemed to shrink the small room even smaller. Overwhelmed, Molly pulled the tea crock from the cupboard, her throat so tight that each word cut like a knife. "It's all right. She's not feeling well."

"Yes, but I raised her better than that." He didn't sound harsh, he sounded concerned that Beth had offended her. "She doesn't take to strangers well."

"Always on the move, without a home, that's understandable." She bit her bottom lip, shocked those words had escaped, but she couldn't unsay them. She clicked the lid off the crock, blinking against the strong scent of tea. "I shouldn't have said that."

"You aren't an unkind woman, I can see that." He paused, as if measuring his words or waiting for her to object. "And it's true, being without a home isn't good for a child her age."

"For a child of any age." Her chest tightened, and she refused to let her own selfish, judgmental words escape. He'd been right. She wasn't a parent. She didn't have the right to judge, and she knew better than most how tough circumstances could change even the most stable of lives.

"Yes, for a child of any age," he said calmly, almost coldly, his words ringing with great sorrow. Then he turned, saying nothing more, leaving the feeling of remorse so great, it hit her like a north wind.

Molly felt ashamed that her life had been so easy these last few years. Had she already forgotten what hardship felt like? Whoever this man was, he hadn't harmed her, and she knew he wasn't going to. Not a man who brushed aside the unruly curls from his daughter's brow with such care, not a man with fatherly love true and clear in his eyes.

The teakettle's shrill whistle startled her, and she spun away to rescue it from the stove top. The image of the man kneeling down beside his daughter filled her with sadness so great she couldn't breathe.

Luke felt the weight and wonder of Molly's gaze as he settled a cushion on the chair for Beth. Washed up, hair brushed and braided, she looked like a princess, he'd always thought so, but he couldn't help the kick of guilt or the defeating burden of failure that settled on his shoulders and squeezed tight in his guts.

"Pa, I don't wanna." Beth rubbed one fist over her eyes.

"Aren't you hungry?"

She didn't answer, tension freezing her little body tight as she watched Molly set a bowl of steaming biscuits on the table.

Molly's gaze caught his, and he knew she hadn't missed how pale Beth looked and the hint of fever shining in her eyes. Maybe a good breakfast and a day of rest would help. The girl didn't appear to be too sick, and she claimed her throat didn't hurt.

Molly returned with two platters, one of fried eggs, sunny side up, and the other sporting thick slices of ham. Good ham. His mouth watered; he couldn't help it. "It smells good."

"I'm a middling cook at best. Some people have a gift of it, but I manage to make due." She set the salt and pepper on the table, and the concern in her gaze was unmistakable.

He didn't know how he could repay her for her hospitality. He'd already cleaned up the mess, patched the bullet holes in her wall the best he could and repaired her door, but dark circles hugged her eyes, marring the fragile beauty of her face. She hadn't slept well last night, worrying about what kind of man she'd rescued from the storm. How could he repair that damage?

She looked at him with distaste, and he couldn't blame her. There was no hiding that he was a hunted man. They ate in silence with the tension uncomfortable. The click of silverware on the purple and blue flowered plates rang above the continuous roar of the wind. It made him nervous, sitting still like this, knowing Moss was close. Too damn close.

What if Hammond had marked his trail? All Moss would have to do was follow it... He'd worried about it all night. Apprehension snapped through him. He was glad for the extra revolver tucked into his boot.

"I could make Beth something else." Molly broke the silence, her voice dulcet and questioning. "If she doesn't like my cooking, I have some oatmeal—"

"I don't like oatmeal." Beth lifted her chin, staring hard at Molly over her untouched plate.

Damn. This wasn't the time for Beth to start acting up. "Hey, I think Molly was very nice to cook for us. You need to apologize to her."

41

"It's all right." Molly reached for the teapot and poured a second cup. "She's tired and not feeling very well."

"No, Molly. You deserve better." His touch was gentle as he caught hold of his daughter's elbow. "Beth, you have better manners than that."

The child hung her head and stared hard at the pattern of lace draping the table.

Anger beat in his chest, anger because of the situation, because he understood what was behind Beth's behavior.

"She looks feverish," Molly said quietly as she stirred honey into the full cup. "Can she drink the tea?"

"Don't want tea." Beth's jaw was set.

Luke's chest tightened. He kept waiting for the sound of steps outside the door, and because he couldn't bear the reason behind Beth's behavior, he stood up and released the ties on the curtains, letting them close.

Molly got up and left the room, back straight, shoulders a tense fragile line as she carried the empty ham platter to the sink.

"I don't want anyone looking in," he explained quietly, kneeling down to lift Beth from the chair. "Anyone with a gun."

"You could have asked." The way she looked at him, as if he were a caged animal ready to break through the bars, hurt like nothing had in a long time. Here, in this tidy world of flowery porcelain plates and matching curtains, he felt hemmed in and too damned big, as if he only had to turn around and he'd break something.

Beth leaned against him and sobbed. She felt hot, too damn hot. She couldn't get sick with a bounty hunter on their trail and a week's more travel through the bitter Montana cold.

"I'll put a touch of whiskey in some honey tea." Molly's quiet offer touched him.

"That would be a great help." He heard the clink of the teakettle and the rush of pouring water. Beth wrapped her arms around his neck crying in misery, and all he could do was carry her back to bed.

"You won't leave me, Pa, will you?"

"Just sleep, darlin'. I want you to feel better." He laid her carefully on the warm flannel sheets, his heart breaking anew. "You lie back and rest."

"Don't leave me, Pa. Please, please, don't leave me." She held on with surprising strength, her fingers locked together around the back of his neck.

"I won't leave you today." It was all he could promise, and he hated it. Hated that he had to abandon Beth all over again. Hated that he was almost to Canada and hadn't found one place good enough to leave her. Or maybe, he hadn't tried hard enough. How could he let her go? Love for his girl sliced like a serrated knife through his chest—sharp, keen, precise—leaving him bleeding inside.

"Oh, Pa." Beth's sobs broke into helpless whimpers as he unlocked her fingers and straightened away. "Don't go."

His heart broke again as he sat on the plump feather tick beside her, tears gathering into a hot hard ball in his throat. A ball he couldn't speak past. Memories assaulted him, images of the deputies breaking down his door in the middle of the night, how he'd startled awake and reached for his revolver, thinking he was being robbed. How they'd shot him, beat him, cuffed him, and dragged him away while Beth watched from her bedroom doorway, tears streaking her dear face, sobs wrenching her little body. She'd cried for him then, too, and he knew she must have cried for him during the long year in that harrowing orphanage where he couldn't hold her, help her, or comfort away the hurt and tears.

He'd failed her, and bitterness beat like a battering ram in his chest. The horrors of hard labor hadn't destroyed him, but knowing his little girl had needed him, and he'd failed her, almost did. How could he leave her again? And with who? Who could be good enough to raise his daughter, who wouldn't neglect her, use her as a servant? Who would show a child not their own a lifetime of caring and kindness?

And because he hadn't found her that home, she was sick, weak, and miserable, afraid he was going to leave her here, just like that, and disappear into the blizzard forever.

Maybe it would be better if he did.

Molly's careful step tapped on the polished wood, and her shadow blocked the light from the parlor. He turned, unable to control his gaze, his broken heart thudding at the look of her, the concern in her shadowed eyes, the steaming cup cradled in her hands. The quiet sadness in her drew him in, made him see not just another woman but her, the shades of her, like daybreak when the light turns gentle along the horizon and before the sun breaks forth. That's what she reminded him of—that shy light of faint pinks, peaches, and lavenders before the bold yellow broke over the horizon.

"Beth should drink all of this. Does her throat hurt?"

Luke watched Beth's spine grow rigid. She was afraid he was going to leave her here, he knew. She was afraid of strangers, afraid of being abandoned. Afraid that by accepting Molly's kindness, her father would be free to leave.

"She's been coughing." He rose from the bed to take the steaming cup in hand, recognizing the scent of lightly steeped tea, heavy honey, and a splash of whiskey—a good home remedy for a cold. "I think it's safe to say her throat probably hurts. How far is the doctor from here?"

"About a mile and a half." Molly brushed past him, her petticoats rustling, trailing the faintest scent of lilacs, her concern quiet but steady. She gazed down at the bed, hands empty. "It's too dangerous to try to fetch him. Besides, the doctor won't come out in this weather. He's old and it's too risky."

"Great." Luke set the cup on the small night table. "What do you know about doctoring little girls?"

"Enough for a woman who's never had a child of her own." Quiet words, and her gaze never left Beth. "I'll make her a solution to gargle with. It should help her throat. We'll start with that."

She left the obvious question unasked, and he was grateful for it. His wife had always cared for Beth, had known what to do for childhood illnesses and fevers. He'd been the one working long hours to keep a good roof over their heads. He felt inadequate now, his capable hands useless.

Once again, he would have to rely on this woman, this stranger.

"Don't worry, Beth," she soothed, reaching out and then stopping short of stroking the girl's head in comfort "We'll have you feeling better in no time."

"I don't like tea," she whined.

Molly's face fell, not in anger, but in hurt. She released a sigh but not a frustrated one. "I didn't like tea when I was your age. When you feel better, I promise to make you a big cup of hot chocolate."

"Don't like chocolate either."

"I see." Molly's acceptance was gentle like the grace of dawn each winter morning, and she turned away. "I'll mix the solution for her throat."

"Wait." Luke stood, daring to wrap his hand around her wrist. He felt the soft cuff of her wool sleeve, soft as kitten fur, and the feminine heat of her skin. She was so fragile he could feel the bones in her wrist, and so tiny he towered over her like a bear contemplating his morning meal.

"I understand. I'm a stranger, and she's not feeling well." She wouldn't meet his gaze, probably because she saw the monster in him, too.

"It's not you, Molly." The ball in his throat expanded, making his words hurt, making his voice raw and exposed. "She's afraid I'm going to leave her."

"Why would you do that?"

He read the steady question in her simple words, spoken without accusation but holding a world of it. She had no children; she wouldn't understand the guilt of failing a child or the guilt of breaking the taken-for-granted promise of providing love and safety. "I'm a wanted man, Molly. A fugitive on the run. Why do you think I have two bounty hunters chasing me through Montana in this weather?"

She swallowed, her eyes growing huge. Big, brilliantly hazel, threaded with bronze and gold. She froze, her chin lifted. "I already figured that out. My concern is for the child."

"Mine, too." He hadn't meant to speak harshly to her. He hadn't spoken more than a few polite words to a woman since the night he'd been arrested. "She feels real hot all of a sudden. She wasn't like that when I checked on her this morning."

"Children can get ill very fast. I see in it my school-room all the time." Molly took a wary step back as if determined to keep a certain distance between her and a convicted felon. "I'll do everything I know. I'm sure it's just a touch of quinsy. Children get sore tonsils all the time."

Why would she offer him that small piece of comfort? Her mouth curled just a bit, her eyes warmed, and for a moment the world didn't seem cruel and bitter and alone. Then she turned, her russet braids swaying with her gait, brushing the delicate dip of her waist and arrowing toward the fullness of her skirts.

His pulse kicked. He couldn't help looking, even though he didn't have the right. His daughter was ill, and he had no business eyeing a woman's backside, wondering if she felt as soft as she looked.

The hard lump in his throat hurt until he couldn't breathe, and he returned to Beth's side. The dog was there, nosing the girl's face, trying to squeeze in a few doggy kisses even though Beth tried to hide in the pillow. Then she spotted him.

"Don't leave me ever again, Papa," she whispered, flying into his arms now that Molly was gone. She held him with force, as if she never intended to let go.

He pulled her onto his lap, this precious child of his, and held her against his heart. Her hair caught on his unshaven chin, and he fought the tenderness in his chest, fought the love for her so sharp that it left him weak. He didn't know how he was going to give her up.

I'm a wanted man. A fugitive on the run. Those words echoed through her thoughts as Molly prepared a gargle solution of warm saltwater. He'd bolted both front and back doors well, and the closed dining room curtain troubled her now—he was expecting more trouble.

She still didn't believe anyone, even a hardened bounty hunter, could make it through the storm, but as she walked through the house she closed the curtains against the blinding whiteness so no one could look in. *A fugitive.*

She ought to be terrified of him, but she wasn't, not now. She could see him clearly, for he'd lit the bedside lamp. He cradled his daughter in his arms, his hard face soft with unmistakable concern. Those big, killer's hands were tender as he held the cup for his daughter to drink from. Tears gleamed on her face. The poor child was still crying.

"My throat hurts," she whispered for her father, although Molly could hear. "You're gonna stay right here with me, right, Pa?"

"Absolutely." He pressed a fatherly kiss to her brow with remarkable tenderness. He looked as hard as stone and as tough as a Montana blizzard.

Where did his gentleness come from?

Molly stepped into the room, unprepared for the weight of his intense, overpowering gaze. She'd felt the same way once, when she'd stumbled on a lone wolf in the woods. The wild creature's eyes were hard and measuring, wild and merciless, and he'd boldly studied her as if he could see every inch of her—body, heart, and soul. Just the way the fugitive in her house looked at her.

She didn't like it; she didn't like him. And yet... She deliberately forced herself not to look at his perfectly honed male form, at the muscles that rippled beneath the too-small shirt, at the soft cut of his mouth no longer hard and unforgiving as he placed another kiss on Beth's brow.

Lady wagged a polite hello from her position on the floor at Luke's feet, ever watchful of the child. Molly appreciated the friendly face and set the warm glass on the nightstand. She didn't know what to say. Beth took one look at her and buried her face in her father's chest. Luke's gaze felt intimidating and far too powerful, and she turned away, chest tight.

He let her go without a word, holding his daughter, who clung to him so tightly.

What kind of father was he? He was loving now, gentle in front of her, but why would any father allow his child to be caught in a blizzard? Why would a child fear her father would leave her?

I'm a wanted man. A fugitive on the run. His answer had troubled her. Why did he have a child with him in the first place? It was hard to keep the question and the accusation from her voice when she returned with hot compresses for Beth's throat. The little girl cried when her father laid her down in the bed, still trying to cling to him, and the child's pain tore through her like the leading edge of a blizzard, leaving her shaking and cold and confused.

She left the room and sat down before the fire, where the flames needed more wood. Stacking the fresh split pine in the grate gave her something to do, but it didn't stop her heart from feeling or the anger roaring like fire.

"Molly?" His voice brought her back, and she realized she'd been sitting, watching the flames flicker around the wood, for a long while. "Beth feels hotter to me. She's in a lot of pain."

"I'll come see." She climbed to her feet, the anger and emotion remaining as she brushed past him in the doorway. He smelled pleasant, but she didn't let her body respond as she knelt at Beth's side.

The child's brow felt hotter to the touch. The girl's eyes were glazed when they looked at her, pleading quietly for help. Then Beth rolled away and started crying for her papa. He came, fast as lightning and as bold as thunder, settling his steel-hard body next

47

to hers. His arm jammed against her shoulder, not with force, but with presence. They hardly touched, but she could feel his iron-like shoulder, arm and chest against her back. She ached at the contact, at the simple act of one body touching another.

He leaned across her as if unaware, laying one huge hand between Beth's shoulder blades. He began to rub in gentle circles, as if to comfort a crying baby, and soon Beth's sobs became hiccups. Then the hiccups faded into a wheezing, fitful sleep.

Luke's body burned long after Molly moved away, her step tapping as lightly as a dancer's on the varnished puncheon floors of her cozy parlor. The nearly silent whisper of her flannel petticoats beneath the soft wool dress grated along his heightened nerves, and he gritted his teeth. When he should be thinking of his child and only his child, his senses felt raw-edged and exposed. His groin thrummed from the pressure of her bottom, and heat snapped across his chest where her soft, willowy woman's body had brushed his.

He hadn't realized he'd been leaning over her. His concern for Beth had riveted all his attention. He hadn't noticed he was wrapped around gentle Molly until his blood felt like molten lava spreading through his veins. *What's wrong with you, McKenna?* He had no business looking twice at a woman like Molly, and he certainly had no right to press the length of his body to hers.

Hell, he was rock hard and trembling. Didn't he have better self-control than that? Anger lanced through his chest, but not sharp enough to carve away the memory of Molly against his chest.

What kind of father did that make him? He laid his hand over Beth's brow. She was even hotter; he'd swear to it. She was too damn hot. Her breathing rasped like sandpaper against wood.

He felt fury rake through him, all the way down to his soul. Beth was sick because of him, because of his actions and his choices, because he'd failed her in the most profound way. He hadn't kept her safe from the cruel world, and not even from a blizzard that had made her this ill.

Don't let this be pneumonia. Luke had lost his wife that way; she'd been too ill and weak at the end to even recognize him. Would Beth suffer that way?

He paced the dark room ignoring the pain stabbing hot and

steady through his side and radiating down his left leg. He'd felt worse than this, hurt worse than this in prison; he could certainly endure it now. If only he knew what to do for Beth.

The blizzard beat against the outside wall, sounding more violent than he'd ever heard wind, outside of a raging Texas twister. There had to be a doctor in town, but could he make it there? That, he didn't know.

And if he did head to town, then he'd be leaving Molly and Beth vulnerable to a killer like Moss, who would use them any way he saw fit. *Any way.* Luke's guts twisted hard, and he stopped pacing. He thought of all the ways Moss would hurt a woman, and Luke's blood turned to ice. What were his choices? He rubbed the heel of his hand against his aching brow. He couldn't send Molly out in this dangerous storm, and he couldn't leave this house unprotected.

He could hear Molly's movements in the kitchen above the crash of wind and snow. The stove lid rattled, the teakettle whistled, and a cabinet door snapped shut. What did an unmarried woman know about treating a sick child?

Next to nothing, he'd wager. And if he combined that with the trifle he knew, then he could only hope Beth's fever didn't worsen.

"Pa?" she croaked painfully, her dark curls clinging to her damp forehead.

"Hey, darlin'." He eased down on the mattress beside her, ignoring his own pain and weakness, seeing only the sweet angel's face of the little girl he loved more than his own life.

"I'm real thirsty."

"Lucky for you, Molly left a pitcher of water right here on the nightstand." His heart was beating like he'd run ten miles full out, but he couldn't let that show on his face. He filled a glass with water and held it to his daughter's lips.

Beth sipped, swallowing with obvious difficulty. "My throat hurts," she said at last, collapsing back onto the plump pillows.

Lady eased up and licked Beth's hand in comfort.

Luke set down the glass and brushed damp bangs away from his daughter's brow. Lord, she was even hotter; he'd swear to it. Panic vise-gripped his guts. His hand trembled as he pulled the quilt to her chin. *I can't lose this child, not this way.*

Beth moaned in her sleep, fitful, the fever bathing her in a light sweat. The wind whipped harder against the thick outside walls, a sign the blizzard was worsening as dark fell. Hopelessness wrapped around him like drifting snow on a fence post.

This night, there was no more running, no quest for freedom and the Canadian border. For the first time since his uncle's death and the night the deputies had hauled him from his bed, he had to face the man he was and what he'd done.

All the running in the world hadn't saved Beth, not if she died here. And all his promises to her, his vows to find her a safe home to grow up in, all felt as cold now as the snow in that twister-strength wind.

He'd lost his livelihood and his home, his dignity and his freedom, his life and his soul. He could not lose this child too, the only hope that lived in his heart, the one true thing he had left in this merciless world.

CHAPTER FOUR

olly listened to the beat of his step, a faint *clump-clump* above the storm's howling fury. McKenna was coming back. Her skin prickled with both warning and memory of how he'd felt spooned against her at Beth's bedside, his steady masculine warmth as hot as flame, as dependable as day. Why was her body remembering the feel of his?

Before she could figure that out, McKenna filled her senses as he approached. She heard him, felt him, saw him, and like a lone wolf, he blended with the shadows in the parlor so that only the uneven gait against the braid rug marked his progress.

He clung to the darkness as if afraid of the light, and all she could see of him was the dark mop of his tousled hair and the broad span of his chest.

McKenna flexed his hands, loose at his sides. "The fever's worse."

She set down the pestle, breathing in the bitter scent of crushed yarrow. "I'll brew her some tea."

"How will more tea help? My daughter needs real medicine or she might well die."

"This is the only real medicine I have on hand." Her heart twisted at the sight of him, lost in the shadows, with only the right half of his face brushed by the faint glow of the table lamp.

"That isn't good enough—"

"It will have to be." She heard the sharp twist of her voice and winced, then picked through the drawer for her measuring spoons. "The storm is getting worse. Not even you could get to town before those winds froze you solid."

His step whispered on the floor, stealthy and as lethal as a hunting wolf. "I'd hoped that you meant what you said. That you knew enough to help my girl. But tea's a drink, not medicine."

Molly felt his presence in her kitchen. Tiny flames of awareness snapped to life along every inch of her skin, making it impossible to think. She dropped the measuring spoon and had to sweep the crushed leaves off the clean counter with her hand. "This is yarrow."

"Yarrow? That's a weed."

"It's a plant with medicinal value." She brushed the last leaves from her fingers and dropped the tea basket into the empty pot with a clink. "I meant what I said. I know enough to help your daughter."

"She needs help, and you said—" He pounded toward her. The lamplight flickered across his face, across the furrow of concern on his high brow and the unmistakable gleam of fear in his eyes. "Maybe there's a neighbor who can help. A woman nearby with children who knows about tending fevers."

"The McGraths are half a mile from here."

"Half a mile?" His face twisted. "It might as well be a hundred in this weather. Look, the wind has already whipped snowdrifts higher than your doors. I didn't bring Beth all this way just to have her die of a fever in a spinster's house."

His face hardened with anguish, and the muscles in his neck corded. He looked like a man at the end of his rope, at the verge of losing everything that mattered, and it surprised her that she could see this in his hard, glittering eyes, that she could see softness in a man as hard as winter.

Memories of her childhood flashed like moonlight on snow, dark and glittering. She lifted the rumbling teakettle off the red-hot stove and kept her back to him.

"I lived half of my childhood in an orphanage near the Dakota border." She poured the steaming water with care, holding back her heart, keeping so much locked away. "The older children were expected to take care of the younger ones. Treating their illnesses was part of the job."

"*You* were in an orphanage?" It wasn't an accusation or astonishment, but a quiet acknowledgment. "I'm sorry."

She lowered the kettle to a trivet with a thud, the strength draining from her arm, memories nudging at the ragged edges of her spirit. "It's a time I don't like to remember."

"No, of course not." His voice was molten steel, a fluid strength and sympathy that made her throat tighten.

This was a fugitive, a killer, a criminal. She had to remember that. But he was still a man, and the sound of caring was something she'd never heard from a man before.

When she faced him, she saw a real flesh and blood man. Pain and exhaustion paled his hard-edged features. Her pulse roared in her ears, drowning out the storm and her fears and memories too painful to recall. He reached out with one hand and caught hers. His touch was callused but gentle.

"It's been a long time since I've been able to trust anyone." His throat worked. "But I'm placing my trust and my daughter's life in your hands."

He was afraid, and she could feel him tremble with it, this man as lethal as a killer wolf. Afraid and trusting her, like the wild deer that came to her stable, knowing she would feed them, not hunt them.

His fingers felt so big against hers, and the width of his palm engulfed her whole hand with ease. He could crush her with the strength in those fingers, but somehow she knew she could trust him. That, until this storm eased, they would have to trust one another. Beth needed them both.

Molly stepped away, withdrawing her hand, but the heat and texture of McKenna's touch remained.

◦◦◦

"I don't want her tea." Beth turned away from the cup. "I don't want it, Papa."

"I know, but you have to drink this, darlin'." With patience driving his words, McKenna set down the cup gently. "If you won't drink this on your own, then I'll have to help you. Molly said this tastes bad, but it will make you feel better."

"I don't want her here, Papa." Tears brimmed Beth's eyes and trickled down her fever-pinkened cheeks. "*Please*, Papa. I don't want her."

"I heard you, Beth, and that's enough." His jaw tensed, but he didn't scold the child as he gathered her into his big arms. "I want you to drink this all up. Every drop."

"No-ooo." Beth started coughing, the sobs and coughs racking her frail body until she cried harder in pain and heartbreak.

The poor little girl, so sick and hurting. What difficulties had she been through with a father running from the law? The child clung to him with both of her small hands fisted in his shirt as if holding on for dear life. Beth clearly loved her papa.

Sympathy for the child gathered in Molly's chest. Beth had no home, no bed of her own, and not even a doll to hug tight. Judging by the way that the little girl clung to her father, she had no one else in the world.

"Drink up, darlin'." He spoke like an archangel; both strength and gentleness laced his whiskey-rough voice. With Beth cradled against his chest, he lifted the steaming cup to her lips and urged her to sip.

Beth cried, murmuring something that Molly couldn't hear. McKenna dipped his head low, his dark locks tumbling over his brow to hide his eyes, but she could hear the warmth of his tender words, mumbled, too, so low they sounded like a lullaby, rich and sweet. Beth hiccuped, nodded, brushing her raven curls up and down her frail back, and then sipped from the cup.

Molly had never seen a man be so tender with a child.

"That's my good girl." His praise came like summer thunder, and the hard lines carved into his face eased and faded until his was the face of a father holding a daughter with love, bright and rare.

Molly's throat ached at the sight, and she lowered her gaze. She stood outside the circle of lamplight, outside the intimacy of a family's love. The flame on the wick flickered as she moved toward the night table, sending the golden light dancing across father and child.

"Don't want no more," Beth complained on the end of a deep cough. "It tastes bad."

"I know, darlin', but you have to drink all the medicine." He was both firm and kind, and the little girl did as he asked. When she was finished, Beth leaned her forehead against the hard comforting plane of her father's chest and rested, her breath painful, her face flushed. McKenna set aside the cup and wrapped both of his arms around his daughter.

Molly took a step back, hearing the kettle rumbling in the kitchen, feeling the cinch of her heart. It looked like Beth had everything she needed—her father. Empty-handed, Molly pivoted and stepped through the shadowed threshold. She didn't know why emotion hurt like a wound within her, but it did.

The fire snapped in the parlor's hearth and illuminated the lonely room as she tapped through it. The dining room felt just as lonely. Sure, there was furniture, but that was all this house held— her and her possessions. It was a house not a home, no matter how she'd worked to make it one.

Loneliness wrapped around her like the dark and felt as harsh and cold as the storm outside. The image of the big dangerous man cradling the frail child in his iron-hewn arms lingered, taunting her with every step. Tenderness. She wouldn't have expected that in a man so ruthless and desperate, in a fugitive on the run.

The teakettle shrilled, and she swept it from the burner. There were compresses to make, and herbs to crush and mix for Beth's throat. Molly may have discovered a layer of tenderness inside the fugitive called McKenna, but she didn't have time to dwell on it now. The storm raged, and Beth was very ill. There was no doubt she needed a doctor's care, but that simply wasn't possible.

Please, let my skills be enough. It had been a long time since she'd tended an ill child. She pulled open the cabinet doors, and the labels on the bottles blurred as she remembered the row upon row of cots in the orphanage's second story. Freezing cold in winter, boiling hot in summer, and always filled with sorrow. She thought of her mother's letter and her mother's rebuke, and fury and pain melded in her chest. She snapped the bottles onto the counter with too much force.

What was wrong with her? She was an adult now, in control of her own life, not a child dependent upon the whims of a selfish mother. It was her choice that she lived alone and chose not to marry the man her stepfather had chosen for her. It was her choice that she had no husband or children to fill the empty places in her life, her house, and her heart.

As she twisted open the lid of the small bottle, mint sweetened the air. She tapped the strong oil into a small basin and set to work measuring out the menthol. Still, the image of McKenna and his child lingered in her mind.

When she returned to the extra room, she saw that he'd

returned Beth to her bed. The child was crying in misery, apparently unable to sleep, her small fingers curled around McKenna's with white-knuckled need.

Molly could remember what it was like to be a child, ill and afraid. What it was like to need love and care from a parent. The lamplight was turned low, but the stubborn flame tossed a sepia pool of light across Beth's pillow and onto her angel's face streaked with tears. Her cheeks and brow were deeply flushed, her skin damp, her dark lashes spiky with tears. Every breath sounded scraped from her throat.

"Papa," Beth twisted to look at her father. "I don't want her here. Please?"

The child's words hurt; Molly took a deep breath remembering that Beth was very ill. Maybe she only wanted her father, as any sick child might. Again, memories from the years spent in the orphanage surfaced. She remembered how ill children cried for parents long dead. How she once cried out for the mother who'd simply left her.

McKenna's answer was a low, comforting rumble, and Molly held her heart still and tried not to listen. Her eyes teared from the stinging steam in the basin she carried.

"Papa, I don't want her," Beth whispered, her words as harsh and filled with pain as her breathing. "You promised, Papa. You promised."

"I know." Luke rubbed his hand over his daughter's brow, wishing. Just wishing. He was too old and too world-weary to believe in wishes.

"Papa, you said I could pick. You said—" She collapsed into a coughing and wheezing attack.

Fear bolted through him and he pulled her against his chest, rubbing one hand in circles on her tiny back. He'd never been this afraid. Not when his quiet-natured wife had died. Not the first night he'd spent in prison. Not every night after that.

A black consuming panic whipped inside him as he felt Beth's reed-thin body spasm, fighting for air. "She can't breathe."

"This will help." Calm as Christmas morning, Molly knelt beside him, her skirts whispering, and pushed the small basin into his hand. "Beth, honey, breathe in the steam. It will help you to feel better."

"No." Beth managed the single defiant word between her fits of coughing. Tears welled in her eyes, and she tried to push the basin away.

"Beth." He kept his voice gentle, trying to lull away her panic and her fears. He knew exactly what she was trying to do. He pressed a kiss to her temple, her damp hair smelling like soap and little-girl sweetness. Oh, how he loved this child. "I want you to breathe this in. Come on, now. I'll breathe with you. In."

He let the fragrant mint and eye-stinging menthol bathe his face. He felt Beth's defiance slip away, and she bowed her head over the basin. Her breath was a grating sound that rattled all the way to her lungs. Exhaling, tears dripped into the basin with tiny splashes.

"That's right, darlin'." He pressed his brow to the side of her head and stayed there. "Good job. Breathe in again. As deep as you can."

"Hurts," Beth cried, but did it just the same.

"That's my good girl." This terrified him, how fast the illness had struck her. Surely, this wasn't a good sign.

What if Molly's home remedies couldn't stop the fever? What if this vapor didn't break apart the congestion in Beth's lungs?

"She's burning up, Molly." He could feel the increased heat of Beth's skin, feel it radiate from her body. "And she's sweating hard."

"I see." Molly reached out one gentle hand, but then hesitated, as if remembering that Beth didn't want her touch or her care. "I want her to keep inhaling the vapor until the plaster cools enough to apply to her chest."

"And then what?"

"Then we'll see." Dark russet curls tumbled into her eyes, hiding her face but not her concern. Her mouth narrowed, her shoulders drooped, and he knew that Molly felt it, too.

There was nothing they could do, not really. They needed a doctor and real medicine. It was as simple as that. And, damn it, no mint steam and weed tea was going to save this child's life.

He looked up, surprised to find Molly leaving the room. "Where are you going?"

She stopped, and her shoulders tensed. "To move my bed into the parlor for Beth. It's warmer than in here."

"I'll do it."

"No, stay with your daughter. The mattress isn't too heavy. I can do it. Besides, Beth wouldn't accept me." There was no judgment in Molly's words, just a statement of fact. She moved away, her skirts rustling, her step light and her shoulders tight.

He couldn't let a woman haul around a heavy mattress. He swept Beth onto his hip and kept the basin steady as he stood. Pain lashed like a whip through his side and groin, backlashing down his leg as he crossed the room. What did his pain matter when compared to his daughter's illness?

Lady trailed behind him, a silent guardian. When he sat Beth in the wingback chair by the hearth, the dog sat at her feet and laid her chin on the girl's knee. Luke set the basin on the corner table and scooted it close, so Beth could breathe in the steam.

"Papa?" The unspoken question in her chocolate-brown eyes burned steadily.

"I'm not going to leave you, darlin'." He brushed the damp, tangled bangs from her hot brow. "Not right now."

"Okay." She nodded once and rubbed her eyes.

He heard a loud thump coming from behind him, from Molly's bedroom, and got there just in time to hear a swear word cross her pearl-pink lips.

"I guess you caught me." She blushed and straightened away from the mess at her feet.

"What were you trying to do, break all your toes?" Luke saw at once that Molly hadn't been strong enough, even though she'd wanted to be, to hold the bed together when she'd unhitched the corner of the frame. "You're damn lucky this didn't land on your feet."

"I'm quick. I jumped back." She pushed a wild tangle of curls from her face. "I really can do this by myself. You should go back to your daughter—"

"This will only take a moment."

"Then we do it together." The footboard began to wobble, and she steadied it with one slim hand.

They moved the bed quickly, working together. She surprised him. He hadn't expected her to carry an equal share of the mattress, but she did so with a toss of her head and her jaw set. She was one determined woman, he realized as they set the feather mattress into place. Beth cried out for him, and he left Molly to put fresh sheets on the bed, and he lifted his daughter against his chest.

There were no words, just Beth's misery as she buried her face in his neck and struggled to breathe. Heat radiated from her pink skin. Her hair was damp, and the shirt she wore as a nightgown was wet through.

Agony tore at him. He pushed aside the curtains and saw only a hard-packed wall of snow covering the glass. They were as good as trapped, and he hated it.

"I hurt bad," Beth cried, thrashing her head side to side, bitterly hot, seeking relief where there could be none. "Real bad."

"I know, darlin'." Her wet curls caught on his stubbled chin. He looked over her head to watch Molly smooth the top sheet with a practical but elegant movement of her arm and hand. A thoroughly female movement that set his teeth on edge and drew his gaze.

"Let me go check on the plaster." Molly plopped the pillows into place. She bustled off, her skirts whispering.

Beth saw Molly return with a pot in hand and started protesting. Knowing it had to be done, Luke laid his girl on the clean flannel sheets and stood back, giving enough room for the woman to work. Molly unbuttoned the shirt Beth wore and smoothed the warm mixture of mustard and onion across her chest with gentle care.

Beth turned her head, refusing to look at the lady tending her, but Luke watched. Yes, he watched and noticed every line of concern in her brow, the troubled purse of her lush mouth, the way she pulled her bottom lip between her teeth and worried it.

Every touch was tender, meant to bring comfort. Beth might refuse to acknowledge it, but Luke had looked upon a world unbearably harsh until he could stomach no more, and this softness, this gentleness from a woman toward a child not her own chipped at the ice that was once a part of his heart.

"Close your eyes and rest, Beth," Molly urged as she set the pot aside.

Sleep, tea, and mustard plasters weren't going to break this fever, Luke knew. He watched, heart aching, as Beth closed her eyes, so tired and miserable as her body shook with fever and her chest struggled with each breath.

Molly wrung a cloth in cool water and draped it over the child's brow. Softly, so softly he could barely hear her over the pulse of the storm and his own fears, Molly began to sing a lullaby, soft and sweet.

Beth sighed, and her eyelids fluttered. He watched as sleep

claimed his little girl, and still Molly kept on singing as she wrung out a fresh cloth, wiped the cold poultice from Beth's chest and started anew.

His daughter struggled for every breath, and delirium slowly changed her dreams, and Molly's singing never faltered, her tender, loving hands never wavered.

Luke felt pulled to the edge of endurance, at the precipice of all that he could possibly feel without exploding into pieces. The chair scraped against the wood floor as he stood too abruptly, and he stalked away from the fire and light, away from Molly's innocent melodies.

He didn't stop until he'd shoveled through the hard-packed drift covering the back door and stepped out into the storm. The blizzard's fierce winds buffeted his face, and the shroud of night cut him off from even the happy golden glow from Molly's windows. In the bitter cold he found what he was looking for—no feeling, nothing at all.

Oblivion. It was safer. He let his heart freeze, letting the painful cutting edges of emotion settle into ice before he gathered an armload of wood and went back inside.

Beth stiffened every time Molly touched her. Lady eased up along the bed and laid her nose against the girl's face. That pink tongue darted out, earnestly trying to comfort, and the girl relaxed.

Molly wrung out excess cold water from the cloth and folded it to Beth's brow. Then the girl, half coherently cried out for her father. Poor child.

The fever kept growing in strength. Night had fallen. The darkness was no comfort, and the howling wind beating at the walls held no answers. What if the fever continued? What if Beth died?

The possibility felt as cold as a blizzard's wind.

Lady lifted her head, cocking her long silky ears. It was *him*. Molly could hear it, too, the quiet shut of the door, the uneven staccato tap of his boots against her floor. He clung to the shadows, but she knew the instant he entered the room.

"I convinced her to drink more tea," she said into the darkness. "Yarrow should help her sweat out the fever, but—"

"It doesn't seem to be working. I know." Like a lone hunter he stalked the perimeter of lamplight, keeping to the dark. "Should we start icing her down?"

"That would be my next suggestion."

Silence was his only answer. Molly wrung out another cloth as she listened to the renewed tap of his gait. He knelt before the fire, a shadow brushed by eerie orange light, and loaded the grate with new cedar. The flames rose, greedily consuming the moss and bark, casting more light on McKenna, who somehow seemed untouched by it as he patiently unloaded the rest of the wood onto the floor.

His head rolled forward and he remained, shoulders hunched, still and dark. "What's this on your hearth?"

She had to twist to see over the curve of his arm to the shadow on the stones, a safe distance from the open fire.

"Oh, it's holly. I cut it to decorate my schoolroom for Christmas."

"Christmas?" He shook his head. "I'd forgotten. I guess it is December."

Molly watched as he stood, brushing the bark from his jacket onto the hearth.

"Where are your spare buckets? I'll haul in the snow."

"I could help—"

"Beth needs you." He turned, towering above her, limned by the bright firelight behind him, but his face remained in shadow. "I'd rather start icing her before the fever worsens."

"I feel the same. The buckets are in the pantry. There's an oilcloth in my closet, folded up on the upper shelf."

He nodded, already moving through the darkness. Her heart beat hollowly in her chest. She laid another cloth on Beth's brow and wiped the last of the plaster from her chest.

Luke's footstep whispered behind her on the braid rug. She looked up and saw the sorrow stark on his face. Saw in him a man who'd already lost too much.

The oilcloth dropped at her feet. "I'll be back."

"Papa," Beth cried out, but she wasn't looking at the man who bent over her bed to brush his hand along the curve of her cherub's face. The child's eyes were closed.

As if Lady sensed their fears, the hound laid her chin on Beth's limp hand and stayed there, gaze on the little child, who began muttering again, thrashing back and forth on the pillow.

"Papa, Papa," she choked out, lost in dreams. "No-ooo."

It was a heartbreaking sound. Molly gathered the child in her arms, holding her tight, not knowing what else to do. The child cried so hard that her entire body shook. She felt frail, like a bird, hardly any substance at all, as if she were already leaving them.

Tears blurred her eyes, and she pressed a kiss into Beth's hair, inhaling the little-girl and soap scent of her. What a precious life to hold and far too precious to lose. Grief shattered her, and Molly couldn't hold back the burning tears. They sheared through her chest and ached in her throat, filled her eyes and warmed her cheeks.

Footsteps charged through the parlor; and then he filled the threshold, a flesh and blood man, power and determination. Snow clung to him, dripped from his hair and plopped against the floor. He'd gone out without a coat, by the looks of it, but the cold didn't seem to touch him. He shook the oilcloth over the bed and smoothed it.

"Lay her on it." His order was terse, determined, but Molly was already laying Beth's shaking body onto the cold canvas.

"Papa, Papa," she cried, desolate, without hope.

His face contorted as if looking at a nightmare, one that haunted his soul. He grabbed the bucket from the floor and poured the snow in a neat circle around Beth's shivering, thrashing body.

"Stay with her." He pounded away, determination a hard knot below his sternum. He'd made a promise to Beth. He wasn't going to fail her. Not ever again. He buried his fear and his grief and burst out into the storm. Ice struck like sharp glass against his hands and face, but he filled the bucket and dove inside.

Beth's mournful cries echoed in the parlor above the tick of the clock, the snap of the fire, the blizzard's remorseless roar, and it nearly ripped him in two. He'd broken his promise to her, broken everything he held dear. Hell, what did he think he was doing? He never should have brought her with him. Even though he didn't know what else he should have done.

Broken, Luke shouldered through the threshold and froze, his jaw dropping at the sight of Beth in the woman's slender arms, Molly's elbows planted in the freezing snow. The child cried in delirium, and Molly held her close, murmuring gentle comforting words that made the shadows less dark and the emptiness in his heart fill just a little.

"She's still burning up." Russet curls tumbled over Molly's face, hiding the delicate cut of cheek and jaw from his sight. "Here, give me one of the buckets."

She reached out, beautiful fingers meeting his rough callused ones to take the cold metal handle. It was heavy, but she didn't complain. Tears shimmered on her cheeks, priceless and genuine, as she circled the bed and lifted the bucket.

She's not what I thought. Not at all. Luke ducked his head, paying close attention to his work. Soon, the buckets were empty, and Beth lay feverish and beyond his reach.

"Want Papa," she murmured in anguish, sounding as if she'd lost everything in the world. "Papa-aa."

He wondered if she were reliving the night he was arrested, or any of the miserable nights in the orphanage, alone. So very alone. Bitterness filled him, and when he drew the chair closer, it almost bubbled over in a sharp strident anger that had no place here. No place at all.

He took Beth's hand in his and laid the other on her forehead, caressing her with tenderness so that she could feel his love, and maybe that would soothe her nightmares. Fear dove into his heart and stayed there, expanding with each heartbeat until he couldn't breathe, until he couldn't speak.

Molly slipped from the room, leaving them alone. But not before he'd seen the look on her face, one of longing, one of sorrow. Both touched him, and he knew what lived in this woman's heart.

"We're going to lose her."

Molly looked up at McKenna as he scooped his child out of the melted snow and into his big arms. Defeat shadowed his face. He eased down into the chair and cradled the girl against his wide chest. Beth lay limp, her head bobbing against him, her dark curls tumbling everywhere. Restless and lost, she thrashed and moaned. Lady padded close and licked one small hand with great affection.

"The yarrow has had enough time to work," Molly said stubbornly past a throat tight with fear. "That fever should be breaking soon."

"Open your eyes." His throat worked, and the cords in his neck rose in prominent lines. "She's dying."

"She isn't going to die." Molly caught the end of the oilcloth and let the melted snow sluice into an empty bucket. "Maybe I should make more tea."

"Tea isn't going to save her." He leaned forward to lean his brow against the crown of his daughter's head. He swore, his face twisting with what looked like pain and rage.

Beth's rasped breathing, like the scrape of chalk on a blackboard, filled the room. Every breath became shorter and more shallow.

Molly's throat tightened with grief, with a horrible sense of failure as she snapped the water-flecked oilcloth over her mattress. "I want to ice her down one more time. She's too hot—"

"Damn right she is." Grief thundered in his voice, a dark failure that made him seem less of a lethal criminal and more a man. He darted out of the chair, cradling his daughter in his arms. "Here, you take her. I'll get the snow."

Molly took one look at the child's face, bright red and beaded with perspiration. "I think you should stay with her."

McKenna's dark gaze latched onto hers, and he nodded slowly, hearing the words she couldn't say. He nodded once, lowered his gaze, and carried Beth toward the wing-back chair, warm near the fire but cloaked in shadows.

It was too late. The medicinal tea hadn't worked. Maybe the fever was too swift and lethal for home remedies. Molly headed for the door, the buckets in hand, but she could not forget the fugitive who cradled his dying child in his arms, laden with a father's grief and a man's heartbreak.

Swallowing her tears, fighting against self-recrimination, Molly remembered her early arrogant promise to McKenna that the girl would be all right, that Molly knew exactly what she was doing.

She may have done everything right, but it hadn't made a difference. It hadn't relieved Beth's suffering, and it wouldn't save her life.

Molly fought her way through the snowdrift and felt the tears freeze on her cheeks. The night felt so fierce and heartless. The wind roared with an inhuman voice. She filled the buckets with snow, holding her heart still and cold, knowing she had to go inside and face how she'd failed a helpless, homeless little girl.

The clock chimed midnight, hiding the sound of her step. Molly hesitated in the shadows, looking at the man and his child. Exhaustion hung on him, slumping his great shoulders and drawing down his chin. His unshaven jaw looked tensed, as if he were holding all his fear and heartbreak inside. The fire popped in the grate, the flames flaring higher, tossing enough light to brush McKenna's profile and the sheen of tears on his cheeks.

Was the child dead? Molly's chest tightened, and a cry tore from her throat. The buckets tumbled from her fingers and slammed against the floor with a shocking tinny rattle, and McKenna snapped his chin in her direction.

"The fever broke."

"She's alive?" Molly couldn't believe it Beth lay so still in her father's arms, like a rag doll, limp and lifeless.

"She's having trouble breathing." He looked so vulnerable and so invincible at the same time, a part of her wanted to comfort him even as a part of her was still afraid. He swiped one hand across his face, wiping away the traces of tears, and he looked once again the tough man who'd rescued her from the bounty hunter with a single lethal shot.

He might be a killer, but he was also a man—Molly could never forget that. Somehow her wobbly knees managed to carry her to Beth's side and she laid her hand on her brow. Yes, she was much cooler.

Molly's heart broke and she sank to the floor. Life was so fragile, a child's life more so. She buried her face in her mittened hands. The wool absorbed the wetness of her tears.

❧✺❧

"Thank you." McKenna's voice stroked like a touch, gentle with understanding and comfort as he rose from the bed, where his daughter slept in a dry shirt on fresh sheets. "Beth owes her life to you."

"When I came back into the house, I thought she'd died." She swiped at her eyes, embarrassed, but they continued to brim over her lids and roll down her face. Beth wasn't her child, but she simply couldn't help the cold wave of relief that left her shaking like a tree in the wind.

"It was you, Molly. You saved her life." He placed one hand on her right shoulder. His fingers curled around the rise of muscle and bone and held her, a touch of comfort and tenderness. Then he lifted her chin to meet his gaze.

He had wolf's eyes, but a man's heart. She could see everything inside him—the weakness from his wound, the exhaustion from two nights without sleep, the hunger, the restlessness, the fear.

He wasn't a safe man, but there was gentleness in him and an unyielding love for his daughter unlike any she'd known. Odd there could be this softness in a hunter's heart.

"Beth still needs care." Molly swept her chin from his touch, but her skin still burned and tingled. Her entire being remained aware of his hand on her shoulder. "I'll need to boil another plaster for her chest."

"I'll stay with her." McKenna withdrew, leaving her cold somehow, leaving her strangely exposed.

She watched as he pulled a wooden-backed chair across the braid rug to the bedside and folded his big frame into it. He said not one word about the dog who'd dared to hop onto the foot of the bed, watchfully keeping an eye on the ill child. McKenna simply watched his daughter sleep, nothing more than a darker shadow in the dark room.

Molly couldn't see his expression to know what he was thinking, but she could feel his relief and his anguish. She could feel how he hurt for his daughter, a father's love tender and true.

Holding back her feelings, Molly headed for the kitchen, stopping to light a lamp to guide her way. The night wasn't over yet, and there was still more work to be done. As she chopped onions and fried them into an eye-stinging pulp, adding ground mustard so tart it made her gasp for air, she couldn't remove the image of McKenna and his daughter from her mind, from her heart.

As the plaster steamed, cooling on the counter, Molly prepared another pan of mint and menthol. While waiting for it to boil, she couldn't help peering around the corner where the faint glow of low fire drew her gaze through the house to the bed where Beth lay, struggling to breathe. The light burnished the line of his shoulders and arms, braced protectively, watching his daughter while she slept.

"How's she breathing?" Molly asked, carrying the steaming basin into the room.

"Still rough." He paused. "Will this turn into pneumonia?"

"Not with my trusted onion and mustard plaster." Molly skirted him and circled to the far side of the bed. "You might not believe me—"

"I do. I was wrong before, and I'm sorry." He sounded like a man who didn't apologize often.

She was a woman who'd received few apologies in her life, and it touched her now, like sun to snow, melting some of the ice life had brought to her heart. "I wasn't sure myself if she would pull through. I'm just glad she did."

"I don't want to lose her after this."

"I'm sure she'll be fine." Molly set the steaming basin on the corner table, and the soothing scents of mint and menthol fogged the air between them.

"Do you always get blizzards like this?"

"I understand they're common in these parts. I've just been here since August myself."

He nodded, watching as she stood. "That's why this place still smells of pine."

"Fresh logs. My uncle oversaw the construction for me."

"You have family in the area?" He lifted one brow, betraying an interest that surprised her.

"Yes." His gaze felt too intense, too penetrating, and she whirled away. The lamp perched on the dining room table flickered as she swept past.

She took refuge in the kitchen, checking the cooling plaster; then she dug through the pantry for a few things. Why was her pulse churning as if she'd been running three miles?

Her hands felt unsteady as she balanced the plates, two glasses, and the small kettle. He rose as fluid and quick as a wild animal, his big frame and long legs carrying him to the edge of the parlor before she could protest.

He took the pot and the glasses from her, leaving her speechless and her entire body thrumming. Why was she reacting to him like this? Beth moaned in her sleep, her chest rising shallowly. Each breath sounded torn from deep within her.

"The plaster will help," she promised the sleeping child, knowing Beth couldn't hear her, knowing the girl wouldn't want her help if she were awake.

"How long will Beth need to recuperate?"

"I don't know. A couple of weeks, maybe."

He swore, a low bitten oath that twisted his features and turned him into shadows. The light retreated, and he covered his face with both hands. "I don't have that kind of time."

"I don't know what the answer is. But you shouldn't have had a child this small and fragile outside in a blizzard in the first place. You nearly cost Beth her life because you chose to run from the law instead of—"

"Lady, that was a bounty hunter who wanted me dead for the money. Understand that?" He stood, stalking through the dark shadows like a wild animal getting ready to fight. "What do you think would happen to Beth if Hammond had gotten ahold of her? He had his hand around your throat. Do you think he'd do less to a helpless child?"

"No. But look at the danger you're exposing her to. I don't understand how—"

"I'm worth a lot of money, lady, dead or alive, so I've got to keep moving. I'm sure you're smart enough to figure out what happens if I don't." Despair settled over his face, and it was the cold lost look of a man without hope. "I'm responsible for that little girl. For better or worse, I'm all she has. There're no relatives or in-laws I can leave her with, and that means she's with me or she's in an orphanage."

"An orphanage?" Molly choked.

"You must know what those places are like and how they treat kids. How they hire them out for field work." His voice broke, and he looked away. His jaw worked, as if he were holding back more than his temper, more than his heart.

"If I don't run and keep running, then that child has no place else to go. If a bounty hunter finds me or the law catches up with me, I'll be killed or arrested and Beth will be tossed into a home— and that's if she's lucky after being alone with those men. If she winds up in an orphanage, she'll be made to work for her keep. I'll be damned if I'm going to let that happen a second time."

Molly felt small in the wake of his admission. She unbuttoned Beth's shirt and tried to concentrate on her work, but those memories too painful to recall threatened to well up, and she shivered. "Beth was in an orphanage?"

"While I was in prison. I don't care what it costs me, I'll never let that happen to her. Not ever again." Muscles strained in his jaw and throat.

Molly stared hard at the dull yellow paste she was spreading across Beth's chest. What did the future hold for this little girl?

The burning wood popped in the hearth.

McKenna took a breath. "I know you understand."

Molly nodded and wiped off her fingers on the edge of her apron. The child slept, every breath rattling; she was still sick enough for concern. Molly resisted the urge to brush away the curls falling into the girl's face, and held back the sympathy for this child's fate.

And failed.

Luke watched the tears shine like silver as they dampened Molly's cheeks. Emotion, long unused and unnamed, weighed down his chest like an anvil. Molly watched his daughter sleep, and Luke knew that she, this woman with russet curls and a house filled with porcelain and lace, was what he'd been searching for.

CHAPTER FIVE

The dog started barking just after the clock struck three. Luke left Beth's side, heart pounding, adrenaline pumping, and stole the revolver from the mantel. The wood and metal weapon radiated heat against his palm.

Molly's eyes widened as she carried a steaming basin from the kitchen. "You don't need your gun. I told you, no one can make it through the blizzard. We're safe enough until the storm breaks."

"Fine." He pushed past her, concentrating on the sounds of the winds outside the cabin and how they could disguise the knell of a boot heel on the porch. The storm was dying down some, and that could mean trouble. "Check the bars on the doors."

The dog's sharp bark echoed again in the parlor and the animal loped past in a hurry to reach the back door.

"She hears something I can't." *Moss.* He was out there somewhere and Luke would find him. He grabbed his coat, knowing what he had to do, knowing he couldn't let this woman and his child down. "I won't go far. You don't have to worry. I won't let another bounty hunter use you for bait."

She paled and turned to watch her dog paw at the back door. "It's probably just the deer."

"The what?"

"The white-tailed deer have figured out I'll feed them."

Lady barked, the warning sharp and undeniable. Hair ruffled

along the length of her spine as she stared up at the ceiling.

Luke shrugged into his coat. "Just do what I say. Stay inside with Beth. Bar the door."

"But the blizzard—"

"I'll be fine." He cut her off, and he watched her take a step back from him. Trust was a funny thing. As they'd taken care of Beth together through the night, the fear in Molly's eyes had faded away, but now, as night melted into morning, she would see the man he truly was.

A man who had killed and who would be killed, unless his luck held.

"I'll be back." He pulled on a hat and gloves and headed through the house, turning his back on the woman who watched, confused and lonely, and the child who slept near the fire, safe and warm.

There was only one way out of the house with the high snowdrifts, and Luke took it. Steeled and ready, he eased into the cold winds, but Moss wasn't lying there in wait. *The bastard has to be out here somewhere.* Luke kept his revolver cocked as he prowled across the hard-packed snow, scanning the dark yard with precise care.

Through a veil of heavy snow, tall shadowed firs danced in the wind, but that was the only movement he could see.

Damn it, he knew Moss was out there. And he couldn't afford to make a mistake now. Exhaustion dulled his senses, blurred his vision, and made him feel slow and numb—a distinct disadvantage.

Don't mess this up, McKenna. Beth and Molly needed protection, and he was the only one to do it. He took a deep breath and willed his eyes to focus and his body to obey.

He searched against the thousand shades of the night but there were no tracks on the snow. The flakes that fell now whirled and danced along the crusted surface, and Luke couldn't even see his own boot prints in the world of night and storm.

He smelled trouble before he saw it. The thick, dank scent of smoke fused with the wind. Moss, that rotten lowlife, was nothing more than the faintest shadow on the steepled roof moving against a gray-black curtain of snow. A dull orange gleam flickered in what had to be the chimney.

Trying to smoke me out, huh, Moss? Anger consumed Luke as he knelt, raising his Colt. At least the bounty hunter hadn't figured out that he wasn't alone. The storm and night consumed the gunman from Luke's sight again and he waited, heart thundering in steady staccato beats. He needed only one clean shot. That was all.

The gust of wind faded and the snows parted, and weak flame glowed orange at the chimney's mouth, but there was no man on the roof, no sign of Moss anywhere.

No doubt the bastard had hunkered down into position at the back door—the only exit from the house that wasn't covered by six-foot drifts. Then all Moss had to do was pull the trigger.

But where the hell is he? He had to stop Moss before Molly and Beth came out that back door. The north wind died against his back, and the sky opened above him, casting faint starlight over the backyard. No footprints, no tracks, no sign of the man who wanted him dead.

He's close. I can feel him. Luke lingered in the shadows, fingers brushing both triggers, tensed and ready. The last snowflakes fluttered to earth, and the night drew silent and still. An owl hooted, and in the distance a coyote yipped, lonely and chilling. He peered around the edge of the house and saw only the silvered peaceful landscape and the majestic, snow-clad firs.

Where would be the best spot to sit and play shooting duck? There, behind the fence line. The drifts were high, and the shadows from the trees would make him invisible. Moss would be thinking that he'd be making an easy five-thousand bucks, but he was wrong.

Moss was about to die.

The snow scrunched with Luke's careful step, an audible squeak in the hush of the night. He shucked off his boots, gritted his teeth against the unbearable cold, and raced on stocking feet behind the stable and around the line of trees.

He heard the crunch of snow up ahead—the sound of someone crouching down for a better view. Moss. There, in the deepest shadows was the man's bulky form, his buffalo coat a furry hump against the polished snow. The rifle he held in his hands, a repeating Winchester, rested on the top rung of the fence, now only a few feet above the snow line, aimed directly at the back door.

Luke heard the squeak of hinges and Molly's voice, low and soft as evening birdsong. She was coming, probably with Beth in her arms, and damn it, he wasn't close enough to take out Moss. He started running as Moss swung the rifle and leaned in for the shot.

"Molly, no!" Rage licked at him like flame, and he aimed, still too damn far away.

He fired, knowing he missed even before the report shattered the silent night. He thumbed back the hammer, still running, watching as Moss turned from his post. Sur-prise and pleasure twisted Moss's face into a killer's smile as he pivoted the rifle in one fast sweep and fired. Straight at Luke's heart.

Luke tumbled to the ground, already firing. The bullet grazed past his shoulder, taking only cloth. He struck the cold ground belly first and rolled, head up, aiming again.

But a man towered over him. Moss's rifle jammed against Luke's chest, forcing him into the snow. On his back, he stared up at death. At the man who'd been hunting him since the Montana border. He saw Moss's gloved finger begin to squeeze the trigger. Luke dropped his gun, grabbed the barrel with both hands and tore it from his chest. Fire burned his palms as the bullet plowed into the earth an inch away.

Surprise narrowed the gunman's eyes, and Luke took advantage of it. He ripped the rifle from the bounty hunter's grip and rolled. Out of the corner of his eye he saw Moss draw from his hip, and he brought the rifle around, both hands on the barrel, and clubbed the gun-man's shooting arm. He heard wood splinter, bone crack, and Moss's sharp cry of agony.

Then Moss's gaze turned black and cold, lethal with the promise of violence. Luke knew what was coming. He swung the broken gun out of the way. He grabbed the Colt from his boot, but the bounty hunter also had another gun.

Finally, he had the advantage. Luke thumbed back the hammer, running for cover as he aimed and fired. Ice sprayed as the bullet plowed through the drift. A grunt of pain rumbled through the night. Moss stumbled behind a snow-topped stump.

Was he dead? Luke ducked behind the thick trunk of a pine, revolver cocked and ready. He could win this now. It didn't matter how weak he was or that his bullet wound had torn open and was bleeding again. He'd been a sharp-shooter for ten long years. All Moss had to do was ease up over the top of the stump to take a shot and Luke would have him for good.

"I did my research on you, McKenna." Strain marked Moss's voice—maybe he was wounded, but not fatally.

"Then you know I'm going to walk out of here alive. And you aren't." Luke took a slow breath, keeping focused and the Colt steady.

"I know what you were, McKenna. What you did." Moss's sharp cynical laugh echoed in the quiet night "I know there's no way in hell I'm gonna win a gunfight against you. But then, I don't have to. You're gonna surrender. I can see that little girl of yours from here."

Was he lying? Luke couldn't chance it. He saw the nose of a gun lean across the top rail of the fence, wobbling a bit, gleaming dark and deadly against the night-brushed snow. He couldn't see where Molly and Beth were through the thick grove of trees, but what if Moss could?

Luke fired. He didn't think, he didn't consider the consequences, he just acted. He watched the revolver fly from the fence rail to the ground. Moss's curse rose on the wind, and Luke started to run. Out of bullets, damn it, and he had no time to reload. Moss tumbled over the fence, heading for the gun.

Ten yards, nine yards... Luke pumped hard, closing the distance. But Moss was reaching out, bloody hand stretching toward the revolver half buried in the snow. Six yards, five... He wasn't going to make it. Moss's hand closed over the wooden grip. He pulled the gun out of the snow.

Luke leaped over the stump, flew over the fence rail, and tackled Moss. They tumbled together, fighting for the cocked revolver in midair. Luke hit first, the back of his shoulder slamming into the hardpacked snow. It was like hitting granite, and the impact rocked him. Moss landed hard beside him, still fighting for control of the revolver.

"You bastard," Moss growled, elbowing Luke hard in the throat.

Pain exploded in his Adam's apple.

"I want that five-thousand-dollar reward on your sorry ass, and I'm not going to die for it." Moss turned the revolver downward. "You are."

The muscles in Luke's arms burned as he struggled. He fought, but Moss was stronger. The nights without sleep, the wound, they took their toll. Luke struggled, eye to eye with his enemy. His arms began to shake, and blood warmed the side of his trousers. He couldn't keep Moss from pushing the gun toward his chest.

Luke could see the triumph in Moss's eyes, smell his own death in the air, and hear the distant thump of Molly running hard. "Luke," she cried, the fear in her voice sharp with horror.

Black fury exploded in his chest, the sound tearing up his throat, snapping through his body. He wouldn't die like this and leave Molly and Beth unprotected.

Moss's finger brushed the trigger. With the last of his strength, Luke twisted the revolver's nose as the weapon fired.

The flash of gunpowder nearly blinded him; the thunder nearly deafened him. Luke felt the gun tumble into his hands. He looked and saw Moss dead, eyes sightless, surprise stark on his ruthless face.

"Luke!" It was Molly kneeling beside him, her touch gentle on his face. He lay back, out of breath, hurting and dizzy, and her thighs pillowed his head; her arms wrapped around him. "Are you hurt? Did he shoot you? I tried to get him in the rifle's site, but I couldn't fire. I was afraid of missing and hitting you. I—"

"It's all right." He pressed her hand to the side of his face. She felt like warm woman and silk, like forgiveness and redemption, like everything he could never deserve again but couldn't help wanting. "Where's Beth?"

"I wrapped her up in a blanket and left her on the porch. I thought she'd be safe from stray bullets there."

Molly took the revolver from his hand and pushed his coat aside to look at the blood on his shirt. "Look at this. Luke, you're really bleeding."

"What about the chimney?"

"He used wet branches from one of the trees in the yard. They're smoking pretty bad, but they're too wet, and I figured the fire would burn out. I was more worried about you winding up dead."

Was that concern in her voice? Not polite, but genuine and heartfelt, as if she cared that he was hurting. His throat ached with uncomfortable emotion, and he turned away from her touch. He couldn't accept her tenderness, didn't deserve it.

He gritted his teeth against the pain, against wounds and exhaustion and relief that left him trembling and weak when he stood. Molly, brushed by starlight and surrounded by silvered snow still crouched on the ground, her skirts draping her slender thighs, her head tipped back. She was delicate beauty and heart, and with her rich curls she looked like a china angel his mother once had, kept safe behind glass.

She was softness and light, goodness and grace, everything he'd lost faith in. He wanted to hold her and breathe in her warmth and sweetness, hold her until the world ended.

A wolf howled nearby, a lone hunter scenting the blood of the kill. Grim, Luke held out his hand to help Molly up. Her fingers curled around his. His heart kicked with a longing so sharp, it nearly knocked him off his feet. A longing for safety and shelter and a life he could never have again.

Moss lay dead in the snow, not three feet away. Twice now, Luke had killed a man in front of Molly. Twice now, he'd become what he despised—a violent man.

How could he look at her? How could he endure seeing the tentative trust and honest caring on her face pale and change into nothing but horror? Shame filled him, and he turned away from her touch, away from her quiet caring that felt like a welcome light on this dark, cold night.

❧ · ❦

The closed door had stopped the smoke from entering the spare bedroom, so Molly laid Beth in the bed there.

"Is my papa gone yet?"

"He's outside." Sympathy tugged at Molly's heart. She eased down to her knees beside the bed, knowing something about loss, about need and losing a parent. "He'll be right back, I promise."

"No, he won't. He's gonna leave me and never come back."

Misery teared her eyes, and then she plunged face first into the pillow and succumbed to a harsh coughing fit.

What fears did this little girl have? She would have so many, losing her father to jail, being tossed into an orphanage, and then on the run, her father a fugitive, with danger around every turn.

"Your father loves you, Beth," Molly soothed when the coughing was over because she sensed the child might need to hear the words.

Molly laid her hand on Beth's back and rubbed in slow circles. The little girl wheezed and coughed but didn't relax. Her spine remained stiff as steel until Molly realized there was no comfort she could give Beth, or none that the child would accept, and withdrew her hand.

"Your papa will be here soon," Molly promised. It was the only solace she could offer as she left the room and closed the door behind her to keep out the smell of smoke.

Her parlor was slightly damaged with a thin layer of smoke, but only because she'd thought to bank the fire. Now the chimney was once again drawing, and she stirred the coals. McKenna had fixed it, just like he'd promised.

She grabbed a hot pad and went in search of the warming irons. They weren't on the hearth next to the grate. He must have moved them, she realized. The heavy iron was only mildly warm, sitting off to one side next to the cut holly heaped in a pile on the floor.

His footsteps knelled in the eerie silence. "I'm sorry about your house. I brought trouble to your door twice."

"I'll find a way to forgive you." She laid the iron near the heat, then reached for the wood box.

"Let me." He knelt beside her like a warrior in the dark. "It's the least I can do after ruining your home."

"Building up the fire won't fix my parlor."

"No, but you've done enough work on my behalf."

"It wasn't so hard caring for your daughter."

He took her hand in his, and she felt the rough calluses on his palm and the male heat of his skin. His touch burned, and she felt branded. But there was only a quiet acceptance in his voice when he spoke. "I've been running all the way from South Texas and do you know what? You're the only one I've come across who helped us. The only one. That's a long way to go without seeing the smallest kindness, believe me."

His words, the depth of them stymied her, left her feeling inadequate, twisted up inside and ashamed. "I wasn't that kind. I was barely kind at all."

"You saved my daughter. You made sure she was safe from Moss. That is everything."

She saw the goodness in him, the love for his daughter that burned brighter than any light, truer than the most constant star. She was no longer afraid. "I'm glad I made a difference. Sometimes I feel as if..."

She closed her eyes. What was she doing? He wasn't a man who cared about her private sorrows.

"Tell me."

He might be as strong as a knight of old, but there was heart in

77

him, too. Molly swallowed, trying to find the words, grateful that he cared enough to ask. "As if my life has no useful purpose. I teach children to read. I like the work I do. But if I disappeared from the face of this earth, it wouldn't matter."

"Surely you have family who cares?"

"No." Her throat constricted, remembering her mother's letter. "My parents and I have had a falling out, and my stepbrothers are on my parents' side."

"You're not close?" He sounded surprised.

She shook her head.

"How did you wind up in an orphanage?"

"I was in the way." Those words hurt, and she didn't want to say more.

His arm brushed hers, filling the grate with sharp, dry pine. Exhaustion hung on him like a heavy coat, slumping his great shoulders and spine. His unshaven jaw looked tensed and his eyes as black as coal. The firelight caressed his face, bruised with fatigue and lined with pain.

How could this man be a fugitive? How could he have committed any crime? She'd seen him kill two bounty hunters in self-defense and yet she couldn't see him killing in cold blood. She wondered about him as he stood, unfolding his big body and limping toward the closed bedroom door where Beth slept.

"I'll bring her some broth I have warming on the kitchen stove."

He kept walking, his step heavy, his limp pronounced. "That'll be fine. She must be cold."

"I'll have her warm in no time." Molly brushed her fingertips across the weight of the iron, then wrapped it in a linen. "Here, take this with you. It will chase the chill from the sheets."

He paused, swaying for a heartbeat, before his big, masculine body crumpled to the ground.

"McKenna!" She dove to his side. Had he been hurt in the gunfight? She pressed her fingers against the side of his throat and gave thanks for the rapid but weak pulse fluttering against her fingertips.

Yes, this man of steel and might was made of flesh and blood, as vulnerable as any man.

And he needed her like no one had in a very long time.

H is eyes snapped open. He saw only darkness, heard only silence. He was lying between warm flannel sheets that were so soft they felt like heaven. Beth. Was she all right? He tried to sit up, but pain streaked through his side and traveled in white-hot bolts down his leg.

He was lying on a floor, warm like he hadn't been in longer than he could remember. Flannel shifted as he tried to move again. The pain convinced him to lie back in the pillows and catch his breath for a few minutes.

He sensed her presence, for there was little to see in the black shadows of the bedroom. It wasn't hard to recognize the faint, gentle scent of lilacs. Soft rustling sounds came from the corner of the room. A drawer squeaked.

"I'm awake."

"Oops. Sorry about that. I didn't mean to disturb you." The drawer squeaked again, and fabric whispered as if she were digging through the drawer. "I just need a few things."

He remembered the dizzy spell in her parlor. He remembered the floor rushing up to meet him before everything went black. "How did I get here?"

"I'm stronger than I look. I brought you in here." Molly closed the drawer with a squeak and a clink of a handle.

"How's Beth? I have to see her." He tried to sit up again, but the pain drove him back down.

"She's sleeping." He heard a rustle of cotton and the pad of feet against the floor, and then Molly knelt at his side.

"Her chest—"

"The congestion is better. I stayed with her until dawn. She's going to be just fine."

"Thank you." The words felt so small for all this woman had done. "I should have been the one—"

"You were too busy collapsing, remember?"

His chest ached at the warmth in her voice and at the thousand accusations and faults she didn't mention or name. "The question is, how are you feeling?"

"Good."

"You lie." Her accusation felt warm as the silk heat of her fingertips brushed across his brow. "No fever yet, but you're a lucky man. You need some bedrest, too."

"The storm's over. There's no time to waste." He moved away from her touch because he had to. "I need a horse."

"You need to let your stitches heal. You tore them open. I did my best, but you were still bleeding the last time I changed your bandage."

"I'll live." Nothing had killed him yet. He swung both feet free from the tangle of sheets. Pain seared up his calf, bit through his thighs, and spun up the rest of his spine. He gritted his teeth to keep from crying out as he shifted his weight and stood, but a moan escaped and echoed in the room.

Cool air skidded across his exposed skin—across the tops of his thighs and higher. Luke watched as Molly turned her back and started for the door with a swish of skirts.

He was naked. He wasn't even wearing socks. She must have stripped him down last night. Hell, he hadn't even realized...he reached down for a sheet to cover himself and winced as pain tore through him like hooked claws, leaving him weak and gasping for air.

"I took your clothes and washed them. They're too wet to wear right now. I guess that means you'll have to rest and take care of Beth today."

"Molly, I can't go around naked. I need my clothes."

"I left something folded up on the bureau for you." The door swung open, and the small wash of light tumbled over her, illuminating the wool dress that clung to her willowy woman's body like a man's hungry touch. She twisted toward him, the movement emphasizing her narrow waist.

He couldn't help it. Need thrummed through his groin. He could feel the blood gather, and he squeezed his eyes shut. "You said my clothes are drying?"

"By the fire." She hesitated. "I left breakfast in the oven for you and Beth. Her congestion is still breaking up, so I left a cough mixture on the counter and compresses—"

"Are you going somewhere?" The storm had ended, and she knew his secrets. "You wouldn't go to the sheriff, right?"

"I've got to head to town and open up the school."

"There's school today?"

"As long as there's no blizzard. The good people of Evergreen don't pay me to stay home."

"What would the good people of Evergreen say if they knew a fugitive had spent the night in your bedroom?"

She merely lifted one slim shoulder. "I guess they don't have to know, do they? I can see you're about ready to fall over. I can stay home—"

"No." That would raise questions, and maybe bring someone from town out to check on her. "I'm tough, Molly. A year of hard labor didn't kill me. This won't."

He stood and laid a hand on her shoulder, feeling kitten-soft wool and delicate woman. Need kicked through him, heady and bold and he drew away. "I know you won't tell the sheriff about me. It would hurt Beth."

"I would never hurt a child." Molly brushed those rich shimmering curls from her brow. "And I want your word on something, too. Beth is too fragile to travel. She won't make it to Canada if you're thinking of running off today."

"That's not my plan now."

"I don't believe you're a bad man. I don't know why, but that's what I think. So there's no need to run." She bowed her head, a vulnerable, troubled gesture that left him at a loss for words.

He stood weak and shaking with pain, but all he saw, all he felt, all he knew was this woman. His heart stood still while she walked away.

His throat ached, and the ice in his chest felt ready to crack. Books sat in a neatly tied pile on the corner of the dining room table—he could just see it from where he stood.

"I'll see you this afternoon." Her promise rang with the quiet strength of a hymn.

Then she gathered her books and tucked them into the curve of her arm. She tapped through the shadowed kitchen and out of his sight. The door whispered closed, and he leaned heavily against the door frame, thankful that they'd stumbled onto Molly's property and into her life.

Dismissed for the noon meal, thirty-seven pairs of feet bolted down the aisles, and the door slammed open with a hard bang. Molly winced as the sound echoed through the schoolroom. Children's voices rose in jubilation—the musical chatter of little girls and the booming challenges of little boys.

Good, maybe they could run off some energy and be able to sit without much fidgeting through the rest of the afternoon. Molly opened her bottom drawer and pulled out her lunch pail. Already it had been a long day, and she'd gone without sleep the night before, keeping vapor for Beth to breathe and compresses on her chest

How was the girl doing? Maybe McKenna had found the sandwich makings she'd left and the frozen pot of stew against the back wall of the pantry.

"Molly?" a woman's voice rang in the tiny vestibule. Heeled boots clomped delicately on the wood floor, and Aggie Grant swept into the classroom. "Goodness, you're a sight for sore eyes. I was near to making myself sick, worrying about you trapped in that blizzard all alone."

"In my house, not lost on the mountainside." Molly pushed out of her chair and circled her desk, arms open to accept her aunt's hug. "I was perfectly safe."

"You must have been terrified. Your first mountain blizzard." Aggie held Molly tight. "Why, I told my Russell that we just had to move you in with us for the rest of the winter. I couldn't live with myself if anything happened to you."

"I'm fine." Molly stepped away, touched by her aunt's affection. "You just sent your last daughter off in marriage. The last thing you need is me hanging around your house."

"I need you more than you know, dear heart." Aggie stepped back and tugged at her coat buttons. "I'm glad you have a good stove in this schoolhouse. Are you sure you're all right? You don't look like you got a good night's sleep."

Molly chuckled; she couldn't help it. "You're fussing over me again."

"There it is, that independent streak of yours. Well, I know how it is to be young." Aggie pulled up a chair. "And heaven knows with the family you have, being an independent sort is a good thing."

Molly thought of the letter she felt too ashamed to tell her aunt about. Aggie was Ma's sister, and the bad feelings between them would only continue. More family strife was the last thing Molly could stomach. "How did you and Uncle Russell weather the storm?"

"Just fine. My, I must say the blizzards are worse up in these mountains than we were used to on the plains." Aggie piled her reticule and hat on a nearby desktop. "Now, just call me nosy, but I wanted to know what plans you have up your sleeve for a Christmas pageant. I know Reverend Mills is planning a lovely to-do. The choir has already started practicing."

"Already?"

"Well, Christmas is fast approaching." Aggie rose from her chair and rescued the newly bubbling teapot from the red-hot stove. "This being the town's first Christmas celebration, why, the first celebration of any kind, we want to do it up right. We're all practically strangers here, just getting to know our neighbors. Think of the good that could come out of a wonderful shindig."

One thing Aunt Aggie wasn't short on was enthusiasm. "I was thinking about a recital."

"Oh, just the thing. Scholarly, but seasonal. Where's the holly? I'll help you start decorating. I picked up a sack of the tiniest nails over at the mercantile."

Molly thought of her holly and of the disaster the bounty hunter had made of her parlor and nearly everything in it. "I put the holly on the hearth—"

"Goodness, did you scorch it? Well, I can come over this afternoon and help you cut more—"

"No." Molly nearly dropped the sandwich she was unwrapping. "You don't need to make a trip all the way out to my place. I cut the first batch of holly. I'll survive cutting the second."

"Stubborn. Independent." But a gleam of pride sparkled in the older woman's blue eyes.

"Fine, now you're making me feel guilty. Come over here tomorrow, and we'll decorate."

"There, now. That sounds grand. As long as we don't get another one of those blizzards. Goodness, I hope the entire winter isn't like this. I'm glad the mayor had enough sense to send someone to shovel out the school this morning. I've never seen such drifts. And with only one storm."

Family ties. Molly felt the pull as Aggie launched into a dozen vivid descriptions of damage from the storm and then right into plans for a town Christmas tree. The older woman's warmth beckoned her like a fire on a cold night, warm and radiant and so welcome she felt touched no matter how far away she tried to keep herself.

Affection frightened her. She'd been estranged from her aunt for years when she'd accepted their offer to apply for the town's first school teaching position. When family had meant duty and more pain than her heart could take, Molly had hesitated, but Aggie had welcomed her with a hug, a kiss, and an acceptance Molly didn't quite understand. But she appreciated her aunt's caring more than she could find the words to say.

Aggie stayed until recess was over, leaving with a hug and a promise to come to supper one night soon. Molly called the fifth math class up to the front, and the afternoon sped by correcting multiplication errors and making sure the little girls in the front row weren't writing notes to one another instead of practicing their letters.

The classroom was quiet for the last thirty minutes of the school day, and Molly's thoughts kept drifting. She couldn't help remembering the man and child staying in her house. Couldn't keep from being moved by McKenna's devotion to his daughter, and how the child clung to him.

Would they be there when she returned? Would her house feel full and not empty?

Molly remembered the sight of McKenna clutching the sheet in the shadows. It had been too dark to see him, but she'd felt his raw masculine presence and she could feel it still. On her skin and in her blood.

She might not believe it, but the fact remained that he was a fugitive and a condemned criminal. Truly a man to be feared. So why did she want him to stay now that the storm was over?

CHAPTER SIX

The dog lifted her nose from her paws and quirked her long ears. Luke eased up from the floor, scrub brush in hand. Pain burned through him as he tugged back the edge of the curtain. Fading sunlight cast sharp bright rays through the glass pane, and he had to squint toward the faraway road. A movement through the trees told him someone was coming.

The guns at his side reassured him. He knew Moss had worked with only one hired man. There probably wouldn't be another bounty hunter on his trail so damn soon, but Luke couldn't afford to let down his guard. Not with his daughter's life at stake.

"Papa?"

"In a minute, darlin'."

He waited as the dog hopped up from the fire and gave a loud bark. Then a golden mare ridden by a woman wearing a gray cloak broke out of the line of trees. Molly. The tension coiled in his muscles relaxed. He hadn't realized what time it was. He resnapped his holsters and grabbed the mop and bucket from the middle of the floor.

"Papa?" Beth rasped, and the gasp of pain told how much it hurt for her to speak.

"I'm right here, darlin'."

"I'm hungry."

"Don't worry. I'll get you what you need." He kissed her brow, thankful, so very thankful. All signs of the fever were gone, and all that remained was a sharp cough.

But that didn't mean she was ready to head out into the wilderness. No, he'd brought her as far as he could. This town was the last he'd come across for nearly a hundred miles. Canada was due north. The safest route for him was straight through the rugged Montana Rockies, and that was no place for a child too ill to travel.

Luke grabbed a plate of cookies from the kitchen after putting away the mop and bucket. Pain hammered through him. He felt as if a herd of stampeding buffalo had run right over the top of him, but he wouldn't rest now.

He didn't know how much time he had.

The dog scratched at the door, and he let the hound out. Lady's buff coat gleamed in the weak sunshine as she bounded down the steps and across the snow.

"Is that *her*? " Beth asked.

"Yep. It's Molly, home from town." Luke held the cup to his daughter's lips, and Beth's small fingers curled around his. So small and trusting, this child who depended on him to provide her with a good life.

And he would give it to her.

"Molly's a schoolteacher. Did you know that?"

Beth didn't answer, intent on nibbling on the cookie. But he recognized the look of her down-turned eyes.

"She's an awfully nice lady, don't you think?"

"I don't like her, Pa." Beth pushed the plate away, tears in her eyes. She was as pale as the sheet behind her, still too weak to do more than sit up in bed.

"Well, now darlin', she's got a nice dog."

"I hate dogs."

He had to bite back his smile on that one. Lady had shared the bed with Beth all day. Beth's hands had hardly strayed from the hound's silken head. Well, there would be time to talk tonight. Plenty of time. Time for both of them to face what lay ahead.

The door creaked open, and the sound of a bouncing dog and a woman's soft step resounded from the back of the house. Luke took the plate of cookies from his daughter. "Want more?"

"Nope." Beth shook her head, scattering dark curls across her brow. "Papa, promise you won't leave."

"You know I can't make that promise, darlin'." His heart broke saying the words and seeing the fear tighten her pretty face, but he wouldn't lie to her. He wouldn't make promises he couldn't keep.

"Is anyone home?" Molly's soft Northwestern accent lured him from the shadows.

He leaned against the door frame, waiting, listening to the rustling sounds as she slipped out of her cloak. The tiny hairs on the back of his neck stood as she swept into sight, and he tried to remember that what he felt was simply *gratefulness*. Anything else—lust, admiration, yearning, why, there was no future in it.

No future at all.

"How's Beth?" Concern furrowed across her brow and drew her soft mouth into a worried line. "Is she doing better?"

"Thanks to you."

"I'm so glad—" Molly stepped into the parlor and froze. "I can't believe this. Look what you did. And with your injury..."

"I'll live. Besides, I couldn't go off and leave your house a mess like that. It got that way because of me."

"The walls, the floor, even the furniture." She spun around, and the green wool dress swirled around her, hugging her trim figure, emphasizing the curve of her breasts, the dip of her waist, the flare of hip and thigh. Lamplight gleamed like aged bronze in her russet curls and made her hazel eyes shine. "You did this. I'm speechless. I... I've just never known a single man in my entire life who knew how to clean."

"I've done my share of floor scrubbing in this life. My wife was sickly, and I helped her often." The way Molly shone, like a newly lit candle, bright and beautiful, pleased him. "I couldn't get all the smoke off the mantel, though. I figured I didn't know what soap to use."

"I hardly noticed." She ran her fingertips over the out-cropping of gray stones.

"I saved everything but that stack of holly. I figured I'd cut you more, if you wanted. I noticed the tree out back."

"It must have taken you all day."

"Just a part of the afternoon. Beth mostly slept, so I had the time."

"You were supposed to be resting." She waltzed toward him, as graceful as flurried snow, her hem sweeping the floor, her heeled shoes whispering against the braid rug. "You look pale."

"I'll live."

"I can't thank you enough."

"You don't have to. You're the one who's owed a world of thanks. More than I could possibly repay." His pulse skipped at her nearness. He could smell her soft lilac scent, see the bronzed threads in her hazel eyes, and hear the hush of her breathing. "You saved us, and I'm not through asking for favors yet."

"I figured as much." Her smile came like dawn on Christmas morning—slow, quiet, life-changing. "Is Beth napping?"

He stepped aside so she could ease into the room. Her skirts brushed his ankle as she passed. His entire being seemed touched by her. His skin tingled and his blood burned.

The room was dim without lamplight. Weak, gray daylight filtered in through the partly opened curtains, enough to illuminate the frail child tucked beneath the ruffled quilt, her dark curls stark against the snowy pillow slip, her breathing light and regular.

Her eyes were screwed shut, so she couldn't be sleeping. But Luke figured Molly didn't realize that as she gazed down at the child.

"She looks like an angel. She's such a pretty little girl." Molly eased away from the bed. "She must be old enough to go to school."

"I don't suppose the orphanage would have spared her for that. Since she's been with me, we've been on the move. I always planned on her getting an education." He tried to keep the bitterness from his voice, the bitterness over what should have been for his Beth. "If you want to keep an eye on her, I'll head out and get a start on the holly."

"I don't know what to say." Her smile beamed like a rare brilliance he'd never seen before, and it changed her from pretty to beautiful.

Get your mind back on business, McKenna. Moss might be dead, but Luke wasn't out of danger. No, the price on his head was too high, and he knew damn well that there was a Texas Ranger hunting him. Maybe Fletcher would give up; then again, maybe he wouldn't.

And if Luke wanted to make it alive to Canada, he couldn't waste time aching for what could never be. A woman like Molly wouldn't want him anyway. Best not to complicate matters any more than they already were. He would keep his fly buttoned, pack up, say what had to be said, and be on the road tonight.

He slipped into Beth's room, leaning his shoulder against the wall. The child had fallen back asleep, safe between soft flannel sheets, kept warm by the handmade quilt. The pillow beneath her head was plump and comfortable, the pillow slip a snow white, embroidered with small lavender flowers and edged with delicate matching crochet work.

Her breathing was congested, but normal and deep. She was such a little thing, and he couldn't help laying his hand across her brow. She coughed, and her reed-thin body quaked with its force.

No, she wouldn't make it over the harsh mountain trail to Canada. Not a chance. He wouldn't risk her life that way. Not when he'd finally found what he'd been looking for, ever since their brutal run from Texas.

The watchful dog lumbered into the room and jumped onto the foot of the bed. She settled down, one eye closed, the other winking open to check on the child A dog, a kind woman, and a pretty house warm and safe in a small town tucked away in the middle of Montana. What else could a child need?

His decision made, he headed outside where the cold wind and gray light were no consolation to the pain in his heart.

Molly carried a basket in one hand and her sheers in the other. An early dusk bled the last of daylight from the sky, and she found McKenna in the shadowed line of trees, his back to her, hacking off lengths of holly with an opened pocketknife.

He didn't turn around to face her, but kept his back to her, muscles bunching and flexing beneath the layers of flannel and wool. She knew what he looked like beneath those layers of clothing—hard, bronzed, breathtaking.

"A storm's on its way," she said, trying not to look at him. "I thought it might go quicker if we finished this up together."

"A job is always easier at a pretty woman's side." He reached with a bare hand through a thatch of dark green holly leaves, the prickled edges digging into his skin, and clipped off more branches.

"I didn't know fugitives could be so charming."

"It's a rare trait, but I'm blessed."

He worked with fast efficiency, and she knelt to snip at the lower branches. The crisp scent of freshly cut holly tickled her nose. The cold from the snow beneath her feet seemed to seep through her heels and through her layers of wool. She shivered but kept working.

She didn't *want* to like him, but she couldn't seem to help it. Any more than she could keep from remembering last night when she'd washed the blood from his body. She'd draped him with a sheet— but she'd been aware of his nakedness and his masculinity beneath that thin layer of flannel. Remembering how he'd looked like a warrior even while unconscious in her room, awareness flashed through her. Blood coursed through her body, and a fluttering settled right behind her breastbone.

He looked just as handsome now and as invincible as night. She shouldn't let down her guard. She was lonely, that's what this irrational attraction to him was. She didn't *want* to feel this way about any man.

"I buried the bounty hunters' bodies out in the forest a ways." He nodded once toward the thick copse of trees where pine and fir shed the thick mantle of snow from their drooping branches.

Regret flickered across his profile, a chink in his armor. Molly's hand trembled, and she focused hard on cutting more of the sharp-smelling holly. "Is anyone going to show up here looking for them?"

"Not a chance. They weren't the kind of men anyone was close to. On the wrong side of the law more times than not." He clicked the razor-sharp knife closed and slipped it into his trouser pocket. "There could be more men hunting me. I don't know if Moss left word which part of Montana he was trailing me through."

"But you just said no one would look for him—"

"Word with the Texas authorities." A muscle in his jaw snapped. "They don't care about a bounty hunter, but I'm a wanted man. There's no changing that. No escaping it. If there was, believe me, I'd do it for the sake of my girl. She's not safe if I leave her. She's not safe if I take her."

"She's too ill to move right now."

"I know." He tipped back his Stetson, exposing more of his face to the dimming light. The regret etched there in the pinch of his dark eyes and the set of his mouth had doubled, making him appear both warrior-cold and vulnerable man. "My guts tell me to get going and keep moving. Moss and his man were the only ones close on my trail, but there could be others. Not tomorrow, not a week from now, but the men after me aren't going to stop. Not unless I head for the mountains and keep going."

"Beth needs time to recover. You can't—"

"I never said that I'd endanger my daughter, regardless of what you think. I had no choice when I found her at that miserable excuse for an orphanage. I had to take her with me."

He tossed fistfuls of holly into her basket. "Don't say it. I know what you're thinking. What you've thought all along. The bullet that hit me could have struck her just as easily. It was all my fault she was caught in that damn blizzard. Don't think that I haven't agonized over it."

"Surely there's some relative somewhere?"

"None to count on." He looked bitter, he looked like a man waging a losing war. Knowing it, and hating every second of the losing.

She knew what an orphanage was like. She knew the lonely nights, the hopeless days, the horrible longing for the love of a parent long gone. To be alone without a single soul who cared if you lived or died.

"There wasn't a spot of trouble this whole trip." Snow started falling in airy, teasing flakes. "The Rangers figured I'd head straight to Mexico. They were waiting for me. So I ran north, and they figured I was dodging them, still intending to head south. I figure I got a hell of a lead until Moss crossed my trail. Now I'm here, not one hundred miles from Canada and freedom, but I can't take Beth through those mountains."

"It's a dangerous trip, even if she were well."

"I know." His gaze lanced hers with heat and promise. "Everything I owned was on the horse Moss shot out from under me. I need time to get supplies and a new mount. I need your help, Molly."

How could she bear it? She was starting to care, darn her foolish lonely heart anyway, and now he needed more than shelter from the storm. She thought of the child asleep in her house and how close she'd come to dying. How could she not help? How could she not care?

McKenna trailed her back into the house. She could feel the heat of his gaze on her back and the intensity of his determination radiating like heat from a stove. He was a powerful man. And he wanted something from her—she could feel it.

A man always wanted something. Hadn't she learned that the hard way? Disappointment seeped through her. For a few brief instances she'd seen in him a greatness of love and heart that she'd never witnessed in a man before.

She opened the door and stepped into the warmth. Sugary bits of snow clung to her cloak and hair. They melted at the touch of her hand.

The movement was so feminine, it set Luke's teeth on edge. She shrugged out of her cloak, and he stepped behind her to help her. As his fingers curved into the finely worsted wool, it hit him hard what he was doing. That he'd forgotten so easily who and what he was.

"I want to leave Beth here with you, Molly."

"What?"

"She needs a home. A real one. I've brought her all this way. I thought I could find something better than that orphanage she was in, and I finally have." He lumbered forward and set the basket on the edge of the counter. "I found you, Molly."

"I can't just take a child."

"But I thought..." He watched Molly reach with unsteady hands and lift the coffeepot from a trivet on the stove; the rich warm scent filled him with longing and regret. Too damn many regrets. "Molly, I need you to raise Beth for me."

She didn't look up, not even when he leaned one shoulder against her polished pine cabinets. Her pretty mouth drew tight and fire sparkled in her eyes. Her small hands worked fast as she spooned sugar into two cups and poured, the steam rising up to brush her cheek.

For some ungodly reason he wanted to touch her like that, as light and as hot as steam. To feel the peach satin of her skin and know the way her cheek felt beneath his fingertips, to feel the cut of that jaw delicate but steeled.

He knew he could count on her. He knew it.

She placed the cup on the counter with a clink. Every muscle in her body looked rigid. "I know what you're asking. I can see why you're asking it. Men are after you, and you can't take Beth over those mountains. I'm not a fool, McKenna."

"I know."

Molly bowed her head, dark russet curls tumbling over her shoulders. The coffee steamed, the clock in the parlor ticked, and

Beth called out for him from the other room.

"I need you, Molly. Beth needs you." His hand found her shoulder, felt warm woman and silken steel. "Say you'll do it"

Her eyes clouded with what looked like memories, what gleamed like tears. The dog's bark rang through the house just as Luke heard it too—the crunch of shod horses on the hard-packed snow.

Don't let it be more trouble. Luke unsnapped his holsters and headed for the window. Between the ruffle and lace edges of the curtains he saw shadows spirit between the trees, then turn the corner and take shape.

A matched pair of blacks, manes streaming in the wind, pranced toward the house, drawing a high-backed sleigh. No self-respecting bounty hunter would be caught dead in the fancy polished vehicle, but a local lawman might

Just how far north had his wanted poster circulated?

Molly sidled closer. Her breath caught. "Oh, no."

"I can handle it. Keep inside with Beth and stay away from the windows." His fingers curled around the smooth walnut grips of his reliable Colt .45s.

Molly's hand caught his wrist, stopping him with a feather-light touch. "Guns won't help. Not with this visitor." A faint smile teased her mouth. "It's my aunt."

How was she going to explain the man in her house? Molly closed the door behind her with a resounding click. Aunt Aggie couldn't have come at a worse time.

If word got out that Molly was letting a handsome virile man— let alone a wanted fugitive—sleep unchaperoned in her house, why, it could ruin her reputation. She could get fired, and the incident would create a blemish on her teaching record that could keep her out of the classroom for a very long time.

"Molly, dear, you look positively exhausted." Aunt Aggie nearly flew down from her elegant sleigh, her fine black wool dress with the wide skirts and hoops flowing around her. She swept a covered basket from the floor of the sleigh. "I knew I should check up on you. You don't feel safe at night all alone out here. I know. I was just like you when I was your age. Wanted independence and adventure, but this world is a big and frightening place."

"I'm really doing just fine." What would happen to McKenna if word got out he was here? What would become of Beth? "Honestly. You didn't need to come all this way in a storm."

"Goodness, it's hardly snowing. Be a dear and put my horses in the stable for me. I'll go right in and put some of my homemade beef-barley soup on to warm—"

"Aunt Aggie, I—" Molly stopped at the caring in the older woman's eyes, alight in her aging face. She couldn't chase this woman away. Maybe Aggie would understand about helping McKenna. She always was a sucker for a lost soul and a lonely child. "There's something I need to tell you first..."

The door behind her swung open, and she heard his step knell with authority and male predatory power. What was he doing? Molly turned, half afraid that she'd see cocked revolvers in his sun-browned hands, but they were loosely fisted at his sides as he strode down the swept clean steps into the snow.

A faint smile touched his mouth. The slight breeze ruffled the dark shanks of hair falling across his high brow. Snow flitted across his face, the unshaven stubble making him look deliciously handsome.

"Ma'am," he held out his hand, a gentleman and not a fugitive.

"My goodness." Aggie extended her gloved fingers. "Molly, you didn't tell me that you had a gentleman caller."

"You didn't give me the chance."

"Just call me Luke, ma'am." He drew Aggie's fingers to his lips and kissed them lightly. "A real pleasure to meet you."

"My, I don't recognize you, and I thought I knew everyone in town." Aggie stepped back, beaming, her cheeks flushing with pleasure.

"That's because I just arrived."

"Do you like beef-barley soup?" Aggie hugged her basket tightly.

"It's my favorite, ma'am. Here, let me carry that inside for you." He reached for the basket like any well brought up man. "I'll see to your team for you."

"What a gem you are." Aggie clasped her hands together and pressed them against her breastbone.

McKenna nodded, managing a shy grin, as if the older woman's praise embarrassed him, and lumbered into the house, giving them a view of wide snow-dusted shoulders, broad back, and firm backside.

Molly couldn't help watching. Who was this man with a honeyed voice and a gentleman's manners? The more she saw of him, the more she saw a man at odds with being a fugitive.

Luke, that was his first name. It suited him. Strong. Tender. He was no outlaw, no criminal. She knew it now for certain. Not because of the hot flickers of attraction snapping through her blood and not because of her loneliness. But because she could feel it like the wind on her cheeks and the snow on her lashes.

"I can't believe you didn't tell me about him," Aggie whispered. "He's absolutely the most handsome man I've ever met. I might be married and a grandmother, but I'll tell you this: the day a woman stops appreciating a fine-looking man is the day she's dead."

"He's not that handsome," Molly couldn't help teasing.

"Not that handsome! I don't think even God is that handsome. Truly." Aggie loosened her top buttons. "It must be another hot flash. Either that, or I ought to head back home and tell my dear Russell he's getting his dessert before supper."

"Aunt Aggie!" Molly felt the blush creep across her face. Her aunt was teasing, wasn't she? Surely sex couldn't be all that good. Not from what she'd heard whispered from her married friends back home and all the sage but somber advice on the marriage bed she'd received from Mother. "I didn't tell you because this could get me fired from my job."

"That's right. The morality clause." Aggie unbuttoned her coat altogether. "Well, I remember what it was like to be young. No one will hear it from me that you've got the most handsome man in six Western territories courting you."

"I don't think he'll be here long. He's just—"

The door swung back open, and Luke McKenna filled the threshold, all man but something greater, something that made her feel alive.

"I'll see to your horses now, ma'am." A Stetson hid his eyes, and he tipped the hat, easing past them. His voice was low and soothing as he reassured the horses and led them through the falling snow, fragile bits of heaven filtering down to cover her yard, washing away all evidence of the gunfight the night before.

Washing away every trace of a fugitive on the run. The man with the slight limp leading two horses to the log stable peered at her over his shoulder and winked.

Oh, he thought he had everything figured out. A man always did, she supposed. That was why she'd sworn off the breed, broke her engagement, and set out to build her own life.

But no real anger came, only a soft sympathy as quiet as a winter's eve for this man unable to come in from the cold, a man sentenced to a life away from the daughter he deeply loved.

"Now tell me the real story. What's he doing here? Courting you?" Aggie bustled through the back door. "Goodness, it smells like smoke in here. And lye soap."

"The house needs a good airing out. I had a small chimney fire. Nothing to worry about."

"Do you mean the chimney fire or the man?"

"Both." Molly reached to take her aunt's cloak.

Aggie lifted the cover from her basket and took out a plate of fresh bread. "Oh, this is perfect timing. A suitor, Molly. After the way Albert treated you, I'd given up all hope of you finding happiness."

"Few people find happiness in marriage and you know it." Molly avoided the truth by biting her lip and by hanging her aunt's snow-damp coat on the peg closest to the stove.

"Molly, you can't fool me with that attitude of yours. I know what you want. What you've always wanted." Aggie's voice dipped, understanding as gentle as the affection gleaming in her eyes.

Some things weren't meant to be. Molly knew that. And she knew the fault was her own. "It was good of you to come out to check on me."

"What else would you have me do? You're my only sister's child, and even if she doesn't have the time with her dinner parties and lady's meetings, I have plenty of time to care about you." There was a clunk as Aggie set a pot on the counter. "You'll get used to being fussed over. Until then, tell me you love my cooking and you're thrilled I stopped by."

"I think you are just a nosy old woman who wanted to check up on me." Molly winked as she lifted the pot to the stove. "You want to stay for supper?"

"Now, why was I hoping you'd ask? Russell has his councilman's meeting tonight, so he won't come straight home from the mill." Aggie reached into the basket and hauled out one covered plate and another small sack. "Is he the reason why you broke off your engagement with Albert?"

"Aunt Aggie. Of course not."

"I know everyone in town, but I never saw your Luke get off the train."

The truth felt heavy on Molly's tongue. She couldn't lie to the only family she had right now. She just couldn't. But the truth was McKenna's to tell.

Aggie's hand settled on her arm, her touch tender and comforting. "Now don't get me wrong. I think your Luke is a charming, virile man, and I know exactly why you're attracted to him, but tell me he's new to town today. That he hasn't been staying here—"

"He came to my door during the blizzard, and I couldn't turn him away."

Aggie's brow wrinkled with concern. "Tell me he didn't sleep in this house—"

A small figure inched into the kitchen. "Where's my papa?"

Beth. Her curls were tousled from sleep and her crumpled face was peaked, but there was no mistaking the terror in her eyes as dark as her father's.

Molly's heart twisted. "He's right outside tending to my aunt's horses. Beth, this is my aunt, Aggie."

Those dark somber eyes lifted upward. "I don't want her, either." The words were whispered so quietly, Molly hoped that only she'd heard them, and her heart twisted again until it hurt to breathe.

Beth knew her father was planning to leave her. Molly knew what that was like; her own mother had told her as they'd packed her satchel for the orphanage what was going to happen. That ride had been terrifying, and seeing the cold fear marking Beth's face, Molly wished she could draw the girl tight and hold her until all that pain melted like snow to sun.

She held out her arms, but Beth took a determined step back.

Molly lured the child closer with one of Aggie's fresh-baked cookies—a sugar cookie in the shape of a Christmas wreath.

Beth's eyes lit at the sight of the brightly iced cookie, but the wariness didn't leave her as she snatched the treat and then stepped back into the shadows.

The child retreated to the window where she stood and watched for her father's return.

I need you to raise Beth for me. McKenna's words echoed in her mind. Sadness rocked her for the little girl who watched, desperate to see a glimpse of her father.

Molly remembered doing the same thing at Beth's age, standing at the orphanage's windows, staring out toward the road wishing, and wishing. Every visitor and delivery wagon brought hope that would always be crushed. Every birthday and Christmas she would wish and pray and wait.

For a love that never came.

The thought of Beth waiting and wishing nearly broke Molly's heart. She turned away, briskly feeding small cedar sticks into the fire, and caught the sad look on Aggie's wise face.

Snow tickled the back of his neck and sneaked down his collar to melt against his too-warm skin. Low clouds hid the rugged mountain peaks from view. They were so close he could hear them calling. His guts cinched hard. What was he doing standing here? Why was he hesitating when he damn well ought to be heading out, escaping while his tracks would be wiped out in the storm.

Molly would take care of his girl. An unexplained child might cause her a few problems, but she was a bright woman and a compassionate one. She'd think of something.

He had his guns and enough clothes on his back, but the wind was picking up and it was a mean one. Should he head for the backcountry and risk getting caught in another blizzard?

Hell, living didn't matter. Not anymore. Whatever happened, he sure as hell wasn't going back to prison with no window to see the sky, with nothing but darkness.

The presence of rats, roaches, and snakes weren't even the hardest part of sleeping in a place like that. Living without hope, without heart or soul—that was the worst.

He wasn't going to be worked like a beaten dog until it killed him.

He was going to die one way or another. He might as well choose the mountains.

The sharp wintry smell of holly clung to his sleeves, and the scent reminded him of Christmas. Of a time when hope lived in his heart and love filled his days.

What if the old woman decided to open her mouth? Mention

his presence here in town? Maybe the sheriff had a *Wanted* poster. Maybe Luke wouldn't have a chance in hell of escaping if he didn't leave now. What would happen to Beth then? Molly didn't have any legal right to the child. Would the authorities step in and take the fugitive's daughter back to another hellhole of abuse and neglect?

Golden light shone like hope in the glass windows. He could see past the delicate lace edging the ruffled curtains and into the dining room. Beth's angel's face looked out on the other side of the glass, watching for him.

His heart melted at the sight of the small girl lost in the way-too-big white blouse, her black ringlets tumbling wildly around her peaked face. She swiped at her eyes with her fists, as if tears were sliding down her cherub's cheeks.

Hell, he couldn't leave. Not yet. Beth wasn't ready, but she was going to have to accept the woman he'd chosen, the one with the yearning in her eyes whenever she looked at his little girl.

Behind Beth, Molly knelt down and bowed her head close. Russet curls tumbled over her shoulders and veiled the side of her face. Lamplight burnished those locks with a rich bronzed brown that rekindled the fire in his groin and made him rock hard before he could draw his next breath.

Molly offered a cookie to Beth and then looked up as if she'd felt him watching. Their gazes collided through the glass and falling snow. She nodded once, as if to let him know everything was fine. That he was welcome on this dark day as daylight ebbed from the sky and shadows fell thick and icy against the glittered snow.

He knocked the snow from his boots on the back porch, gathered up the last of his courage, and tried to remember all of his manners. He would pretend to be one of Molly's suitors, but inside he felt dirty and shameful as if nothing, not the pretty house and polite manners, not this tentative freedom or the encouragement of Molly's quiet smile could hide what he'd become. He felt as if the stain of prison still clung to him and would never be washed away.

Worse, he was sure that if anyone looked close enough, they would see it.

The door swung open and Beth flew into his arms. The dog yipped after her, and he guided both of them back into the warm kitchen.

"I thought you was gonna leave me," Beth sobbed in a whisper.

"There's two of them."

"Two women?"

"I don't want the old one, either."

"Women scare me, too," he teased. "Let's you and I go hide in the stable. The horses are friendly."

"Papa." She almost smiled. Her arms wrapped like a tourniquet around his neck. "You're gonna stay with me."

"I'll do my best for a little while longer."

When they entered the room, both Aggie and Molly bounded to their feet. They'd spread rolls of red ribbon and holly across the surface of the lace tablecloth. The scent of warming soup lifted with the stove's heat and made his stomach rumble.

"My aunt has kindly offered to help me with the classroom decorations," Molly explained.

"Decorations?"

"For Christmas. The students will be contributing, too, but I thought red bows and holly would make the schoolroom festive. These winter days are dark and cold, and a little brightness might make those long division lessons go more smoothly."

He shrugged off his coat, and Molly took it from him, her touch light, her eyes steady. He figured she was afraid of what he'd say next and that was why she was hovering. But she didn't need to worry. He wouldn't do anything to shame her. This was like coming home, a dream he'd never thought he'd see again. The kitchen felt cozy with the cheerful lamps, fragrant food, and the fire chasing the chill from his bones.

"Luke, I can call you Luke, can't I?" Aunt Aggie asked as she lifted a plate from the counter. "Molly is just no help at all, since she's family and she's far too careful of my feelings. Tell me what you think of my cookies."

"Cookies?" He could only repeat the word and stare at the plate crammed high with four different types of Christmas cookies, colorfully iced and decorated.

"I could use a man's opinion." Aggie persisted, wiggling the plate enticingly.

"Don't try the white ones, Papa," Beth whispered. "They don't taste good."

The women burst into laughter. If this were a dream, then it was the one he wanted for his girl. He chose a gingerbread man all dressed up in white icing and licorice drops. The sweetness that broke apart on his tongue reminded him of better times, of memories long buried. And of hope.

Molly smiled as if she felt it, too.

CHAPTER SEVEN

"Goodness, the wind's kicking up." Molly watched her aunt rise from the chair by the fire. "The time is flying, and I've been chatting up a storm. I ought to be going before that turns into a full-fledged blizzard. Are you and your daughter coming too, Luke?"

Luke's gaze riveted on Molly's. "In a bit. Let me get your team hitched for you."

"Wonderful." Aggie tilted her head to one side, ready to tease. "Here, let me hold that precious little girl. Even if she didn't like my macaroons."

"She's a little wary around new people." Luke laid his daughter carefully in the cozy wingback chair he'd abandoned.

Molly retrieved an afghan from the spare room and offered it to Luke. Their fingers met in a brush of tingling heat. She watched him shake out the crocheted blanket and tuck it gently around his child, the child he'd asked her to raise.

How can I say no? How can I say yes?

"He's a charming man," Aggie whispered as Luke's steps echoed through the room. The back door snapped shut and they were alone. Her gaze narrowed. "A lawman, by the looks of him. I would have known if he'd rented a place in town. I'm the head of the welcoming committee."

"I don't want to lie to you." Molly reached for the emptied teacups.

"Then I'm right. He hasn't rented a place in town."

The cups in Molly's hands rattled against their saucers. She headed for the kitchen, but she couldn't escape. Aggie tapped determinedly behind her.

"He's staying here?"

"For now."

"Sleeping here?"

"His daughter is recovering from an illness. You heard her coughing. She's too sick for even a ride to town." Molly slipped the cups on the counter with a clatter. "I couldn't kick them out into the blizzard."

"And now the girl's too fragile to leave. I see."

"No one in town has to know. He won't stay here for much longer."

Molly jumped when her aunt's hand settled on her shoulder, a loving touch, one that made everything in Molly's heart hurt fresh and new.

"I know what you want. I saw the way you were raised." The shadows seemed to close in on the well-lit kitchen, draining away the brightness, but not the warmth. "You're still wanting a family of your own. I know. I watched a lonely little girl being shuffled from relative to relative and then to an orphanage. I did my best for you, but my sister, your mother, was a spiteful woman. She wouldn't let you stay with me."

"I know. I remember." Unbidden memories battered her like a boxer's fists. Images of the summer she'd spent with her aunt when she was six. Of climbing trees in the orchard and picking fresh apples and plums off the trees, the fruit so plump and ripe and sweet that the flavor exploded on her tongue. Almost twenty years later she could still remember the taste. Not just of the plums, but of sunshine and happiness.

"You've been wanting to belong all your life, Molly. I don't know what happened between your fiancé and your parents, but I can see it hurt you. You've given up on your dreams."

"I made new ones."

"But still yearn for the old. I can see it in you." Aggie's touch became a hug. "Be careful not to act too swiftly and grab the first chance at those dreams. Mr. Luke is a heart-stopping man, but is he right for you? And staying here, risking that others might find out, what about that?"

Molly wanted to explain, but the words tangled with the emotion in her throat and with too much grief. "I don't want those dreams anymore."

"You don't want a family to belong to, a family to need you?"

How did she know it wasn't possible? If she hadn't learned it as a child, from her own family and seeing all those unwanted children in the orphanage, then she'd learned it during her engagement. She simply wasn't lovable. "I'm not going to spend the rest of my life waiting for someone to love me. I have a new job and this land. My own land. That's more important to me than anything."

Aggie said nothing more, just squeezed a little harder before stepping away. Her mouth was pinched with sadness, and Molly couldn't stop the feeling that she'd somehow disappointed this woman who'd been the only relative who ever cared for her. Who cared now.

"I'll see you tomorrow to help decorate your schoolroom."

"I can get the students—"

"Nonsense. Don't you know I'll do anything for my dear niece? Now, let me get my basket and I'll be off." Clearing her throat, blinking her eyes, Aggie snatched the wicker basket off the countertop. "Let me know what you're planning for your school pageant. I want the town of Evergreen's first Christmas to be one everyone will remember."

The back door opened, and Luke called out in his rich, rumbling voice that the horses were waiting in the cold wind. The weather was worsening, so Aggie's good-bye was quick, but not without feeling.

"I want you to keep this in mind: you're not alone." She pressed a kiss to Molly's cheek and hurried off, complimenting Luke for seeing her safely to her sleigh.

Molly saw them through the kitchen window, Luke tipping his hat, Aggie laying her hand to her bosom as if charmed. The horses sped off, leaving Luke alone in the yard. His big shoulders slumped, and for all his steely might, he looked lost. He stood in the falling snow a long time, hands fisted at his hips, gazing off toward the mountains hidden by night and snow.

"I want my papa." Beth padded into the kitchen, rubbing her

sleepy eyes. "He's not s'pose to leave me."

"And he hasn't." Molly regarded the one child she hadn't been able to win over, not even with a plate of Christmas cookies. "Do you want me to warm some hot chocolate?"

Beth folded her arms over her chest. "My papa can do it."

"He might be outside for a while." Molly reached into the pantry for the tin of chocolate. "I'm going to make some for me. Just say the word and I'll heat up enough milk for you, too."

Beth bit her bottom lip and didn't say a word.

But the little slip of a girl didn't look as rigid, and those brown eyes didn't look as leery as before. Maybe there's a chance, Molly realized, a chance for Beth's acceptance. She poured milk into the saucepan and placed it on the stove to warm.

When she turned around, Beth had retreated to the dining room window, watching over the yard where she could see the road. Maybe watching to make sure her father wasn't riding away.

Beth smothered a cough in her fist. Lady padded close and curled up at the girl's feet.

Be careful not to act too swiftly. To grab the first chance at those dreams. Molly remembered Aggie's compassionate warning. And her own stubborn response.

This is your last chance to mend the shame you've caused us. Mother's words written in black and white on the parchment was proof enough that she wasn't going to find her dreams.

She might never have a child of her own, because what man was going to love her? Love her truly, for who she was, and not because she was a wealthy man's stepdaughter?

She'd left Helena and Albert and turned her back on her parents because she wouldn't spend her life trying to please a man who said he loved her, but didn't. She wouldn't let her heart break and become hard like her mother's from the breaking.

All he's asked is for you to raise his child. Molly fished a spoon out of the drawer and stirred the heating milk. Steam curled off the white surface in foggy coils.

She wanted a child, but not a husband and not love.

Maybe this could be the perfect solution.

Beth didn't move from the window, her nose pressed to the frosty glass, silently watching and fearing.

Molly spooned the powdered chocolate into the milk and stirred. The sweet fragrance teased her with memories of all she'd never had in her childhood. Of all she had to give to a child. Laughter and safety and coziness. Lit Christmas trees and caroling and happiness wrapped up in big red bows.

Molly filled a cup and set the pan on a trivet. Rich chocolate steamed the air, a sweet comforting scent that made Beth turn from the window.

Molly carried the cup into the dining room. The girl watched with wide eyes.

"I always like to read and sip my chocolate." Molly balanced the cup carefully and headed toward the parlor. Even empty, the room retained the coziness from Aggie's visit. Fat poofy bows littered the top of the pine chest that sat between the sofa and the chairs. Holly, strung together on green yarn, sat heaped in a basket on the floor.

On impulse, Molly tugged a children's book from the shelf tucked in the corner of the parlor. She heard the whisper of footsteps behind her, tentative and ghostlike. Good, Beth was curious.

"Oh, my favorite Christmas story." Molly peered over her shoulder.

Yep, Beth was standing in the dining room, watching with her hands clasped together and a quiet wish in her eyes. But the wariness hadn't eased.

Beth didn't want a new mother, and it was easy to see why. She had a father who loved her. What else could a child want? How could a child let go of a father's love?

Molly sat down on the sofa and opened the book. She read the words written on the thick paper in a voice just loud enough to draw the girl closer. By the time Luke threw open the shutters, Beth had eased around to the corner of the sofa and was leaning against the stuffed arm.

"Have you heard this story before?"

A tentative shake.

"It's better with a cup of chocolate. Mine's cool enough to drink now, but I'm reading. Would you like it?"

Beth looked longingly at the steaming cocoa. Molly knew without asking that there had been no treats during her time spent in the orphanage. The delicious fragrance of melted chocolate drew Beth another step closer.

Molly lifted the cup from the pine chest and offered it to the child.

The girl inched forward, drawn by the temptation, but unable to let go of her fears. She reached out and took the cup, and Molly breathed again.

She returned to her book, the glow in her heart warm and true, and read aloud of how Santa slid down the chimney by laying a finger against his nose.

Luke eased through the house like a wolf on the hunt. He felt cold to the marrow of his bones, but the warmth of Molly's voice drew him out of the darkness toward the light.

He saw her profile as she sat on the damask sofa, her forest green skirts tucked around her slim legs, her russet locks tumbling over her shoulders to brush the fine curve of her face. The book propped on her lap, held by slender hands, looked brand-new. The spine creaked and the crisp paper rustled when she turned the page.

Beth perched on the very edge of the sofa. Both of her small hands were wrapped around one of Molly's pretty cups. He could smell the chocolate in the air. Lady uncurled from Beth's feet and padded toward him.

"Papa!" Beth set down the cup and came running. Her arms wrapped hard around his knees. "I waited and waited for you."

He ran his hand over her head, ruffling her dark curls. "I missed you when I was outside. Did you know that deer come to Molly's stable, hoping to get some hay."

"Real deer?"

"Yep. Come with me and I'll show you." He knew Molly was watching as he scooped his little girl into his arms and carried her to the kitchen window. He turned out the wicks and held her up to the dark window. "Do you see? At the back of the barn?"

Shadows moved against the canvas of the night.

"Can I pet 'em? Can I, Papa, please?"

"They're wild creatures, darlin'. They aren't used to people being around them. But I bet if you're patient, you could get close enough to feed them one day."

"Not now?"

"No." He tucked her under his chin, against his heart. Her gossamer curls caught on his chin stubble. It was sweet simply holding her. He breathed in her little-girl scent—she smelled like a sugar cookie—and memorized it for safekeeping.

"Did you like Molly's story?"

"No." Her arms tightened around his neck, nearly cut-ing off his air supply.

"It sounded like a good story to me."

"It ain't true. Not one word." Beth sighed. "Santa didn't come last year."

"I know, darlin'." He'd spent last Christmas in his dark cell. There had been no carols, no magic.

No salvation.

"It will be different this year." The vow burned inside him.

The clock bonged the late hour. It was well past the child's bedtime. Beth coughed into her hand, reminding him she needed a lot of care. He hauled her to the necessary room to brush her teeth and change into a blouse of Molly's that would make do for a nightgown.

"You won't leave me tonight, right, Papa?"

"Right." Against all better judgment.

Molly had turned down the covers. She avoided his gaze as he carried his girl into the room and laid her down on the soft sheets. He spied a bed warmer wrapped in a thin towel at the foot of the bed, to keep Beth warm, and gratefulness flooded his chest until he couldn't breathe.

"I brought my book," Molly said casually, patiently, as she smoothed the sheet up to Beth's chin. "In case you want to hear the rest of the story."

"I guess." Beth rolled her eyes, as if she weren't all that interested, but Luke wasn't fooled. He recognized her sharpened interest carefully hidden behind a frown and a defiant chin.

Lady hopped onto the foot of the bed and settled down to watch over the child, and Molly began reading. Her voice lifted like the first strains of a song, quiet and refined.

The wind gusted against the side of the house, rattling the windowpanes, and he watched as Beth fought sleep, yawning once, twice, then three times as Molly read to the end of the story.

A hollow feeling settled in the place where his heart beat.

"She's sleeping." Molly closed the book with a quiet creak and eased out of the chair. The wood joints squeaked just a little, but didn't wake the girl.

He followed her out of the room and closed the door. "What about your aunt?"

"She wouldn't say anything to hurt my reputation." Molly slid the book into place on the shelf. "She's a good person."

"I noticed." The kind of woman who would accept Beth as part of the family, he'd wager. "There's a lot to settle between us."

"Tonight?"

"I don't know a better time." He stalked closer, the hollowness inside him expanding until it swallowed everylast emotion, leaving him barren and empty. He'd do what had to be done, no matter what it cost him. "I figure I have enough time to buy a horse and supplies. A day, maybe two, unless a blizzard hits."

"A blizzard would wipe out all the tracks?"

He nodded. "Any that Moss might have left that would bring another bounty hunter or a ranger after me."

"Is there a danger that they might try to grab Beth?"

"That's what we need to talk about."

"I see." She knelt on the floor in front of the pine chest and began stacking the fat red bows into a roomy basket. "You would leave your child in danger?"

"No. And not you, either." He paced close like a prowling wolf, and his intense blade-sharp gaze felt as if it could slice her in two. "I can't leave her without knowing for certain she's safe."

"Everyone in town knows I don't have a child." Molly held her heart still. She kept stacking the bows one by one. "How do I explain Beth? I don't have the right to keep her, Luke. You can't hand over a child like she's a bartered cow."

Molly's heart hurt for Beth, and she squeezed her eyes shut before Luke could see more. She hurt for any child alone and afraid, and yet with this little girl... The warmth in her chest remained. She'd loved reading Beth to sleep and wishing her sugarplum dreams.

"I have to admit I never thought this far." McKenna braced one hand on the edge of the mantel. "I couldn't get past the idea of leaving her somewhere. My little girl."

She heard what he didn't say. All the pain. All the grief. He rubbed his hand over his face and sighed.

What would it be like to give up a child?

Suddenly an inhuman force exploded against the north side of the house with such power it blew out the dining room lamp. Fear bolted through her as McKenna drew, the glint of the Colt's metal barrel swinging toward the front door.

"It's a blizzard, Luke."

"Another one?" He released the revolver's hammer, his shoulders visibly slumping. "Looks like luck is with me. Again. But I don't trust it to last."

"You're not an optimistic man, are you?"

"And something tells me you're not brimming with optimism, either." He eased down next to her, bringing with him the scent of the woodsmoke and radiating a different kind of heat.

Her blood roared in her ears, and she stared hard at the bows she was stacking. Her hands shook. Could he tell?

"I want some assurances from you."

Molly knocked over the basket. "From me? "

His big calloused hands gathered up those lustrous satin bows gleaming in the firelight. A wry grin crooked one corner of his mouth. "I know, I'm the fugitive, but I need your word. I need to know when I leave here that Beth will have the kind of life she had before I was arrested."

"I won't treat her as if she's not wanted, if that's what you mean." The whip of pain made her draw in breath. "I'll do everything in my power to make sure Beth doesn't feel as if she's just taking up space in my house."

"You must know something about that."

"A bit."

"Tell me about your mother who put you in an orphanage. And how she could bear to give up a pretty thing like you."

"Now you're trying to charm me again." She was no fool, but his words felt like a balm to decades of wounds. "She couldn't support her daughter as a widow."

"She used the time to find a husband?"

Molly took one look at his crooked brow and the sadness at his mouth. "A very wealthy husband. It wasn't so bad. I had so much more than a lot of children. I don't mean to complain. At least my mother came back for me, and I had a beautiful home to live in."

"But no love?"

Molly stacked the last bow into the brimming basket.

"I see love in you, Molly Lambert. I know you have enough in your heart to see my daughter through the life ahead of her. I don't know how I got so damned lucky, but I'm grateful I found your door. I'll always be grateful."

"Now you're making me into something I'm not."

"I don't believe that for a second." He reached out, and his touch was like silver, liquid-hot and rich. "You are the reason I can leave her. I don't know how you lured her into a cup of hot chocolate and a story, but it only goes to show I'm right. You'll be good to her. If you marry and have kids of your own, I know you won't put her aside."

"I would never do that."

He heard what she didn't say—that she would come to love his child. Overcome, he gazed down at her, measuring the fierce protective flicker in her hazel eyes. In eyes that glowed luminous and true and could not hide the size nor strength of her heart. Tenderly, he stroked his knuckles down the warm silk of her face, drawn to her like he'd been to no other woman.

Just a few inches separated them. He only had to bend forward to taste Molly's bow-shaped mouth. The tip of her tongue darted across the luxurious span of her bottom lip, and he choked on a moan of pure hunger to taste and kiss that sweet dampness.

McKenna, you have to be crazy. But he couldn't help it, honest, he couldn't. Like the leading edge of a blizzard, unexpected and intense, hunger for her pounded through him, and he leaned in, closing the few inches between them. A groan broke low in his throat the instant their lips met.

Heated velvet. Fine silk. Responsive woman. Luke drank her in, crushing his mouth to hers and sucking her full lower lip between his. She tipped her head back and her hands splayed on his shirt. Her fingers curled into the cotton, holding on tight.

She likes this. He had no doubt. Her lips moved against his, caressing and supple. A soft moan rumbled through her and into him. Fire licked through his veins, and he wrapped one hand around the curve of her neck, winding through her reddish brown curls. Wanting more, needing more, he stroked his tongue along the seam of her lips, and she yielded willingly with a small gasp. Her fists tightened on his shirt as he dove inside, tasting mint and heat

He was rock-hard and breathing like he'd run ten miles uphill. Luke laid one gloved hand on the swell of her left hip and pulled her body to his. She swayed against him like a windblown willow, and he planted his hand on the small of her back, holding her full length against him. Her breasts pillowed his chest, and her stomach pressed the hard ridge of his aroused shaft.

Her tongue worked a slow caress along his bottom lip, tentative, tasting, gauging, and then she kissed him fully, with mouth, teeth, and tongue. A groan of pure lust and building desire whipped through him like a firestorm, and he fought to keep from reaching for the tiny pearled buttons marching down the front of her bodice. He tore his mouth from hers, gasping for air, desperate to continue, but closed his eyes, stepped away, and counted to ten.

It wasn't enough. He could count to a hundred and he'd still want her. Blood beat through his body in quick punches. The need for her hammered every inch of him, and his erection strained against his too-tight trousers. He wanted her like the air he breathed. He shook from chin to ankle with a relentless desire. Even though they were no longer touching, he could still feel her body against his, taste her kisses, feel her matching need.

"Luke?" One gentle hand splayed against the center of his chest, directly over the crazy, wild beat of his heart.

"I'm sorry." The words hurt like blows. He wasn't sorry he'd kissed her, but he'd taken advantage of her and he shouldn't have. He opened his eyes, struck by the sight of color high on her cheeks.

She looked embarrassed...and she looked aroused. Her eyes were midnight-dark, adding fuel to the fire in his veins. He cleared his throat, but his voice sounded thick and raw. "It's been so long since I've been in the company of a woman, I guess I lost some of my manners."

"Manners? So, you're telling me that was an unmannerly kiss?"

"Yes, ma'am." The thoughts running through his head and pounding through his body were anything but polite. His entire being thrummed with the need to take her. He breathed deeply, fighting for control.

She withdrew her touch, leaving a tingling heat in the shape of her handprint against his sternum. Remembering how she'd responded to his kiss and how she'd pressed her sweet body to his, want jolted through him. Those pearl buttons gleamed on the curve of her breasts, breasts that would be creamy-white and heavy in his hands. All he had to do was reach for the top button...

But she lifted the basket on her slim hip and swept away, all beauty and grace, her russet locks swaying with the speed of her gait.

"I haven't begun to think about the enormity of all this." Her voice came strained, without music, without light as she placed the basket on the table. The darkness swallowed her, veiling her from his sight.

Damn. He shouldn't have kissed her. He had better control than that. Luke rubbed the heel of his hand over his brow, hating the hard, tight feeling that gathered in his chest. He was no green boy, inexperienced and eager. He'd been burned enough times to know what happened when a man played with fire. The last thing he wanted to do was anger Molly. He needed her. Beth needed her.

Just cool it, McKenna. And hope the lady forgives you.

"It's scary, thinking about being responsible for Beth, but I know the alternative." Molly eased closer, stepping out of the shadows. "I don't want that for her."

Lamplight burnished her locks with a rich bronzed brown that left him breathless and rekindled the fire in his blood. He was still rock-hard from wanting her.

"But I can't take her unless she agrees." Molly's lush mouth pinched, her soft pink lips narrowing. "I don't want her feeling abandoned. I don't want her staying with someone she doesn't want."

"I know she's tried pretty damn hard to push you away."

"With good reason." Fondness in her chest warmed like melted butter on a stove, remembering. It had been hard for Beth to accept the hot chocolate and the story tonight. "I need your word, Luke."

"I'll speak to her, but she already knows how it is." He stared into the fire, the red-orange light limning his profile and teasing his jet-black hair. "I've been honest with her from the start of the journey. There's no way we can be together. Not even if I make it to Canada. The arm of the law is a long one, but revenge, why, it doesn't respect borders."

She couldn't bear to look at him and know what trouble haunted him. She couldn't believe he was a wanted man, now that she'd gotten to know him. And why had she kissed him like that? Her lips still buzzed with the heat of his. Her entire body tingled with awareness and life, and it left her breathless and confused.

She'd never felt this way about Albert. Not one single man had ever set her on fire the way Luke McKenna did. It was like new territory, undiscovered and filled with dangers.

Molly laid her hand over her heart, and it was still beating fast. "It's getting late. If the blizzard blows itself out during the night, I'll need to be at school in the morning."

"And if it doesn't?"

"I still want to get to bed." Molly could still feel the heat of him on her skin as she breezed past him. "You said you needed a blizzard to cover any remaining tracks."

"I came north from Idaho and kept to the mountains. Stayed away from towns. No eyewitnesses and no sharp-eyed lawmen. Moss stumbled onto me by blind luck. Tonight I scouted your property and both directions down the road. I didn't see anything to concern me. Only your aunt knows that I'm here."

"Then we have time enough to figure out what's best for Beth, blizzard or not."

"Are you mad at me? About the kiss?"

"No." But she wasn't likely to forget it. She took a step toward her bedroom. The last thing she wanted was for him to see the ache in her heart—for a man, for a child, for love.

He isn't the right man, Molly. But she wanted him to be. With all her heart, all her soul, with every wish she'd ever made. And she didn't know why.

Mr. McKenna is a heart-stopping man, but is he right for you? Aunt Aggie had asked her.

Molly knew the answer. She knew it with certainty as she closed her bedroom door and sat on the ladderback chair to unbutton her shoes. Luke McKenna was the wrong man for any woman.

But the smallest hope crept into her heart, and she hated this weakness in her. This yearning for love that could never happen to her. Not ever. No matter how much she wanted it. She was too old, and she'd given up hope.

The blizzard shrieked like a wild animal outside the stout log walls. Molly closed her eyes and tried not to mind that she was alone.

M olly might have enjoyed their kiss, but she hadn't wanted to look at him. Luke was surprised he could feel disappointment after the last year. It was a miracle he could feel anything at all.

Beth coughed in the next room. A deep and painful-sounding cough that reminded him her health was still frail. He banked the fire in the grate by covering the gleaming hot coals with a thick blanket of ashes.

Beth erupted in another longer string of hoarse coughs. Before he could climb to his feet, Molly's door opened. Her ghostly white nightgown fluttered around her slim form as she whisked the short distance to Beth's door.

He fought every urge to follow her. His every instinct cried out for him to check on his child. But another part of him, disciplined and hardened, told him to stay back. Beth would have to get used to Molly's presence in her life. There was no one else to leave her with, and he doubted if he could find someone better if he searched for a whole year.

"I want Papa." So thin and helpless, that voice, and he could hardly hear it above the sounds of the brutal storm.

Molly's answer was muted, and he wondered how much fight Beth would give them. But it was late, and the girl broke into another fit of coughing.

Molly appeared and breezed past him as if he were no more than a part of the furniture and began banging pots in the kitchen. She wouldn't even look at him. When she returned with a basin steaming wisps of menthol into the air, she ignored him, too.

She thinks you're a murderer, McKenna. What did you expect?

"I want my papa," Beth cried.

Molly appeared in the shadowed threshold. "She needs you."

Luke held his breaking heart still, rigid with the pain of what was to come. Beth needed him and always would.

Soon, he would be riding away forever. Forever was a hell of a long time.

"Papa." The worry lines digging into Beth's brow eased when she saw him walk into the room.

Whatever lay ahead in his life could not be as good as this child. With regret huge enough to choke him, he knelt down to rub those worries away from Beth's brow. She snuggled against his hand and closed her eyes, the scent of mint and menthol warm in the air.

Molly didn't look at him when she swept from the room. With the click of her door, she left him alone. He waited until Beth fell back to sleep, and then he unwound her fingers from his hand.

The blizzard moaned like a wild animal clawing to get in, and he felt trapped in this porcelain and lace prison. He felt restless and edgy in Molly's fussy parlor. He might have his freedom, but he was a long shot from being free. Shaking out the afghan, he draped it on the overstuffed sofa.

He didn't know how much time he had—a day, a month, a year—but he knew that if he wanted to make it alive to Canada, he couldn't start dreaming of what-might-have-been. He had to let go of his child, and he couldn't be distracted by Molly's goodness and his long-denied need for a woman.

Damn, he never should have kissed her.

As long as the blizzard raged, he would be a polite gentleman. No more kissing or touching. Not even the most private yearning. He had no right to connections—emotional, romantic or otherwise.

He'd concentrate on caring for Beth, on savoring this time with her, and preparing her for her new life with Molly.

It was the right thing to do.

Troubled, he curled up on his side on the sofa and tugged the afghan over him. The cushions were soft, the scent of wool from the blanket tickled his nose. The clock ticked, and the scent of fresh-cut holly lingered in the air, a false sense of comfort in this cold world.

He fell into a fitful sleep filled with hopeless dreams.

CHAPTER EIGHT

"You know I have questions," Aunt Aggie began the instant she set foot inside the schoolhouse's vestibule.

"About my Christmas pageant?" Molly lifted one brow as she tottered on the wooden chair.

"Hardly, my dear."

"Well, it was worth a try." Dreading the interrogation to come, Molly climbed down, leaving a long spray of holly dangling down the center of the window. "I know what you're going to ask and, yes, he did spend the night. On my sofa."

"Molly, I'd work up a moral outrage, but I can't say that Russell didn't warm my bed before our wedding day." Aggie's cheeks grew warm, and she fanned her face. "Goodness, it's hot in here. The schoolroom sure does have a good stove."

"Luke won't be staying for much longer." She was never quite sure what to think about her aunt, who was a marked contrast to Molly's quiet, cold mother. "Here, let me hang up your cloak."

"I'm not going to be distracted." Aggie's quick wink said she wasn't going to blame her, either. "You care for him?"

"More than I should." At least that was the truth. Throughout the day-and-a-half long blizzard, she'd been cooped up in the house with him. With his slow-burning presence, his inscrutable, downturned eyes, and the memory of their inappropriate kiss tensing the air between them.

He'd spent the time studying a map of the Montana Rockies and whittling toy horses for Beth out of chunks of firewood. Beth clung to his side the entire time, watching Molly less warily.

She'd spent the duration of the blizzard trying to figure out how a man's kiss could feel that good. And why it affected her even after it had long ended. Her skin felt on fire just from being in the same room with him, and it didn't make sense.

She'd never had this physical reaction to Albert, and she'd almost married him.

Aggie pulled over a chair and climbed onto it. Wood creaked, and she gave a small gasp. "Why, speak of the devil. There's your handsome Luke right now, riding a black gelding into town."

Molly spun toward the window so fast, she nearly dropped Aggie's basket of strung cranberries. "He's got Beth with him."

"Is she well enough to be out in that cold air?"

"I don't know, but I'm going to find out." Molly dropped the basket on the chair and rushed to the vestibule. She snagged her cloak from its hook and bolted outside. Cold air and watery sunshine brushed her face as she cut through the yard.

Luke had pulled up his mount and watched her, tipping his hat to protect his eyes from the glaring sun. He sat tall and straight in his saddle, and with his dark jacket and matching Stetson, Aggie was right. He looked like a lawman. A noble, courageous man who gazed out on the world intent on protecting it.

Not on causing harm.

Her heart dropped like a rock to her ankles, and her entire body began to burn in slow, sizzling agony. What was wrong with her? She ought to be angry with him for bringing Beth to town, and not just because of the cold.

What if Luke were in danger? What if coming here...

"Moss's horse," Luke explained when she'd skidded close enough to step into his shadow. "I ran into your neighbor on the way here. Nice old guy."

"Mr. McGrath knows about you?"

"He knows I'm new to town and that I know the new schoolteacher." His dark gaze narrowed and met hers for the first time like a cold, penetrating spear. "Nothing more. Beth's doing better. I wanted to take her to see the doctor. Just to be sure. She's still wheezing when she breathes."

"Good idea. Looks like you've got her bundled tight." Molly

looked at the little girl who was tucked into the saddle in front of her father, holding onto the saddle horn with bright yellow mittens. "Hello, Beth. There are some girls just your age playing near the schoolhouse steps. Do you see them?"

Beth's mouth buttoned shut, but her gaze slid over in the direction of the schoolhouse.

Luke hugged his silent daughter. "I'm going to get the supplies I'll need so I'll be ready to head out."

"What are you going to say if anyone asks who you are?"

His mouth twisted bitterly, as if without hope. "I'm not sure. Hate to admit I'm just passing through. We've got to figure out a way to explain Beth."

"And to ensure I can keep her." It was really going to happen, and over the last day and two nights this decision had time to sink in. Could she take care of a child on her own? Could she do a good job? What if Beth couldn't accept her? She feared Luke was running out of time.

The brutal, wintry mountains awaited him.

"I'll think of something. Maybe no one will even ask." He knuckled back his hat.

"Oh, someone will ask. Trust me." Evergreen was a new railroad town, founded only this last summer. The pioneer spirit was still high and made the first residents a friendly and rather nosy group.

I'll let you know how it goes." He lifted the reins, sending the sleek horse toward Front Street.

The memory of his kiss felt like a ghost on her lips, cold and barren. Her first real kiss with a man—real because she'd enjoyed it, because it touched a place in her heart that she hadn't know she had—and it had been with a man all wrong for her.

A horse and sleigh slid by. Mrs. Neville called out a welcome, and Molly waved. The town stretched out before her, the brand-new boardwalks gleamed honey-gold in the sunshine. Women shopped, carrying toddlers on their hips. Men hurried to a stop at the hardware store or the blacksmith's. Horse-drawn sleighs and sleds lined the sides of the street, tied in front of new buildings bright with fresh coats of paint. A man hurried out from the bank to greet his wife and sons on the boardwalk and escorted his family into the diner.

Luke halted his horse in front of the mercantile and

dismounted. He swept Beth into his arms and held her there. Molly watched as father and daughter climbed the steps to the elevated boardwalk.

She closed off the part of her that still dreamed and saw Aggie's worried face through the schoolhouse window. The sun slipped behind a cloud, and the watery brightness disappeared, leaving only grayness and shadows.

" 'Afternoon." The shopkeeper looked up from his inventory list as Luke walked through the door.

" 'Afternoon." Luke nodded and made only brief eye contact. He set Beth down on the floor and took her by the hand.

"Got some good specials goin' today," the man, about Luke's age, said from behind the counter. "Got them tacked up on the wall behind me, but a lot of folks around here can't read. Got a real good price on red licorice ropes."

Luke had to hand it to the shrewd merchant Beth gasped, and although she didn't ask, hope lit her eyes. How could he say no? He tossed a penny on the counter, and Beth clapped her hands.

"You can pick two." The shopkeeper smiled and held down a big jar.

Beth reached in and pulled out two two-foot long ropes. "I'm gonna put one in my pocket and save it."

"Gonna give me a bite out of the other one?" Luke ruffled her hair.

She tilted her head back to look at him. "Yep. I'll share only with you, Papa."

"Good." He thanked the merchant, who kept watching them. That made Luke damn uncomfortable. The tall aisles of shelves looked like a good refuge, and he led Beth toward the back of the store.

"Here you go, Papa." She'd twisted off a three-inch piece of candy.

He knelt down to take it. "Thanks, darlin'. Reckon you can help me pick out some new shirts?"

She nodded. "Maybe we should pick out some ribbons, too."

"Well, as long as I can find some to match my new shirts," he teased.

"Oh, Papa." Beth almost smiled.

Almost. It was a start.

The bell above the door chimed with the arrival of another

customer. Luke caught sight of the tin star on the man's leather jacket before the shopkeeper could call out, "Welcome, there, Sheriff. Did you see today's specials?"

"I see 'em, Drew."

Luke felt the lawman's gaze like cannon fire and dipped his chin. The Stetson's brim hid half his face. That was the best he could do for now. That and act calm.

"Papa, there's a whole lotta ribbons right here." Beth pointed with her fistful of licorice. "The yellow one's awful pretty."

"It sure is." He knelt down, keeping his back to the sheriff and studied the display case holding dozens of spooled ribbons.

"It's got flowers on it and everything." Wistfully, Beth leaned against his shoulder and sighed.

The year at the orphanage had been tough. He knew exactly how that felt. "We'll have to ask the shopkeeper to cut us a good length when we get ready to go."

"Truly, Pa?" A faint smile touched her Cupid's mouth.

The lawman's step knelled on the rough wooden floorboards, drawing closer. Luke's pulse skipped, and he turned his back toward the display table of men's ready-made garments. Beth must have sensed his tension because she grew quiet and leaned hard against his knee.

He pulled a blue wool shirt in the right size out of the pile and slung it over his arm. The boards beneath his feet wavered slightly as the sheriff approached. *Keep moving, Sheriff,* Luke thought as he pulled a second shirt from the pile.

The lawman halted at the same display. " 'Afternoon to you."

"Good afternoon." Luke's heart felt ready to beat its way out of his chest. He gazed hard at the shirts and grabbed an ugly green one, just to appear at ease.

"Drew's always got the best merchandise this side of Butte, but the picking's been real slim lately." The sheriff shook his head. "Hey Drew, got any more 38s in this store?"

He doesn't recognize me. At least, I don't think he does. Maybe the *Wanted* posters hadn't reached this part of Montana. Luke released the breath he didn't realize he was holding. Relief sluiced through him like ice water. Maybe Cousin Fletcher believed he was heading up through Idaho and hadn't received word from Moss to think any differently.

The shopkeeper gave a snort. "Hey, don't blame me. It's the

train's fault. I put in an order about a month ago, and it hasn't come in yet."

"We got a problem with the new train," the sheriff admitted to Luke with a casual shrug. "Built a railroad and towns along the line, and then the train can't run because too much snow falls on the tracks. Say, I haven't seen you around here before."

Luke's spine stiffened. "Just rode in."

"Rode in, you say? Through Walker Pass? This time of year?"

"Wasn't too tough." He folded up the green shirt and slipped it back on the pile, hoping the sheriff couldn't hear the lie in his voice. "Since the train isn't running, I didn't have much of a choice," he added and laid a protective hand on Beth's shoulder.

The sheriff shook his head. "Shoot, I tell you, newfangled transportation isn't what it's made out to be. Give me a horse any day."

"Ain't that right, Sheriff," Drew the shopkeeper added with a chuckle.

Luke turned on watery knees toward the pile of packaged long Johns and sorted through the sizes. Beth's free fist was balled tight into the denim fabric of his trouser leg. She'd stopped eating her licorice.

Just keep calm, he reminded himself, quelling the urge to run while he had the chance. The sheriff wasn't looking for a fugitive passing through his town, or he would have paid more attention.

He ambled through the store, deliberately keeping his pace slow and unhurried. He picked up enough clothing items and foodstuffs to see him through the mountains. Remembering Molly, he added a few extras to his purchases and asked Drew to cut Beth a length of the ribbon she favored.

"Where are you stayin'?" the clerk asked as he counted back Luke's change. "I'll have our delivery boy run this right over for you."

"I don't have a place yet."

"No? Fine, I'll just wrap this up, then."

The sheriff lumbered up to the counter, but there was nothing easygoing in his sharp, lawman's gaze. "With this cold weather, don't tell me you don't have a roof over this pretty little girl's head."

Luke forced his spine straight. He couldn't very well admit the truth, so he improvised. "I'm staying with Aggie Grant."

"Is that so?" The sheriff's sharp-eyed scrutiny faded into easy acceptance. "Why, Mrs. Grant is one of our founding citizens. Her husband started up the sawmill the minute it was learned the railroad was coming through. This is their last watering and fuel stop before they reach the pass, and I tell you, Russell Grant is a full-fledged genius. Can't speak highly enough of the Grants. They're good people."

"Yes, sir, they are at that." Luke hoped he'd be forgiven for those small lies, spoken to protect his child. Drew finished tying the white string around the brown paper and pushed the heavy package across the counter.

Luke took a deep breath, tipped his hat, and managed a smile. "Good meeting y'all."

Sweat sluiced down his brow and froze against his skin in the cold wind. The door jangled closed behind him, and he kept going as if nothing were wrong.

A bell, crisp and silvery, chimed above the distant whine of the sawmill, the hubbub of traffic on the snowy street, and the roar in his ears.

The schoolhouse bell. Class was in session. The thought of Molly sent his pulse back up to a thousand beats a minute. Shame tore through him; he'd hardly looked at her when she'd crossed the schoolyard to greet him. This good-hearted woman had graciously agreed to raise his child, a child not her own, a child she hardly knew. And he couldn't act like a gentleman around her.

Even now as he checked the sign in the doctor's front window and saw that he was still closed for dinner, Luke could feel Molly's lips hot on his. She was heat and velvet, spice and sweetness. The memory of her soft, firm woman's body pressed against him nearly made him drop his package. He shoved his purchases into his saddlebags and reminded himself he owed Molly Lambert a world of respect.

He had no right wanting to bed her.

A fancy dressmaker's sign caught his eye. They had time to kill waiting for the doctor, so he scooped Beth up into his arms. "What do you say we find a few pretty dresses to match that new ribbon of yours?"

Beth gazed up at him adoringly, and his heart broke all over again.

Through the holly encircled windows, Molly saw Luke approach, spine straight, shoulders broad, his Stetson in a no-nonsense tilt. He looked more grim than usual, and her stomach fluttered. Something was wrong.

The minutes ticked by as she fired test questions to the eighth-year mathematics class. As the hands of the clock moved closer to three o'clock, the shuffling and fidgeting increased, and she had to ask for quiet. Expectant tension filled the pleasant room, now decorated with strings of holly and plump red bows, as the big hand crept closer to the mark.

Finally, she praised the students on their work, sent them to their seats, and penciled down their grades. With only a few seconds to go, she closed the stove's damper. "You're dismissed."

Chaos exploded. Boys leaped out of their seats. Little girls hopped from behind their desks. Molly reminded them to be orderly, but that merely slowed them on their way out the door to freedom.

"Miss Lambert's beau is here!" a boy's shout rang loud and clear.

Molly grabbed a clean towel from the stack and began wiping down the blackboards. The chalk dust fogged the air as she swiped over the smooth surface. She heard McKenna's step and felt his presence.

The skin on her back prickled, and she peered over her shoulder. "I'll have to remember to rap that boy's knuckles with a ruler."

One dark brow quirked in amusement. "I bet you rule with an iron fist."

"Absolutely." The chalk dust tickled her nose. The schoolhouse seemed to shrink as he stalked close with Beth on his hip, his hard-edged gaze piercing like an arrow to her heart.

"How did the trip to the doctor's go?"

"Fine. Beth is pretty much over the croup." He halted near the window, close but not too close. Framed by gray light and dark holly, he looked like a wild wolf trapped in a cage, restless, edgy. "I didn't realize you and your aunt were so popular in town."

"I couldn't call it popular." She finished wiping down the board.

"Then call it well-known." He cleared his throat, a gruff and impatient sound. "The mercantile went all right. I only told a few small lies, nothing major, just enough to keep the sheriff from looking at me twice."

Molly set down the towel. "The sheriff?"

"The real problem came when I stopped at the dressmaker's. For Beth. Seems Miss Wilson is a close personal friend of yours and Aggie's. Wanted to know just how well I knew the town's beloved schoolteacher."

"Beloved is going a bit far. Most people hardly know my name."

"Then," Luke ground out, "I took Beth to the doctor. Old Doc Stanton is a councilman with your uncle and assumed I was your fiancé come to beg your forgiveness and win back your heart."

"Oh, dear." Molly reached for the broom. "I never told a soul in this town about my broken engagement and what happened back home."

"Something tells me your aunt might have let it slip once or twice because the doc definitely knew. If I told him different, then I'd raise the question of who I am and why I'm in town."

"I'm sorry, Luke." Molly gave the floor a hard swipe with her broom. "Aggie had no right mentioning anything."

"I don't see how it can hurt. Maybe it will help." He eased Beth down to the ground. The little girl took one look at Molly and bit her lip, unsure.

"Do you want to draw on my slate?" Molly pulled out a chair from one of the front-row desks.

Beth nodded and wordlessly sat down.

Progress. It was a good thing, and warmth gathered in her chest for the child she wanted to love. She set the slate and stylus on the desk in front of Beth.

"She loves to draw." Luke smiled, a slow curve of his hard mouth that softened his face until there was brightness in his eyes and in her heart. He made her want to believe...

His smile faded, and he gazed out the windows where the town stretched like a shining jewel draped with a mantle of white. "At least no one is wondering what I'm doing here. That's good. I've been keeping an eye on the sheriff, and he didn't race back to his office after meeting me. He didn't organize a posse to bring me in."

"Maybe you're safe for now. Maybe—"

"Hell, I can't let up now. My suspicious nature is the only thing that's kept me alive since my fellow inmates dynamited the back wall of Rockville Prison."

"The train isn't running, and the telegraph line up this way isn't completed yet." Molly took a breath. She knew dangerous men were after him; she'd seen them with her own eyes. But surely the blizzards had buried all the tracks a bounty hunter could possibly find. And if there was no danger of the sheriff recognizing him... "Maybe you could stay for a few more days."

"Molly, I—"

"No, listen. Beth isn't ready to stay with me. I can't take her against her will. I won't do that to her."

He lowered his voice, pounding toward her. "What if a bounty hunter shows up and puts a bullet through me? What then?"

"You know I'll keep Beth. And protect her."

"Then what's the difference if I leave now, before I'm shot?"

"Because we both know how dangerous those mountains are in the winter. Avalanches aren't the only way to die up there. Wild animals are hungry this time of year and will hunt a man. Sometimes one bullet won't stop them. Or a blizzard could blow in suddenly and you'd freeze to death. The chance of your making it to Canada isn't all that great."

"I know." A muscle jumped in his jaw, and he continued staring out the window at the town, at the last of the children playing as they walked home, at the shrouded peaks so close, they filled the entire skyline.

Keeping her back to Beth and her voice low, she asked, "What's the difference if you die up in those mountains tonight or a week from now?"

He swept off his Stetson. "Damn it, Molly, I don't intend to die up there. Or be shot down in front of my daughter."

"She's not ready for you to leave."

"When will she ever be?"

"You can stay. A week. Two would be perfect."

His throat worked. "Staying won't help. It would make it harder for both of us, wishing for what could never be."

She saw the pain in his eyes, heard it in his voice. "It's Christmas in two weeks. Surely you could stay that long. Or at least, you could try, couldn't you?"

"Christmas." He glanced at his daughter, who sat quietly drawing, mouth pursed into a frown, her brows furrowed with concentration. "I can't."

His words echoed with a depth of hopelessness that felt like a glacier's leading edge, cutting the life from the land it smothered. He splayed one broad hand against the wall, right next to one of her red poofy bows, and swore.

"I don't have the heart for that," he told her, then stormed out the door.

He heard the click of the lock in the door and the tap of Beth's shoes on the schoolhouse steps. Molly's skirts rustled in the brisk wind, and he could feel her nearness like a candle's flame. He wanted to turn toward her, reach out and hold her. To feel like a man again.

"I've already spoken with your aunt," he said, never letting his gaze stray from those mountains.

"Aggie? When?"

"Just came from her house. I told her I needed some help. Goes against my grain to do it, but I don't want your reputation damaged. For your sake and for Beth's."

"Did you tell Aggie the truth?"

"No. I couldn't do it. I met her gaze and..." How could he explain? Aggie Grant looked at him and saw a man, a whole man. Not a criminal and a fugitive. How could he say one word to change that? "Besides, she let your story about the broken engagement slip."

"I know." Molly sounded disappointed as she swept past him, the edge of her skirt's ruffle brushing his trouser leg. "What did you tell her?"

"Something as close to the truth as I could manage. I didn't want to hurt your reputation. She offered to let Beth and me stay with her for a while. Said her house is lonesome ever since her youngest girl left home to be married."

"Aunt Aggie's been trying to talk me into moving in with her since she wrote me about the position here at the school."

"I took her up on the offer." He let out a breath, wishing, just wishing he could face Molly and be proud of the man he was.

"You're moving out?"

He nodded and knuckled back the brim of his hat "The blizzards wiped out all traces that I found my way to your house. You'll be safer with me gone."

"And my aunt?"

"There's no danger right now, Molly. I don't know how long that will last." He studied the clouds veiling the mountain peaks from view. A storm raged there, not twenty miles away, keeping the pass closed to the train and most likely to the men wanting his death.

"You don't have to worry. By the time trouble shows up, I'll be gone, and they'll follow me right out of here."

"And they won't know about Beth?"

He sighed. That troubled him more than he wanted to admit. The plan had seemed simple when he'd spied Beth in that field beneath the brutal Texas sun.

"Go ahead, move in with Aggie. It's for the best." Molly sounded sensible and accepting...and she sounded mad. She stomped away, skidding along on the ice. "I need to get my mare."

Beth leaned against his knee and said nothing, just held on tight.

Molly walked away with much unspoken. Her skirts snapped in the wind as she crossed the yard. Although he tried not to look, in fact he commanded his eyes not to look, he couldn't help watching her, willowy and womanly. The breeze tore at her russet locks that were twisted into a disciplined bun and battered her butter-colored skirts. She moved like music, looked like poetry, and he hurt from head to toe simply watching her.

With the way he was feeling, it was a damn good thing Aggie had taken him in.

He didn't want to spend another minute around Molly Lambert, to look, smell, hear everything about her when she wasn't his to touch.

⁓⋅⃝⤳

"Oh, so you're the man Elise Davis saw talking with Molly Lambert after school." Russell Grant, Aggie's husband, tugged a pipe out of his jacket pocket near the red-hot stove in the Grants' cozy kitchen. "Elise said she was just driving by, but she figured it was my nephew, my sister's boy, come all the way from Kansas to help me run the mill."

"I didn't see anyone in the schoolyard, sir." Luke set Beth down so she could run over to Aggie, who was trying to charm her with a plate of gingerbread cookies. "There was just Beth and Molly and me."

"Now, Elise was probably riding on the road in front of the school in her brand-new sleigh." Russell slipped the pipe into the corner of his mouth and fished a tobacco pouch from his other pocket. "We're a small town and close-knit. There isn't a one of 'em who won't notice if you're wearin' brown socks or black, believe you me. Then the rest of the town will know by sundown."

"If you're expecting your nephew, I can move—"

"Nonsense, Luke," Aggie trilled from the table. "There isn't room at the boardinghouse, and the hotel isn't even halfway close to being built yet. Besides, a little girl needs a home, not a boardinghouse."

"Especially if you're courting our niece." Russell tapped a wad of tobacco into the mouth of his pipe.

"Oh, no you don't," Aggie admonished. "Don't think just because we have company you can smoke that filthy thing in my kitchen. Go out on the porch and freeze your toes if you have to. Honestly. Men. Remember this Beth. When you grow up and get married, you can't give 'em an inch or the next thing you know, smelly pipe smoke is in your clean kitchen."

"I'm not gonna get married." Beth picked a licorice button off the chest of her gingerbread man. "Not never."

"You intend on being like Molly, then? She says the exact same thing."

"Don't want Molly." Beth bowed her head.

Luke felt Russell's question like a spear to his chest. "Beth's worried about getting a new mother."

"It's a worrisome thing." Aggie clucked in agreement, all sympathy and concern, and hugged the little girl tight.

Beth stiffened, but didn't move away.

"Luke, come outside with me," Russell invited. "Do you smoke?"

"Used to." Before he was thrown in prison. Stomach tight, Luke grabbed his jacket from the coat tree and followed the older man outside.

"I've grown mighty fond of my niece over the years," Russell began once the door clicked shut and his pipe was lit. "She's a good girl. Didn't have much of a family, that's for sure. It's a wonder how she turned out good like she did. We're real proud of her, teaching the school up here. All the parents in town are pleased as punch with her, and the kids love her."

Luke waited for what came next, sensing it like the snow on the wind.

"Seein' how Molly's father died when she was just a bit of a thing, littler than your girl, I try to step in when I can. When she was younger, her mother didn't always like it or allow it, but now that Molly's a grown woman I like to be the one who looks out for her."

Luke waited for the lecture, and he was ready. Ready to assure Mr. Grant that he wasn't out to break Molly's heart.

Russell took a deep drag on his pipe and blew out a long stream of smoke. "Do you have yourself a skill, young man?"

A skill? Young man? Luke felt old of heart, weary of soul. What was Russell getting at?

"I didn't have much when I was your age, I'll admit it. Thought I could make my way as a logger. I was young and cocky and a handsome cuss, I'll tell you that. But you know what I'm sayin' about supporting a family. You have a child you're responsible for. I know you know what I'm saying."

Then it dawned on him. With his mind on the men after him, the price on his head, and being forced to leave Beth, it had taken a while. But he chuckled; he couldn't help it. "You're worried I can't support Molly."

"I have the right to ask."

"I suppose you do, sir." Luke watched the tiny flakes of snow falling dizzily through the swath of light from the kitchen window. Freezing fog hugged the earth, and the dampness in the air made the most fragile, airy flakes he'd ever seen. "I used to be a Texas Ranger."

"A lawman." Russell nodded approvingly. "You got the look of one."

"But a bullet in the knee made riding tough, and I gave it up for ranching."

"Cattle or sheep?"

"Cattle."

Russell nodded again. "Good. Wouldn't want a sheep-man in the family. Got to keep up the standards."

Although the older man was teasing, Luke failed to smile. He opened his mouth, the words ready on his tongue to straighten out the misunderstanding, and then he stopped.

What would it hurt to keep letting everyone think he was

courting Molly? Maybe it would be the best way to hide Beth from his cousin.

Luke breathed in the bitter night air, and for the first time in months, he didn't feel without hope on a dark winter's night.

The house felt so empty without them. Molly looked up from her sewing and watched Lady sigh, brown eyes downcast, a frown drooping the hound's entire doggy face.

The evenings had always been the loneliest, filling the hours between supper and bedtime. As Molly stitched the basted skirt seam on a dress she was sewing for Beth, she remembered how she'd hurt Luke today when she foolishly suggested that he could stay. As if he could, when dangerous men were following him.

The blizzard was protection for a while. The mountains were vast and the towns few and far between, except for the new railroad spur. But she didn't know what Luke had been through and didn't know how determined the men were who hunted him.

She'd only witnessed the fear in Luke's eyes when she'd suggested it.

Lady barked, leaping to her feet, scurrying across the polished floor to the back door.

Was it him? Molly set down the dress and hurried through the house. After what she'd said, he probably thought he needed to talk with her. And that was good, because she wanted to apologize for her words today.

If only she could figure out a way to hold back the warm feeling in her heart when she looked at him and erase the memory of his kiss.

"Mr. McGrath." She tried to hide the disappointment at the sight of her elderly neighbor on her porch step. "Is something wrong? Is Mrs. McGrath—"

"Fit to be tied. That's why she sent me over here with a plate of cinnamon rolls and an apology." He managed a beleaguered shrug. "Can I come in?"

"Certainly. Lady." The dog smelled the treats, and Molly curled her fingers through the hound's collar. "Come in, and here, I'd better take that plate before the dog decides it's for her. I've got tea water hot."

"No, thanks. Got to be headin' back." McGrath tugged his knit wool cap off his head, revealing rumpled and thin gray hair. "Wanted to tell you the storm brought down a tree and busted the fence on our property line. I was fixin' it when your fella come by and helped me out. I didn't realize he was your intended."

The plate slipped from her fingers and clinked on the countertop. "*Luke?*"

"The missus started knitting you a wedding present this very day when she heard the good news."

She opened her mouth, but not one sound emerged.

"No sense of being modest, young lady. Nothing wrong with a fella admitting his mistakes and trying to mend his ways. Looks like an honest man. Glad to know you've forgiven him. A man like that's got some good in him."

Molly stammered. She couldn't think of one single thing to say. But she knew what she was going to do— strangle Aunt Aggie the first chance she got. First thing tomorrow morning right before school started, if she had to.

"Well, got to get goin'." McGrath backed toward the door. "Hope we're invited to the wedding."

"But—"

The door closed, and she could only stare at it. Shock pelted through her like ice in a fast wind. There was no way in good conscience she could let Mr. McGrath think—Goodness, it was too impossible to think—

She tore open the door. "Mr. McGrath! Mr.—"

"He's already gone." A man strode out of the darkness and into the spill of light through the door.

"Luke." She knew she shouldn't sound so eager to see him. "Has Aggie run you out of her house already?"

"Took the broom to me. Got a bruise over my left eye from her chasing me off," he quipped, and for a moment with the darkness behind him and facing the light, he looked younger, less dangerous, like a tall honor-bound hero and not a fugitive on the run. "You might take your broom to me, too, when I tell you what I've got on my mind."

"Come in, but only if you're going to tell me you aren't leaving tonight. The trains still aren't running and—"

"That's not why I'm here." He bounded up the steps, all might and muscle, and he took her breath away.

She stumbled back as Lady barked and leaped in welcome. Luke crowded through the threshold, so close she could smell the winter wind and snow on his jacket.

"There's only one thing on my mind and I don't know any other way to say it, so here I go." His gloved fingers curled around hers, holding her tight.

A moment of panic fluttered in her chest. "Luke, is something wrong?"

"Not wrong. Something is finally right." The left corner of his mouth crooked into a tentative, dazzling smile. "I've come tonight to propose to you, Molly. I want you to be my wife."

CHAPTER NINE

"Your *wife?*"

Uh-oh. She didn't look too happy. "It makes sense."

"No, it certainly does not make sense." Molly spun away, shoulders rigid, spine stiff. "I know why you're asking this. My neighbor was just over here, letting me know about the fence. He congratulated me on my upcoming wedding."

"I know. Five of Aggie's committee meeting friends stopped by after supper desperate to hear the real story." Luke watched Molly bow her head forward, a painful sigh rattling her slim frame. Her russet curls parted, revealing the slim, pale column of her curving neck, vulnerable and sweet. His chest kicked. "I see a way out, here. I knew you wouldn't like it. I was hoping you'd go along with it."

"So you think you can stroll in here and control my life?" She marched away, fury and heartache.

He wished he knew what was hurting her so much. "You said you'd raise Beth."

"How do you even know that I can do a good job?" She grabbed the poker and knelt in front of the giant stone hearth. "All I've done is teach other people's children."

"You seem to do a pretty good job with that. Russell told me how proud he was of you. He gets a lot of compliments from parents."

"Raising a child is a lot different than teaching spelling and multiplication."

"I have all the faith in the world in you." He knelt at her side, feeling the scorch of heat from the snapping fire and her despair. "Are you going to change your mind? Is that what this is about?"

"No, it's just—" She jabbed the poker hard into a crumbling log in the grate, maybe to hide her shuddering sigh. "I spent half my childhood in an orphanage or being farmed around to relatives."

"Then you know better than most what's at stake." Luke covered her hands with his over the hard iron handle. He took the poker from her grip and laid it on the hearth.

"The rest of my childhood was spent with a woman who didn't know she hated being a mother until it was too late. What do I have to give anyone, much less a child?"

"Everything." His grip remained on her, steady and reassuring.

Molly's heart broke. "Maybe Beth would be better off with Aggie. It would be easier to explain. She could claim she was taking care of an unwanted child. She's done it before."

"Easier isn't my way." He eased her back from the scorching heat and against his chest, into his arms. His voice vibrated straight through her when he spoke. "I like Aggie, but she's getting up there in years. Beth will need someone with a good twenty years left in her. You know, like a good horse."

"You're a bad man, Luke McKenna." She liked that he could make her laugh, sheltered against his chest, held against his heart. "I just want to be honest with you. I like Beth. I know I can love her."

"I have no doubt. Not a single one."

No one had ever had so much faith in her. Admiration and desire and yearning swirled together, and she tilted her face up to look at him. The firelight brushed his rough-hewn features, handsome and rugged and intensely masculine. For one brief moment, she couldn't help wondering what it would be like to be loved by a man like this—powerful but tender. To spend every night nestled against his protective chest.

"You're the woman I want, Molly. For my daughter."

She'd almost forgotten. Strangely disappointed, she straightened away from him, although she secretly longed to stay. Lady scooted close and nudged her hand. "I'm not sure marrying would be a good idea. It's not like I can take your name or anything."

"No one said we had to use my real name." He bowed his head.

"It would be best for Beth. It would give her anonymity. As far as anyone in this town knows, I came courting, married you, and got caught in a blizzard while hunting in the mountains. I'm not Luke McKenna to them. Yet."

"I noticed you didn't give my aunt your last name when you introduced yourself."

"Didn't give it to anyone. I don't intend to." The fire popped like a gunshot, and his gaze strayed around the room, scanning the polished furniture and the cushions that still smelled vaguely of smoke.

"The thing is, if I just left her, everyone would think I'd abandoned her. What could you use to explain her presence? Before, I had this vague notion that no one would know much about you. That you could explain the child away as a niece or something. But everyone in this town seems to know everything about you. Please, Molly. I'll behave myself. I won't make demands on you."

Sex. He was talking about sex. She closed her eyes and felt the heat creep across her face. Remembering their kiss, remembering how he'd kept his distance from her when it was over, she whirled away from him.

Lady barked excitedly, dashing toward the back of the house. Luke hopped to his feet, unsnapping his holsters, bounding across the room like the hounds of hell were after him.

"It's probably just the deer come for a late-night snack," she told him.

He didn't answer, but stalked through the kitchen and put out the light. Darkness cloaked him. "It's the deer all right."

"I told you." She tugged her cloak off the peg and stabbed her arms into the thick sleeves. "Are you planning on heading back to town?"

The ruffled curtain whispered through his callused fingers. "You haven't answered my proposal."

"I know." Taking a stranger's child was one thing. Marrying him was different.

She pushed open the door and let the bitter temperatures chase the blush from her face. The snow crunched noisily beneath her shoes as she headed toward the barn, Lady bounding ahead, barking happily.

The deer milled nervously, even though the corral bars kept

Lady from them. The hound's thrill at seeing deer up close echoed like joy through the solemn, shrouded night. Fog made the deer seem air bound as they pranced and jumped in the shadow of the stable.

The determined crunch of boots on the snow behind her told her Luke wasn't going to let her get away. Unhappiness gathered around her, cold as the freezing fog. She heaved the heavy door open, but Luke's fingers curled around the wood above her own and lifted the weight easily.

His nearness burned, and she stormed into the stable. The scent of sweet alfalfa and warm animals soothed her. Honey lifted her golden head and whickered a gentle welcome. The mare nosed out over the wooden rails, begging for attention.

Molly reached for the tin of matches and lit the lantern hung on the center post by feel. The door eased shut, cutting out the cold night. The stable shrank in size as the flame caught, illuminating Luke as he stalked toward her, a wolf on the hunt, and she felt like soon-to-be-caught prey.

He tracked past her and grabbed the wooden-handled pitchfork from its resting place against the back wall. There was the sound of iron scraping against wood and the rustle of alfalfa settling into place. A hinge squeaked, and cold rushed across Molly's face, but she was spell-bound by the sight of Luke's hardened shoulders and arms moving with masculine grace and effortless power as he forked gigantic forkfuls of feed through the open half door.

"I've thought about what you said. About staying." He kept pitching without a break in his rhythm and without a hitch in his breathing. "I gave it some real serious thought."

"You were right. It's dangerous."

"There's no telling if I'm safe as can be or if I'm about ready to be surrounded and nailed with a bullet in the back."

"I understand. But if we get married like you want, that will take time."

"A week. I can stay that long. There's another storm in the mountains, and if Moss didn't send word when he spotted me, then I might have time."

"A week."

It was so little; it was so much. Luke's throat closed tight, and he figured the deer had enough to eat, so he leaned the pitchfork against the wall.

Bitter-cold air seeped through the open half door, and he shivered "I don't think I'll ever get used to this cold."

"Did you live in Texas your whole life?"

"Yep. Was born near Abilene. Flat, rolling hills, the sky as blue as a bluebonnet, and it goes on forever. And the sun, it'll bake you to the bone, but I loved it."

"I've heard Canada is colder than Montana."

"So have I." His heart was showing, the core of who he was, and he backed away, closing off those memories. "The sun isn't likely to bake me like dried bones where I'm headed. You know, I thought about circling back south. Thought maybe if I kept moving after enough time passed they'd give up, and Beth and I could settle down someplace remote and quiet. I could find work and raise her myself."

"Then why head to Canada? Why marry me?" A muscle jumped in her jaw. Pain, not anger, shadowed her as she pried up the lid to the grain barrel with her thumb.

"The man after me doesn't want me caught. He wants me dead. It's personal, and I don't know if he'll ever give up." He shouldered up to her and dipped a small pail into the molasses-and-corn mixture. "I don't like running, and I don't like staging a marriage, but it's easier. And it will protect Beth a lot better than anything I can think of."

Molly's throat worked as she swallowed. "I never wanted to be a convenience. That's why I broke off my engagement. That's why I've given up on the notion of marrying."

"Think of the favor I'll be doing you, then."

"Favor?"

"Sure. You can be a widow the rest of your life if you want. Your aunt will stop trying to match you up with all her friends' sons because you're in mourning."

"Then you've sold me on the idea."

"You mean it?"

"Yes."

Relief left him almost smiling, and the burdens of a lifetime lifted from his weary shoulders. He set down the pail, disregarding the whinnying demand of the horse for grain, and cupped her face with his hands.

She was silk and angel, real and true, and he never thought he'd touch a woman like this again. "You aren't a convenience, Molly.

You're wanted and needed. I swear to it with all my soul."

Her eyes glittered, sparkling rich and rare. "I know you have to say those things, even if they aren't true. Just be careful and don't overdo it, OK? I'd hate to start believing your blarney."

"Let's get one thing clear right now. I know you look at me and see a man who doesn't deserve to walk on the same earth as you, but when I tell you something, I want you to believe it."

"See? This is what I'm talking about." Doubt dulled the bronze gleaming in her eyes. "And by the way, I'm glad you're on this earth, Luke McKenna, because I would never have gotten to know you. And because of you, I get to share my life with a child, a dream I'd given up."

A hard ball of emotion shattered in his chest, like a glass ornament tumbling to the floor, scattering the shards of his bitterness. Somehow his mouth was on hers with want and need. She tasted like hot chocolate and desire, smelled like lilacs and snowflakes, and felt like heaven, like nothing he'd known before. He twined his fingers through her hair and wrapped one hand around her nape, tipping her mouth open.

She was warm, willing, and he laved his tongue over her velvet lips and surged over her pearled teeth. Desire roared in his ears and pumped in his veins as he plunged into her mouth. A moan tore through his throat, the intimacy of the kiss thundering through him. She was wet, warm silk and passion, and the sweet tip of her tongue laved over his, slow like sunset, luscious like dawn.

He fit one hand on the small of her back and drew her against him. Her breasts pillowed his chest, and the curve of her stomach trapped his erection between them. He was hard, thrumming and aching. A primal need speared through him, arrowhead sharp, and he knew he was on the edge of losing control.

But instead of pushing her away, he wrapped his arms around her and crushed her to him. Her moan was one of pleasure, and he lost all rational thought and every speck of common sense. There was only her—the taste of her, the scent of her, the feel of her woman's body against his. The way she leaned in to his kiss and in to him.

He backed her against the wall. Cold air from the open half door breezed against the back of his neck. Outside the dog barked and alfalfa rustled. But those sensations were dim, like light through fog. His skin tingled with her every breathless gasp, the gentle way she caught his bottom lip between hers and sucked, and how she seemed to want him.

Her cloak gaped—she hadn't buttoned it—and his hand found its way down the graceful column of her neck to the point where her collar met the hollow of her throat. He could feel the flutter of her pulse beneath his fingertips as he unhooked the first button. The flutter quickened as he unlooped a second button and a third. Fabric gave way to heated skin that tasted like cream. His mouth settled there in the place where her collarbones met, and her heartbeat raced because of him.

There was no need for words as he slid one hand inside her blouse and beneath her woolen undershirt. She was heat and forbidden softness. Her pebbled nipple thrust against the center of his palm as he covered her breast with his hand. A groan tore from his throat, a sharp, raw sound that cleared his head enough to think. He pulled back before he could pluck that sweet pearled nipple with his tongue.

Need pounded through every vein in his body, a driving keen ache for completion—for mating, for connection, for sanctuary. Luke took a deep breath and stepped away from her.

Her hair had fallen from its loose knot to tangle in abandon around her shoulders and exposed throat. Head tipped back in surrender, chest rising and falling with shallow breaths, she opened her eyes. She stared at the rafters and then at him. It wasn't disgust that saddened her eyes and drew her up straight. It would have been better if it had been that.

He cleared his throat, trying to find the right words. "Here I promise you that I won't make demands on you if you give me the greatest favor of a lifetime, and the first chance I get, I—"

Anger soured his mouth and tasted bitter on his tongue. He swung away from the sight of her shadowed breasts lifting and falling with each breath. Instead of kneading her with his hands, he snared the grain bucket and up-ended it above the palomino's trough.

Out of the corner of his eye he saw Molly drawing the placket of her blouse together. Her fingers shook as she worked the buttons into the loops.

She had to be angry with him. She had to be disgusted. Her eyes were wide and revealed nothing. No condemnation, no fury, no outrage. But it had to be there.

He reached for the door, but his fingers hesitated on the latch. "I'm sorry, Molly. That won't happen again. You have my word on it."

"I see." She hugged her cloak tightly around her. She looked tousled and vulnerable and small in the shadowed corner. "Can I ask you something?"

"Absolutely." He braced himself, knowing she had the right to lash into him.

"What don't you like about me?" Her thin question hovered in the air. "I mean, you keep stopping and walking away from me. I know I'm not pretty..." She gestured helplessly with one hand. "Never mind."

She came off the wall and pushed past him, marching away from him as if he didn't exist.

"Molly?"

She kept going. The snow had iced over and was too slick to run, but she slipped and slid toward the house, where golden lamplight glowed through fog. Her safe haven. Her sanctuary from fear and rejection. All she had to do was run inside and bolt the door, and she'd be able to pass this off as a bad mistake.

But Luke was running after her, and even though he still limped, he was gaining. His long-legged pace was quick and easy, and he caught the edge of the door before she could snap it shut.

Her mouth flamed from his kiss. Her breasts tingled and sparkled from his touch. Her body felt as if someone had kindled a fire inside it and added fuel. She didn't want him to know how she still wished he would touch her breasts again. Glitters of sensation left her ashamed and wanting. What would he think if he knew?

"I know what kind of man you think I am." He wedged open the door. "You look at me and see the worst of men, and I don't blame you. I—"

"I don't see the worst." She whirled away before he could somehow see that she still wanted him to touch her. "I've told you what I see."

"I remember." His hand curled around her elbow. "But the day they threw me into Rockville State, I stopped being a man. I spent too much time there, enough time that something got beat out of me."

"You were innocent of whatever crime they accused you of, weren't you?"

141

His jaw dropped as if he'd been slapped, and he passed a hand over his eyes. His great shoulders slumped, and the fight seemed to go out of him. "Why do you say that?"

"I've never known a more selfless man. I know there are men who love their children the way you do your daughter, but I've never seen it. A man who can love that much can't cause harm. I don't believe it."

His throat worked. "Since the moment I was arrested, there was only one person on this earth who believed I didn't murder my uncle for his money. One person, and he'd known me all my life. He was the foreman on my father's ranch, and he'd always looked out for me. When I escaped, he was the one who told me what happened to Beth and gave me enough money to make it to Canada."

Maybe Luke needed someone to see the good in him. She dared to lay her hand against his stubbled jaw and look into world-weary eyes. "Did you get a fair trial?"

"It was fair, all right. I was framed, and there was no way to prove it." He leaned his cheek against her hand and closed his eyes. "I was my uncle, Lee's, heir after his son died—he was a ranger, too. Lee was a lot like Russell, fatherly and good at heart. He was also a millionaire many times over, and my cousin was pretty furious when he was cut out of the will."

"Did you say a millionaire?"

"It's a lot of money, I know, and my cousin wanted it. Bad enough to murder Lee and make it look like I did it. He used my knife and my gun; he stole my horse while I was sleeping. A dozen cowhands saw a man on my white Arabian stallion race off across the hills minutes before Lee was found dead. I was home in bed, sleeping, when the deputies kicked in my door and arrested me. I didn't even know why."

"Oh, Luke." She held him tight.

"There wasn't a speck of evidence that I could use to defend myself with, and I was sentenced to hard labor, which was better than death." He rested his chin on the top of her head, his rum-rich voice rumbling through her. "Fletcher just grinned at me the whole time he was in the courtroom, and I knew he'd done it just for the money. For all that money."

"I can't believe what you've been through." She wanted to hold him forever and keep him safe, to give him back a home and a life, his freedom and his future.

Then he released her and turned his back. "And no, Molly, there's nothing wrong with you. Not one thing. Any man ought to be proud to have the right to love you."

"I don't need flattery, Luke. Just the truth."

"That is the truth. You are beautiful and desirable, and if I could, I'd stay right here and try to make myself into a man you could want."

"But, Luke, you already are."

He didn't move, didn't even appear to breathe. The lamplight caressed his black locks and the line of his unyielding shoulders. The tick of the clock seemed unnaturally loud as her heart raced, and the dog scratched at the door, asking to come in.

Maybe she shouldn't have said that, opened up to him. Maybe, after what he'd been through, he didn't have the heart for it, just like he'd said.

Then Luke pulled her into his arms and held her so tight, she couldn't breathe. And she didn't doubt.

Morning dawned with fresh snow and intense cold, but Molly hardly noticed it as she rode to town, the wind in her face, snow clinging to her cloak and hood, because she felt toasty inside, snug from being held in Luke's arms.

He'd held her, nothing more, and yet it had quieted all the ache inside her. He needed her; she knew that. She knew his concern for Beth's future was what motivated his every act, except maybe his kisses and the way he'd touched her in the stable, and even then, he'd feared he'd alienated her. Not only because of her sensibilities, but because of Beth's needs.

Molly tried not to let that bother her. She was, after all, a plain woman. She had lines on her face and a waist that not even her corset could make fashionably small. She was too short, too quiet, and too ordinary. Albert had said she wasn't enough woman to inspire passion in a man.

But she'd inspired it in Luke last night. She smiled against the rough knit of her scarf that protected half her face from the subzero temperature. For the first time in her life, she realized why Aggie had always spoken of a married couple's relations with a wink and much enthusiasm.

When she rounded the corner into town, she saw gray smoke pluming up from the pipe in the schoolhouse's roof. Uncle Russell must have been there for her this morning. Her heart warmed, grateful for Aggie and Russell, who looked out for her in the way her own mother wouldn't. What would she do without them?

She left her mare standing at the bottom of the steps and she ran inside to stock the stove with more coal. Frost still hung on the nail heads in the wall and gathered in the creases of her cut holly garlands. She closed the door tight behind her and nosed Honey through town. The thermometer on the wall of the mercantile read thirty-eight degrees below zero.

A man looked up from his work shoveling off the snow from the boardwalk in front of his feed store. " 'Mornin', Miss Lambert."

"Good morning, Mr. Potter." She slowed Honey to a walk. "Your little girl is the best speller in the entire fourth class."

"Glad to know it. You're a fine teacher." Mr. Potter beamed, straightening from his work. "Hear you might get yourself a wedding ring for Christmas."

"You shouldn't listen to nasty rumors, Mr. Potter," Molly teased and earned a chuckle.

Aggie's two-story house was shielded by a stand of old growth fir and mantled with white. Movement on the front steps caught her eye.

"Luke." She tried, but knew she failed to keep the warmth from her voice.

"Why, it's my beautiful fiancée." He straightened up and leaned on the shovel's handle. "I didn't expect to see you this morning. Russell and I went over and started up the stove for you."

"And shoveled the steps. I noticed." She felt the tension of last night's encounter between them—he with his fears and she with hers. "You said Beth was pretty well recovered. I wondered if she wanted to go to school with me today."

Luke tipped back his hat, scattering snow off his brim. "So, you've come to steal my daughter from me."

"You bet." Molly's breath caught as he stalked close, and the fire banked inside her rekindled, remembering last night, remembering his touch. "Beth is going to be my whole life."

Luke's hand found hers, and through the wool of their mittens for a brief moment, she could feel his warmth. Then he withdrew his hand. "Dismount, and I'll take your mare to the stable to keep warm. Aggie's starting breakfast."

She dismounted, careful of her skirts. Luke's sure hand helped her to the icy ground, even though she didn't need help. Still, it was a nice gesture. He took the mare's reins and led her away. Snow gusted hard, driving away the warmth within. She shivered, feeling bereft, watching him disappear from her sight.

"Luke told us the good news," Aggie announced over the sizzling of bacon and sausages, spatula in hand. "I have to admit, I'm pleased but concerned."

"Oh?"

"Yes, concerned." Aggie turned the bacon, and the sizzling grease snapped and popped into the silence between them.

How did she tell her aunt a lie? Even one to protect a child? Molly shook the snow from her wraps and hung them up near the stove, wishing Luke were here. Wishing she knew what he'd told them.

"I know your mother's rejection hit you real hard. It would anyone." Aggie turned the sausages, her head cocked to one side as she worked, her love unmistakable in her voice. "But I care about you, Molly. I only want to know you're not grabbing hold of the first man who comes along, ready and able to fill up your life. If you love him truly, then I'll shut up and spend the rest of my days being happy for you."

"I don't love him." The truth cut like a sharpened knife. "He doesn't love me."

"You want the child, don't you?" Aggie sounded sad as she forked the bacon onto a waiting platter. "The good Lord knows Beth is a keeper. She's sure afraid of losing her papa, though."

Molly caught Aggie's shrewd, measuring glance. "Yes, I noticed."

"Do you happen to know Luke's last name? It's funny, but he's never mentioned it to us."

"He hasn't?"

"Not once."

Panic whipped through her, and she darted across the room. "I'm going to look in on Beth. Maybe she's well enough to attend school today."

"I didn't hear but a few coughs last night. And while you're at it, plan on coming with Russell and me this afternoon to get our tree. We're having a sleighing party."

"I suppose Beth would like that."

"My thoughts exactly." Aggie bent to slip the platter into the oven to keep warm, her chin jutted, her mouth a tight line. "Are you sure you know what you're doing?"

"I'm sure." Molly laid her hand on the newel post, knowing she owed more to this woman. "Trust me."

"I do without a doubt."

With those treasured words, Molly climbed the stairs. The bright red ribbons wrapped around the polished banister added a festive cheer to the house. The evergreen garlands coiling through the posts smelled like a winter forest, fresh and new.

She saw one of the guest-room doors ajar and heard the shuffle of a child's footsteps.

"Come here, kitty," a child's voice called from behind the door.

Molly leaned her forehead against the door frame and watched Beth trot after Aggie's house cat, a friendly black and orange calico. The cat gave a gravelly meow and collapsed in the center of the rag rug.

"You want me to pet your tummy, Mrs. Whiskers?" Beth dropped to her knees beside the begging cat and, head bent, brushed her small hand along the cat's side.

Mrs. Whiskers purred with pleasure.

Beth was a lovely child. A more healthy color now blushed her face, and her dark eyes gleamed. Her Cupid's bow mouth was stretched into a charming smile, and she looked so small and dear in the new yellow-checked wool jumper Luke had bought for her. A white blouse with a lace-edged collar was a snowy contrast to her black hair.

She's going to be my little girl. Molly's heart filled at the thought. Maybe there was a way the two of them could be a real family. It didn't hurt to hope.

Beth looked up and her darling smile faded. An uncertain wariness drew the sparkles from her eyes. "Papa said I had to be polite. I said I'd try."

Molly pushed open the door all the way, but she hesitated at the threshold. "Do you like Mrs. Whiskers?"

"I used to have a cat before I lost my papa and my house." Beth ran her fingers through the calicos fluffy fur.

"Maybe we could get you a cat come spring when new kittens will be born."

"I guess."

Well, she'd hoped the kitten bribe would work. Molly took another step into the room. "I came by to ask if you wanted to go to school today."

"No."

But Molly heard the waver of uncertainty in Beth's voice.

And Luke must have, too, because his step tapped into the room behind her. "That's a mighty fine offer, Molly, inviting Beth to go to school. Isn't it, darlin'?"

Beth bowed her head. "I guess."

Molly watched Luke pace closer, and the love in his voice, his manner, and his eyes was unmistakable. He knelt beside his daughter, the big powerful man and the small child.

"You know, there are little girls just your age who go to Molly's school." He ruffled his daughter's curls as black as his own with so much affection that it left no doubt—he thought this child was the most precious in the world.

That's when Molly knew she was falling in love with him, with this man of might and tenderness she could never truly have.

"Papa, do I really gotta go?" Beth asked with a trembling whisper as the schoolhouse loomed ahead of them.

"This is your new life, darlin'." He drew back on the reins, halting the gelding. "Don't you want to get started on it?"

"No."

In truth, neither did he. It was damn hard handing her down to Molly, but the light in the woman's eyes told him everything. She was falling in love with his daughter. It was as simple as that. He'd found a good woman to give his daughter what he couldn't.

"You're comin' back to get me, right, Papa?" Beth's mouth crumpled, as if she were fighting off tears. She clung to Molly's hand with a white-knuckled grip that had to be cutting off Molly's circulation.

"Count on it, darlin'." Two boys were tromping through the vacant lot, tossing snowballs at each other. He knew it was time to let go. "You do what Molly says."

"Yes, sir." Beth rubbed at her eyes. "I'm gonna be polite."

"That's my girl."

"I'll take good care of her. Don't worry." Molly's hand caught his in a quick squeeze of reassurance. Snow dappled her russet hair, and all he could see was the woman from last night tucked in his arms, holding him tight.

His body, however, remembered something different. The passion of her kiss, the taste of her skin, the weight of her breast settling into his hand.

Damn. What in blazes was wrong with him? She was everything he could never deserve, and he owed her as much respect as he could give her.

Molly flashed him a beautiful smile and led Beth away by the hand. The little girl watched him over her shoulder, the longing and fear so stark on her face, it was all he could do to sit still and watch her walk away.

He had work to do. He had to search the forest for a sign—any sign—that men had followed him despite the storms. He didn't feel safe. Maybe he'd been running too long, but he couldn't relax. He wouldn't relent. He had Beth and Molly to protect.

When he looked back, he saw his daughter's face in the window, inside gazing out at him. He waved and she waggled her fingers. The plea in her eyes asked him to rescue her, but she knew how things were going to be. Hell of a thing for a six-year-old, but the world he knew wasn't a kind one.

He laid the reins over the gelding's neck and headed out of town.

"Papa!" Beth raced down the steps, her new shoes clacking against the wood board with her urgency. She flew off the bottom step and into her father's arms.

"I guess you missed me." He swung her through the air before settling her back on the ground. "You liked school?"

"No."

Luke's amused half smile met Molly full force, and she nearly dropped her keys. "You're late. I expected you the minute school was over."

"I meant to be." He squeezed Beth's hand in his before he lifted her onto the back of the horse. "Went out searching for bounty hunters, and the ride home was farther than I figured."

"You're taking every precaution."

"Absolutely."

He made her feel safe. He made her believe in him. She'd never felt this way before, as bright as a Christmas star every time she looked at him. She didn't want to feel this way. She really didn't.

"I'm about to head over to the church. Aunt Aggie's coerced me into agreeing to take Beth to a sleighing party."

"Wouldn't you know that she charmed me into going along, too?" A dimple flirted in his left cheek as he fought a grin. "Seems she said something about needing a big strong man with muscles to help chop down the trees."

"She asked the right man."

"You noticed my muscles?"

"Not really." Molly bit her lip to keep from grinning. "But I guess an older woman like Aunt Aggie might think you were firm in comparison."

"In comparison to what?" He mounted with one powerful masculine motion and knuckled back his hat.

"Older men."

His laughter followed her across the street.

Every step she took, she felt him beside her, towering above her on the horse like a flesh and blood Western hero. With every breath she took, the strange flash of brightness in her chest increased tenfold like air to flame.

"Why, look who's here." Mildred Smythe, the mayor's mother, broke away from the small crowd gathered on the front steps of the Evergreen Community Hall. "So, this is the man who's come to claim our schoolteacher's heart."

It was only pretend, and that knowledge hurt like a wound. Molly managed a bright smile and accepted Mildred's warm hug. "I'm a fortunate woman to have snared a good-looking man like Luke."

"You bet." Mildred's gaze scanned Luke's hard-muscled form with female approval. "It's as easy to marry a handsome man as an ugly one. So you might as well pick one that's going to be easy on the eyes."

"I wish I'd thought of that," Aggie teased as she wrapped Molly in her arms.

"Hey, I heard that!" Russell called out, and everyone laughed.

"When's the wedding?" Marguerite Rutledge bounced forward to ask.

"Yes. I'd be happy to sew your wedding dress." Joy Wilson, the town seamstress, stepped forward. "Congratulations, Molly. This will be the first wedding in our new town."

"A cause for celebration," Mildred added.

It was all too overwhelming. She watched as Luke handed Beth to Russell. Questions from her friends rose in the frosty air—Is that his little girl? When's the wedding? How on earth did she keep a relationship with a man like him secret?

Molly felt like she was drowning. She answered the questions she could honestly and dodged the others. She saw Luke surrounded by a half dozen men and wondered if he was doing any better than she was. He looked across the heads and shoulders of some of Evergreen's first citizens and shrugged, as if to say, well, who knew this would happen?

Warmth coiled around her, a feeling of belonging.

"Look, here come the hay sleds!"

Mr. McGrath and the mayor appeared around the corner of the livery. Two pair of draft horses drew each long, flat sled, and the wooden beds were spread with soft sweet hay.

"Put the lovebirds together!" Mildred Smythe's suggestion was met with great enthusiasm.

The next thing Molly knew, she was being escorted toward the second sled with Aggie holding one arm and Joy Wilson holding the other. Molly couldn't get away, and no one would listen to her protests. Snow and merriment mingled in the crisp December air, and the next thing Molly knew, she was seated in the soft hay with her feet swinging over the end.

She leaned back against a steeled chest.

"I hear we're having a big wedding," Luke's rum-rich baritone rumbled against her ear.

"We are?"

"According to Mayor Smythe, it's a good thing they invested the town funds into building the community center. The town's population has grown so that the church wouldn't be big enough to hold the wedding."

The gleam of warm humor made her smile. "Have they set a date?"

"I wouldn't be surprised."

The sleigh jerked into motion. Laughter filled the air as the crowded sleighs eased down the main street. Beth held her father's arm and didn't let go.

Snow tumbled from the sky in perfect white flakes, and the gleaming new storefronts gave way to pristine forests of fir and pine, their evergreen boughs slung low with mantles of white.

Aggie's hand curled around her arm, and Molly twisted backward to face her aunt. "Was the community hall your idea?"

"Now, don't look at me like I'm a meddling old woman."

"Why not? That's exactly what you are."

Aggie's eyes twinkled. "Fine, I'm guilty. But I was telling Mildred the good news, and she was the one who suggested the community hall. Isn't that grand?"

"You're actually proud of yourself. You're impossible."

"No, just proud of my niece and can't keep my mouth shut about it." Aggie's fingers squeezed, a loving gesture.

And Molly treasured it. All her life she'd wanted to belong, and now she did. The afternoon sparkled with good-natured chatter and jokes. The sled whispered over the snow with dizzying speed, and Luke put his arm around her shoulder, holding her against him.

He gave her a wink, and she knew it wasn't real. But her heart skipped a dozen beats and she wished, how she wished she weren't falling in love with him.

What had Luke said to her? *Any man ought to be proud to have the right to love you.* Flattery, she knew, spoken from a good man who needed her for his daughter, but still, the words healed something dark inside her and gave her joy.

Even Beth looked like she was having fun. Her dark eyes sparkled, and pleasure pinkened her face. She peered over her shoulder silently. "Where are we goin', Pa?"

"To get Christmas trees."

"Real Christmas trees?" Her mouth dropped into a surprised O. "For us, Pa?"

"For everyone. They're making it a party."

"Then we really do get one? Honest?"

"Aggie said she was going to put it up in the middle of her parlor for you to decorate."

Beth's face crinkled into a smile.

Luke's arm tightened around Molly's shoulder, and she leaned against him. A hot thudding sensation zinged through her blood, and her chest filled with warmth.

She loved this man. How on earth was she going to hide it from him? From everyone?

Mayor Smythe, seated next to his wife at the front of the sleigh, started the first verse to "Jingle Bells." A dozen voices joined in. It was a perfect afternoon.

Snow tumbled from sky to earth in a gentle dance. The sleighs glided low to the ground, and it felt wonderfully free to be flying so far and fast. All her friends were around her, and Aggie's slightly off-key soprano voice warbled above the others. Molly wanted to laugh with happiness.

She was seated beside a wonder of a man who looked at her with sparkles in his eyes and a grin on his mouth. Beth snuggled close, and they sang together as they dashed over snow-covered hills.

Nothing in Molly's life had ever felt this right.

How he was ever going to explain that he wasn't marrying their beloved schoolteacher on Christmas Eve, even if Aggie had suggested it, he didn't know. He would find a way. His arms ached from the bite and kick of the ax he swung, but as he watched Beth playing in the snow with the mayor's daughter, he felt happy for the first time in years.

This is what he'd struggled and fought for. What he was willing to die for.

"You're a strong cuss, son." Russell leaned his ax, handle up, against his knee and took off his wool cap. "And a hard worker, too. Good thing my Aggie thought to invite you along."

"I can't remember the last time I've had this much fun."

"You don't get out much, do you?" Russell chuckled.

Luke hefted the ax and drove its blade deep into the fir's trunk. Russell didn't know what he had here. Maybe none of them did. A handful of children played, while the women passed out hot cider in tin cups. A bonfire blazed in the big yard, not far from a town council member's ranch house. The women stood close to the fire, chatting and keeping warm.

"Mildred thought you looked a little frozen." Molly swept into his peripheral view. "I was urged by all the women to take my handsome fiancé some cider before you freeze solid as an icicle."

"They figured the southern boy isn't tough enough for this weather, is that it?" The ax blade chucked and bucked, and he had to pump the handle to loosen it from the deep cut in the trunk. "I can't hide my accent."

"I lied and said you were from Denver, which is where my former fiancé is from. No one said a thing about your drawl." She held out the steaming cup. "I think they really wanted to see us together. Look, they're watching."

"It hurts you to deceive your aunt this way, doesn't it?"

Her brow furrowed. "People marry for all different reasons. It doesn't have to be for love."

"Sensible. That's what I like about you." He took the cup from her, careful not to brush her fingers with his. Over the ringing *chunk-chunk* as Mayor Smythe took his turn at a tree, Luke sampled the steaming cider. "I'd forgotten how good this tastes."

"I'm glad you like it." Tiny russet curls had worked free of her hood and spilled in unruly abandon around her heart-shaped face. She was pink from the cold air and laughter, and haloed with falling snow. "Oh, I almost forgot. These are fresh from the fire. Mildred's first batch."

She tugged a folded cloth napkin from her cloak pocket. The gingham fabric fell open to reveal roasted chestnuts, so hot the steam rose in great white curls.

His mouth watered. "Why don't you give mine to Beth?"

"Aggie is already taking care of that." Molly gestured with the lift of her slim arm to where Beth and little Jessie Smythe sat side by side near the fire, munching away.

Snow clung to Beth's new yellow hood and cloak. She leaned close to Jessie and giggled at something the other girl said.

"She's made a new friend." Molly laid a cracked chestnut into the palm of his hand.

"Because of you." He felt the heat sear through the wool of his glove, and it was similar to the burn scorching the rest of him.

"Beth and Jessie share a desk. I couldn't help it. I thought the girls would suit. I might have to keep an eye on them, since they're getting along so well, but this is exactly what I wanted."

Molly was an angel, no doubt about it. The crown of snow clinging to her gray hood might well have been a halo. She'd saved them, given them her family and her future. She was sweetness and grace, like everything good in this world.

Then she tilted her head back to look at the sky. "It stopped snowing."

The position reminded him of last night. Her neck was extended, her head thrown back. His tongue remembered the forbidden spice of her mouth, the sweet silk of her skin. He couldn't forget the sight of her blouse gaping open and the warm weight of her breast filling his hand. Need blasted through him, but it was a need he couldn't satisfy.

So instead, he peeled the tender meat from inside the chestnut's shell. Surprise flashed across her face as he stepped close enough to see the bronzed threads in her hazel eyes and smell the faint scent of lilac in her hair.

"For you." Heart pounding, he placed the sweet morsel on her tongue, and the intimacy of the act left all his senses reeling.

CHAPTER TEN

S omething was wrong. Molly felt it the instant they circled the final corner toward town. Her stomach fluttered, and foreboding settled like a hard ball in her chest. Dusk had fallen, casting the streets in blue shadows.

Lights burned brightly from dozens of windows and gleamed on the snow, and this settlement tucked in the valley between the high peaks of the Rockies looked like it had been painted on an artist's canvas.

As the horses drew them down Front Street, she tried to pinpoint what was wrong. Children played on sleds on the side streets, their merry laughter ringing like happy bells. Women were hurrying home from the mercantile or butcher's to prepare the evening meal. Men hauled fuel or feed on huge sleds, or paced along the boardwalk, eager to finish the day's business and go home.

Nothing looked different. Nothing looked out of place. Not one thing.

Luke's arm against hers was steeled with tension. Did he sense it, too?

"Come have supper with us." Aggie leaned close, mischief twinkling in her voice. "I could use help with the decorations for the tree."

"Of course she'll come." Luke's hand closed over hers. "Right,

Molly?"

Anger speared through her, and this time she couldn't keep it in. "I don't need you to speak for me. I'm perfectly capable of doing that for myself."

"Still, I want you to spend time with Beth."

He was good-looking and powerful, and Molly didn't doubt that like any handsome man, he was used to having women obey him. He probably expected it of a woman about to be his wife.

Too bad for him he was dead wrong.

"I haven't decided what I'll do," she said quietly, so her voice wouldn't interrupt the last verse of "We Wish You A Merry Christmas" that rang in the air behind her. "I have the recital to plan."

"You can plan at Aggie's house."

"I intend to plan any darn place I want."

The sleigh squeaked to a stop in front of the community center. A light in the adjacent building shone in a long swatch across the dark boardwalk and into the street, illuminating the snap of a muscle in Luke's jaw and the fists of his powerful hands.

"I want you to spend more time with Beth," he ground out, not mean, but unbending, and then hopped off the sleigh with ease.

He held out his hand to aid her, but she hopped the short distance to the ground herself. She didn't look at him, but felt his displeasure as he swung Beth to the ground.

"Bye, Beth." Jessie Smythe waved as her mother led her down the boardwalk.

"Bye, Jessie." Beth shone with happiness, even though her face was peaked from the outing. She coughed into her fist.

"It's time to get you inside, missy." A line of concern creased Aggie's brow as she shot a questioning glance at Molly and took Beth by the arm. "Uncle Russell and your papa will see that our tree gets home safe and sound. Let's go make some hot chocolate while we wait for supper to heat."

"A big cup of hot chocolate?" Beth sounded uncertain.

"The biggest cup I have."

"Okay." Beth sighed, squaring her shoulders, as if giving up a part of her fight to keep women at a distance. "What are we gonna decorate the tree with?"

"You'll see. Molly, please come. I would love the help."

"I would like to, but—"

"Need to prove a point to him. I understand." Aggie gestured to where Luke stood in the shadows unchaining the cluster of trees from the back of a sled. "But this is your first Christmas without your parents and my first without my girls. I'm so lonesome for them, I could curl up and cry like a baby. Having you and Beth to make new memories with would be a gift. Please?"

"Now how am I going to say no to that?" Molly wrapped her aunt in a hug. She and Luke would talk later, but right now her aunt needed her. "Do I get a cup of hot chocolate, too?"

"I think I can arrange that."

"In a big cup?"

Aggie laughed.

The snow crunched beneath their boots as they started out. The men's voices as they were seeing to the trees and horses rumbled in the crisp, clear air. Beth twisted around, walking backward, searching anxiously for her father.

He would have to leave soon. Molly knew it. She figured Beth did, too.

When she looked over her shoulder, Molly's gaze was drawn to him like the moon to the earth. Dressed in black, he blended with the shadows, and even though she could hardly see him, her pulse surged through her veins, and she remembered the feel of his lips at her throat.

Her day had been filled with him, made better by him, and her heart ached with an emotion she didn't understand at all.

The door next to the community center opened, spilling a wide path of lamplight onto the dark boardwalk. Two men ambled out into the cold, strangers who looked rugged and mean. The light reflected off the revolvers holstered at their hips.

Bounty hunters. Her blood froze. Luke. Did he see them? And worse, could they see him? She wanted to warn him, but there was no way she could without drawing attention to him.

Instead, she grabbed Beth from Aggie and pulled the child in front of her skirts.

"Are those the bad people?" Beth asked in a whisper.

"I think so, so we have to hurry." Molly nudged the child toward the street corner.

"But what about Papa?" Beth grabbed Molly's skirts and held on. Her whisper broke with fear. "Are they gonna take my papa?"

"I hope not." Molly could feel Aggie's unspoken question like a dagger in her side. "We have to get you safe so your papa doesn't worry, OK?"

Beth sniffed. Molly hiked the child into her arms and was surprised when the girl clung to her and didn't let go. The shadows hid them from view, but the sound of steeled hooves on iced snow rang directly behind them.

Molly shielded Beth with her body as Aggie ducked through Mrs. Rutledge's shadowed front lawn. Heart thundering, Molly pressed Beth into Aggie's arms as soon as they'd rounded the corner of the house, then turned to peer through the tangled Oregon grape bush at the dark street.

A single horse and rider stopped in the middle of the road. It was one of the men who'd been in the sheriff's office, who looked from the top of his battered hat to the tip of his scuffed boots like the bounty hunters she'd seen before.

He scanned the street and yards, dark as night fell. A gaggle of boys broke out from between one of the houses, snowballs flying. The gunman wheeled his horse around and headed back to Front Street.

It was too late to save Luke, but she would protect his child. Molly followed Aggie through the alley and Mrs. Kemp's backyard, making certain no one followed.

Luke kept his head bowed so the brim of his Stetson would hide his face. The chain holding the base of the trees clattered free, snaking to the icy ground. He'd seen Molly take off with Beth, and he was grateful to her.

"Any trouble, Sheriff?" Russell stepped into the light of the open door.

Luke didn't take his gaze off the bounty hunters meeting at the edge of town. If they recognized him, they gave no sign of it.

"A fugitive loose, from the sound of it."

"Out of the territorial prison?" Mayor Smythe strode forward, not wanting to be left out. "Seems those escapees don't come this way, too busy heading due north for Canada."

"This one's coming up through Idaho. Was spotted in Twin Falls buying winter gear. Could have a little boy with him, I guess, from the sounds of it."

"A hostage situation?"

"No one knew for sure. The bounty hunters ran out of Wanted posters a few towns back. A killer named McKenna."

Luke's hands were shaking so badly, he didn't dare try to pick up the chain. The rattling alone would give him away. They were looking for a man and a boy. That was a stroke of luck.

He knew damn well up close no one was going to mistake Beth for a boy, but he'd bought her a boy's coat at a mercantile in Twin Falls because it was thicker and warmer than the little girls' coats. The manufacturers must have figured little girls belonged in the house and not in the high country.

Luke stood, stepping back into the shadows. He heard the mayor comment that it was a good thing no fugitive had passed through their town, and maybe they ought to swear in a few deputies to keep an eye out.

"We might not have any trouble at all," the sheriff answered. "I'm more worried about those gunmen in our town."

Luke felt the hair on the back of his neck prickle. Had the bounty hunters recognized him? Had his freedom come to an end?

"Are you going to tell me what's going on?" Aggie asked from the stove over the steaming milk. "That little girl won't talk to either one of us and won't do more than sit in the corner and shake. Is your Luke in some kind of trouble?"

Molly concentrated on slicing the bread in even slices. She wouldn't say a single word that was a lie to her aunt. Too bad she couldn't think of a way to answer.

"He introduced himself to Russell as Luke Jamison, but when I met him out at your ranch, he only gave me his first name." Aggie lifted the saucepan from the stove and filled three waiting mugs. She set the rest aside to stay warm. "Now, that makes a body wonder what's going on. If you need help, you know I would do anything I could."

"I know." Molly set the knife aside. "Beth needs this marriage. That's all I'm going to say."

"Fine." Aggie sighed and managed a small smile. "She sure had fun today. Opened up to us a little."

"I noticed." She took two mugs from the counter and stood shoulder to shoulder with her aunt. "You're right, you know. All I've ever wanted is a family to belong to."

159

"That almost got you into a bad marriage with that Albert fellow."

"I know. This situation is different."

"I trust that you're right." Aggie's touch to her cheek was like a mother's love.

And Molly didn't step away, didn't allow that old familiar uncomfortable feeling to settle around her heart. She'd found her family here in Evergreen, Montana, and she wasn't alone. Not anymore.

Beth jumped when Molly entered the parlor. The cat in the little girl's arms gave a startled *meow*, but caught in a tight grip the calico couldn't escape.

"Those bad men have my Pa." Beth's whisper came harsh with fear. "I'm never gonna see him again."

Silent tears rolled down pale cheeks.

"Uncle Russell will take care of him the best he can." Molly held up the mug. "It's Aunt Aggie's biggest cup."

"My tummy hurts. I don't want it now."

"I'm worried, but hot chocolate help makes worries go away. See? I have a cup, too."

Beth nodded and released the cat. Mrs. Whiskers remained, her *purr* raspy and contented, as the little girl took the big mug in both hands. She sipped.

"Feel better?"

"A little."

As good as hot chocolate was, it couldn't take away every worry.

"You're gonna take care of me if my papa doesn't come back." A sob racked Beth's small frame. "Right?"

"That's what I promised your father." Molly's heart nearly broke with affection. "Is that all right with you?"

A small nod. "No."

Footsteps tapped on the polished wood behind her. "Here comes Russell and Luke with our Christmas tree."

"Luke? Are you sure?"

"Looks like him." Aggie pushed open a corner of the heavy damask drape. The lit room reflected back at them as Molly joined her, squinting through the glare.

She recognized Russell's tall, lanky shape and Luke's wide-shouldered frame. Relief swept through her, leaving her shaking.

Aggie squinted again, then shook her head. "Hope they brought the right tree. Beth, dear, run to the front door. Hurry."

The little girl threw open the door with a bang. "Papa? Oh, Papa."

"Good to see you, darlin'," a familiar voice rang through the night. "Stand back now, so we can get this tree through the door."

It was Luke. Molly's heart soared at the sight of him holding his half of the six-foot spruce. He carried it easily in one hand, while poor Uncle Russell was panting and red in the face.

"It's good to see you, Molly." Luke's gaze pinned hers with an odd steadiness, like both light and dark, parting and greeting, and she understood.

The bounty hunters hadn't spied him, but that didn't mean he was out of danger.

"Bring that right over here." Aggie led the way to the already cleared space in front of the window. "Wait, let me pull the stand into place."

Cold air breezed into the house, carrying the crisp, homey scent of pine. Boughs rustled, and boots tromped across the floor. Molly shivered and closed the door against the night. He was safe now, and that's what mattered most.

She heard a rustle at her side and felt a small hand creep into her own and hold on tight.

"That's it, Luke." Aggie bustled around, the supervisor in charge of the tree raising. "A little to the right."

"Here it goes." He straightened, and the beautiful spruce tipped into place with a rustle of its majestic boughs. As soon as he was done, Beth raced to him and held him so tight around the knees that he couldn't move.

Molly took a step forward, but she stopped as Luke managed to sweep his daughter into his arms and cradle her close. He kissed her brow, so infinitely tender. Tears filled Molly's eyes, and she turned away.

She couldn't love this man. She *wouldn't* love this man. But she knew it was too late.

Beth clung to Luke through supper, and his stomach was coiled so tight he couldn't enjoy Aggie's roast beef. The flavorful food turned to sand on his tongue. He couldn't get what happened out of his head.

Molly leaned close when Russell and Aggie began a playful argument about another helping of meat and gravy.

"Jamison." Her breath fanned across his cheek like the sweet kiss of winter sunshine. "You could have told me."

"I should have told you. I've been a tad distracted." He watched as Aggie rose to refill the meat platter. "It was my mother's maiden name."

"What happened with the bounty hunters?"

"I'll tell you later." He cut his fork through a soft, mushy potato and tried not to look at her.

He remembered how she'd felt snug in his arms as the sleigh swayed back and forth over the uneven ground. With the wind tousling his hair and the landscape as peaceful as heaven's grace, he'd felt like a man. One good enough for a woman like Molly.

'Course it had only been wishful thinking, but still, the day would never be forgotten.

When Russell was finished with his second helping, Aggie decided to leave the dishes and led the way to the parlor. She was a grandmotherly woman, and Luke liked the way she fussed over Beth, making sure the child had gotten enough to eat.

Molly remained silent, and he remembered the heat of her question against his skin, the fear in her eyes when he'd shown up with the Christmas tree, and her anger before that. Whenever her gaze met his, he could read the question in her eyes as plain as day—what happened?—but other questions were not as obvious, and he couldn't guess at them.

He knelt to add fuel to the fire; the scent of dry cedar and the texture of the wood against his fingers seemed real. This world where people were friendly on the street and where strangers invited a man and his child into their home, he knew it wasn't real and he couldn't relax. Couldn't believe in this dream. Because that's all it was for him—a dream.

"Perfect," Aggie praised as she studied the well-proportioned spruce. "My, this is the most beautiful tree we've had yet."

" 'Course we had our pick this year." Russell swiped off his cap. "It was good of the Wilsons to donate trees from their ranch. That way the townsfolk won't go cutting down any owned by the town for beautification purposes."

"It's the most beautiful tree ever," Beth whispered.

Luke softened at the sight of his daughter. This dream world felt foreign to her, too, after their hardships.

"We've never had a Christmas tree before, have we, darlin'?"

"Never, ever."

"Looks like things are about to change."

She almost grinned, and the ice around his heart broke into a thousand tiny pieces of grief and happiness. Something settled on his arm—Molly's hand.

"No one does Christmas like Aunt Aggie. Beth, you're in for a real treat."

Beth's brow twisted in thought as she stood frozen in the middle of the parlor—caught between wanting to hold on to him and being drawn by the beauty of her new life.

Aggie held out a small box filled with tissue paper, her face soft with kindness. "Sweetheart, come see what I have. Molly, be a dear and bring in the bowls of popcorn I made today. They're in the pantry."

"Sure." She crossed the room and drew his gaze.

Desire for her sluiced over his skin like a spring rain. She returned with each arm crooked around a bowl heaping with pristine white kernels. Every step she took made the blood throb in his veins. Every breath she took made her shapely bosom rise and fall. She moved through him like wind through fog, leaving only the clear light of day.

Beth oohed as she lifted a delicate glass snowflake from the bed of tissue paper. The lamplight caught the crystal and cut the light into a thousand rainbows that sparkled and danced through the room.

"Help me get all these unwrapped, hon," Aggie suggested and instructed Beth to lay the ornament on the coffee table.

Molly handed her uncle one popcorn bowl before curling up on a rocking chair with the other. "Luke, you look overwhelmed by all this. I know just how you feel. When I was small, we lived near Aunt Aggie, and she would invite us over for Christmas Eve."

"Still intend to," Aggie added with a determined gleam.

"It was a shock coming from my mother's house." Molly pulled a spool of thread from her pocket and uncoiled an arm's length. "It was like walking into a dream."

"So you do know how it feels."

Her lush mouth opened, but no words came. Her eyes filled and burned like a new flame, and for the life of him he wanted her in his arms, in his bed, to bury himself in this angel-woman.

"That mother of Molly's has a dried up raisin for a heart; that's why she hates Christmas." Aggie helped Beth set the last ornament onto the table, ready for placement on the tree. "She's my sister, so I can talk about her like that."

"It's true. Ma doesn't like Christmas." Molly threaded a needle with a flick of her wrist and knotted the thread. "It was like any other day."

"That's why Molly's lacking in the Christmas spirit," Aggie added from two rooms away.

"I am not," Molly protested. "Look who has too much."

"Nonsense. There can never be too much Christmas spirit. Russell, give me that bowl. I'll show Beth how to make a popcorn string if you want to get out your fiddle. I think we need some Christmas cheer in this room."

"Christmas carols would be just the thing," Russell agreed, his rocking chair creaking as he climbed to his feet.

"Here, give this a try." Molly's fingers pressed against Luke's, giving him a needle and thread and pushing the popcorn bowl between them.

"Angel, I know I'm going to fail at this before I even try."

"Do it like this." Her warm silk fingers curled around his hand, holding the needle high. She pressed a fragile piece of popped corn onto the sharp edge and eased it down. "That simple."

In his experience, nothing was ever that simple. Not one thing. Especially the way he felt when he looked at her. She could tie him up in knots if he let her. Make him forget what he'd been and where. Make him believe in a life like he used to have once and thought was gone forever.

Molly began working her own string, and across the room Beth cuddled with Aggie on the couch. Woman and girl leaned over their needles together, the old teaching the young. Beth tried hard to string the popcorn, her brow furrowed and her bottom lip puffed out in concentration.

Luke took a white corn from Molly's bowl and tapped it onto the tip of his needle. The fragile piece of fluff crumbled into pieces in his hands.

The fire crackled, and the sweet homey scent of pine filled the air. Russell plucked his fiddle strings, tuning them.

Molly leaned close to Luke, breathing in his pine and winter scent and noticing the day's growth on his jaw.

"Tell me the bounty hunters aren't a problem," she whispered.

"They didn't see me, and the sheriff told them that he didn't know of a stranger passing through his town. They rode out of town. Headed up the tracks toward Liberty. I couldn't ride after them to be certain, but those kind of men are aggressive. If they knew I was here, they would have come after me."

She trusted him. If Luke said the bounty hunters were gone, she believed him.

Russell finished with his tuning and the sweet verse of "Silent Night" filled the cozy parlor.

"It was like in the story book." Beth snuggled beneath the colorful handmade quilt in Aggie's spare room. "Are we gonna have a real Christmas, Pa? Like in the story Molly read to me?"

He remembered the tale of *A Visit From St. Nicholas* filled with sugarplum wishes and presents under a shimmering tree. "Christmas Day is a while away yet, and you know about the bad men who are following me."

"Yeah." Beth's arms curled around her pillow. There was no doll or stuffed animal to hold for comfort, and he'd have to put a few of those under the Christmas tree.

"I want the story."

"You want me to read to you, darlin'?"

"No. I want to be *in* the story."

"I see." Tucked safe in bed, presents under the tree, a family together for Christmas. "Molly is going to give that to you. Christmas is coming soon, and look how Aggie's already decorating not just her house, but the town."

"The whole town?"

"She's in charge of the Christmas committee. I hear there's going to be a town tree lit up for a big Christmas party. Rumor has it Santa himself will be stopping by."

"Papa?" Beth rubbed her eye with her fist. "Santa never came at the orphanage. Mrs. Fines said that's because Santa doesn't exist. It's a story, not real."

His cousin's greed had robbed Beth of a part of her childhood Luke knew he could never return to her. He remembered how she'd looked the day he'd stolen her—so thin, her shoulder blades poking through the back of the flour-sack dress, trudging in a line with the other children, hopeless and broken.

"I won't lie to you." He brushed those dark ringlet curls off her brow, like fine silk against his palm. "In a way, Santa Claus is a story. It makes for a pretty fine one, don't you think?"

Beth nodded, her eyes dark and clouded.

"But in another way, the story of Santa Claus is true." He remembered how his mother had explained it to him, a gentle country woman with wisdom and heart, and the remembering warmed the frozen places inside. "It's the spirit of Santa Claus that's true. Or it can be true, if we believe it. And if we believe it hard enough, then maybe we can make the world into a place where little children won't be forgotten, even if it's just one day out of the year."

Beth's brow wrinkled.

Maybe she was too young, but it had been a long time since he'd remembered his mother's words and felt them in his heart.

A board creaked in the hallway behind him. He turned and saw tears in Molly's eyes.

"Y ou don't have to see me home," she told him at the kitchen door, where the soft lamplight gleamed like bronze in her russet curls.

How he ached to wind his fingers in those locks again, to curl his hand around her nape and never let go. "It's dark and a long way to your land. I ∫ see you there safely."

"Oh, back to thinking you have the right to boss me around, I see." She took a jaunty step back so he couldn't help her with her cloak, and shrugged into the garment all on her own. "Aggie, it was a wonderful evening. Your tree is going to be the prettiest in town."

"I sure hope so." Aggie beamed as she covered up a plate of cookies. "Don't forget the committee meeting tomorrow at noon."

"How could I?" Molly thanked her aunt and tucked the basket under her arm. She gave Luke a scowl when he beat her to the door and turned the brass knob before she could grab for it.

A little thrill of victory rolled through him as he snared his jacket off the coat tree. "I won't be long."

"I'll keep an eye on our girl," Aggie called, then closed the door behind them.

The frigid air breezed through his layers of clothing, and he started to shiver. Aggie waved good-bye, snug and warm behind the glass window, limned with the golden glow of lamplight. Molly waved back, then tromped through the snow with a practiced gait. He took off after her, heading toward the stable where Russell had brought her mare over from the livery.

"I can saddle my own horse," she told him as she tugged on the stable door. It didn't budge.

He curled his fingers around the edge of wood and pulled against the small drift of impeding snow. The door opened and she slipped past him. She didn't say thank you.

"I never said you couldn't saddle your horse." He grabbed two blankets and shook them out. "But I'm going to be your husband and it's my job."

"*Your* job." Molly stole one of the blankets from him and draped it over her palomino's withers. "This isn't a real marriage, in case you've forgotten."

"That would be hard to do. I know what a marriage should be." The black sidestepped at the sight of the blanket, and he soothed the gelding with a few low words.

"You loved your wife."

"Yes, I surely did. She was my high-school sweet-heart." The pain of her loss had vanished, like a candle burned to a stub. The memory was now just a faint impression after the hardship of the last year that had taken all the light from his world. "It feels like a lifetime ago; our love was a sweet one, two kids in love."

A vast sense of loss stretched inside him, and the sweet flame of his first love was overshadowed by his feelings for this fiery angel of a woman, a woman he was deter-mined to honor. "I don't care what you say, Molly. I'm saddling your horse."

He hefted the sidesaddle from the sawhorse, and to his surprise she didn't protest. Nor would she look at him as he sidled up close and eased the leather contraption down on the well-smoothed blanket. He bent to buckle and pull tight the cinch.

"I was never sure love really existed," she confessed when he disappeared into the shadows. "But I see it between Aggie and Russell, and I realize that it's rare. There are marriages based on duty and power where there is no real love at all."

"But it doesn't have to be that way." He emerged from the shadows carrying a saddle hooked on one shoulder. "Ours, for instance, will be very happy."

"And brief. You're leaving."

"Well, there's that." He turned his back to her as he lowered the saddle onto the impatient gelding.

She buckled the bridle and led her mare toward the door. "I suppose there will be more bounty hunters?"

He tugged hard on the cinch, then pulled the gelding into the aisle and tugged again. "Being your beau has sheltered me better than I'd hoped. The sheriff didn't consider me a stranger in town, but a friend of the Grants."

"I'm glad." She headed outside and waited for him to join her in the yard. The frigid temperatures felt like spring thaw when she saw him amble toward her. The cut of his profile and the tilt of his hat were familiar now and cherished.

She waited until they'd mounted and were on the road out of town. "I heard what Beth said, about wanting to be in the Christmas story."

"She wants a dream. Who doesn't?"

"She wants you to stay for Christmas."

"She wants me to stay, period." The darkness seemed to swallow him until he was only a shadow riding beside her. "It's impossible."

"If the bounty hunters rode on, maybe you're safe."

"Maybe I'm just lucky. A man can't count on luck."

"It's better than nothing."

"True." He fell silent, and the night felt huge.

The *clomp* of hooves on the crusted snow, the call of a coyote in the forest, the hush of winter soothed her. The snow gleamed like onyx and silver. The wind smelled of ice and evergreens.

Slowly, her knotted stomach eased. "Before we get married, we need to talk, Mr. *Jamison*."

"I was afraid of that."

"When Aunt Aggie invited me to supper, you answered for me."

"Beth needed you to stay."

"You tried dishing up my plate at the table."

"Just wanted to take care of you."

"You saddled my horse when I was perfectly capable."

He chuckled. "All right, I give. I'll be rude to you from now on. Let you trip in mud puddles and let doors slam in your face when I don't hold them for you."

"That's not what I mean." She remembered all the ways he'd tried to make things right—protecting her, cleaning the smoke damage from her parlor, repairing her door, helping the neighbors, making her look like a woman loved and cherished.

"I just want you to treat me like a grown woman." She led the way off the road toward her dark house tucked amid the silent pines and firs. "You should have told me about your made-up last name."

"Hey, I already apologized for that one, angel." A smile shone in his voice. "Can't try me twice for the same crime in this country."

"Then don't commit a second offense and I'll be lenient."

"I'll try to behave." His laughter rumbled like winter thunder.

Lady bounded down the drive, barking a welcome. It was dark and it was late, and the poor hound acted as if she'd been disowned and abandoned.

"I can rub down your mare and feed her, if you want to look after your dog." He stared out at the night and the dark line of trees, studying the pristine snow marked only by Lady's paws. "Notice I'm offering, not assuming."

"You're a quick learner. I just might marry you after all."

"Lucky me." His saddle creaked. "I take it you're going to stable your own mare?"

Being alone with him wasn't wise, and yet here she was alone with him, her foolish heart, and the memory of his kiss. "Since you asked so politely, I'll let you do it."

"Gee, thanks." His gloved hands took the reins from her. He was so close she could feel his heat.

Her blood zinged in response.

"We've set a wedding day, but I suppose you know that." He cleared his throat, as if he had more on his mind but couldn't find the words. "I've heard the rumor we're getting married on Christmas Eve, but I had something sooner in mind."

"Rumors can be so untrue."

His strong hand cupped the side of her face with infinite tenderness. "Did you see how happy Beth was, helping Aggie decorate the tree?"

"It was hard to miss. She seemed like a different child, all smiles and laughter."

"That was the child I remember. You've had a healing effect on us. I didn't think it was possible, but I'm almost seeing the man I used to be."

How sad he sounded, and his touch became a caress so tender, it brought tears to her eyes. His mouth slanted over hers, and in the space between one heartbeat and the next, she rose up in her stirrups to bring her lips to his. She might have started the kiss, but his hand curled around her nape and held her to him.

He tasted crisp and intriguing like the night, like spice and man and something thrilling she couldn't name, but it spiraled through her blood, spilled into her muscles, and left her shaking, weak. His mouth devoured her, his lips both possessive and giving at the same time. When she opened to the velvet heat of his tongue, he hauled her off her saddle with the strength of one arm and settled her on his lap.

He tugged at her scarf, exposing her chin and throat to the brush of his lips. "I noticed kissing wasn't on the list of offenses you just read to me."

"No, I guess it slipped my mind." She melted as his hand caressed the length of her arm. Even through bulky layers of flannel and wool, her skin flamed as if they were skin to skin.

"I know I shouldn't be doing this." He popped open two of her cloak buttons and he tore off his glove with his teeth, then folded it into his jacket pocket. His hand at her nape didn't relent, holding her against his chest.

The slow gait of the horse rocked them together, and she could feel the thick ridge of his arousal hard against her hip. Excitement spiraled through her with such force, she felt as if she were melting from the inside out.

More of her buttons gave way, and frosty air skidded across her sensitized skin. Her flesh rose in tiny goose bumps, and she could feel her nipples tighten into hard points.

Luke's brow met hers, and they were eye to eye, breaths mingling. The heat of his palms chased away every goose bump. Her nipples remained taut and pebbled as he cupped her and weighted her.

Pleasure fanned through her breasts, and as he began to knead and caress, it melted into a liquid heat. She caught his mouth again, her kiss as urgent as his caress. His fingers plucked and stroked her breasts until she cried out.

Then he chuckled and his mouth left hers to settle where his fingers had been. The cold air and his hot mouth closed over her nipple, coaxing a sensation sharp like pain but luscious like pleasure. She wrapped her hand around his nape and held him there.

The rocking stopped—the horse had reached the house. Lady scratched at the door. Molly didn't want this pleasure to end, but he moved away, and cold air rushed across her damp, sensitive nipples. Her breath rose in great hot clouds as Luke straightened and fastened her buttons.

She was hot and trembling everywhere, and the very center of her felt hot and expectant. And he was stopping?

Then he claimed her mouth with his. His kiss was deep and slow, sweet and satisfying. She smiled when he pulled away and in the shadows it was too dark to read what he tried to hide as he tipped his Stetson back into place.

But she could feel it in his heart. It beat beneath her hand as crazily as her own. His breath came fast and shallow, and he groaned when she shifted. He was iron-hard.

He swept her to the ground easily with the strength in one arm, and even though her feet contacted earth, she swore she was floating.

"You, my lady, are a dream." His lips brushed her knuckles. "My very own dream."

He tipped his hat and rode away toward the shadowed stable.

How in the world was she going to keep from falling any more in love with him?

CHAPTER ELEVEN

"Afternoon, Jamison."

"Drew." Luke greeted him with a nod. "Good-looking window display you got there."

"Thanks. I'm tryin' to get into the Christmas spirit."

A guffaw rose from the center of the store, where a handful of old men sat around a red-hot potbellied stove. "Sure, Drew. You're just tryin' to raise profits."

"Then you'd better fill up those shelves. They're gettin' too damn empty."

"Tell that to the railroad company."

The bantering continued, the old men discussing the trains that were still stuck on the other side of Walker Pass and the fool Easterners who were responsible and how the shelves were picked over and that didn't bode well for winter.

Luke found what he was looking for in the back near the yard goods. Drew had a fairly good toy selection, considering. He chose Beth's gifts with care and tried not to give in to the suffocating sadness that threatened to claim him. Even if he couldn't be with his daughter for Christmas, she would have beautiful presents from her pa under the tree.

Molly wasn't so easy to shop for.

"Heard you've got a wedding coming up tomorrow." At the counter, Drew added up the purchases. "Now my sweetheart's

172

thinkin' we should tie the knot, too. Talkin' on about how romantic the two of you are and some such."

"That's me, Mr. Romance." Luke gestured at the bowl of peppermint candy. "Give me half a pound of those."

"Sure thing."

Luke took some good-natured ribbing from the old men jawing around the stove before he paid for his purchases. He'd envisioned a quick and private ceremony, but Molly wanted time to find a new dress, and in a town this small, keeping the news private was proving impossible.

He stepped out onto the covered boardwalk and into a thick layer of new snow, driven by a mean wind. As much as he missed the Texas sunshine, he wouldn't complain about the weather. The heavy storms had become nearly continuous, and while some bounty hunters would travel in this weather, the passes remained closed, and the train couldn't run. He wouldn't get safer than that.

But he still scouted the outskirts of town for danger every day.

"If it isn't the groom." Mayor Smythe bypassed a patch of ice on the boardwalk. "Got cold feet?"

Luke chuckled, liking the easygoing family man who ran the tailor shop by day. "This is the second time around for me, so I know what to expect."

"Ignorance is the only reason we marry the first time. The second time I imagine you're just numb." Smythe's eyes laughed.

"Yeah, it looks like you're a man suffering with that pretty wife and those children of yours."

"I try to put up a good front." The mayor had the look of a contented man. "I reckon you'll wind up just as miserable as me."

"I'm counting on it." Luke's chest tightened, for his words were true even as he lied. He stumbled and nearly slid on the ice as he circled around his new vehicle.

"Got yourself a new sleigh." Smythe hopped off the boardwalk.

"Figured it would be easier for Molly to take Beth to school." He lowered his packages to the floor of the new sleigh and covered them with a corner of the fur lap robe. The mayor was heading over to the school, too, to pick up his daughter, so they walked together.

Over the past few days, the town had transformed. Garlands of pine and holly wrapped around banisters and awning posts. Christmas displays gleamed in the merchant's windows and wreaths on their front doors. Even the schoolhouse looked cheerful with Molly's decorating touches.

The front door slammed open, and children stampeded down the front steps, their noisy clatter and shrill shouts shattering the peaceful afternoon. His chest swelled with pride when he saw his daughter hopping down the steps beside Jessie Smythe. The two where giggling and chatting. Beth looked happy, and her new blue dress and cloak were as nice as any other child's.

And he owed it all to Molly. She gave him a small wave through the window and then disappeared from his sight. Sensation swept through him like sun across snow, glittering and sparkling, and he felt alive, the way a man should.

"Papa!" Beth ran up to him, and he held her tight.

The pinecone candleholder that Beth made in school sat in the place of honor in the center of the supper table. Molly had found a pretty red candle in Aggie's junk drawer and lit it. The flame flickered merrily, and everyone complimented Beth, but she'd hardly said a word or touched the food on her plate.

She wandered upstairs while Molly and Aggie did the dishes and discussed the arrangements for the wedding tomorrow. Russell slipped outside to smoke his pipe, so Luke seized the opportunity and crept upstairs.

He found her sitting on her bed, holding the old calico cat on her lap. The animal's rusty *purr* filled the room as Beth rubbed her fingers across the top of the feline's head.

"I guess you know things are going to change come tomorrow." He sat on the soft feather mattress, and the ropes squeaked in protest.

Beth stiffened. "I know."

"This is what we talked about all the way from Texas."

"I know."

He wasn't getting anywhere. Beth's chin lifted stubbornly, and she looked so bleak; all the happiness he'd seen in her today when he'd picked her up from school had vanished. "I found a new mother for you, just like I promised."

"I don't like her."

"Now I know that's a lie."

"I don't *want* to like her." Beth's bottom lip thrust out. "I *won't* like her."

Her defiance felt as impenetrable as stone. Luke stood and paced to the window. "We've run clean out of other choices, darlin'."

"I don't want you to go, Papa."

"Disliking Molly isn't going to make me stay."

"You can't leave me if I don't got a new mother." Beth's voice broke with tears. "I don't ever want a new mother."

"Oh, Beth." He crossed the room in three strides, and she was in his lap, cat and all.

"I'll be real good." She buried her face against his chest. "I promise. I won't make any trouble. I'll be real quiet."

A sharp pain axed through his chest, and he hung on to her and to his resolve. "Molly's going to love you from now on."

"No, Papa."

"You have to make me some promises. Some really important ones."

"I wanna go with you, Papa. I won't cry if I get c-cold." Her reed-thin body quaked with a harsh sob.

He pressed kisses into her sweet-smelling hair. "You have to promise to treat Molly as if she's your real mother. You have to obey her. You have to love her."

"Noooo," Beth broke down, shaking so hard it nearly tore him apart.

"You have to do this for me, Beth. Remember what I'm telling you." He kissed her again, breathing in her little-girl scent, sweet like cookies, warm like sunshine. "I need you to be a grown up girl from now on. Will you do those things for me?"

"No." Her fingers curled into the fabric of his shirt, holding on tight. "I love you, Papa."

"I love you too, darlin'." How he loved her. He felt ready to break into a hundred-thousand irrevocable pieces, and he would the minute he rode away into those mountains.

He heard a shuffling sound and the softest rustle of fabric. Was Molly out there, heading back down the hallway to give them privacy? But his heart stopped when Aggie walked into the room, the set of her jaw and the measuring squint to her eyes telling him exactly what she'd heard.

"Here, let me take her. I'll get her calmed down and put to sleep. It's early, but it's been a big day." Aggie lifted both the wretched little girl and the cat from his arms.

He felt empty, just like that.

Tomorrow was the last day on earth he'd ever get to spend with his daughter.

Christmas was coming. She had Aggie to fuss over her, Russell to protect her, and Molly to give her a whole new life.

Beth was going to prosper here. And it was time he start letting that happen. He rose and left the room. He didn't look over his shoulder; he just kept walking.

Molly heard the creak of the loose board on the stairs and the steady rhythm of Luke's gait. She swiped at her tears. "Before you ask, yes, I heard what she said. About not wanting me."

His step faltered. "She didn't mean that."

"I know what she meant."

"She doesn't want me to leave her, that's all."

"I know." She watched the candles flicker on the Christmas tree and felt so empty inside. "I told you I wouldn't marry you unless Beth accepts me."

"She'll accept you just fine after I leave." His hands came around her shoulders. "Trust me."

"I can't."

"Try." His hands locked around her waist, holding her against him, his chest to her back, as solid as tempered steel.

She closed her eyes and leaned against him. His strength held her up, met her inch to inch from her nape all the way to her ankles. All she could feel was him...and the ache in her heart. "I don't want her spending the rest of her childhood gazing out my windows staring off at the mountains, wishing you'd come back to her."

"She knows how it is."

"She's six years old. She only knows how she feels."

"I wish things could be different, too." His regret rumbled in his chest, passing into her like a cold wind. "The only real question is: do you think you can love Beth anyway?"

"Absolutely."

He held her and pressed kisses along her throat. "She might be gazing out the window for a long while; she's only a child, but I know you'll be there comforting her. I know she'll grow up to be a beautiful women in the light of your love."

Tears filled her eyes and made her throat hurt. Big, horrible, wonderful feelings flickered to life in her heart. This love she felt for Luke became sharp and hurting and too huge to bear, and yet left her changed, left her filled.

"I need you to marry me, Molly." He kissed her with endless tenderness. "I want *you* to marry me."

With those words, Luke won every last piece of her heart.

He couldn't sleep. Russell had insisted on taking Molly home tonight, and sensing the older man's disapproval, Luke wondered what Aggie had told him. He would ask, but Aggie had gone to bed, and Luke wasn't about to knock on her door.

Beth had cried herself to sleep. Hell, he just might tonight, too. The wind had kicked up, threatening to turn into a fullfledged blizzard at any moment, and the last thing Luke needed was to prolong his stay.

He raided Aggie's Christmas-cookie stash and took his handful of macaroons and gingerbread men into the dark parlor. The tree, candles snuffed, stood like a silent observer, arms out, holding strings of popcorn and cranberries, ribbons and bows, and those expensive glass ornaments.

Presents were already under the tree, gifts from Aggie and Russell to each other, he figured. He had a few more to add before he left. Gifts for these kind people who felt like family.

Tomorrow he would marry Molly. And the next morning he'd arranged with Russell to head out early to go hunting. It would be easy to make sure they became separated, and then it would only be a matter of losing himself in the mountains.

With the way it was snowing, people would just think he'd become disoriented. What else would they think? He'd accepted Russell's job offer, so he had employment, his child, and a lovely new bride to live for. What man would ride away from paradise?

Only one who didn't deserve it.

The wind gusted, blasting against the windowpanes hard enough to lightly jostle the tree. The ornaments jingled; the boughs rustled. Luke thought of the story he'd told Beth about Santa Claus.

The spirit of giving—of generosity, of love. He'd certainly walked into that when he'd stumbled in to this town. So weary of heart and old of soul he didn't think he could believe in anything again. But he was wrong.

The house felt so empty. Molly tied the sash on her housecoat and listened to her movements echo in the bedroom. When she'd first come here, she'd cherished her solitude. Now, that solitude felt like a dark place in need of light.

She'd felt this way ever since Luke and Beth had moved in with Aggie.

She shuffled through the dark parlor, Lady trailing. A covered plate of Aggie's cookies sat on the corner of the kitchen counter, and she helped herself to a few. Listening to the hush of her nightgown and the pad of her feet so loud in the stillness, made her feel even more alone.

Maybe she was just anticipating tomorrow night. Her heart thumped at that, and she pulled out a dining room chair and folded herself into it. Lady sat at her feet, politely begging.

"Soon you'll have Beth to feed you everything off her plate." Molly laid the cookies on the edge of the table, keeping one to break apart. "What a lucky dog you're going to be."

Lady accepted the edge of the macaroon neatly and didn't bother to swallow, already begging for another bite.

Molly broke off a chunk of the cookie and popped it into her own mouth. The sweetness teased her tongue, but as good as it was, it fell far short compared to Luke's kisses.

Maybe he'll kiss me like that again. She hugged the thought close. She didn't know what Luke had in mind to do on their marriage night. He'd been both gentlemanly and ungentlemanly in his conduct to her.

She remembered how he'd unbuttoned her bodice twice now and created a pleasure in her breasts she would never have imagined existed—not in a hundred years.

I want you, he'd said earlier tonight when they were alone in Aggie's parlor, his arms around her, his kiss sweet and spicy on her lips. He wanted her.

She hugged that thought close and wished, how she wished he could be her husband for real.

Morning dawned, and for Luke it had been a sleepless night. By the time he finally gave up the struggle and climbed out of bed, the house was nearly empty. Russell was out on a mill emergency, Aggie's note said, and she'd gone to pick up Molly and bring her into town.

He heard the faint tap of Beth moving around in her room upstairs, getting ready to face the day. This would be their last day together. Beth would stay with Aggie tonight—on the older woman's twinkling-eyed insistence—and he'd be gone the next morning.

His guts clenched like he'd been punched, and he felt physically sick. How was he going to find the strength to walk away from his child forever?

Luke pulled out a chair and sat before his legs gave out. He'd worked in a quarry for sixteen-hour days beneath the hot brutal sun. The first week had been the worst. By the end of the workday, he'd been nauseous with dehydration and shaking with exhaustion. His hand and knees had sluiced blood, and his back hurt so much every time he took a step that lightning bolts of pain streaked down both legs.

Gradually, he'd gotten used to working that hard, and in the end, it hadn't bothered him. But still, that pain and exhaustion was nothing compared to the hard ball of grief ready to rip through his entire being right now.

He was going to have to leave Beth.

It's a good thing, he tried to tell himself. *She'll have a much better life than I could give her on the run.*

And some of his pain eased a bit, but only a bit.

Finally, he found the gumption to stand and discovered that Aggie, efficient as usual, had left a platter heaped with food in the warming oven. Since it was nearly eight o'clock, he filled two plates and carried them up to Beth's room. He found her staring out the window, dressed in a blue-checkered dress that made her look as cute as a button. Her long black hair fell down her back, tangled from sleep.

"Maybe a great big blizzard will come." She swiped loose curls from her pixie face with the flat of one hand. "Then there can't be the wedding."

"Well, that could happen, I guess." He eased into the room and set the plates on one end of the bed. "But maybe we'll be able to make it the few blocks to the churchyard."

"But I want the blizzard."

He heard what she didn't say. "Yeah, me, too."

He heard the back door open downstairs, and women's voices murmured through the floorboards. Beth stiffened and looked like her whole world was about to end.

But it was really just beginning.

He firmly believed that. He had to, or he couldn't go on. He rescued a plate from the bed and invited her to sit down with him. She sighed and dragged her feet across the floor.

They ate together, side by side, just like they'd done on the trail for the last two months. But this time there was nothing to say but good-bye, and neither of them seemed ready for that.

So they ate in silence.

The knock on the door didn't sound like Aggie's knock. Molly whirled around and pulled her dress off the bed to cover herself with. Sure enough, Luke filled the doorway, and his hungry-looking eyes didn't miss her bare shoulders or the rise of her cleavage.

"Beth's helping Aggie pick out a dress." He stepped into the room and shut the door. "I guess there was a missing button crisis and another dress had to be chosen. That's why she isn't here yet."

"And so you took the liberty of trying to see me in my underwear."

"I'm a tricky devil." He winked and lifted the garment out of her hands.

She watched his pupils dilate. The exposed skin along her shoulders, arms, and the tops of her breasts felt charged. Her nipples tightened painfully, anticipating. Remembering. "I'm supposed to be changing into my wedding dress. Since we're to be married in about an hour, I figured I'd better start getting ready."

"I like this better." His hot finger traced the curve of her shoulder.

"Yes, but I'd get cold this time of year."

"Still, the view is something to behold." That clever finger glided across the top curves of her breasts.

Her entire body burned. "My aunt is going to come in here any minute."

"I know." He dipped lower and their lips brushed. Just once. "I'm trying to be a good boy."

"You mean you're capable of it?" She laughed as his hand skimmed down her back and settled at her hip. "This is only a pretend marriage."

"We don't have to pretend completely." His mouth touched hers and claimed her. Hot, wet, deep.

Desire curled through her in delicious spirals. She felt as if her whole body would melt right there.

"I just wanted to make sure we're still on, that you haven't changed your mind about this." His mouth brushed hers, half kiss, half talk. "Considering everything I'm costing you, I want you to be sure."

Even though he'd been teasing her earlier, she could feel his sadness, feel his need. "Not only do I want to marry you, I'm going to."

The gratitude in his eyes couldn't be mistaken. But it was gratitude. He liked her, he lusted after her, and heaven knew she loved him far too much for her own good.

The door snapped open.

"You scoundrel." Aggie stormed into the room, skirts flaring, mouth pursed, and eyes laughing. "What do you think you're doing accosting my niece in my very own home? You'll have time enough for that sort of thing after the ceremony. Now, get downstairs."

Luke chuckled and shook his head. "Shoot, I was just trying to sample the merchandise and you know it."

"Not in my house. This is a decent, proper home."

"Sure, that's why Russell's always whistling in the morning." Luke ducked out the door before she could swat him.

"That man." Aggie's eyes sparked as she closed the door. "You'll have to keep a tight rein on that one, mark my words. He's a handsome devil, and he knows it."

"I plan to try my best to stay in charge of him, but he's awfully hard to resist."

"My, I can't believe you've managed it so far." Aggie tugged open the wardrobe door.

Molly blushed, and she didn't know what to say.

"I might not believe it if I didn't know better, but I wouldn't take you for the same serious young woman who moved to town five months ago. And now you're about to discover the good part of life."

Molly had to hope—this wasn't a real marriage, but could it be a real love?

"It's comin' down pretty darn hard," Russell observed as he knocked a new layer of snow from his hat brim—the third time in a block. "It's not too late to change your plans. Heaven knows Reverend Thayer is a reasonable man. I'm sure he'd be happy to open the doors of the church."

Molly tipped back her head to get a good look at the sky. Thick, cold flakes landed on her face and in one eye. It tumbled fast and furious, so that she had to squeeze her eyes shut and dust the flakes from her face. "It's coming down just a little hard, but I think we'll be fine."

"A little hard? You call this a little hard?" Luke, tucked beside her on the sleigh's backseat, shook his head, scattering the snow that had accumulated on his brim. "If it precipitated this hard in Texas, I'd call it torrential rain. We'd be dashing for higher ground before a flash flood swept us away."

"You're exaggerating."

"I'm dead serious. We'd better have the ceremony inside so the snow doesn't drift over us and bury us while we're repeating our vows."

"While the rest of us freeze to death," Aggie added from the front seat, hugging a very quiet Beth on her lap. "Need I remind you that half the town is turning out for this blessed event? Right in the middle of all the hustle and bustle of the Christmas season."

"Yep." Luke continued with the joke. "I'd sure hate for all the townsfolk to freeze up solid on our wedding day and miss out on the upcoming Christmas celebration."

"We could always decorate them like the other snowmen," Molly quipped, shivering.

Luke slid closer on the bench seat and slipped his arm around her shoulders. Beneath the lap robe, the side of his thigh pressed against hers. Heat curled through her body, and she didn't even notice the cold.

"Better?" his baritone rumbled in her ear.

"Hey, what are you two doing back there?" Aggie admonished, but her eyes were laughing.

"I'm just warming her up, ma'am."

"For the ceremony or after?"

"Aggie!" Molly felt color spread across her face.

Russell pulled the sleigh to a stop in front of the thirty-foot-tall fir towering between the white steepled church and the boxy community center. Lit candles flickered through the heavy veil of snow, and beneath it a crowd of well-wishers had gathered.

"Miss Lambert." Reverend Thayer broke through the throng and extended his hand to help her from the vehicle. "It's snowing quite heavily. Shall we move everyone inside?"

Molly climbed out, careful of her new dress, and stared up at the giant Christmas tree. The falling snow cast the majestic fir in shades of gray and white. It stood quiet, old and wise, and she couldn't find a better witness to this union that was made for the sake of a child.

Luke's hand found hers, and he led her through the parting crowd to stand before the solemn tree. The snow fell in a reverent hush, like a blessing from heaven, and their breaths rose like fog in the cold air. She was shivering, and he kept knocking the fastly accumulating snow from his hat brim every few minutes during the ceremony. When they said their vows, it was as if the entire world silenced.

Standing before the ancient tree, in front of family and friends, she became Luke's wife.

A fterward, they celebrated in the town's only diner. Luke received more congratulations than he knew what to do with. Russell, looking pale and worried, lifted his cider glass in a toast, wishing them prosperity and happiness, and added that he was glad Luke would be starting work on Monday to relieve some of his workload at the mill. Everyone chuckled, and Luke could barely meet the older man's gaze.

By leaving, he was going to disappoint—and maybe even hurt—this kind and generous man.

Sadness filled him so that he couldn't take it anymore. He slipped through the kitchen and out the back door, where the alley was quiet and the frigid cold leeched all the pain from him, heart and soul.

Then he felt a child's small hand slip into his palm. Beth didn't say anything as she leaned against his knee, just leaned there. Her rich ebony curls shone with luster and beauty; he'd brushed those tresses himself this morning. Aggie had added a matching blue barrette that held those thick bouncy curls from her face.

"I kept my promise to you, Beth." He knelt down to meet her eye to eye. "I got you a new mother who will love you."

"You could love me." So wistful, that voice.

"I always will, darlin'." He pressed a kiss to her brow. "Never forget that. You are the best thing that has ever happened to me. Better than Christmas. Better than all the presents in the world combined."

"I don't like her, Papa." So much sadness.

"You are going to love her. You'll see." He hauled his little girl against his chest and stood, holding her tightly, wishing to God that he would never have to let her go. But it was cold, and she wore no coat, so he headed inside where the noise of the dinner crowd rose to a crescendo. The waitresses were bringing out a cake made especially for their wedding.

He'd known nothing about this. It had all been Russell and Aggie's gift to Molly. And what a gift it was. Molly shone with happiness and with all the congratulations she'd received. Joy shone like a soft, steady light in her eyes, and when she caught sight of him holding Beth just inside the dining room, her loving smile nearly knocked him to his knees.

"Something wrong, Luke?" Russell appeared through the door behind him, smelling of fresh pipe smoke.

"Beth and I just needed some fresh air."

"Aggie was looking for your little one."

Beth turned her face into Luke's chest and held on with bruising force.

"This is a lot for her to get used to," Luke managed to say past the cold, hard lump of pain wedged in his windpipe. "She withdraws when things get too much for her."

"She'll be fine with us for tonight. Aggie's got a special evening planned." Russell rubbed the back of his neck with one hand. "Let me grab my wife. She'll want to make sure Beth gets a big piece of that cake."

"I'll come with you."

Luke wove through the crowd, and it was slow going because it felt like every other person stopped him to congratulate him on catching the prettiest woman in the county. His conscience was hurting worse than his heart. These sincere, good people had chipped in to buy a wedding gift—a box of fragile Christmas ornaments for his and Molly's first Christmas together.

And worst of all, he was deceiving Russell and Aggie, who'd helped him without question and intended to love his daughter as part of their family.

He left Beth alongside Jessie Smythe and another little girl he didn't know and headed back outside. This time he grabbed his jacket, and not even the cold air could chase away this shame growing inside him.

"You have the look of a troubled man." Russell joined him in the middle of the quiet alley. "I hope you're not having regrets over marrying my niece."

"No, but I have regrets." Luke shoved his hands in his pockets. There was no one around. The noise from the diner drifted out onto the twilight street and would disguise whatever he chose to say. "You'll be taking care of my girl tonight, while I'm with Molly. But there's something you should know, something I haven't been honest about."

"I knew there was something." Russell stiffened, his shoulders taut. He looked troubled and fierce, understanding and fatherly, and he didn't deserve to be deceived.

"I'm only marrying Molly so Beth will have a mother." He hated the way it sounded—as if he were using her, using them all. "I'm a fugitive trying to make it to Can-ada, and I've got no family to raise my daughter. She can't make it through those mountains, and it's no longer safe for her if word gets out where I am. Those bounty hunters who came through town were looking for me."

Russell took a slow, deep breath, then released it just as slow. His mouth thinned. His face crumpled into a mass of hard lines. "Does Molly know this?"

"Molly knows everything." The wind kicked up, rattling a loose edge of the diner's tin roof and driving the cold straight to the marrow of his bones. "I'm trusting you, here, Russell, not to turn me in."

The older man nodded once. "A bad man doesn't raise a daughter as good as your Beth."

It was the only answer Luke needed. He didn't realize he'd been clenching every muscle in his body. "Those bounty hunters know I have a child with me. I keep an eye and an ear open all night."

"Hell, son, you've been getting up every few hours and heading outside, and now I know why."

"I could have put you in danger." Luke rubbed the tension at his brow with the heel of one hand. "I know it looks bad, but I wouldn't have let anything happen to you. On my life."

"You're just trying to do right by your girl. Can't find fault in that." Russell thought about it, and for a moment he looked even more troubled; then he shrugged. "You've been spending time in my house, and I've gotten to see something in you. You don't look like any criminal I've ever met."

Luke stared hard at the ground.

"You're family now. And by God, that means something to me and Aggie. I've never seen Molly look so happy, and if you can give her that for the rest of her days and treat her well, then that's more than she's gotten from anyone else. Whatever you need from us, you'll have."

Luke tried to tell him that he didn't need anything, but it wasn't true. He wanted a family. He wanted safety. He wanted to live in Molly's log house in the woods and never leave.

"Luke." It was her voice, soft as a Christmas carol and filled with as much hope. She stepped into the slash of light from the open back door. "Everyone's ready to leave."

He wanted to melt just looking at her. Her hair was loose, tumbling over her shoulders, half wild, half sweet, and one-hundred-percent beautiful. The pretty white dress she wore adorned with tiny red ribbons and holly leaves hugged her curves the way he wanted to.

Heat shot straight to his groin. She was his wife now. His to touch.

"It's time to head home." She held out her hand, and the promise in her eyes could have incinerated him on the spot. "I hope Uncle Russell hasn't been pressuring you to start work first thing on Monday."

"He's mentioned it."

"Hey, I'll be honest. I need someone to help me run the place. I'm getting too old, and that nephew of mine is never going to show up." Something strange rang in Russell's voice.

And Luke recognized it. The old man wasn't just offering him a job. He was offering him a partnership. Just like that. His throat filled, and he couldn't find the words.

"We will talk on Monday," Russell promised as they reached the end of the alley, where the noisy din of a small crowd echoed against the two-story buildings.

"Here they come!" someone shouted.

Applause thundered as they ducked out from the alley, and someone made a comment about it. Good will and endless cheer melded with the falling snow as he led his bride to the awaiting sleigh—his sleigh drawn by the black gelding.

He held tight to Molly's hand, so slim and substantial against his. She was shining like a winter star, quietly beautiful and gracious. She thanked her friends for sharing this day with her, but Luke's chest was so tight he couldn't breathe, much less look at the people he was deceiving.

True, it was for Beth's sake, but it didn't lessen the sting. He'd always prided himself in being an honest man, at least in gentler times, before his cousin's betrayal and a lifetime sentence.

Molly didn't notice the sleigh until they were speeding away from town. "This isn't Uncle Russell's sleigh."

"Do you like it?"

"It's beautiful, small and cozy." She sighed, leaning against him when he drew her close. "It rides as smooth as silk."

"That sounds like you like it. Which is a good thing, since it's yours." His grin was half sheepish.

"Mine?"

"Yep. Yours."

The snow flew in her face, and the sleigh sped along the ground with so much speed and grace, it felt as if she were flying. "Remember when I explained to you that I was capable of thinking for myself."

"I have a vague recollection."

"I'm also perfectly capable of buying a sleigh if I need one." She couldn't be truly angry with him, not on this beautiful, sad and happy day. "Maybe I wanted a bigger one."

"You just said it was cozy."

"Yes, but maybe I wanted brown instead of black."

"You're going to torture me about this, aren't you?"

"Only a little."

His lips brushed hers. "I only want to take care of you the best I can, while I'm here."

"I know." And she finally did. She didn't need to give up her independence to be loved. True love didn't take, it only gave.

"Now, we're coming up on your driveway, and that means we're going to go into your house in a few minutes, and we'll be alone together. All night." His hot breath fanned her forehead and smelled faintly of rum. "I'm not asking for anything you're not willing to give me, Molly. Not one thing."

"I already know that." She kissed him, this man of heart and strength. His arms came around her and pulled her onto his lap. She leaned into his heat and hardness.

The snow tumbled over them, and the silent evergreens lining the road watched with nodding approval.

It was the perfect night for love.

CHAPTER TWELVE

Luke carried her into her bedroom, holding her close to his chest. Her hair tickled his cheek as she leaned into the curve of his neck and shoulder. She smelled sweet, like lilacs and snow, and the minute he saw the bed he thought about all the things he wanted to do to her.

"It had to be the McGraths who lit the fires for us." Molly eased out of his arms as he set her on the bed. The ropes squeaked slightly, and he fully intended to make them squeak again. "I saw a folded afghan on the dining-room table. Wasn't that thoughtful?"

"I didn't think there was a place on earth friendlier than Texas, but Montana seems to beat it by a long shot." He didn't want to talk about the neighbors, so he reached for the match tin he knew Molly kept on the nightstand. He lit the lamp, satisfied when the healthy flame cast soft lemony light over half the bed.

"See? There you go again. Deciding what to do with-out asking me." She stretched one slim arm across his chest to turn down the wick until the flame almost went out. "There, that's better."

"Now, how come your way is better?" He caught her by the wrist and pressed a kiss to her open palm.

"We could have compromised, but you blew it." Her breath caught when he laved his tongue across the base of her thumb. "Just be glad I didn't turn out the light completely."

"I guess I'd better behave from now on." He sat down on the

shadowed bed—hell he could hardly see her—and ran his hand up the row of buttons marching along her back. "I'll do anything you say."

"Anything?"

The button at her nape gave beneath his fingertips. "As long as we're in this room, angel. You want it, I'll do it."

"Hmm, this could be fun." Her breath caught as his lips settled on her bare skin. "I love to be in charge."

More buttons gave way. "I didn't say you were in charge."

His kiss trailed down her back with slow, restless heat, making progress with each unfastened button. Blissful sensation tingled on her skin and danced in her spine. If his kiss brought this much pleasure, what would his touch bring?

"This is a pretty dress." His words fanned her damp, sensitized skin. "I could see it a lot better if I turned up the wick. It'd be nice to admire all its beauty."

He scooped the dress off her shoulders, smoothing it down her arms, and she forgot to laugh. Fabric puddled at her waist, and his hands curled around to cup her breasts. Twisting pleasure coiled through her abdomen as he kneaded her with his fingers and ran his thumbs across her nipples.

"Forget the light." She laughed as she melted back onto the bed.

"If you insist." His hand splayed across her rib cage and tugged the dress over her hips. "I'll just have to go by feel."

And he did. His fingers blazed a trail of liquid heat down the outside of her arm, and he bent close to press a kiss to the inside of her elbow. Flares of pleasure exploded inside her, and he did the same to her other arm, then her palms and all ten fingers.

When his mouth descended on her nipple, which was tightened and painfully waiting, a moan tore from her throat, and she held him there, her hands on the back of his head, his silken hair wound between her fingers, and she didn't let him go. The taut cord that twisted through her body coiled ever tighter, and he switched to her neglected breast.

"You are definitely my dream." No more humor in his voice, just solemn truth. He kissed her stomach and ran his hands over the swell of her hips, taking her drawers with him.

Goose bumps multiplied over her exposed skin. Anticipation buzzed through her as his fingers burned an imprint on the inside of her thighs. She'd never been so vulnerable, so open to anyone. A sharp fear shot through her and vanished as Luke's gentle hands trailed along the inside of her thighs and lingered at her knees, rubbing the sensitive skin and urging her legs wider.

"You can trust me." His reassurance skidded over the stimulated skin of her inner thighs. "Remember, the light's so damn low I can't see a thing."

Then he kissed her with his smile. White-hot streaks of pleasure burst through her entire body, originating where his hot mouth stroked over her most sensitive, swollen flesh.

"Luke." His name tore from her throat as her back arched. The burning pleasure doubled and seeped through her chest to radiate through every part of her. She felt his fingers open her, stroking with the same slow, steady pressure of his tongue. Her body drew ever tauter. The unbearable pleasure coiled tighter. Then release slammed over her in hot, sharp, thrilling waves that tore her apart, then put her back together again.

"You're smiling." Luke stretched out on the quilt beside her.

Heavens, they weren't even on the sheets. She was still wearing her shoes, and he was fully dressed except for his loosened top button that showed the hollow between his collarbones and a tuft of dark hair.

"You're smiling, too." She plucked at his buttons and smiled even wider at the sight of his powerful chest. Even in the shadows she could see the ridge of muscle and the sprinkling of downy hair that gathered at his sternum and arrowed down toward his belt.

"What do you think you're doin', ma'am?" He leaned on one elbow. "I'm a proper gentleman and not used to being accosted like this."

"I want to see your chest," she admitted. *And maybe a lot more.*

"Now you're treading on dangerous ground," he warned with a low, lionlike purr when her fingers closed over his belt buckle. "I never planned on going any farther than this."

Her hand faltered. "You don't want to go any farther?"

"That's not what I said." His fingers caught hers. "I want you, Molly. I definitely want only you."

Her heart caught at those beautiful words. "All we have is tonight, Luke. I've never been m-married before..." She blushed and couldn't look at him, so she stared at a block of her patchwork quilt instead. "I've always wanted a man to love me. To really love me."

Luke heard what Molly didn't say. She wanted more from him than sex, and he wasn't certain he could give her what she wanted. But he ached in his body, in his heart, and in his soul for her. "I want you to know that I won't leave you pregnant. I made sure I bought what we needed when I was in Drew's Mercantile. Just in case."

She didn't smile. Instead she bit her lush bottom lip and helped him out of his shirt. She was still breathing hard from her climax, and even in the deep shadows he could see the evidence of her excitement—the flush on her face and chest, her pebbled breasts, and the dampness at her thighs.

His senses spun with the lilac scent of her skin, the light flutter of her rapid breathing, the taste of her on his mouth, the shadowed curves of her body as she lay back and tugged once again on his belt buckle.

He didn't hesitate. He pulled the condom from his trouser pocket and unbuttoned before she could do it for him. Throbbing and heavy, his shaft sprang free, and he watched Molly's eyes widen. Her mouth parted just a bit, but it was enough to drive him over the edge.

"I still have my shoes on," she whispered when he rolled on top of her.

"Just don't kick me with 'em." He caught her mouth in a frantic kiss, and she returned it, all passion and need and a quick, eager tongue.

Need broke him, and he knew he should touch her more, heat her up again, but she seemed as frantic as he was. He was already between her thighs, his shaft thrumming and trapped against the curve of her belly. She lifted her hips; he rose up and nudged inside her silken folds. Her hands caught his lower back and pulled him deeper into her.

"Easy now, angel." He gritted his teeth as he sank into her tightness, trying to go slow because he was afraid of hurting her.

"Oh, that feels amazing," she cried against his lips, eyes glazed, and threw her head back. Russet curls tumbled everywhere, and her mouth opened as she moaned once, twice, and he couldn't take it any longer. He thrust hilt-deep.

Amazing wasn't the word. She lifted her hips before he could and started rocking against him. He let her set the rhythm, determined to see to her pleasure before his, but she was hot, tight silk and passion, and he fought against his body's urgent demands.

Tendons strained as he tried to hold back, but every thrust brought a new level of sensation. Tenderness, hotter than the pleasure bolting through him, burst in his heart. She cried out, this beautiful passionate angel of his, and her release brought his own. Heat fired through every inch of him: heart, body, and soul, and he cried out, unable to keep at bay the sweet painful pleasure that left him weak and spent.

Her kiss to his brow gave him enough strength to climb up on one elbow and gaze down at her. Sweat dampened her brow, and her hair was every which way on her hand-made quilt. But her smile, it went heart-deep, and he kissed her gently, kissed her slowly.

"The box has a whole dozen condoms," he told her.

"Is that all? I hope we don't need another box." Her hand touched his face, brushing the hard line of his cheekbone and jaw, and the way she touched him made him feel treasured.

He kissed her long and slow, although he was already iron-hard. For tonight, she was his—wife, lover, and angel.

Molly awoke warm and sated—and naked. The soft flannel draped her sensitized skin still tingling from the long night of lovemaking. Remembering, she grew warm and smiled. She'd never guessed being joined with a man could bring such stunning pleasure. But as she smiled, her heart cooled.

Faint gray light teased at the edges of the curtains. Dawn approached and with it her last and only morning as a bride.

She washed in the necessary room and pulled on her favorite winter dress—a deep cranberry wool jumper with an ivory flannel blouse beneath. When she caught her reflection in the mirror, her jaw dropped at the woman she saw. There was a new sparkle to her eye and a satisfied grin to her mouth, made that way by her husband's love.

The house was empty, although a fire snapped merrily in the grate. She whistled, but Lady didn't come. He wouldn't have left already, right? He wouldn't have left without saying good-bye. At the panicked thought, she pulled back the kitchen curtain and saw Lady leaping and running in the snow out by the corral, her long ears flopping.

Relief fluttered through her, and she grabbed her coat from the wall peg, where Luke must have hung it up for her early this morning. She took a brief look around the kitchen—the stove was lit, coffee made, a kettle steaming and set on a trivet. In the corner she spied the full firewood bin and Lady's water dish brimming. Her chest ached at his thoughtfulness.

The snow had stopped falling, but the sky hung low, cold and gray. Her boots crunched, the air smelled like snow and pine, and Lady's happy bark rang through the yard. A snowball exploded through the line of trees and sailed high.

Lady barked again, mouth open in a doggy smile, eagerly dashing after the snowball. It crashed into the earth, and Lady turned head over heels trying to grab it with her mouth. She rolled onto all fours, silky hair dappled with snow, tail wagging, eyes shining.

"Where's Luke, girl?" she asked, and Lady ran up to her, leaped up for a midair pat on the head, then took off, tongue lolling toward the stand of trees behind the stable.

Luke saw her coming and straightened, snow heaped in one gloved hand. He looked younger and more relaxed than she'd ever seen him, with the morning breeze ruffling his black locks and his face chapped by the cold. His black jacket, denims, and boots made him look like a rancher, not a fugitive. The ease of his smile hinted at a man with hope as he patted the snow in his hand into a compact ball.

Lady leaped at his glove, barking and begging. Luke pulled back his arm and threw. The white sphere arched high overhead and speared through the tree boughs. Lady dashed off, yipping with delight.

Molly took a step toward him, suddenly feeling shy after last night. "I haven't seen Lady play like that since she was a puppy. Of course, I can't throw a snowball that far."

"She kept bothering me while I was chopping down your tree. I guess she thought my ax was a toy." Luke scooped snow into his glove. "I haven't played with a dog since I was a kid. I couldn't resist."

"I see." She watched Lady tumble breathlessly toward them. "What tree?"

"Your Christmas tree." He pulled one strong arm and shoulder back and threw. "I noticed you didn't have one up yet. I figured you shouldn't be chopping it down by yourself, so I took it upon myself—"

"Without asking what I wanted?" Warmth filled her simply from looking at him. He was humor and might, day and night, and she couldn't summon up enough ire to be annoyed with him.

He gave her a guilty little smirk that sent her senses reeling. "You were asleep, so I figured that it would be OK."

"You just figured it would be all right because I wasn't there to protest or offer my opinion?"

"That's right. You just want everything your own way, Mrs. Jamison." He strode toward her, apparently forgetting about Lady's next snowball, his lone wolf pace intimidating but his dark eyes sparkling with humor. "You'll just have to be satisfied with the tree I picked for you."

"What if I'm not?" She couldn't give in too easily or he might lose respect for her. So she bit the inside of her lip to keep from laughing.

"I've got another hour before I need to meet Russell. I might carry you inside, toss you down on the bed, and do whatever it takes to change your mind." He pulled her to his chest and gave her a cocky grin.

"There's an idea I like."

His lips slanted over hers with a claiming heat. On a moan, she opened to the brush of his tongue. She felt as if they belonged together, as if they were made for one another. What would her life be like without him?

Lady dashed up and rammed into Luke's knee. The hound leaped again, begging for another snowball. The dog was so expectant and happy, that Molly couldn't bear to disappoint her. She suspected Luke couldn't either, and so she stepped back.

"This is the last one," Luke warned Lady, who was oblivious and took off the second the snowball left his glove. Her yapping echoed in the yard, a happy sound on this peaceful morning.

But when Molly turned back to Luke, she saw the truth in his eyes. And the sadness. A tree lay upright, tilted against a sturdy pine, and he grabbed the fir by the base, dragging it after him.

The banter was gone, the teasing and the humor. All that remained was this silent knowledge between them.

"Why did you cut me a Christmas tree?"

He didn't answer right away. The snow crunched beneath their shoes as they broke through the low branches of the trees and stepped into the yard. Lady tumbled and rolled as her snowball broke apart, unrecognizable except for her smile beneath all that snow. Dawn came quietly, like snowfall, and the winter birds broke into song.

"I cut down the tree for me." He gave a self-depreciating sigh. "Because I'm riding out in a few minutes, and I'm not coming back."

Pain began to gather low in her throat.

"I brought gifts for you two. I hid them in the stable. Up on the edge of the loft, where it's easy for you to reach but high enough that sharp-eyed Beth won't notice." Sadness settled on his shoulders like an iron weight. "I'd like you to put those presents under the tree on Christmas Eve."

Molly nodded. She would do anything for this man—including letting him go. "We're going to miss you."

"Not half as much as I'm going to miss you." His voice broke. "That's why I want you to put this tree in your house and decorate it. And remember me."

"I'm not ever going to forget you." Tears burned behind her eyes, and it took all her willpower to keep walking.

Leaving was better for him. She could find peace picturing him alive and well someplace safe in Canada. His life mattered to her.

They'd reached the back porch. He leaned the tree against the wall. He moved slowly, as if he were trying to drag out their last minutes together. She wanted to touch him, kiss him until she lost her breath and her heart raced. She wanted to lead him to her bed and make love with him one last time.

But he crossed his arms over his chest and turned his back on the house, where the door beckoned.

"Riding away from you and Beth is going to be the hardest thing I've ever done." He stared at the mountains, crisp and clear this morning as if they were awaiting him. "I'm a man, and it has to be done, so I'll do it. But it's going to tear out my heart."

She wanted to comfort him. She wanted to protect him from this awful pain. When she reached out, he took her hand and instead of pulling her against him, he simply twined his fingers through hers.

"The nights ahead are going to be the worst, and I want to have something to think on to keep me going. If I can think of you and

Beth decorating that tree, and sitting around it in the evening, and piling gifts underneath it, then I'm going to be all right. I'll know everything I'm doing is right."

Molly couldn't speak. She knew what she was losing— a lifetime of nights spent in his arms and mornings just like this. But his loss was far greater. How could he ride away from his beloved daughter, his own flesh and blood?

When he pulled her to him, he kissed her, open-mouthed and deep as if to taste passion one last time.

Lady's shrill bark tore him away, and the sound of a galloping horse echoed in the yard. Luke's hand flew to his hip, but he didn't draw.

When Molly looked up, she saw why. Sheriff Kemp looked imposing and high in his saddle, guns at his hips and a hard look in his eyes.

"Sheriff." Luke stepped forward, alarm drawing him tall and straight.

Molly's heart sank as she caught hold of Lady's collar. Had Jeremy Kemp come to arrest Luke? Terror beat in her chest She couldn't bear the thought of him being returned to the prison that had taken so much of his soul.

But the sheriff spun his stallion around, snow flying. "Luke, Molly. It's Russell. He collapsed this morning when he was trying to saddle his horse. The doc's there now, but Aggie asked me to tell you. It doesn't look good."

Aggie flung open the door and flew into Molly's arms. "He just collapsed right there at the stable door. Oh, it was so awful. I'm scared."

Fear left Molly weak and shaking, but she held on to her aunt, who suddenly seemed so frail. "Let's get you back inside the house where it's warm."

"The doctor's up with Russell now, and I have to hurry back up there to be with him." Aggie stepped away, tears sluicing over her cheeks, and her lower lip trembling. For once, she looked every bit of her fifty years. "What if something happens to him?"

Luke took Aggie by the elbows before she collapsed in the foyer. "Here, let me take you."

Molly's heart broke watching the strong man and older woman

ease up the stairs. Worry for her uncle energized her, and she shut the door, slipped out of her cloak, and headed for the kitchen. She found a kettle whistling, forgotten on the stove, and removed it, then headed upstairs.

She climbed the stairs to her aunt's room. The big window let in the day's gray light and shone down on a sunken old man lying motionless in bed. His chest barely lifted and fell, and it was hard to tell from the doorway if he lived or not.

The doctor was winding up his stethoscope, and Aggie sat in a wingback chair, her hands to her face, tears dripping off her chin and staining the front of her dress.

If love began with passion, as it did between her and Luke, then Molly couldn't fathom how deep and great a love that spanned a lifetime must be.

She knelt on the floor beside the chair and took her aunt's hand. Aggie held on with all the fear in her heart, as the minutes passed and the doctor told them there was a good chance that Russell would live.

There wasn't enough of the medicine in town that Russell needed. It had been ordered, the portly, concerned doctor assured them with great regret. In fact, it was probably aboard the train stuck on the other side of Walker Pass along with the next order of groceries.

"The trains better start running before too long," Dr. Stanton warned, "or we're going to start seeing some serious problems. Fetch me if there's any change. And take care with him—he's fragile."

Luke assured the caring physician he would do just that. He followed the doctor outside, where he untied his gelding and Molly's mare and led them into the stable. There was an impression in the snow where Russell had fallen during his attack. Luke felt gut-punched and sank to his knees.

He heard the turn of a knob and the squeak of hinges. Small steps tapped down the brick steps and along the shoveled pathway. Dark curls hid her face.

"Worried about Russell?"

She kept her head down and wouldn't look at him.

"I am, too. You must have been scared for him."

Her fingers crept along his. Her small hand fit against his palm.

"I thought the bad people got him." Beth sniffled. "Aggie said that no bad men came. Uncle Russell got a pain in his chest and fell down."

"That's right." He knelt, and she curled against his chest like a lost kitten. "The doctor says the pain is going to go away. Russell will get better."

"Are you gonna get a pain in your chest?"

"No, darlin'." He kissed her hair, holding her, just holding her.

After a while, he shivered from the cold, and the horses became listless, but he didn't care. He wasn't ready to let go of his girl.

"I swear, I don't know how I'd make it without you." Aggie patted the back of Molly's hand, ever-present tears in her eyes and fear etched on her face. "You've been like a daughter to me these past months. I love you so much, dear."

"I love you, too." Molly pressed a kiss to the older woman's cheek. "I know you're not hungry, but you have to keep up your strength for Uncle Russell. He needs you."

"I know, I know. I'm not sure if I can stomach the food." Aggie scrubbed the new tears from her red eyes. "Goodness, look at me. I'm a mess. Did Beth get her supper?"

"No, Aggie, I decided to starve her." She squeezed her aunt's hand and headed to the door. "I'll bring up warm water in a bit, as soon as I set out supper for Beth and Luke. I'll help you wash him."

More tears brimmed, and Aggie could only nod.

Molly ambled down the hall, heart heavy. Russell's condition was still grave, and when the doctor visited again just an hour ago, he could give no guarantees how active the old man would be if and when he mended.

The Christmas tree in the parlor was dark—Molly hadn't felt up to lighting it. Beth sat in a corner, holding the cat and staring out the window at the mountains.

Russell's attack had only delayed but wouldn't prevent Luke's departure.

She found him in the kitchen, setting the table that nestled comfortably between the window and the back door. He looked up, a pink flowered plate clutched in midair. She read his concern, saw his question.

"No change," she answered.

The plate clinked onto the polished table, followed by another. "Aggie is expecting me to run the mill in Russell's place. She told me she's glad I'm here to take over. I'm family now, and they're counting on me."

"I know." Molly felt so knotted up inside. "I don't know what to tell her."

"Russell knows the truth. I told him." Luke dug through the corner hutch's silverware drawer. "The thing is, I can't walk away, but I can't stay."

"Maybe I can help out." Molly carried a trivet and the bowl of steaming potatoes to the table. "Hey, don't give me that look. Come Tuesday, the school term is over."

"Why Tuesday?" The silverware clattered to the table.

"It's the last day of the term. My Christmas pageant is that night, and the town celebration is after that. Although it seems sad to think of a party with Uncle Russell bed-ridden."

So much weighed on his mind. Luke shoved the knives and forks into place, debating what to do. Then Molly's hand curled around his upper arm, soft silk and comfort.

"You won't be letting Russell down if you leave." Like her touch, her voice soothed. "I'm here to help him and Aggie. And I'll stay beside them until he makes it through this."

"Russell was good to me. He learned the truth, and he didn't for once think I was a criminal." First Molly, and now Russell. What next? How could he endure it, this faith these people had in him?

He owed Molly. He owed Russell. And he owed it to Beth to be the best man he knew how to be.

"Aunt Aggie." Molly knelt at her aunt's feet, where the older woman slumped on a hard-backed chair at her husband's side. "Come, let me take over. You're exhausted."

"He needs me." Aggie might have looked frail, but her will was as strong as steel. "I won't leave him."

"Think of your health. Uncle Russell will sleep until morning. If there's any change, you'll be the first to know."

Aggie remained resolute. Molly kissed her exhausted, frightened aunt. She looked back at the door, ready to close it tight. Aggie's hand held Russell's, those hands wrinkled and marked by age, and the truth gleaming in tearstained eyes said everything. Molly closed the door and left Aggie alone with her one true love.

"How is she?" Luke looked up from the corner of his bed where he sat, tugging off his boots.

"Exhausted. I'm worried about her." Molly slumped against the wall. "She looks incredibly frail."

"People are." He stood in his stocking feet, came to her with that easy predatory stride, and wrapped her in his arms right next to his heart. "How are you holding up?"

"Much better than my aunt. I didn't almost lose my husband tonight."

"Not yet, anyway. And not like that." His lips trailed across her brow, hot and damp. "Beth's asleep. I read to her, and we talked about what happened to Russell again. She understands that he and Aggie will be part of her new family."

Molly closed her eyes and soaked in the feeling of being held by him, so strong and protective. She thought of all the nights to come when she wouldn't have him to hold. His hands stroked down her back and up again, infinitely comforting. She tipped her head back, and his mouth covered hers with the lightest brush.

"Considering what's happened to Russell, I understand if you think it's inappropriate..." Luke glanced toward the guest bed, a double four-poster with a wooden head-board. "If you'd rather not, I'd be happy to just hold you."

"Life is short, Luke." She unbuttoned his shirt. "Much too short to misspend love."

His throat worked, but he said nothing at all. Not even when he stripped off every piece of her clothing and laid over her in the comfortable bed. Not even when he entered her in one fierce thrust, binding them together in the flame of newfound love.

The strain of the last few days and the worry over Russell's failure to improve had worn Molly's patience thin. She clapped her hands and struggled to modulate her voice at the ten older students in her charge, who were chattering and carrying on the minute her back was turned.

"Grady, finish your recitation please. The rest of you, quiet."

She sounded harsher than usual, and she knew it—or maybe she was frazzled. The surprised students silenced, and Grady finished his part of the Christmas poem.

"How is Russell?" Mayor Smythe looked genuinely concerned.

Molly remembered that he and her uncle both belonged to the lodge. "The doctor is concerned with his irregular heartbeat. It's very serious."

"I'm sorry to hear that." He let out a troubled sigh. "I know Tillie brought by a casserole yesterday and did some laundry for Aggie—"

"You don't know how much we appreciate it." Molly had been speechless when Mrs. Smythe had shown up and could not be discouraged from helping out—and had truly made a difference.

"Russell helped us when we first came to town, and it's good to return the favor." The mayor applauded as the next in line on the makeshift stage recited the final section of the Christmas poem. "Looks like your students are ready for tonight."

Molly listened to the lilt of Marcie Thayer's voice as she wished to all a good night. Everyone clapped, and Marcie beamed.

"The two of you did an excellent job. Not one mistake." Molly clapped, too, praising her best and oldest students. "I don't believe we need to run through the closing recitation again, so that means you're all dismissed."

Noise erupted, and Molly had to raise her voice to be heard. "Remember, be back here in ninety minutes dressed and ready."

But they were already pounding out the door, calling out good-bye to her and to each other. The dark outside made the lit schoolroom seem cozy, and the holly and bows, pine wreaths and paper snowflakes hanging on strings from the ceiling announced that Christmas was fast approaching.

The faint sound of jingle bells rang outside on the street, and another set answered. "I bet that's Luke." He'd picked up the last pair on Drew's shelf just yesterday.

"That's a fine husband you have. A real good man." Mayor Smythe nodded once, respect in his eyes. "He's real concerned about Russell. That's what I like to see in a family. No, don't bother with the damper. I'll close up for you."

The bells chimed and faded to silence right outside the door. "Thank you."

The snow fell in heavy sheets, making it hard to see the sleigh.

Instead of climbing out into the storm, Luke held back the fur lap robe, and Molly stepped into the low-slung vehicle. Beth, sandwiched between them, moved over a little closer to her father.

Molly's heart hurt just a little because she wanted to love her stepdaughter and wanted Beth to accept that love. "Did your papa take you shopping for new hair ribbons to match your dress?"

Beth shook her head. "The doctor came, so we didn't go"

"Luke?" Molly clutched the edge of the fur. "Was there an emergency? Is Russell worse?"

"Yes." He looked hard as stone. A muscle in his jaw jumped. Even in the dark shadows of the street as they sped past shops closing up for the night, she could see the strain on his face—the sharp cheekbones, fatigue bruising the skin beneath his eyes, the worry bracketing his mouth. "He's running out of medicine, and the doctor can't get more."

"Is he gonna die, Papa?" Beth's lower lip wobbled.

"Not if I can help it." Luke wrapped his arm around his daughter and pulled her close against him. The little girl held on to her father tightly, and just looking at them made everything inside Molly hurt.

Christmas was coming. The streets were festive with their new decorations—wreaths and bows, candles and garlands. The Christmas tree in the town center blinked through the thickly falling snow. Old Dick Rutledge was already standing beneath the community center's awning, teasing carols from his violin. "Silent night, holy night," the fiddle sang.

"I was hoping you would take Beth shopping." Luke pulled the gelding to a halt in front of the mercantile, the busiest store in town. "I need to run an errand, and it can't wait."

"But Papa—" Beth started to complain, looked at her father, and bowed her head. "Yes, sir."

"That's my girl." They'd obviously had a talk about this earlier. Luke kissed his daughter and pressed a kiss to Molly's cheek.

Later, his eyes promised her, and she tingled, knowing that after the town's festivities and celebration, she would spend one more night in his arms.

Molly stepped out into the cold wind. The snow battered her as she lifted Beth out of the sleigh. The little girl went stiff in her arms, but she felt as fragile as a lost bird. Molly set the child down on the snow-covered step to the boardwalk and took her hand.

Beth didn't pull away, but she didn't look happy, either. They waved to Luke as he sped off, jingle bells tinkling, and disappeared into the snow and night.

"Let's find something really nice for you to wear tonight," Molly suggested.

Beth sighed and nodded, struggling hard to be brave and polite at the same time.

That was a good sign, right? Molly held the door for her stepdaughter and steered her past the long line of customers at the front counter. The noise in the mercantile was deafening. There were so many people shopping that Molly could barely squeeze down the main aisle.

"Did you hear?" Joy Wilson waved to her from her place in line at the yard-goods counter. "The Northern Pacific has canceled the train service here until after the New Year."

Molly thought about the medicine Russell needed. And she noticed the shelves, which had been steadily emptying over the last week, were now bare as people stocked up.

"They say our little northern spur isn't cost-efficient." The dressmaker looked mortified. "I swear, all companies care about is profit. They built this railroad and put a water and fuel stop right here, and that pretty much founded the town. Now they have the gumption to say we aren't important? How am I going to explain to my elderly mother that this will be the first Christmas she can remember not having cranberries? They're already gone."

Joy Wilson was upset about cranberries, but Molly saw much more. The clerk behind the counter called the seamstress away, and Molly stood disoriented for a moment, watching as the last bag of rice was snatched from its place on the shelf. There were no more beans, either.

Beth clung to Molly's hand. They made their way down the empty aisle, where the shelves were stripped of canned vegetables, to the ribbon display at the far end of the store.

"Oh, Beth." Molly's jaw dropped at the empty spools of ribbon. Everything Christmassy was gone. Only a few spools remained— colors no little girl would want in her hair for her first Christmas pageant.

"I'm so sorry, sweetheart."

"It's okay." She stared hard at her boots. "Didn't want a ribbon anyway."

But it mattered, Molly knew, to a little girl who'd gone without every imaginable comfort. "Your papa promised you something new for tonight. Why don't we look around? Maybe there'll be something else you'd like."

"Okay."

"Come, this way." There was a picked-over display of barrettes in a glass case. "I like the red bows."

Beth bit her bottom lip and splayed her hands against the glass. "I like the lace."

"The lace?" Molly scanned the barrettes displayed on a black fabric background. When Beth pointed, she realized what the child meant. Elegant gold fans in a lacy pattern held two small pearls each.

"Oh, it's the new Mrs. Jamison." Drew's mother tapped close. "Congratulations again on your marriage. And what a pretty daughter you've gained. Here, let me just lift this lid and you can look to your heart's content."

Molly thanked the woman, who scurried off to help a distressed customer. Beth stood on tiptoe to see the golden barrettes Molly began lifting from the case.

"Oh!" Her eyes shone with wonder. "They're just like Aunt Aggie's ornaments. Except better."

"Then you like them?"

"Oh, I do." Beth waited, breath held.

"I think they would look perfect with your new Christmas dress." Molly resisted the urge to brush those dark, unruly curls from Beth's brow.

The child clutched the barrettes carefully in both hands, staring down at them in wonder, as if she'd never imagined having anything so beautiful.

Molly felt the exact same way.

"Let me get a good look at you, darlin'." Luke's heart shattered again at the sight of his Beth descending Aggie's stairs.

Beth stopped midway down and held out her arms. The dress Molly had sewn made his daughter look like a china doll all wrapped up for Christmas. The white velvet dress was trimmed with embroidered ribbon in red and green holly and edged with gold braid. The full skirts swirled when she moved, and with her white stockings and shining black shoes, why, she was the prettiest little girl he'd ever seen.

"See what Molly got me." Beth tipped her head to display the delicate gold barrettes shimmering against ebony curls.

"Did you thank her?"

"Uh-huh." Was it his imagination or was Beth's attitude softening a little? Beth let him hug her, and he held her tight.

He released her only because he couldn't hold on to her forever. "Do you remember your lines?"

"I practiced and everything." Beth looked proud. "Molly said Jessie and me could do a poem together."

"You two will be the best in the recital."

The back door's hinges squeaked, and the flurry in the kitchen could only mean one thing.

"Lady!" Beth took off at a run, new shoes striking the boards, and Luke had to remind her to stay quiet.

Muted laughter drew him toward the kitchen. He leaned one shoulder against the wall and watched Molly struggle to keep her big snow-dappled dog from jumping up on Beth in greeting.

"Come on, Lady. I think you need to melt first." Molly looked exhausted from her extra work for the school pageant and extra time spent helping Aggie, but her voice came as gentle as always, as rich and dulcet as a hymn.

After half dragging Lady, who refused to leave Beth, into the enclosed back porch, Molly cast him a disparaging glance. "You could have helped me."

"Yes, but I thought you wanted to be the boss in our relationship so I decided to let you do all the work."

"Two demerits. I'm going to have to punish you severely when we're alone tonight." She came into his arms, and the loving gleam in her eyes left no doubt what she had in store for him.

He figured he could survive it. He buried his face in her hair. She smelled of crisp air and the apple cinnamon pie they'd had for dessert. She felt wonderful, soft in the right places, firm in others, tucked beneath his chin.

"Something's wrong." She looked up at him, and he hated the worry he saw in her eyes. The worry he'd put there.

"Yes." He wouldn't lie to her. Beth was eyeing the covered pie plate on the counter. It didn't take but a minute to cut her a small second helping and to get her settled at the table. Then he took Molly by the hand and led her into the parlor.

He kept his voice low so Beth wouldn't overhear, but he could see the realization on Molly's face before he said a word

"You're leaving tonight while the weather's clear. Is there another bounty hunter?"

"No. A rider came through the pass today, sent here by the railroad."

"I heard." She rubbed the heel of her hand over her brow. "I have to sit down."

Her petticoats rustled; her skirts whirled around her slim hips and thighs, and she was gone from his grasp before he could pull her back. She chose a wingback chair by the fire and buried her face in her hands.

He knelt in front of her, stared at the plain gold band on her left hand, and watched the firelight dance in it.

"You have to go. I know." Tears gleamed like silver in her eyes. "I'm not going to question your judgment or ask you to stay, no matter how much I want to."

"I'll go anyway." He laid his cheek against hers so they were face to face, heart to heart. "But I'm not heading to Canada. I'm going over Walker Pass to get Russell the medicine he needs."

He felt her quiver and realized she was silently crying. Her fingers curled around his as if holding on for dear life. "If you cross Walker Pass, there could be bounty hunters on the other side. Or lawmen with your *Wanted* poster tacked on their jailhouse walls."

"I know." He kissed her and tasted the salt of her tears. "But I can't let your uncle die. And he isn't the only one in need of the supplies that are stuck on the train that isn't going to be here for a while."

"The shelves were nearly empty in Drew's."

"There are going to be some people hurting over this. Maybe even going hungry. Not everyone, but some families."

Her heart felt like it was shattering for the last and final time. All she could do was hold on to this man she loved more than her own life. "What if some bounty hunter catches you before you can reach Rattlesnake Ridge?"

"I'll outsmart them." Confidence changed him. Made him stronger, better, new. "We both know my odds of making it north through the Rockies alive this time of year aren't good. So if I'm going to die, I might as well do it for my wife and her family."

She wrapped her arms around him. No words came, and she held him until the church bells rang in the distance.

CHAPTER THIRTEEN

"This is turning out to be a fine presentation, Mrs. Jamison," the mayor whispered so as not to disturb the crowd of proud parents and friends watching young Milton Thayer recite a passage from Emerson.

Nine-year-old Milton paused only once, and then looked relieved when Ginny Kemp took over and brought the crowd to a loud round of ringing applause.

"Is it time now?" Beth gazed up at her, her face peaked with worry. She gripped little Jessie Smythe's hand with white-knuckled force.

"Do you want me to go up with you?"

Beth's eyes said yes, but she shook her head. With a shaky sigh, she ambled forward up the aisle between the rows and rows of people. Hand in hand, the two girls went, two little angels, one in white, the other in gold. Their new shoes tapped on the wooden platform the livery owner had built for this event.

Luke's hand came to rest on Molly's shoulder. "That's our little girl."

It sure was. Affection burned in her heart like a new flame—strong and proud. She wished Aggie and Russell could have made it—it was impossible with Russell's condition. They would be proud of Beth, too, standing like a tiny little soldier, eyes wide as she stared back at all the strangers watching her.

The lamplight from the wall scones gleamed on the gold trim of her dress and the barrettes in her hair. Beth trembled so much that the hem of her dress swayed.

Jessie nudged Beth in the side with her elbow. "You'd better start," she whispered a little too loud, and it carried all the way to the back of the classroom.

"Nope. You're supposed to start. Remember?"

Jessie Smythe scrunched up her brow as if thinking. "Oh, yeah."

Molly bit her lip to keep from chuckling as the sounds of muffled laughter filled the room.

"O Christmas Tree with your boughs of green," Jessie began. Then stopped to scrunch her face, concentrating. "Miss Lambert— I mean, Mrs. Jamison, I forgot how it goes."

"Tall and silent..." Molly prompted.

Jessie shrugged helplessly.

"Disaster." Her father, the mayor, slapped his forehead, trying not to laugh.

On the stage, Beth nudged Jessie. "It goes like this: Tall and silent on this oly night."

"Holy night," someone in the front row corrected.

Jessie's brow puckered. She whispered to Beth, "Do you know what comes next?"

"No."

"Neither do I." But before Molly could prompt her, Jessie's face brightened. "O Christmas star shining bright—"

"That's my part, Jessie," Beth informed her. "Guiding us—"

"Guiding us—" Jessie repeated.

"On this oly night," they said in unison.

Then they stopped and stared at each other.

"That's all we remember," Jessie admitted with an angelic smile.

Applause drowned out the delighted laughter, and Molly felt Luke shake with mirth. Shouts of "bravo" and "wonderful" rose as the girls hopped off the stage with a clatter, hands once again tightly locked together as they tripped down the aisle.

Molly sent the next students to the front, where Grady and Marcie took turns reciting the finale of the evening, "A Visit From St. Nicholas." But she couldn't take her eyes off the dark-haired little girl skipping toward them, arms flung out, bright as a Christmas star.

"Did you see, Papa?" Beth ran into her father's arms.

"I sure did. You were excellent."

"I know."

He cradled her against his chest, and his love and pride in his daughter could not be mistaken.

Molly hurt, watching. This would be one of Luke's last memories of his daughter. He would leave just after midnight. His supplies were packed. They would never see him again.

Applause rang out, and to her surprise the last recitation was over. The audience was standing, cheers ringing in the rafters overhead. Both Grady and Marcie blushed with pleasure.

Molly, ready to say words of praise for her students and thanks to the community, stepped toward the aisle, but the superintendent hopped onto the stage and did it for her.

"Let's get out of here before we're trapped in the vestibule. The crowd's starting to head outside." Luke's hand caught hers.

She held on tight.

"Papa, are we gonna get candy now?"

"We'll have to see if Santa's arrived in his sleigh." Luke balanced Beth on one hip and led the way through the growing crowd. "Rumor has it he's supposed to be here by now. Wait, I hear something."

Bells jingled in the distance. The night silenced as the children running and playing in the schoolyard halted and listened to the music growing closer.

"It's Santa Claus!" Jessie Smythe cried out, clasping her hands. "He really is coming."

Little children cheered, Luke right along with them. Hooves tapped on the snow, and suddenly out of the dense forest four draft horses appeared, pulling a small silver sleigh. Bells chimed, and Santa's merry "ho-ho-ho" warmed the chill from the cold winter's night.

"It's Santa! Hey, Santa!" Several of the more energetic boys took off after the sleigh as it flew by, dashing off toward the lit square in the heart of the town, where the candles on the Christmas tree glowed a warm welcome.

"Hurry, Beth!" Jessie cried as she grabbed hold of her father's hand and pulled him toward the road. "You gotta come with me and see Santa."

The little girl shone with belief and excitement. "Hurry. All the boys are gettin' there first."

"Go on." Luke let go of his daughter's hand no matter how hard it was. "Have fun, darlin'."

"I know Santa isn't real," she whispered in his ear. "Doesn't Jessie know?"

"Remember what I told you about him? He's real enough, so don't you say anything to Jessie."

She nodded, brow wrinkling. "You're gonna come, too?"

"I'll be right behind you."

It hurt to watch her scurry away with her new best friend and the mayor, who escorted them safely down the people-filled street. A knot was forming in front of the community center, where Santa was climbing out of his sleigh wearing a buffalo coat and a red cap. His "ho-ho-ho" boomed like thunder drowning out the noisy crowd.

Molly's hand tightened in his. Luke's throat ached with words he couldn't say, so they crossed the street in si-ence. Several people called out hellos and congratulations.

"I don't think I need to worry about my daughter growing up to be an actress," he quipped.

"She might surprise you." Molly leaned her head against his shoulder. "Beth was the one who helped Jessie with her lines."

"That's one performance I'll never forget." Not as long as he lived and breathed.

In front of the community center, he spotted his girl standing in line beside Jessie Smythe. The two girls alternated between whispering and giggling. The line for Santa Claus moved forward, and the girls didn't notice.

"Look, it's almost Beth's turn." Molly pulled him toward the side door, where they had a good view of Santa in a hard-backed chair. Several parents waited there, too, smiling a greeting and making room so they could all see.

"Potter's doin' a good job with them," Drew commented. "The kids seem to be getting a kick out of it."

"And others believe. Look." Molly nodded once at the little girl, about Beth's age, on Santa's lap. The wonder bright in her eyes reminded Luke that all children deserved magic, dreams, and stories to grow on.

Then it was Beth's turn. She hesitated, trying to get Jessie to go first, but the other girl refused. Santa held out his gloved hand, and

Beth dragged her shoes, in no hurry. Her brow furrowed, and she looked around and saw Luke in the doorway. Her smile warmed him all the way to his soul.

"Why, if it isn't Beth." Mr. Potter scooped her up on his knee. "Now speak right up because Santa's hard of hearing in one ear, and tell me what a good girl like you wants for Christmas."

Beth looked at the old man with great suspicion, but his full white beard and spectacles were real. She thought hard for a minute, biting her bottom lip. Then she nodded as if she'd figured out what to say. "I don't want any little girls to go to sleep with their tummies hungry 'cuz it's real sad."

Luke felt Molly's hand slip around his.

"Look, Pa! I got a big sack of candy." Beth ran toward him, holding up her treasure. Then she leaned close and whispered. "Santa looks like Mr. Potter."

"Don't tell the other kids that." He wrapped her in his arms and held her, just held her, this child he loved so much.

"I'll take over now." Aggie's slow step padded through the sickroom. "I hate leaving him for even a few minutes."

"You needed some rest."

"It's nearly midnight as it is. Three whole hours I slept." A crease marked her cheek from her pillow, and her hair was rumpled from her nap. "I feel refreshed, so I can stay with him until morning. This will be your last night to spend in your husband's arms for the better part of a week, and that's if the weather holds."

If Russell lives that long. Molly heard Aggie's unspoken fears.

"You go say good-bye to your husband properly. He's doing a brave thing, crossing those mountains for us. You make sure he knows that, do you hear? You two couldn't have done more for Russell and me if you were our own children. Now, you go. I'll be fine."

Russell looked so gaunt and unnaturally still. Molly closed the door and crossed the hall, trying to hold on to her heart. Her world felt in danger of shattering into a thousand pieces, and nothing would ever be right again.

"I came to check on her, too." Luke stood in the hallway outside Beth's door.

"Did you tell her good-bye yet?"

"I couldn't. She had a good time tonight. She looked the way a little girl should—happy, bright, and magical. I don't want to take that away from her. My leaving is going to hit her hard."

Beth slept on her side with one arm wrapped around Mrs. Whiskers. The calico opened one eye as if to reassure them that she had everything under control. Lady slept curled on the floor on a braid rug—apparently banned there by Mrs. Whiskers.

"After I go, Beth's going to be withdrawn for a while." Luke pulled the door closed. "She'll be quiet and maybe have nightmares again. That's how she was when I found her."

"She's going to grieve for a long while. After all, she's losing a wonderful father." Emotion clogged her throat and hurt in her heart. "I'm losing a wonderful husband."

"Not so wonderful."

"Oh, yes, you are."

"Only because I have the best wife in three territories."

"Only three?"

He pulled her into the bedroom with him and locked the door. Faint moonlight danced on the bed like silver sprinkles as the tree outside the window swayed gently in cadence with the night breezes.

"Love me one last time, Molly. Please." The clock on the wall claimed it was only minutes after eleven o'clock. They had an hour. One hour left together.

He kissed her with sadness and passion. And the bitter-sweet taste left tears in her eyes. She wanted to hold him forever. She wanted to grow old with him.

Every kiss left her crying. Every touch left her aching. They made love in the dappled moonlight. The world and its problems faded away a little more with each desperate kiss, each deep stroke, and the harmony of their beating hearts. For a time, there was just the two of them and the love they shared.

But it couldn't last. Release shattered her. Luke collapsed in her arms, and their time of loving came to an end.

Moonlight filtered through the broken clouds as Luke rode the gelding to the back door. The crunch of the snow, the bitter cold on his face, and the rock of the horse reminded him that he was a condemned man. Molly's love couldn't change that. Nor could the stars that winked overhead, ever watchful, ever vigilant.

The door flew open and Beth dashed outside, half in her coat, her nightgown fluttering in the breeze. He dismounted, and she was in his arms, a wonderful sweetness snuggled against his heart.

"You gotta take me, Papa." Something bulky was tucked under one arm. "I'm all packed, see? I got my warm clothes so I won't cry if I get cold."

"I guess Molly told you I was leaving." Her hair caught on his unshaven jaw, and he closed his eyes.

"I remembered my mittens."

"You remember your promise to me. You treat Molly well. She's your new mother now. She'll raise you the way I always figured to."

"No, Papa. I saved up some of Aunt Aggie's cookies for our trip, and I brought my candy, too."

"Shhh." He brushed a kiss against her brow because he couldn't bear to hear anymore.

Molly wrapped her arms around him, too, and he held them both, daughter and wife. Pain was a sharp-toothed animal caged in his chest, and he didn't know a man could hurt so much and still be alive.

"You take care of yourself, Luke McKenna." Molly's slender hand cupped his jaw. "You are my one true love. And will always be."

He couldn't find the words to tell her the same. The love he felt for her was as wide as the sky and as rare as a blue moon. She'd saved him when he thought no one could. When he'd thought the year in prison had leeched all the humanity from his soul. But this woman had restored it.

If he told her the truth, he'd never find the strength to leave her, the greatest love he'd ever known. So he pulled her against him and kissed her one last time. She was sweetness and fire, angel and passion, and she clung to him silently, afraid to let go.

It nearly broke him, but he tore his mouth from hers, breathless with wanting. The cold air between them froze their breaths, and those clouds mingled, and for one second he let himself believe they could have forever— somehow, someway.

Then he handed Molly his daughter—the other great love of his life.

"Don't forget me, darlin'," he said, kissing her brow one last time, breathing in her cookie and child scent before he turned away.

"Don't l-leave me, Papa." Beth's sob was a whisper, raw and agonizing.

He gritted his teeth and didn't look back. Feeling like he was dying inside, he fit his boot into the stirrup, laid his gloved hand on the pommel, and mounted. The gelding shifted as Luke settled into the saddle.

"Papa, Papa." Beth wept.

He couldn't look at her and see those great big tears. He wanted to protect her from any pain, but in order to protect her, he had to ride away. Dying a little more inside, he closed his eyes and laid the reins across the gelding's neck.

"Don't l-leave me here. Oh, P-papa."

At the edge of the property he dared to look over his shoulder. Beth was on her knees in the snow, weeping silently, her face buried in Molly's skirts.

Across the distance their eyes met, and he saw the sheen of tears on Molly's face.

He kept riding.

"We have to go in, Beth." Molly's heart felt broken enough, but the child's grief hurt even more. "It's too cold for you to be out here like this."

"How could P-papa l-leave me?"

"He didn't want to." She scooped the sobbing child off the cold ground.

"I c-can w-walk." Wrenching sobs shook her. Beth limped up the steps and turned around at the door, scanning the night, hoping her father would return for her.

Lady nudged the door open with her nose and licked the girl's hand in comfort. Then Beth shuddered, her head dropped forward, and she shuffled into the kitchen.

Heart breaking, Molly closed the door. Her hands were red with cold, but she didn't feel it.

Beth was shivering from grief and chill, and tending the child who was now hers alone gave her something to concentrate on.

"Let's get this cloak off you." Molly slipped the wool garment off Beth's spindly shoulders and took the rolled bundle of clothes and cookies. "Those wet socks, too."

Tears streamed down the girl's face. She lifted one foot and then the other. Her little toes were red, not white with frostbite, and Molly dried them and found a clean pair of unfolded socks in the laundry basket.

"Do you want me to make you some hot chocolate?" Molly found a handkerchief and knelt to dry Beth's tears. But there were too many, so she pressed the cloth into the girl's hand. "How about we have some of those cookies?"

No answer.

The clock in the parlor struck one, and the house was so silent the quiet chime bonged like a war drum. Lady startled and ran to the nearest window to inspect the yard.

"Come on." Molly held out her hand. "Let's get you back into bed."

"Papa's gonna c-come for me." Beth snatched her rolled clothes from the edge of the table and clutched the bundle tight to her chest. A broken cookie tumbled to the floor, and the dog bounded over to eat it.

Molly knew exactly how much Beth was hurting. So she didn't argue. She took the girl's free hand and led her upstairs, stopping only to turn down the few lamps as she went. Their steps made no sound on the stairs. The night felt oppressively quiet—vast and empty, like loss.

The line of light slipping beneath Aggie and Russell's bedroom door lit their way down the hall. Beth dropped her pack, and Molly retrieved it and carried it the rest of the way to the little room in the corner.

She lit a lamp and grabbed a book from the shelf. She moved Mrs. Whiskers from the rocking-chair cushion to the blanket on the foot of the bed and settled into the chair. Beth watched her with wide, unblinking eyes and silent tears.

"I always feel better when I read." Molly knew there was no chance she'd find a moment of sleep lying in the room down the hall on the sheets where Luke had just finished making love with her. "Would you like to sit on my lap?"

Beth merely stared at the floor.

Molly opened her book, and the binding creaked as she turned to the first page of *A Christmas Carol.* Dickens's lush prose stared up at her, and she ran her index finger across the precious words. She started reading, speaking softly, hoping to draw Beth in. It was hard to concentrate on Scrooge's plight when she kept wondering how Luke was. Was he cold? Was he tired? Was he safe?

The moonlight shifted from the floor to the wall as time passed, and Beth crept closer until she was curled up at Molly's feet. She kept reading, her eyes blurring and her voice scratchy until Beth yawned and her chin bobbed.

Only then did she put the book aside to lift the child into her arms.

"My papa 1-loves me," she whispered, half asleep.

"Very much." Molly pulled back the covers and laid Beth gently on the sheets.

Even through the hurt, a bright new love for this child burned in her heart. "Do you want me to stay with you? Your father said you have bad dreams sometimes."

"I'm awfully cold," Beth said in way of an answer, and scooted farther away on the mattress. "I guess you could hold me until Papa comes back."

"I'd like that." Molly turned out the lamp and crawled beneath the warm blankets. Mrs. Whiskers sneaked up to take her place in Beth's arms. Lady curled into a ball on the floor, keeping watch.

"Are you gonna 1-leave me, too?"

"I'm never going to leave you." Molly opened her arms, and before she knew it both Beth and the cat were there, tucked under her chin, right next to her heart.

Luke felt as cold and still as the night. The jagged peaks of the Rockies gazed down at him, so close he could tip his head back and they would still fill the entire sky. Those dangerous pinnacles shone with the luster of a new pearl, silvered white and filled with light. His pulse jumped at the lethal beauty ahead.

It wasn't just the perils of avalanches that worried him—it was the humankind he was likely to run into up on that pass. That's how Moss had found him, by lying in wait in the night's shadows on a pass like this one. With the clear weather and full moon, he would make a good target for an ambitious bounty hunter.

A wolf's hungry cry echoed along the crumpled, rugged peaks, a lonely, eerie sound. Luke unsnapped the straps that kept his saddle holster in place. The gleaming Winchester was new, loaded and ready. The gelding beneath him lifted his head, scenting the wind, and didn't appear alarmed. There was no danger from wild animals, then. But who knew what lay ahead?

With the deep snow, it wasn't like he could risk heading off into the trees and forging his own path. He had to keep going as the road narrowed between a steep slope and a cliff's dangerous edge.

No wonder most teamsters refused to cross this pass in a storm. One misstep would mean death. And it was a hell of a long drop to the rocks below.

The gelding's ears pricked the same moment the skin on the back of his neck began to tingle. He was trapped between the steep bank and the drop-off with no way out. The moonlight sheened on the bend ahead, creating shadows, as he swung out of his saddle.

Light reflected on the polished snow that rolled like white porcelain over the hard rise of the mountain's slope. Trees, scrubby and bent, cast long shadows over the approaching riders. Two of them. A bounty hunter and his hired gun, most likely. Only desperate men would be out in this cold in these mountains.

There wasn't enough time for him to turn the gelding around, and his boots skidded on the iced, porcelain-hard snow. It would be suicide to try to outrun them. There was only down or up, and he sure as hell wasn't going to jump.

"C'mon, boy." He swung up into the saddle, trying to figure out how they were going to do this. The slope was steep, maybe too damn steep. But it would have to work. Russell's life depended on him, as well as Beth's and Molly's safety.

He backed the nervous gelding as close to the cliff's edge as he dared and dug in his spurs. The horse bolted, and Luke fought to keep control. Arms straining, he angled the animal toward the bank and spurred him again.

The gelding leaped and skidded, hooves digging for purchase. A panicked *neigh* tore through the silent night. The horse fought; Luke stood up in the stirrups and fought with him. *Just a little farther. Come on.*

He felt the cold night at his back and danger approaching. The gelding pawed and leaped, gaining ground and then sliding back. It was too slick, too hard-packed, and it didn't seem like they would make it. When Luke hopped from the saddle, his boots slid out from beneath him, and he landed on his knees.

It was like climbing up a wet china plate, but Luke grabbed the gelding by the bit and hauled him up the slope with the strength in his arms. They were both dripping with sweat and breathing hard when they reached the top. He tied the horse in the shadows of the trees and reached for his pocketknife. The blade snapped open and he hacked through a slim bough.

The *chink-chink* sound of steeled shoes rang closer as Luke skidded down the embankment on hands and knees and did his best to sweep away the worst of the tracks. He could hear the rumble of voices. He worked quickly, backing up, grabbing a handful of snow off a low bough and packing it into a hole left by the gelding's hoof. He patted it flat and swept it.

The riders rounded the corner. Luke kept working as he glanced up to see the gleam of moonlight off a repeating rifle. He eased into the shadow of a pine and continued sweeping with the branch that erased his trail.

"Keep your gun out, partner," one of the riders warned.

Luke slipped over the embankment and drew one revolver. He palmed the hammer, his woolen mittens absorbing the quiet click of the chamber. The riders were directly below him.

"This pass has been known to hide an outlaw or two. Just last week some bounty hunters came looking for a fugitive in these parts."

The riders emerged from the shadows. Squinting, Luke could just make out the Army coat on the closest horseman. There was a fort northeast of Evergreen by about a hundred miles. He couldn't get a good look at the second rider; he was too far away, but one thing was for sure. They weren't bounty hunters.

"Strange, but I'm sure I heard someone." The sergeant stopped his horse and gazed up the road and then down into the darkness. "I've been ridin' since dawn. Guess I'm gettin' saddle weary."

The two men rode on, but the chill wrapped around Luke's spine remained.

"He's still holding on, and that's what counts, Aggie." The doc's voice was modulated and kind, but it carried out into the hallway.

Molly, arms full of sheets for the laundry, leaned against the wall. Snow had come with the dawn, and she couldn't stop thinking of Luke alone in the vast wilderness with men hunting him. Luke was strong and smart—he had to be safe. She had to believe it or she'd fall apart.

At the sound of the doctor's step, Molly hugged the sheets to her chest and waited outside the door.

"I wish I could do more," he said, his round face pinched. "Make sure your aunt gets more rest or she'll be joining him in that bed."

"I've been trying." At a loss, she looked at the older woman perched at Russell's side, her back straight, her chin determined. After seeing the doctor out, Molly checked on Beth, who was in the parlor, watching the snowfall and cradling a contented Mrs. Whiskers.

The child looked devastated. Her eyes and nose were red from crying and her face pale with grief. She didn't move, didn't blink, and didn't even breathe when Molly stopped beside her.

"I can make you some hot chocolate, if you'd like."

"No, thank you."

Remembering what it was like to sit and wait for what could never be, Molly smoothed her hand along Beth's shoulder, tiny and bird-thin. She busied herself in the kitchen preparing an early lunch and a comforting pot of peppermint tea.

"Oh, goodness." Aggie took one look at the tray and shook her head. "You do far too much for me. Look at this. You baked."

"Just a coffee cake. I know how you like them."

"Russell's being a stubborn cuss as usual and insists on lazing around in that bed." Aggie's bottom lip trembled, and she fought so hard to lighten a day made somber by the doctor's visit. "Since the moment I met him, he's been like that. Always taking his own time to do what needs to be done."

"That's a man for you. Flawed to the core." Molly set the tray on the nightstand, careful to nudge a glass vase, a pitcher of water, and a framed photograph out of the way without knocking anything over.

"That was taken on our thirtieth anniversary." Aggie grabbed the frame and cradled it in her hands. "Right before we moved here from Butte. Russell was being stubborn about getting his likeness taken, but I finally got him to agree. Look at that smirk on his face. He wanted to do it the whole time; he was just making me carry on."

Tears filled her eyes, and she hugged the frame to her heart. "Oh, Molly." She lowered her voice, her whisper broken and raw with fear. "I don't know what I'd do without that man. He's grown on me over the years."

"Men have a habit of doing that." Molly held her aunt until there were no more tears, and begged her to lie down for a bit, but Aggie refused.

It was as if she believed she could will Russell to live.

Molly poured her aunt some tea and left, determined to see if Norma Kemp could talk Aggie into taking care of herself.

"I have an errand to run." Molly lifted the cat from Beth's lap and set the suddenly disgruntled Mrs. Whiskers onto the arm of the sofa, where the feline flicked her tail with great insult.

Beth sighed and said nothing as she slipped into her coat. She showed no protest, no question, no interest in where they were going. It was as if the fight had gone out of her—and the light in her heart, too.

The snow fell in a hazy veil that made the lamplight in the windows of the houses they passed glow with warmth. They stopped at Mrs. Kemp's house, where the gnarled, white-haired old lady vowed to talk some sense into Aggie if she had to use her cane to do it. Molly, seeing the concern on Norma Kemp's face, didn't doubt her.

The town bustled with activity. Horses drawing sleighs of all varieties jammed the main street. A trio of boys raced down the road, tossing snowballs at each other and then disappeared through the town square, their shouts drowned out by the street noise and the mill's distant hum.

Beth walked quietly, chin bowed, hands balled into fists. She only answered a polite, "Yes, ma'am," or "No, ma'am," to anything Molly tried to say.

Two men she didn't recognize dismounted in front of the diner. Their horses looked trail-weary and were flecked with snow and ice. Molly stood on the street corner and watched them across the flow of holiday traffic.

Neither man looked like a bounty hunter—one was clearly in the army. Had they crossed over Walker Pass or did they come from the north? She supposed it didn't matter. Those men couldn't be after Luke. They wouldn't know anything about Beth.

As soon as she spied a break in the traffic, she took the girl's hand, and they crossed. The mayor, just stepping out of his tailor shop for a smoke, called out a hello and asked after Russell. While Molly told of the doctor's visit, she couldn't help noticing the men split up—one went into the diner, but the other, the one dressed in a fine wool coat and cap, headed straight for the sheriff's office.

"Now I wonder what a stranger to town needs with Jeremy?" The mayor tapped the ashes off his cigarette.

Molly wondered, too. The bad feeling in her stomach continued to grow. She wished the mayor a merry Christmas and hauled Beth down the boardwalk and away from those men.

The mill's business office was three doors down from the sheriff, and when Molly pushed through the glass door, she felt as if she were being watched. She looked over her shoulder and caught sight of the soldier staring at her through the window.

A chill raced through her, and she shut the door.

"You're shivering, Molly." Clint Neville stood from behind his paper-strewn desk. "Come warm up by the fire. I have the paychecks for you to sign—the banker told me you had authority now. And you might want to take a look at these invoices."

Molly settled Beth by the stove and began to work, but she couldn't stop the shivery feeling in the pit of her stomach.

"Saw a little girl, like the one you're lookin' for."

"Is that a fact?" Former Texas Ranger Fletcher McKenna shook the snow from his Stetson before he eased down into the ladder-back chair. With an impatient flick of his wrist, he summoned the waitress, who nearly dropped the steaks she was serving.

"A cup of tea, piping hot, and I mean piping." He'd had his fill of small towns and riding snow-bound trails. From the instant he'd crossed into Idaho, the cold seemed to settle in his bones. Nothing—not heat, fire, or a night of paid sex—had been able to drive it away. He shivered and cursed his damned cousin all over again.

The waitress returned with the tea and a cup of sludge that she called coffee for the sergeant.

"Tell me about the girl."

Gaylord Hobart sipped his sludge without adding a speck of

sugar. "Black ringlet curls just like you said. Little heart-shaped face. About yay-high." He held out his hand.

"Too tall." Fletcher frowned at the crock of honey on the table as he measured out a precise spoonful. "Of course, I want to eliminate every possibility. The only word I received is that they were spotted in Twin Falls, and that news simply isn't reliable. I'm looking for a man and his daughter, not a boy."

"Hey, don't blame me. Some folks in these parts are too eager. Money hasn't come in the way the railroad promised it would. The new towns would boom, but the truth is, a lot of us are struggling and aren't too particular when good money's to be had."

"Not good enough, apparently." He'd spread the word to bounty hunters in four territories and two countries, and only one wired back word that he'd spotted McKenna. And that one never surfaced again. They were beginning to give up their search. They said Luke had probably hiked through the mountains to Canada by now and wasn't worth the effort.

Other than the fact that he hadn't been spotted in Canada, that meant the bastard was dead or hiding out in this godforsaken wilderness.

"Hobart, you were a good guide through the mountains. Do you have time to spare before you need to return to your fort?"

"A few more weeks."

"How would you like to make some money?" The tea burned his tongue, but it didn't chase the chill from his bones or the fury from his soul.

Luke was out here somewhere, and someone had to have seen him. A small child couldn't survive a trip through the northern Rockies in winter, so she had to be in Montana. And Luke was with her.

"There isn't room at the boardinghouse here in town." Hobart licked his fleshy lips when the waitress set a plate of fried beef on the table in front of him. "Guess the hotel isn't built yet, so if we want somewhere warm to sleep tonight, we'd better head back over Walker Pass or north to Liberty."

Fletcher frowned at the chicken steak on his plate, greasy and limp. For the hundredth time that day, he missed his Texas home.

"There she is." Hobart pointed with a greasy knife at the window. "Across the street, in front of the barber-shop."

"I can't see her." An old woman was in the way, and there

wasn't a man in sight in front of that shop. "No, it can't be her. There's no way my sonovabitch cousin would let his precious kid out of his sight."

Hobart hacked a huge bite out of his bloody steak. "Why do you want her, anyway? It's a little funny that she wasn't mentioned on the Reward poster."

Fletcher didn't feel the need to point out that he'd been a ranger before he'd gotten his hands on his father's estate.

"Don't you worry about what I want with the girl," he snapped and managed to choke down a flavorless, limp bite of chicken.

On the boardwalk across the street, the elderly lady parted with whomever it was she was speaking to and went on her way. Leaving behind a woman with a little girl at her side—a little girl with black ringlet curls.

"**G**oodness, Lady, stop barking or you're going to make us all deaf." Molly couldn't get Beth, who sat at the window seat behind the kitchen table, to smile or the dog to quiet down. "I think my ears are ringing."

Still no smile. The hound leaped at the door, silky paws battering the wood, her bark shrill and nerve-wracking.

"Sorry, Mrs. Thayer." Molly apologized and hauled the dog back into the house. "Let me lock her in on the porch. She must miss her big backyard to run in. She's getting edgy. If I let her out, she just keeps barking."

"The Kemp's shepherd has been howling up a storm ever since the noon meal. Must be something in the air. Or a doggy form of Christmas caroling." The reverend's wife brushed off the snow melting from her hat and coat before she stepped from the enclosed porch into the kitchen. "I wanted to stop by and check on Aggie and Russell. Oh, here—Merry Christmas."

"Thank you." Molly set the bright red basket on the table, hoping the sweet, homemade candy inside would momentarily tempt Beth out of her sadness.

The little girl didn't look up at the sweet, Christmassy scents.

"Would you like me to stay with Aggie, in case you want to step out of the house for a bit?" Mrs. Thayer shrugged off her coat, her kindness a welcome gift on this cold winter's day.

Molly took the fine garment and hung it carefully on the rack.

"Aggie has been at Russell's side since his collapse. She hardly takes time to rest, and the doctor has warned me that that isn't good for her. She won't listen to me, because I'm family, and she's not even listening to Mrs. Kemp. What do we know?"

"I understand completely. You watch, I'll get her to at least lie down for a bit." Confident of success, the gentle Mrs. Thayer headed through the parlor, waving off all assistance since she knew the way.

The falling snow outside the window caught Molly's attention as it drove to the ground in thick sheets. Her husband was out there, battling the weather and nature and worse. Had he made it safely over the pass last night? Had he found shelter?

Was it going to be like this through the evening, too? Thinking of him, worrying about him, wishing she could touch him one last time? Heartsick, she sat down on the sofa next to the Christmas tree. The candles were dark, and the evergreen branches proudly held up white strings of popcorn, glass bells, and porcelain angels.

It was impossible to believe that Christmas would be here soon, with presents under the tree to open, a special meal to prepare, and carols to sing. The images of the happy holiday she'd envisioned with Luke and Beth in her life faded. A wrapped gift under the tree couldn't save Russell's life or give Aggie back her one true love. A present tied up with a fancy bow wasn't going to give Beth the father she loved or heal the painful void in her heart.

How were they going to make it through this holiday?

Beth sat at the window, staring out at the graying snow. Darkness eked into the late afternoon, for it was one of the shortest days of the year.

"Christmas is nearly here and look at us, sitting around and moping when there are a thousand things to do." Molly marched into the kitchen and threw open the pantry door. "Have you ever had fudge?"

Beth shook her head and hugged Mrs. Whiskers tight.

"Never had fudge." Molly spotted the tin of cocoa and pulled it off the shelf. "Well, today's your lucky day."

Beth didn't look convinced.

Molly gathered her ingredients and plopped them on the table. She found measuring cups, spoons, and a few bowls, and opened the sugar sack.

"Front and center, Miss Beth. You and I are going to make all the Christmas treats Aggie can't get to this year."

" 'Cuz of Uncle Russell?"

Molly nodded and pulled out a chair. "Come right here and I'll let you measure the sugar."

"I don't want to."

"I know. Neither do I." Molly knelt in front of the sad-eyed child, who was now her daughter. "I miss him, too, and I want nothing more than for your papa to come riding back down that road and burst through our front door and stay with us forever. But you know why that can't happen."

" 'Cuz of the bad people."

"That's right. So we're going to do something good for someone else, because Christmas is coming and I don't want to cry anymore."

Beth squeezed Mrs. Whiskers so tight, the cat's purr squeaked. "I don't know how to bake."

"Then it's a good thing I do, because Russell will be disappointed when he gets better if there's no Christmas fudge." Molly held out her hand. "Come on, I'll show you."

Beth sighed, set down the cat, and placed her small hand in Molly's palm. "When I was at Jessie's house, her mama baked us cupcakes."

"I'll bake you cupcakes sometime, too, if you want." Molly lifted Beth onto the chair.

"Chocolate?"

"That's the only kind." Molly handed Beth the one-cup measuring cup and a long-handled spoon.

Lady's shrillest bark echoed on the porch. That didn't sound right, but before Molly could turn around and investigate, a steeled arm clamped her against an equally hard chest. A knife gleamed in the lamplight as it swung toward her throat.

The cold blade slanted across her Adam's apple. "Scream and you're dead."

CHAPTER FOURTEEN

Fear sluiced like ice water in her veins. She didn't need to wonder who this man was—she recognized the army jacket by the brass buttons on the cuffs of his sleeves. She'd seen him in town today and dismissed him as no threat

"The girl's under the table," he said as his accomplice pounded into the room.

Molly couldn't see because she couldn't move her head a fraction of an inch, but she heard the thud of knees hitting the floor and a grunt of exasperation.

"Come out here, you little brat." There was a scraping noise and a tiny mewling sound of fear as the second gunman dragged Beth out from beneath the table.

Molly couldn't see if Beth was okay, if she was afraid, or if the man was holding her roughly. The pressure on her throat increased as the blade bit into her skin.

"Where is he, lady?" he growled in her ear.

The blade felt ready to saw through her.

"Tell me, goddamn it!"

Panic flooded her. Warmth sluiced down her throat.

"I've waited long enough to catch that sonovabitch." The second gunman's knuckles slammed into her cheekbone, and the force tore her from her captor's arms.

Lights danced in front of her eyes, and pain exploded through her skull. A loud buzz rang in her ears, leaving her dazed. The floor rose up to meet her.

"Don't hurt my ma." Beth's cry pierced the roar in Molly's ears. The child shot toward her and wrapped her arms hard around Molly's neck. "Don't you hurt her any-more."

Molly struggled to sit up, but the room spun, and she tasted blood. Nausea vise-gripped her stomach, and she couldn't seem to catch her breath. Her lungs felt ready to explode, and her head roared with pain. The big men stormed toward her, and Beth clutched her fearfully. If only she could reach the gun in her pocket—

A boot stepped on her wrist, and pain cracked through her bone as the gunman pounded her with his weight. "I'm a sharpshooter, and one of the fastest draws in all of Texas. Don't insult me."

Through her haze of pain and fear, Molly recognized an accent like Luke's. She curled her free arm around Beth and held her with all the strength she had left. "Luke isn't here. He left last night. He rode off—"

"He wouldn't leave his precious brat." The raised heel of his boot ground harder. "It's ten degrees below and falling, and I'm not in the mood to wait for him to come home. Tell me where he is, or I'll take the girl."

"He left her with me. The mountains are too dangerous—"

He tore Beth from Molly's arms as if she were little more than a rag doll. Over the girl's sobs, his face turned ugly. "You tell Luke that if he wants his girl to live, I might be in the mood for a trade—his life for hers. *Maybe.*"

"You're not taking Beth." Molly found the strength to crawl onto her feet. "You take me, but leave the child here."

She didn't see the fist coming until it was too late. Pain knocked her to the floor, leaving her breathless and weak.

The gunmen were gone and Beth with them, leaving the door banging in the wind.

"What's all this racket down here?" Mrs. Thayer hurried into the room, then skidded to a stop.

That was the last thing Molly remembered before the world went black.

"I'm going to ask Mrs. Kemp to come spend the night." Doc Stanton knotted the last bandage on her splinted forearm. "Those men worked you over pretty good, Molly. You need to take it easy for a few days. Mrs. Kemp will take good care of you."

"Does Aggie know about this?"

"Not yet. Mrs. Thayer is with her now, and we both thought poor Aggie has enough to deal with. I figured I'd get you patched up first."

"I don't want her to know about this." Molly felt shaky, but she put her feet on the floor anyway, leaned her good hand on the table for leverage, and straightened her knees.

"Sit down, young lady," the doc admonished. He pushed her easily back into the chair.

Her head pounded with pain. The bandage at her throat where the shallow cut still bled made it hard to turn her head, and she cursed not being able to see the clock. How much time had passed since Beth's kidnapping? She had to leave now, while there was a trail to follow.

The doc droned on and tried to get her to take a dose of laudanum, which she managed to avoid. Finally, when he realized she wasn't going to take the painkiller, he headed upstairs to check on Aggie, promising to return.

Laudanum would only put her to sleep, and she needed to be awake and alert for the trip ahead. She levered herself up on her feet, and once she was standing she stumbled across the room to the coatrack. Sharp pain snapped through her broken wrist as she jammed her arm into her sleeve, but she wasn't going to let a little pain stop her.

Beth was with those brutal men. If they could beat and injure a grown woman, what harm would they cause a small child? Fear for her daughter kept her going when she didn't think she could make it down the steps.

She saddled Honey and pulled a pair of Russell's clean long wool underwear off the clothesline in the shed. The itchy wool fabric was freeze-dried and hard as week-old bread. She took a few changes of clothes, a variety of what she could find on the line or folded in the basket, and wrapped them in a wool blanket. Then she mounted up and rode off into the storm hoping beyond hope that the men who'd taken Beth had left some kind of a trail.

She headed her mare toward the mountains as the wind gusted, swirling the snow in her path. A blizzard was coming; she could sense it in the air, but it didn't stop her and she refused to be afraid.

She'd promised Luke to protect Beth with her life—and she intended to keep that promise.

Or die trying.

A group of mountain men were camped on both sides of the road next to the wooden bridge, and Luke cursed his luck. It was night and he was ready to move, and he was stuck. That crevasse had to be at least a hundred-foot climb down and back up the other side and that's what he'd have to do if he wanted to move tonight. With the weather, he couldn't get close enough to see if the men were travelers or bounty hunters.

This time of year, few travelers would brave the wicked mountains, and so Luke decided to play it safe, turn around, and head back to his shelter. He fought wind and ice to claw his way up the steep slope and welcomed the cold that seeped into his bones and stole the warmth from his blood.

His heart began to freeze, all the warm parts cooling to ice. Maybe, without a heart, he couldn't feel. And if he couldn't feel, he wouldn't hurt.

The howling wind hid the sound of the approaching horse, but Luke spied the faint movement against the thousand shades of night. He crouched low not a foot from the road's edge and watched as a horse nosed by. The rider clinging to the saddle looked too small for a man.

Wind-driven snow stung his eyes, making it harder to see. He caught the faint edge of something pale against the light-colored horse's flank, but he couldn't make out what it was.

The horse halted in midstride and lifted its weary head to scent the air. He watched, heart pounding and ready to draw, as the mare swung toward him and nickered, a low, welcoming sound that tore him into pieces. Recognition pounded through him, and he couldn't move as Honey knocked into the stubby, gnarled pine he was hiding behind and pressed her nose into his gloved palm. He saw the hem of a woman's dress and moved to her side.

"Molly." The wind tore her name from his lips, and he laid his hand on her knee, close enough to see the layer of iced snow covering her as she shivered in the saddle.

She lifted her left hand and tried to pull at her muffler, but it wouldn't budge, frozen solid from the warmth of her breath and the driving snow.

She was half frozen herself. Alarm beat through him. "What happened? Did something happen to Russell?"

She grabbed his wrist hard and held on tight, and he could barely understand her as she spoke through the iced layers of wool. "Did you see them?"

"See who?"

"The men who took Beth. They took her."

The blizzard gusted, and black fury hammered through him. He didn't ask who. "Were you following them?"

She nodded, and he couldn't get past what she'd said— Beth was gone. He wanted to roar like the storm.

He took it all in—her white face above the muffler, the hard quaking of her body, the clack of her teeth as she chattered, the way she hunched in the saddle, too weak from exposure to do anything more. The mighty torrent of night-black snow shrouded her as her head bowed forward even more.

He squeezed her knee and wished he could reassure her somehow, but the truth was he didn't know if anything would be right again. He hadn't spotted any suspicious riders on this road— and he'd been out scouting since dusk, trying to figure the best way down the east slopes of these unforgiving mountains. Where was Beth? The bounty hunter who'd snatched her was going to pay for it, that was for damn sure.

With every step up the steep rise, his anger doubled. He was the one to blame, staying in a paradise where he would never belong, wishing for a life he couldn't have. How could he have been that selfish as to risk his daughter? And now Molly was involved, and it was his fault—no one else's.

His rage kept him warm as he pulled the mare up the slippery slope, using the strength in his arms and shoulders to keep the weary animal from sliding back down into the ravine. The struggle across the porcelain-hard crests dappled with slick, loose snow kept him focused and the growing void of despair and fear for his daughter at bay. For now.

The wind blew harder and the flecks of snow punishing. He deserved it, damn it. Russell was depending on him; Molly was in danger of freezing to death; and Beth was out here somewhere at the mercy of a paid killer.

The abandoned prospector's shack was nothing more than walls and a roof, but it was shelter. He tied Honey out of the wind, and Molly tumbled into his arms. She was shaking so damn hard he didn't think she could walk, so he carried her against his chest, her cold body draining the warmth from his, and kicked open the door.

"Let me go," she demanded and twisted, but she lacked any real strength, and he carried her across the dirt floor to the stone chimney in the center of the one-room shanty.

The fire had burned to embers, but the hearth still held heat. He sat her on the stones and winced at each groan she made. Her teeth chattered; she shook from head to toe, and fear for her raged like a firestorm in his heart.

"I h-have t-to f-find h-her." Molly tried to stand, but cried out in pain. She tried again but had no strength left.

Luke poked the embers with a stick, breaking them apart before he added kindling. The cedar cracked, flame leaped to life, and he carefully added a few sticks of dried fir.

"Th-they w-walked r-right into the h-house," she stammered, tears brimming her eyes to freeze on her lashes. "P-people had b-been c-coming in and out all d-day and th-the door w-wasn't l-locked." She sobbed. "I sh-should have m-made sure the d-door was l-locked."

"Angel." He gathered her in his arms, as gently as he could because he knew how much she hurt. She cried out and pressed her face against his throat, shaking with cold and heartbreak.

"How c-can you stand m-me? I l-lost your d-daugh-ter."

The fire flared, casting enough light to see her by. He unwound the scarf that protected her face, and it was so thick with ice it was board-hard and crackled like breaking glass. She turned away from him, but he saw the bruise on her cheekbone, dark purple from a hard, cruel blow.

Guilt slammed into him like a charging buffalo, leaving him weak and drained. When he unbuttoned her cloak, he saw the bandage peaking out above the high neck of her undershirt. When he tugged off the wool socks she was using for gloves, he saw the edge of the splint that stabilized her wrist.

"I d-didn't stop them." Her eyes were dark with sorrow, and tears sluiced down her ice-burned cheeks in silent rivulets. "I tried."

He wasn't good enough to be with her, to breathe the same air, to walk on the same earth. His hands shook not from cold or rage but from something deeper, something greater, as he unbuttoned her dress. Snow had driven through every layer of clothing and froze against her skin. She didn't fight him as he stripped away the last garment.

She stared at a spot on the dirt floor while he shook out his bedroll and spread it in front of the fire. Head down, shoulders slumped, her broken wrist drawn up against her breasts, she didn't acknowledge him when he called her name. She didn't look up when he knelt in front of her and held out his hand.

So he carried her the short distance to where the warm bed waited. She shook hard and buried her face in his makeshift pillow. He covered her and fought the urge to love her until she'd never feel cold again.

Instead, he added more wood to the fire, and hoping sleep would claim her, headed back out into the night.

The blizzard's worsening wind chased him up the slope not an hour later, and he cursed the heartless storm that kept him from figuring out where the riders holding Beth captive had veered off the mountain road. The vicious winds wiped the snow clean of tracks and left him with less than what he started out with—hope.

But his determination remained. Neither the mountain nor the storm could drive that out of him. Beth was out in this cold and on these mountains, and he would find her. The men who'd kidnapped her would be forced to find shelter for the rest of the night, too. The hunt would resume with dawn.

The leather hinges whispered as he opened the door. She'd fallen asleep all right, lying on her side facing the shadows. The dying light from the fire brushed her with a soft sepia glow and highlighted the bruise on her cheekbone.

Holding back both rage and tenderness, he pulled the latchstring and loaded more wood in the fire. The ice on his gloves melted and snow tumbled off his hat brim, but he couldn't feel the heat. Ice-cold, he sat there, letting the fire thaw everything but his heart. Then he stripped down and eased between the scratchy wool blankets warmed by the fire and her body's heat.

She didn't stir when he settled beside her. The even rise and fall of her rib cage told him how deeply she slept. With the curve of her neck and the tiny bumps of her spine exposed, she looked vulnerable and small.

The firelight caressed the curve of her hip, the nip of her waist, and the outer curve of one breast, making his blood pound. He knew those curves well and had loved them with his hands and his mouth. Holding back his heart and telling himself he didn't deserve her couldn't stop his feelings.

He was rock-hard and shaking with the need to love her. It took all his strength to let the blanket fall, covering her nakedness from his sight.

"Luke?" She rolled over, and the blanket shivered down to expose the creamy rise of one breast. The fire-light caressed her the way he wanted to with lazy flicks and luxurious strokes, and her nipple pebbled from the cold air. "I didn't think you were coming back."

"Now where would I go? There isn't a town for fifty miles in either direction."

"How can you stand to look at me? I lost your child. I promised to protect her with my life and I failed."

He pressed a feather-light kiss to the bruise on her cheek.

Tears ached in her throat. "I tried to stop them."

He kissed the slope of her jaw where a smaller bruise darkened her skin.

"You should hate me, Luke."

"Angel, I'm never going to hate you. I love you too much. More than I've loved any woman. You are my heart." He brushed her silk-soft curls from her face.

Burning, aching tears spilled over and trailed in crooked tracks over the bridge of her nose and dripped onto the pillow. His kiss caught them, and she only cried harder. The pain inside built as he eased her onto her back and claimed her with kisses so sweet and tender, the pain inside her broke apart leaving her helpless and weak.

His kisses trailed down her throat, and when his tongue drew her nipple into his mouth, she held him there, powerless to fight the twisting spears of pleasure. He suckled, and she cried out, defenseless as her knees opened and he eased between her thighs. Hot curls of sensation coiled tight inside her and left her breathless.

She didn't understand how he could touch her, how he could even want to look at her again, but his hands swept down the slope of her stomach to curve inside her. She'd hurt this man, failed him in the most important way, and he was loving her with slow intense caresses of his tongue and hands that left her begging for more. Desperate, pleading words tumbled from her lips.

He chuckled, eager to oblige, and released her nipple, gently scraping his teeth along her sensitized skin. His swollen shaft nudged her inner thigh and pushed inside her, stretching and filling her, and she lifted her hips to draw him in more deeply.

With body and heart laid open to him, vulnerable and exposed, she closed her eyes tight. But the tears spilled between her closed lids, and sobs tore from her chest. He rocked into her again and again, his hard length stroking the deepest part of her, his hard body unyielding against hers, his kisses tenderly catching every tear that tracked down her cheeks.

Pleasure pounded through her; heartbreak threatened to tear her apart, and the future was crumbling into irretrievable pieces. But for this moment and this moment alone, she had him to hold on to. Desperate, she folded her body around his, hugging his hips with her thighs and his back with her uninjured arm. His tender-fierce thrusts sent her over the edge. Release shattered them both, and as if they were one, they broke apart together in a pleasure that left her weak and wet with his seed.

Then he was kissing her again, still hard inside her.

"Look at me." His words brushed across her lips and rumbled in her chest.

She met his gaze. He had the right to hate her, even after loving her like this. She didn't know how she could bear to see the disappointment on his face.

"I love you, Molly. I will always love you."

A sob tore from her chest, and she kissed him, open-mouthed and deep. His shaft thrummed inside her, thick and hard, and she rocked her hips. He moaned and met her rhythm, and there was no more need for words. Outside the shanty the blizzard raged, but here in Luke's arms she was safe and warm and loved. She was loved.

"You're not coming." Luke tied his canvas pack and flung it on the floor. "You're going to head back over that pass and go straight home. You don't belong out here."

"Right, but you do."

"I'm her father." He tossed a pair of his trousers and a wool shirt onto the bedroll. "Put those on; that dress of yours isn't going to keep you warm enough for the trip home."

"I'm not going home." Battered and bruised, Molly lifted her chin and grabbed the shirt with her good hand. "I'm going after my daughter."

"You should have let the sheriff handle it, instead of running off on your own trying to get Beth back." He jabbed the charred stick into the fireplace and knocked apart the embers, venting his rage.

He was furious at himself for believing in a dream. He was furious at Molly for being so damn loyal. Even as she fumbled into his shirt, taking care not to knock her bro-ken wrist, she didn't look bowed, not with the defiant jut of her delicate chin. She looked like a warrior woman ready for battle.

"I *am* going." Molly struggled into the trousers. "When you catch up to those men, you'll need me. You'll need someone to take care of Beth."

"Here." He handed her a length of rope from his saddlebag. "Use this for a belt."

She wasn't going. That was the end of it. He had too much on his mind to deal with her independent streak. The first hint of dawn was graying the world, and he had to get moving.

While she was wrapping her wool scarf around her neck and face, he bolted outside. The wind slammed him up against the wall of the shanty, and he fought it all the way to the other side of the building.

The horses were blanketed out of the wind, but that was little protection against the cold ground. The gelding laid back his ears and bared his teeth. Luke apologized the best he could by offering a double helping of grain. By the time he'd saddled both horses, Molly was there, dropping his pack at his feet. His saddlebags were slung over her good shoulder.

He wanted to take her in his arms and protect her. The Montana Rockies in winter was no place for a woman, especially one he loved. She could have frozen to death last night on her misguided journey, although he loved her for the way she loved his daughter.

"I wasn't planning on traveling by day on these roads, but I don't have a choice right now. We'll ride together as far as the pass." He handed her a handful of beef jerky from his saddlebag. "The men who took Beth wouldn't head north. There's no telegraph, no city, and no train. No, they're heading south."

"Then we should be heading toward Rattlesnake Ridge and not back up the mountain. They have our daughter."

"Not for long." Tall on his saddle, he towered over her, a man of might and courage. The snow shrouded the landscape so completely they couldn't see more than a few feet in front of them, but Luke led the way through trees and ice fields back to the main road.

"Avalanche danger," he told her and kept on the road after that.

Molly set her teeth to keep them from chattering and bowed her head against the cutting wind. She'd been cold last night, but it was nothing compared to the temperature this morning as the sun rose in a small glowing ball hidden behind white clouds. The winds rose, stirring the snow, making it more difficult to see anything. Luke made her dismount and walk so they wouldn't ride straight off a cliff.

"This has to be where they cut off." Luke sawed a small limb from a pine and swept at the layers of snow. What he saw there made his shoulders straighten. "This is where we part paths, Molly. Go home. Tell Russell I'll do my damnedest to stay alive and order his medicine, but there's no guarantees."

"That's why I'm going with you." She swept the snow from her saddle. "And don't waste your breath arguing. I've made up my mind."

"Damn it, this isn't the time. A woman doesn't belong in those mountains."

"It doesn't matter. That's where Beth is."

"We could die up there."

"Then that's the risk we'll take." Molly gazed up at the ruthless mountains, unforgiving and dangerous. She'd never ridden in the high country, but she understood the perils.

Sometimes in life, a woman couldn't choose safety or peace. She had to take a stand; she had to take a risk. When it came to family, nothing else mattered.

Luke guided his gelding up a steep embankment, then climbed down to help her lead her mare to the top.

"They took the railroad grade. Look at those snow-heavy peaks. Noise will bring half the mountain down on top of us. We're silent from here on out."

The high country stretched around them, hushed and predatory. A small heap of snow sloughed off not a hundred feet above them, thundered to the ground, and rose like dust in the air.

The back of his neck tingled, and Luke couldn't shake the feeling that death awaited him.

He picked up their trail a mile out of Rattlesnake Ridge. One of their horses had thrown a shoe, and they'd repaired it right there on the trail, leaving behind two men's boot prints and a child's footprint in the new snow.

Two days of solid riding left him exhausted, but as he headed toward town at Molly's side, Luke felt energized. The fury that had driven him across the mountains faded into a cold, deadly focus.

Molly looked too exhausted to go much farther, and as the noise and hustle of the town surrounded them—a jarring shock after the silent mountains—he checked her into the first hotel he saw and sent her upstairs to a hot bath. She protested, but he assured her that Beth's kidnappers were just as cold and weary.

He roamed the streets alone. When he found Dr. Richards's office, he handed the physician a note from Doc Stanton and a hundred-dollar bill. It would be enough incentive to pay for the delivery of the medicine and the foodstuffs on Drew's purchase order, the doctor assured him. Teamsters were hurting for work and some would look past the danger. After Luke was certain the doc would find someone immediately, he headed back out to the street.

It was crowded, but Luke knew where to look. He stopped across the street from a diner and studied the patrons inside, enjoying their noon meals. No luck, so he kept walking until he saw two horses left on the street, trail weary and covered with snow, shivering in the cold.

He turned around and saw through a dirt-spotted window black ringlet curls tangled by the wind and matted from snow. Her yellow coat was torn at one sleeve, and she sat between two men, their attention on the pretty waitress as she jotted down their orders. He didn't recognize the man in uniform, but he'd know the other one anywhere.

His knees nearly gave out, and he grabbed the hitching post for support. Fletcher gave the waitress a charming smile, the same one he'd given in court when he'd lied through his teeth. Luke stepped out of sight when he wanted to burst through the door and tear Fletcher apart with his bare hands, but that wouldn't help Beth. So he gritted his teeth and kept walking.

Across the street, the sheriff stepped out of his office and peered through the veil of snow. Luke ducked into a shop and waited until the lawman went back into his office, but he couldn't shake the gut-deep feeling his time was running out.

He kept out of sight until Fletcher and his gunman hauled Beth across the street to the train depot. Cousin Fletcher must have felt Luke's hatred from thirty yards away because he kept looking over his shoulder.

Good. Let him be nervous. He ought to be.

Luke waited until Fletcher had hauled Beth inside the station and out of sight, before he approached the ticket window. There was only one train arriving in the next few hours—southbound to Cheyenne.

A horse neighed on the street, and Luke ducked around the corner. On his way past the window he saw Beth sitting slump-shouldered on the bench, Fletcher's hand banding her arm.

A pack of deputies fanned into sight, surrounding the building. Luke stepped into the shadows and disappeared just in time.

"Two tickets, please." Molly's hands shook as she laid the bills Luke had given her on the counter.

The scarf tied around her face hid all but her profile, and the wide-rimmed bonnet hid every scrap of her russet hair. The dress Luke had purchased for her was far more elegant than the dress wadded up in the bottom of his satchel. She only hoped she didn't look like herself.

Molly tucked the change into her reticule and crossed the wooden platform. The train stood like a giant bellowing beast issuing a thick column of black smoke that dirtied the falling snow.

"Ma'am." A deputy tipped his hat to her.

For a split second, terror lashed through her, but then he strolled away from her. Still quaking, Molly noticed half a dozen uniformed men on the platform, probably every lawman the town had, watching the crowd. For Luke.

The deputy who'd spoken to her stopped to talk with someone else on the platform. Travelers began to board, and suddenly she was surrounded and swept toward the nearest door. She recognized too late that the deputy was talking with Beth's kidnappers. The well-dressed of the two men had to be Luke's cousin. But where was Beth? Had something happened to her? What had they done with her?

Then she saw a flash of Beth's yellow coat and dark ringlet curls. People cut between them and blocked off her view. Molly turned her shoulder as the crowd pushed her closer. *Please, don't let Beth see me.*

Someone knocked against her side, and Molly turned. Not five feet away, Beth was staring up at her, her sad eyes filling with silent hope. She heard Fletcher say, "I'll double the bounty if you catch him today. I want him dead, Deputy. He's a killer, don't forget that."

Molly turned away. *Please, Beth, don't say a word.*

Then the crowd swept forward, and she boarded the train. She took the closest window seat and watched as Beth and Fletcher boarded the train. They headed to the back and disappeared into the next car.

It seemed an eternity before the train's whistle pierced the air, signaling all aboard. The engines thundered, the wheels clattered, and the platform drifted away.

Luke, where are you? Fear beat in her heart. He had to be safe. Molly took a deep breath and scanned out the window. The town was whirring by at an alarming rate. The trees close to the tracks were a green blur. The telegraph wire swooped up and down between the poles. They were going too fast if Luke thought he could jump onto the train.

Then the front door banged open, and there he was, wearing a gray cap instead of his Stetson and a gray worker's uniform instead of his jacket. Smoke smudged his cheeks and stained his hands. As he ambled down the aisle, his gaze locked on hers and chased away her every fear.

"Hi, gorgeous." He settled into the seat beside her and leaned so close that her entire being sang with his presence. "I paid a man fifty bucks to take his clothes and his place at the coal stop."

"I'm glad you're safe." Molly pressed a kiss to his cheek.

"I wasn't a Texas Ranger for nothing." He wiped his hands on

241

his denims before he took her hand in his. "Did any of the deputies get on the train?"

"None that I saw."

"That's one thing going for us. Did you see Beth?"

"She looked terrified." Molly kissed his knuckles. "She recognized me."

"Then maybe she won't be so afraid." Fury threatened to overtake him. He wanted to hunt down Fletcher and deal with the bastard once and for all. But there were innocent people on this train, people Fletcher wouldn't think twice about harming. "Do you know where she is?"

"In the back of the train."

He released her hand, hating to let her go. "You stay here."

"There you go, giving me orders again." She untied the hat from her chin and laid it on her lap. "Haven't you forgotten I'm not the following orders type of wife?"

"It's damn annoying, too." Tenderness filled all the hollow, angry places in his heart as he watched her untie the scarf and shake her head. Beautiful bronzed curls cascaded over her shoulders to brush the curves of her breasts.

"You can come only as far as I say. I mean it this time, Molly. You have to keep Beth away from any danger. She comes first. Whatever happens, I need your word on that."

"You have it." Her lips brushed his in a brief hot kiss.

He took her by the hand and led her down the aisle. The train rocked from side to side, buffeted by the howling winds. A storm was brewing as they ascended into the mountains. Luke stumbled when the car snaked on the tracks, and the wind howled, rocking the car again.

Several women cried out in fear, but he kept going. He stepped into the last passenger car, shielding Molly from view with his body. Where was Beth? He scanned the faces in the car quickly. In the last seat he spotted a tuft of black curls—Beth was too small to see over the top of the seat.

Wind slammed against the car, shrieking like a wild animal, and daylight vanished. The lamps in the front and back of the car lit the way as he ducked back into the other car and escorted Molly to the nearest empty seat.

"Is she all right?" Molly's eyes widened when he pulled out his revolver.

"I couldn't tell." He checked the chambers quietly, keeping the gun low and out of sight of the other passengers. "There are a lot of people in that car. I can't risk a gunfight with innocent families in the way."

"Then do we wait?"

"We don't reach another town for about an hour."

As the train leaned into a curve, the wind rocked the cars hard from the north. A terrible screeching sound sent some of the passengers into a panic.

"We wait," he decided. "We wait for the right time to take her—when she isn't likely to get hurt and neither is anyone else."

Molly's hand curled around his arm, and she felt so good. He pressed a kiss to her russet curls, inhaling the silk and lilac scent, wishing they could have one more night together. Just one more night.

But he knew in his heart that he wouldn't make it out of this train alive.

The door slammed open behind him, and he turned in his seat, gun in hand. Fletcher filled the doorway between the two cars and looked around before heading down the aisle.

Of all the men who could have entered that car, it had to be Fletcher. Luke knew the instant the bastard spotted him. He heard the hesitant footfall and whisper of a gun drawing from a holster.

"Everyone down!" He burst into the aisle, already pulling the trigger. The car shook just as his gun fired, and the bullet punched a hole in the edge of Fletcher's sleeve and into the window behind him.

Women screamed, and people scrambled for the door. Others collapsed on the floor as bullets filled the air. Luke aimed, and the damn car rocked again, knocking him to his knees. He hit heavily and rolled. A bullet plowed into the floor where he'd been.

Luke drew his second revolver, but it was too late. Fletcher had retreated into the other car where his daughter was. Damn, this wasn't how he wanted to do it. He wanted Beth safe with Molly on the other side of the train, not in the middle of a gun battle.

"Get out of here," he ordered the people who'd dropped to the floor and were paralyzed with fear, now that the bullets had stopped. "Get going. You, too, Molly."

"I'm not leaving without Beth."

"You'll be leaving in a pine box if you don't get on the other side of that steel door." He grabbed her by the wrist. "Do it now."

Before she could answer, the rear door flew open. Luke saw the flash of two guns. Bullets shattered windows and tore through seat backs. He rolled into the aisle, fired, and kept rolling. One of the gunmen dropped to the floor, already dead. The remaining gunman kept firing. Dodging ricocheting bullets, Luke pulled out his third revolver and fired. Heat grazed his shoulder, but the second gunman flew against the back wall and slid to the floor.

"Molly, are you all right?"

"Y-yes."

"Good. Stay down." Taking advantage, Luke stalked the aisle to the back door. Both gunmen were dead—no doubt about that—and he turned his attention to the man inside the last car.

"Fletcher, going to send anyone else out to kill me? Or are you going to try next?"

"I'm a better gunman than you, Luke."

"I'm a better marksman." He could smell his cousin's fear. "It doesn't matter what you do now, Fletcher. You're going to be a dead man for what you did to my daughter."

"I am her legal guardian."

Luke heard the shuffle of feet and fired through the narrow passageway. A body struck the floor with a lifeless thud. Another gunman—Fletcher couldn't have too many more hired guns protecting his back.

"Let's make a deal, Cousin." Luke pulled out his fourth revolver and cocked it. "Release my daughter and the passengers in that car, and I'll let you have me."

"As if I would trust you, you murderer."

"It takes one to know one." Luke aimed both revolvers and held them steady. "What's it going to be?"

"You'll trade your life, just like that?"

"I want my daughter out of there."

Molly uncurled herself from the floor next to the dead gunman. She could see Luke crouching to the side of the door like a mighty wolf ready to spring on his sizable prey. No fear lined his face or diminished the powerful set of his shoulders.

One by one the passengers ran out of the car, frightened the gun battle would resume at any moment. Businessmen, mothers with their children, and fathers carrying frightened infants looked grateful to have their lives. Finally, Beth tripped into the car, holding out her arms to her father.

Molly scooped her up and ran as fast as she could to the other side of the car.

"Papa! Papa!" Beth struggled and kicked, but Molly didn't let go.

She hesitated at the door, but there was no time to say good-bye.

"Drop your weapons, Cousin. It's time to keep up your end of the bargain." Fletcher's words rang with triumph and a note of fear. "I've got my guns cocked and ready because I wouldn't want you breaking your promise to me.

"Go." Luke mouthed the word to her and walked through the door.

The car swayed with the force of another wind gust, and knocked him to his knees. The wheels beneath squealed as iron grated against iron. By the time Luke struggled to his feet, Fletcher fired. A bullet ripped into the floor an inch in front of Luke's left boot.

"Drop the guns, dear Cousin. I expect you to keep to our bargain."

Except for Fletcher, the car was empty. Luke dropped his revolver, grateful for the final one tucked in his boot. "I wasn't sure if you'd bother to come all this way after me. Montana's pretty damn cold this time of year, and I know how you like the Texas heat."

"And I will be returning shortly, after I finish this last bit of business. Turn around."

"So you can put a bullet in my back?"

"That would be my preference." Fletcher holstered one gun, and his free hand skidded over Luke's chest and hips, down his legs and into the top of his left boot. "Thought for sure I'd find one here. Let me check the other—"

Luke drove his elbow straight back, and bone connected with flesh. Fletcher tumbled, and Luke was on him, knocking the gun from his hand and ramming a fist into his cousin's face.

Fletcher's fist caught Luke in the chin.

He returned it once and twice. He tried to reach for his cousin's holstered gun and took another blow to his jaw.

"Keep the damn money for all I care. You could have left me alone." Luke landed another blow.

"What if you found a judge—" Fletcher spit blood.

The car slammed sideways, skidding off the tracks in an ear-splitting screech. The fishtailing sent Luke rolling across the floor.

Fletcher drew and fired. Luke ducked, rolled, and his shoulder rammed into the wall. Pain fired through his neck, and he spun around as another bullet bit into a seat an inch from his head.

The train was skidding downhill; the scream of rending iron filled the air as the car swayed in a free fall from one side to the other, tossing Luke around like a rag doll. He slammed into a seat back, and pain streaked through his ribs.

The car tipped on end and listed to the side. The windows shattered. Luke grabbed the iron bar holding a seat to the floor. At the first impact, metal buckled as it slammed into trees. The car began to break apart.

Fear licked through him, as cold and cruel as the storm, but then it faded when he realized that Fletcher couldn't open the door and escape. It had slammed shut and there was no escape. None at all.

The two of them would die, and Beth would finally be safe.

"Take your seats!" the conductor dashed down the aisle, and Molly could hardly hear his booming instructions above the roar of the engine, the howling blizzard, and iron breaking apart.

"Where's Papa?" Beth cried, her arms so tight around Molly's throat she couldn't breathe. "I want my papa."

"I know." Molly smoothed a hand over Beth's tangled curls. The child's grip eased when they settled down in a seat, but she didn't let go.

The train flew down the incline, and Molly could feel the floor beneath her lift off the tracks. Terror rang through the passenger car as cries, prayers, and pleas added to the general din and confusion.

"Heads in your laps, hold on to your children!" The conductor was gone, barking his orders at the next car of travelers.

We're going to crash. Molly held her daughter tight and tried not to think of what could happen. Beth was crying as the car slammed back to the tracks. The wall of falling snow broke apart, and Molly nearly screamed at the endless space and yawning canyon below. Then the snow swirled, cutting off her view of the trestle they were speeding across between two mountain slopes.

Cries turned to screams as the train curved toward the relative safety of the mountain. The car jerked and flew off the tracks completely. They sailed through air and then hit with a bone-bending jar, skidding along a glacier field in a long, frightening hiss.

Molly heard the screams of horror, and she jumped out of her seat just in time to see the rear end of the train fly off the trestle and break apart. Carrying Beth on her hip, she raced across the aisle and watched the caboose and two cars careen out of sight.

An explosion shattered the last of her hopes. Dark plumes of smoke curled up from the canyon below.

"I was in that car until..." a businessman said into the shocked silence. "There were gunmen..." He broke down and said nothing else.

Luke had been in that car. Molly clawed her way outside and ran to the edge of the tracks. The train lay in a disjointed jackknife, half on the trestle and half on the mountainside. She didn't need to walk any closer to see that Luke wasn't among the passengers lining up to look at the wreckage.

"No one could have survived that." A man held his hat over his heart.

Molly's knees started to shake as the wind drove the acrid smoke over them. Battered by the blizzard, filled with grief, Molly dropped to the snow and accepted the truth.

Luke was dead.

CHAPTER FIFTEEN

"You're a sight for sore eyes." Mayor Smythe stepped off the dark boardwalk, a crying infant on his shoulder. The town Christmas tree was lit and candlelight illuminated the father holding his tiny son. "I know your aunt was worried about you. No one knew where you went."

"I went to help Luke." She held back the truth, a raw personal pain that felt out of place on this holy night. Organ music drifted from the church, where windows were lit against the darkness, and the evening service was in full swing.

"Where is he?"

Molly choked and couldn't answer. She just couldn't. Carrying a sleeping Beth, she crawled out from beneath the fur robes in the teamster's sleigh. Her feet were unsteady as she stood, and the mayor caught her elbow.

"Would you deliver this to Aggie for me?" She pulled the medicine from her cloak pocket. "That is, if Russell's still—"

"He's alive and improving, and the doctor is hopeful. I'm sure this medicine will make all the difference." The mayor accepted the package as his son gave a loud protest. "My mother usually babysits, but she wanted to attend the service tonight. Let me get the door for you—"

"No." Molly untied Honey from the back of the huge sleigh filled with supplies from Rattlesnake Ridge. "I need to get home."

"You don't seem well, Molly. Let me walk you to Aggie's."

"No, I need to be alone." She thanked him and then remembered Lady. She couldn't go home without her dog. Remembering how Luke had played with the hound in the snow made her want to cry, and she mounted up onto the ice-cold saddle.

Drew raced out of the church at the sight of the sleigh piled high with groceries and thanked her. The teamster hauled the load around to the back of the mercantile, and Drew followed, searching for his keys.

The night was still and dark, calm and peaceful. White stars winked in a clear sky overhead, and it felt as if heaven smiled down on the pristine beauty of the earth. The candles flickered merrily, lighting the way as she nosed the mare down the dark street.

The Christmas tree gleamed in Aggie's front window, the flickering candles as magical as a promise made and kept. Glass ornaments reflected the light. Molly almost went to the door, but she waited in the alley as Mayor Smythe trudged up the front porch steps. Lady's bark shattered the stillness, and Molly nearly cried at the sight of her dog rounding the corner of the house. Lady leaped and yipped merrily.

The ride home was long, and Molly's heart sank at the sight of her dark and lonely home. Beth stirred awake, wanting to know if they were there yet.

It was so cold in the house they had to keep their wraps on and stomp their feet to keep warm until the fire had burned hot and long enough to chase away the deep freeze in the rooms. Trying not to think of Luke, Molly put a frozen pot of stew on the stove.

The dark, unadorned tree in the corner of her parlor reminded her of him every time she walked into that room. Of the promise she'd made to him. Of how lonely her life would be without him. How could she bear to decorate that tree now, knowing he'd given up his life to keep her and Beth safe?

"Is this the night Santa comes?" Beth asked over their simple meal.

"It's Christmas Eve." Molly didn't feel like celebrating, and there was no hope in her heart.

Maybe it was just her imagination but she heard something on the wind, a silvery shiver that sounded like...

"Jingle bells!" Beth raced to the door with Lady barking after her.

Sure enough, the sweet chime of sleigh bells filled her yard. Lady lunged at the back door with her big paws. Was it Aggie? Had Aggie come to welcome them home?

Molly pulled aside the edge of the curtain and saw a man climb out of a small sleigh, his shoulders broad and his gait uneven. For a moment, she thought she saw Luke's profile...

No, it was impossible. Maybe Aggie had sent someone from town.

"*Papa!*" Beth ran to the door and flung it open.

"No, Beth. It can't be your father." Heart breaking, Molly ran out onto the porch after the child and the dog. The spill of light tumbled past her and illuminated the face of the man holding Beth in his arms.

Luke! She flew down the steps and held him tight, and he was real, flesh and blood and not imagination, not dream. His mouth found hers in a sweet, hot kiss that chased away every last doubt.

"I missed you, angel," he whispered in her ear and led her into the warm house where the fire flickered and hope lived. "How I missed you."

Her heart felt new. "Let me feel you one more time. I have to know that you're still real."

His lips slanted over hers in a hot and tender kiss that made her remember every time he'd touched her. "I know just how you feel. I'm not a man who believes in dreams, and here I am, I've come home to you."

"Papa, Papa!" Beth tugged on his trouser leg. "Don't ever leave again."

"Well, darlin'." He knelt and took her into his arms. "That's my plan. Tell me why the tree isn't decorated."

"We were just getting around to it, right Beth?" Molly held out her hand.

The little girl smiled. "Right. 'Cuz it says in the story that when Santa comes, the tree has to be decorated."

"Then we've got work to do." Luke watched his wife and daughter cross the room, and a great love built in his heart. He knew it would never leave him but burn more brightly every day of his life.

He believed in dreams, in miracles, and he believed in happy-ever-afters.

It was Christmas Eve, and on this night it felt as if the world were new and life held endless possibilities.

Later that night, Luke rolled her off his hips and wrapped her against his chest. Breathless from lovemaking, Molly cuddled into his side, savoring everything about him—the texture of his skin against hers, the way a dimple carved into his chin when he smiled, and a thousand other things that reminded her he was really here in her bed.

Grateful tears stung her eyes, and she buried her face against his hot skin.

"Hey, why are you crying?" His lips brushed her brow. "Don't tell me I was that bad of a lover."

"You were terrible. It was such a letdown."

"That's why you were making all those sounds of ecstasy?"

"Exactly."

His mouth brushed hers, tentative and tender. Love filled her heart with so much pain.

"I've lost you twice, Luke. I can't stand to do it a third time. I know you're only here for Christmas, and when it's over you're going to walk out that door and take my heart with you—"

"Now, that's where you're wrong, angel." He rolled her beneath him and stretched out over her. He was strength and tenderness, and he made her want to believe...

"What are you talking about? You're a fugitive." Tears filled her eyes as he pressed her legs apart with his knee. His hard shaft nudged against her inner thigh.

"Luke McKenna died in a train wreck along with his cousin. But Luke Jamison didn't." He kissed her long and deep, and then he smiled, truly smiled without fear, without darkness. "Luke Jamison is a free man."

"That can't be true. I couldn't be that lucky." Molly pressed her face into the hollow of his neck, hiding her tears and her heartache.

"No, I'm the lucky one." His lips grazed hers. "I love you, Molly, with all the depth of my soul, with everything I am. You are the love of my life, and I want to spend my future with you."

Overcome, she held him, just held him, her one true love.

The parlor clock bonged twelve times.

Luke filled her in one slow thrust. "Merry Christmas, my angel."

Hannah's Heart

Colton Kincaid reined in the team of horses. Trepidation skidded over him like the fat chunks of falling snow. It wasn't much of a town. Just a couple streets, a handful of businesses, and a few unimpressive houses. But it looked quiet and safe. A real family place. A town where nothing went wrong, men were honest, and, he figured, there would be no need for a full-time sheriff.

Colton felt a tug on his sleeve.

"I'm hungry."

This child was all he had in the world. Colton studied the small boy's round face, and a trickle of hope filled him. Maybe he could find what he was looking for in this forgotten little town. A home for his son. The dream of living again.

Lights shone through the falling snow, warm like a beacon welcoming him home.

Home. Colton craved it like the feel of a hot, crackling fire. He'd been without one for so long. But this was the last leg of a long journey. After this, there would be no more traveling. He snapped the reins. The team broke into a trot as if they sensed the town might mean home, too, and the sled's runners squeaked on the loosely packed snow.

The main street was quiet, perhaps on account of the storm. Only one horse, a fine spotted mustang, stood drowsing at the hitching post outside the only hotel.

"Look at the lights," he told his son. "We can eat in there."

"Want beans."

"Me, too, little fella." Colton reined in the team and climbed from the sleigh, careful to keep cold air from slipping in beneath the thick blankets, careful to keep a tight control on his heart. It would be easy to start putting up dreams, building on them one by one, looking at a peaceful place like this.

Dreams, he'd learned, didn't buy a boy a hot meal and a safe bed for the night. Hard work did. And by God, that's why he was here—to start a partnership with his one-time friend and, in time, buy his own land.

Determined to right old wrongs, Colton lifted the child from his snug nest in the sleigh.

The hotel's front door popped open, and his gaze landed on the woman who emerged with one hand propped on the doorknob. She stopped in the well-lit threshold, her back to him as she laughed with someone inside.

"Rose Carson," she said, light as air, "you stop matchmaking for me. Maybe you should concentrate on finding men for the younger girls in this town. They're foolish enough to actually *want* husbands."

The woman turned, facing him. Lamplight filtered through the window, burnishing her uncovered gold hair. His breath caught at the sight. Her face was heart-shaped, her blue eyes kind.

"What a handsome son you have." Warmth. Gentleness. Those qualities filled her voice like melody and harmony, and she breezed closer.

"Thank you," Colton managed. If he had one pride, it was his son. The quiet, gentle-hearted soul who'd been left in his care after Ella's death. Colton set the boy on the ground, keeping a firm hold of him so his small feet wouldn't slip on the ice.

"How old is he?"

"Two," Colton answered.

Zac held up three fingers.

The woman's laughter made the freezing air feel warmer and easier to bear. "Well, little one, you'll have to come to my Sunday School class. We have two other children who are just your age. That is, if you're planning on staying in town that long." She tilted her face and looked up at him. His heart skipped five beats.

"We sure hope to." He found the air to speak, and noticed the shine of a gold band on her left ring finger. "I'm Colton Kincaid. And this little charmer is my son, Zac."

"It's a pleasure to meet you both. My name is Hannah." She reached into her cloak pocket and withdrew a pair of gray knit gloves. "You must be new to town."

"Yes, ma'am." What was he doing, talking to a married woman, far too fine for the likes of him? Colton took a step toward the hotel, holding on tight to Zac as the boy toddled and nearly slid.

Colton caught him, both hands on those small elbows, and kept him upright. Zac, the trust so deep, kept waddling.

"Perhaps you could tell us if this is the only place to eat in town?" he found himself asking, just to catch her gaze again.

"Yes, it is." Dream-blue eyes brushed his. She wasn't bold or flirtatious, just friendly, and it intrigued him, touched him.

How long had it been since he'd lived in a place where women could greet strangers with such a smile? Such complete faith in the goodness of the world?

All the more proof he was a duck out of water. A man like him, he didn't belong here. But for his son's sake, he would do his best.

Colton nodded his thanks and took a few more patient steps up onto the boardwalk, carefully holding Zac by the forearms so the boy could walk on the ice on his own.

"Rose Carson runs this establishment." Hannah rushed after them, her face pinkened from the harsh burn of the cold air. Despite the bulky winter coat and the care she took on the ice, she looked graceful and gentle. And as well dressed as a fashion plate. "Rose is a great friend of mine. I should introduce you."

So eager. Colton wondered at that. Then he realized she was watching after his son, the small boy determined to follow in his father's footsteps, sliding, but unafraid of falling. It was for the child her eyes shone and her voice rang like melody and harmony.

A knot tightened in Colton's throat. When he studied her now, with a careful eye, he saw the lines of sadness etched around her mouth.

"Thanks, but I think I can manage on my own," Colton said more gruffly than he intended.

Hannah froze, a stiffness settling along her jaw. In her eyes, he saw her own reproach. He'd embarrassed her, he realized. Worse, she must have thought she'd embarrassed herself.

But in his book, any woman who cared so easily over another's child, why, that was a good thing indeed.

"Yes, come inside and introduce me to this Rose." Colton let his voice soften. He felt bigger, better, when a small but sure smile brushed her soft lips.

"I hope she's a good cook," he added.

"I'm hungry," Zac grinned.

Hannah's heart caught. Such a dear child—she could see that about him already, this tiny boy who was the exact replica of his father, with the same dark hair and eyes. The same sense of stoic strength that made heroes of men. At least in myths and legends.

She'd never known a man who was halfway trustworthy, let alone one who could be called a hero.

But she did admire how this man, Colton Kincaid he'd called himself, held open the heavy front door to the hotel with a patience only a father's love could provide. Her throat ached, remembering.

How she'd wished things could have been different, that Charles could have looked with love like that so bright and alive in his eyes at his own child. But there was no changing the past. Certainly not now.

Her whole chest hurt watching the little boy as he ambled on short, chubby legs out of the bitter cold and into the hotel. Her arms felt empty. Her heart felt empty.

"I didn't mean to..." Zac's father paused, "embarrass you, I guess. I think he's something special, too."

"Then you're a good father." Hannah forced a smile. Loneliness wrapped around her as cold as the snow outside but here, in the light of this stranger's presence, she felt less alone. "All little children should be so lucky."

"Not so lucky." A single shake of his head.

Hannah wondered at the swift denial. Then wondered at the man. His chiseled face looked rugged, but handsome. His black hair was long, falling just past his collar to touch his shoulders. And the shadows in his brown eyes, they drew her. As if he, too, had lost hope long ago.

Remorse shivered through her. Small lines hugged his eyes,

etched his face. Hardship had placed them there. And time.

And here she had been longing after his child like...like a kidnapper. Blushing, ashamed her feelings rose too easily to the surface, Hannah only took a step past the door he held for her. She caught a fresh scent of pine and outdoor air that clung to his coat, to him, and it was as rugged and as attractive as the man.

She cleared her throat, determined to leave before she could embarrass herself further. It just hurt, being so alone. Having such empty arms.

"Rose," she called out into the warm and well-lit parlor. "You have customers."

"In this weather? Oh, my!" Rose bustled out from the back door of the kitchen, wiping her hands on her crisp, ruffled apron. "My, what a handsome little boy. Hannah, are these friends of yours?"

She felt the man's gaze on her, sure and steady, bold as a touch. Had she given him the wrong idea? "No, I just met them myself. I wanted to recommend your wonderful cornbread and baked beans."

"Beans," Zac repeated wistfully.

The big, powerful man, handsome as the devil, pulled off the tiny boy's knit woolen cap. A simple brown, nothing special, made with a mother's love.

Hannah wondered if they were alone. If Mr. Kincaid was a widower. Then she shook herself, determined to stop letting her dreamy nature get the best of her. Whatever Mr. Kincaid was, he wasn't her business. Never would be.

"I've got to get home, Rose," Hannah called out to her friend. But Rose was already kneeling down to talk to little Zac as his capable, broad-shouldered father unwound the boy's dark muffler.

"Thank you, ma'am." Colton's words rattled through her like a thunderstorm, low and dark and powerful.

"Good luck to you." She managed the words, thankful she sounded normal. Thankful her heart didn't show, for she was determined to hide it.

" 'Bye," Zac turned, lifting his mittened hand in a cute, childish wave.

Her heart collapsed. Would the pain always be with her? Lord knew she'd tried so hard to bury it. But there it was again, always raw and hopeless. She supposed she would have to try harder.

More determined, Hannah closed down her feelings, dug a little deeper, and laid the yearnings in her heart to rest.

"Good-bye, Zac." She tried to smile through the words, but couldn't. Not really. So she stepped out into the cold and let the freezing comfort of the snow wash over her.

Mrs. Rose Carson's wholesome beans, honeyed ham, and fresh cornbread did the trick. It had taken the edge off his hunger and driven the cold from his bones. Colton sat down on the edge of the double bed, neatly made and the tick freshly stuffed—he could smell the clean straw—and gently tugged off Zac's shoes.

Tummy full, the boy's eyes had closed the instant Colton had laid him in the bed, more exhausted from the trip than Colton had figured. In truth, the cold ride out from Missoula had been a grueling one this time of year. He hadn't thought cold weather would come so soon in these mountainous foothills east of the Rockies, but he'd been wrong. Had he known, he would have started for these parts weeks earlier.

But in his letter, Charles had promised there was no hurry, that the job would be waiting for him—and the opportunity. It was too damn good to be true. The knowledge of what he stood to gain calmed the guilt of how hard the trip had been for little Zac. He was so young now, but if Colton played his cards right and worked for all he was worth, the boy would have land to call his own one day. He wouldn't have to make his living the way his father had, at the cold end of a gun.

A light knock on the open door spun Colton around. It was only Mrs. Carson, harmless in her blue gingham and ruffled apron, a smile lighting her eyes. "He's a precious one. Is he sleeping?"

"Hasn't even stirred." Colton set the tiny shoes on the hearth to stay warm and turned to pull the hand-crocheted afghan over his son. "Thank you for the meal. I know it was late, past dinner time. You were cleaning up your kitchen."

"I always have food for a weary traveler, especially one so small." There was no censure in Rose's eyes. Maybe a question. And he could guess it. What was a man doing out in such weather with a child?

Colton was appreciative that the woman didn't ask. "The town looks shut down because of the storm."

"It is." Rose leaned against the threshold. "Folks are used to the snows around these parts, but it's the blizzards that come up and can kill a man. Last winter ranchers in these parts lost most of their cattle. The winds were so cold and hard and the snow drifted so high it smothered entire herds."

That was not news to Colton. When Charles had written late last spring, looking for a partner and extra cash to help save his ranch, he'd written of the terrible storms. Of the tremendous losses that had sent him—as well as many other cattlemen—into neck-deep debt.

"The mercantile's open, though," Rose continued, as if his silence didn't bother her in the least. "The Bakers live on the second floor above the store, so it's good for business because they can stay open no matter the weather."

"Yes, ma'am." Although he wasn't by nature a talkative man, he rather liked this woman's pleasant chatter. He was hungry to know more about the town. "The lady I met outside today, the one who introduced us, mentioned Sunday School classes."

That had struck his interest. Zac needed to be around children his own age. And church sounded like the right place to take the boy. It felt like he'd landed on his feet this time. A small ray of hope burned in Colton's chest.

"Yes, Hannah Sawyer—she teaches the littlest ones every Sunday. She has a gentle hand with them."

"Hannah *Sawyer*?" Realization ran over him like a speeding train. The woman he'd met, with the angel's face and the ache for a child in her eyes, this woman was married to Charles?

His mind reeled. He hadn't put the pieces together. Couldn't even remember, in fact, if Charles had written his wife's name in his letters. Now he resisted the urge to dig through the small packet in one of the two satchels sitting on the floor and find out

"Charles Sawyer, why, he was killed just a few months ago."

"Killed?" Charles, who'd offered him a partnership in his ranch, was dead? "That can't be—"

"Terrible accident. Has left Hannah in difficult straits." Rose's voice dipped in genuine sympathy.

A terrible emptiness echoed through Colton's gut, and his hopes for his son faded.

ABOUT THE AUTHOR

Jillian Hart makes her home in Washington State, where she has lived most of her life. When Jillian is not writing away on her next book, she can be found reading, going to lunch with friends and spending quiet evenings at home with her family.

6945471R00152

Made in the USA
San Bernardino, CA
18 December 2013